Piranha

ALSO BY CLIVE CUSSLER

DIRK PITT® ADVENTURES

Havana Storm (with Dirk Cussler)

Poseidon's Arrow (with Dirk Cussler)

Crescent Dawn (with Dirk Cussler)

Arctic Drift (with Dirk Cussler)

Treasure of Khan (with Dirk Cussler)

Black Wind (with Dirk Cussler)

Trojan Odyssey

Valhalla Rising

Atlantis Found

Flood Tide

Shock Wave

Inca Gold

Sahara

Dragon

Treasure

Cyclops

Deep Six

Pacific Vortex!

Night Probe!

Vixen 03

Raise the Titanic!

Iceberg

The Mediterranean Caper

FARGO ADVENTURES

The Eye of Heaven (with Russell Blake)

The Mayan Secrets (with Thomas Perry)

The Tombs (with Thomas Perry)

The Kingdom (with Grant Blackwood)

Lost Empire (with Grant Blackwood)

Spartan Gold (with Grant Blackwood)

ISAAC BELL NOVELS

The Assassin (with Justin Scott)

The Bootlegger (with Justin Scott)

The Striker (with Justin Scott)

The Thief (with Justin Scott)

The Race (with Justin Scott)

The Spy (with Justin Scott)

The Wrecker (with Justin Scott)

The Chase

KURT AUSTIN ADVENTURES

Ghost Ship (with Graham Brown)

Zero Hour (with Graham Brown)

The Storm (with Graham Brown)

Devil's Gate (with Graham Brown)

Medusa (with Paul Kemprecos)

The Navigator (with Paul Kemprecos)

Polar Shift (with Paul Kemprecos)

Lost City (with Paul Kemprecos)

White Death (with Paul Kemprecos)

Fire Ice (with Paul Kemprecos)

Blue Gold (with Paul Kemprecos)

Serpent (with Paul Kemprecos)

OREGON FILES ADVENTURES

Mirage (with Jack Du Brul)

The Jungle (with Jack Du Brul)

The Silent Sea (with Jack Du Brul)

Corsair (with Jack Du Brul)

Plague Ship (with Jack Du Brul)

Skeleton Coast (with Jack Du Brul)

Dark Watch (with Jack Du Brul)

Sacred Stone (with Craig Dirgo)

Golden Buddha (with Craig Dirgo)

NONFICTION

Built for Adventure: The Classic Automobiles of Clive Cussler and Dirk Pitt

The Sea Hunters (with Craig Dirgo)

The Sea Hunters II (with Craig Dirgo)

Clive Cussler and Dirk Pitt Revealed (with Craig Dirgo)

Piranha

CLIVE CUSSLER
and BOYD MORRISON

MICHAEL JOSEPH
an imprint of
PENGUIN BOOKS

MICHAEL JOSEPH

UK | USA | Canada | Ireland | Australia
India | New Zealand | South Africa

Michael Joseph is part of the Penguin Random House group of companies
whose addresses can be found at global.penguinrandomhouse.com.

First published in the USA by G. P. Putnam's Sons 2014
First published in Great Britain by Michael Joseph 2015
001

Text copyright © Sandecker, RLLLP, 2014

The moral right of the author has been asserted

Printed in Great Britain by Clays Ltd, St Ives plc

A CIP catalogue record for this book is available from the British Library

HARDBACK ISBN: 978–0–718–17874–1
TPB ISBN: 978–0–718–17875–8

www.greenpenguin.co.uk

MIX
Paper from
responsible sources
FSC® C018179

Penguin Random House is committed to a
sustainable future for our business, our readers
and our planet. This book is made from Forest
Stewardship Council® certified paper.

Piranha

PROLOGUE

Martinique
May 8, 1902

The steamer SS *Roraima* was sailing toward the Apocalypse.

From the bridge of the Canadian cargo and passenger ship, First Officer Ellery Scott peered through a gray snowfall dirtier than anything he'd seen during a sooty London winter. Although it was 6:30 in the morning, the light from the rising sun could do little to penetrate the ash drifting over Saint-Pierre's harbor. The outline of "The Little Paris of the West Indies," as Martinique's commercial center was known, resembled less a thriving city of thirty thousand and more a blurred Impressionist watercolor recently fashionable in the Caribbean town's namesake.

Scott absentmindedly stroked his silver whiskers as he turned toward Mont Pelée, the volcano looming above the harbor. Although he normally bore a jovial demeanor that made him well liked by officers, crew, and passengers alike, today he could manage nothing better than a wary frown. He'd been a sailor for twenty years, aboard every kind of cargo vessel, at sea through murderous gales and towering rogue waves, but the stout old sea dog had never seen anything as ominous and foreboding as the mountain only three miles to the north.

Rolling thunder pealed from beneath its depths at regular intervals, as if a great roaring beast lay within. Darkness shrouded the peak, and a sulfurous odor permeated the air. Scott could imagine the Devil himself taking up residence in such a place.

"What do you think of this weather, sir?" Scott asked with a casualness he hoped did not betray his apprehension.

Captain George Muggah, his face etched with lines carved by years of salt and sun, and his upper lip hidden by a bushy mustache, glanced up from his log and squinted at the otherworldly tableau.

"Stay the course, Mr. Scott," he said, his voice steadfast. "Unless I hear different from the harbormaster, we're going to drop anchor."

"This ash might foul our equipment. It could delay our sailing this evening."

"Then I leave it to you to make sure the crew sweeps the decks and keeps our machinery clean. There are eighteen other ships at anchor. If it weren't safe, they'd be long gone."

The thick coat of ash floating on the water made it look as though the ships to either side were moored on dry land. At the risk of seeming impertinent, Scott persisted. "What of the explosion we heard two nights ago?"

They had been at anchor off Dominica fifty miles north when a blast at four in the morning rocked the ship so vigorously that cups and dishes crashed to the deck.

Captain Muggah went back to scribbling in the log. "I'm inclined to agree with the Portsmouth telegraph operator, that it relieved the pressure inside the volcano. It may continue to belch, but I'm sure nothing will come of it."

Scott wasn't as sure, but he kept his tongue still.

After they found their berth and dropped anchor, the harbormaster and doctor came aboard to check the ship and make sure the crew and passengers carried no contagious diseases that might infect the island. Both of them downplayed the continuing volcanic activity and bolstered Muggah's supposition that Pelée's growl wasn't dangerous. The current activity was nothing more than the mountain's last gasp.

Because it was Ascension Day, all the laborers would be at morning Mass, so Scott and Muggah headed down to the officers' mess for breakfast. They discussed the day's lading schedule—unloading lumber and potassium from New Brunswick, loading rum and sugar bound for Boston—but nary a syllable was spoken of the volcano, even though its rumblings continued to make it impossible to ignore.

After finishing breakfast, Scott went up on deck to receive the local agent who would be supervising the stevedores.

The 340-foot cargo vessel was a simple design, with holds fore and aft of the midship bridge topped with a single funnel. Masts equidistant toward each end were used for lifting heavy cargo. Every inch was dusted with Pelée's bountiful output. As Scott walked, his treads left prints on the deck.

Passengers crowded the railings for a view of Saint-Pierre's menacing backdrop. Some of them were sweeping ashes into envelopes and tobacco tins as souvenirs. Two women raised parasols to keep their dresses from being dirtied.

One man Scott recognized, a meek German named Gunther

Lutzen, was even setting up a tripod so that he could photograph the scene. He'd boarded two days before in Guadeloupe, and Scott had rarely seen the man without his camera.

"A fine day for pictures, Mr. Lutzen," Scott said.

"Yes, I am very interested," Lutzen replied in halting English.

"Is this for your scientific expedition?"

"No, that is complete. But I will be pleased to add this photo to my . . ." He paused and pulled a German–English dictionary from his pocket. "*Ach*, what is word for *Sammlung*?" He leafed through the pages.

"'Collection'?" Scott offered.

Lutzen smiled and nodded vigorously. "Yes, of course. 'Collection.' English is my new language. I learn still. My sister in New York gives me child's books to read."

Scott patted him on the shoulder. "You're doing well. It's better than my German."

Lutzen laughed and put away the dictionary so he could jot in his ever-present notebook. Scott went on, nodding greetings to other passengers as he passed.

When he reached the forecastle, he saw Monsieur Plessoneau, the local agent, coming up the gangway that had been lowered to his boat. Plessoneau, a gaunt man dressed in a white suit and straw hat, shook hands with Scott.

"Good to see you again, *monsieur*," Scott said. "I see that your angry mountain hasn't hurt business." He nodded to the other ships stretched out across the crescent-shaped harbor.

The Frenchman pursed his lips and blew through them. "*Oui*, but we are hoping the worst is over."

Scott frowned. "What's happened?"

The comment elicited a rueful chuckle from the agent. "We have been hearing from Pelée for over a month now. The ants and centipedes at the sugar mill in Usine Guérin were the start of our troubles."

"Ants and centipedes?"

Plessoneau made a face. "I will not miss them once I return to France. We call the ants *fourmis-fous*—crazy ants. They swarm over everything, biting in a frenzy. The centipedes are even worse. One foot long and black, a few bites will kill a man. It took every mill worker to save the horses. Then the snakes arrived."

Scott's eyes widened at the mention of snakes. Insects were one thing, but he could not bear the idea of facing a snake.

Plessoneau nodded in return. "Hundreds of *fer-de-lances*—pit vipers—suddenly appeared four days ago out of the forest in northern Saint-Pierre. Fifty people and hundreds of animals died. Then a day later a mud slide destroyed the mill. Fortunately, it happened at night, but we still lost many men."

This was sounding more like the coming of the Apocalypse that Scott had imagined as they sailed into the harbor.

"Perhaps we should leave and stop here on our return trip instead," he said.

Plessoneau shrugged. "I was going to suggest that since it is a holiday, many of our men won't work, and you might continue on to Fort-de-France and come back tomorrow. You will need the harbormaster to give permission, though, and he may not let you."

"Why not?"

"Because the governor has ordered troops to keep people from fleeing the city. There is an election in three days, and he is worried that it will not happen if everyone leaves. Some got out, but peasants are coming to Saint-Pierre from farms on the mountain slopes, so it's as crowded as I've ever seen it."

"Suppose we leave anyway?"

"Only one ship has so far, an Italian barque called *Orsolina* that had loaded only half its sugar cargo yesterday. The harbor-master refused permission to depart until they'd finished loading, and he threatened the captain, Marino Leboffe, with arrest. Supposedly, Leboffe, who is from Naples, told the harbormaster, 'I know nothing about Mont Pelée, but if Vesuvius were acting the way your volcano is this morning, I'd get out of Naples.'"

"He might be right."

"It is your captain's ship, but another leaving without permission may cause a panic with the others. A French cruiser just arrived in Fort-de-France, the *Suchet*. She might be called on to stop you."

"Let's see what Captain Muggah thinks," Scott said, and led Plessoneau to the bridge.

The captain listened to the agent's tales but was unmoved. He waved a copy of *Les Colonies*, the city's newspaper, which the doctor had left with him.

"The editorial in here says the mountain is safe. That's good enough for me. Now, prepare the ship for unloading."

There was no arguing with the captain. His decision was final. Scott gave him a curt, "Aye, Captain," and escorted Plessoneau back to his launch.

Scott bade him adieu and made his way back to the quarter-deck, where he found the third mate gazing at the city in rapt silence.

"Mr. Havers," Scott said, "what's caught your eye?"

"Well, it's a peaceful sight, isn't it, Mr. Scott? Gray, but bathed in a bright sunshine."

Scott grudgingly agreed that the sight was mesmerizing. But "peaceful" was not the word he would have chosen. To him it still seemed ominous. "We have work to do. The captain wants this deck to sparkle by the time we leave."

"Aye, sir. But do you mind if I take just one photo before we get started? My camera is on my bunk."

Scott took out his pocket watch. 7:49. What with the dock-hands at Mass, a few minutes wouldn't hurt.

He smiled and nodded. "But hop to it."

"Thank you, sir," Havers said with glee, and ran toward the crew's quarters.

Scott had moved only two steps toward the bridge when it seemed as if the sun had been extinguished. With dread, he looked toward Pelée. The sight that met his eyes caused him to be rooted in place as if his feet were trapped in cement.

A massive plume of black smoke and ash shot straight up into the sky like the expulsion from a battleship's cannon. The side of the mountain blew apart, and a second mass of ash churned down the slopes of Pelée in a glowing avalanche of superheated gas. The deadly flow was aimed directly at the city of Saint-Pierre. At the rate it was going, it would engulf the town in little more than a minute.

Still, Scott couldn't move. He was mesmerized by the appalling view, which was silent until the deafening shock wave arrived and blasted him backward. He would have remained pressed against the bulkhead until he was taken by the deadly cloud if not for that unholy sound. Thrown off his mark, Scott came to his senses. His first impulse was to get the ship to safety, so he sprinted toward the bow.

As Scott came amidships, he met Captain Muggah running in the other direction. The captain must have had the same idea as Scott.

"Heave up, Mr. Scott!" the captain yelled as he raced past toward the bridge.

"Weighing anchor, aye!" Scott yelled back. The third mate

who'd gone off to get his camera joined the captain on the bridge, ordering the boilers up to full steam.

Scott reached the anchor chain and engaged the steam-powered donkey engine to raise the anchor. Passengers around him screamed in terror and ran in every direction, unaware of how to protect themselves from the coming rain of fire. Most of the crew fared no better, and despite Scott's shouts for help, none came to his aid.

He counted fifteen fathoms of chain retrieved when the lethal cloud of ash rolled over the northern edge of Saint-Pierre, setting everything it touched aflame and blowing apart stone structures as if they were made of matchsticks.

The cloud continued to roll out over the harbor, where it met the cable-laying ship *Grappler*. She did not have time to catch fire before she was capsized by a wall of water. The tsunami swept toward them, smashing one ship after the other.

With fifteen fathoms of chain still to go, Scott knew getting the *Roraima* out of the harbor in time was hopeless. He scrambled to find shelter. With only seconds until the fire reached him, all he could do was snatch a large tarpaulin from one of the ventilator covers, flip it over to create multiple layers, and pull it over his head. He threw himself to the deck and huddled beneath the tarp, with only a tiny hole to see through. He could see Captain Muggah barking out orders on the bridge, defiantly trying to save his doomed ship.

Scott felt the heat before the blast wave. It rose to such a degree that he thought he would be cooler inside one of the ship's boilers. The layered tarp deflected the worst of the heat; without it, Scott was sure he would not survive. It was confirmed when he watched in horror as the captain's mustache, hair, and clothes were set on fire. The captain wailed in unbearable agony, and

Scott was spared from seeing more when Muggah dropped from view.

Hot stones and mud pelted the tarp, some of them smaller than buckshot, others as big as a pigeon's egg. None of them were traveling at a speed that would injure Scott, so he simply endured the hail of stones, listening to them hiss as they splashed into the water beside the ship.

A moment later, the blast wave reached the *Roraima*, causing the tarp to be nearly ripped from Scott's hands. Both masts were sheared off two feet above the deck as cleanly as if they'd been cut by a saw, and the smokestack snapped in half. The tidal wave struck the side of the ship, initially tilting her to port before jerking her so hard to starboard that the ship's ice rail dipped into the sea.

Fearing that he'd be pitched into the water, Scott cried out and scrabbled to find a handhold. He slid down the ash-covered deck, still under the tarpaulin, until his feet slammed into a cargo latch. For a second he thought the ship would capsize like the *Grappler*, but the old girl held strong and bobbed back up, though she still carried a heavy list.

Scott opened his eyes, peeked through the tarp's hole to get his bearings, and saw that he was just opposite the forecastle. He was about to make a try for it when the door swung wide and two sailors, Taylor and Quashey, reached out and dragged him inside.

They closed the door and covered the portholes with mattresses, trunks, anything they could find. When the room was sealed, they huddled beneath the tarp and blankets, waiting for the end—either of the firestorm or their lives.

After what seemed like an hour but could have been no more than ten minutes, Scott felt the heat abate. Hoping the worst to be over, he stood and opened the door.

With one look, he realized that the worst was just beginning.

The deck was littered with charred corpses. Men, women, and children were burned horribly or coated with enough ash that they appeared to be frozen in concrete. He could not tell passenger from crew.

He stepped gingerly around them, searching for any signs of life, when he found someone facedown, the back of the clothing burned away. The poor wretch was moaning in pain. Scott gently turned the person over and reeled backward when he saw the awful visage.

The man's hair was gone completely, his skin blackened and his nose and ears misshapen and melted to his face. The only reason Scott knew it was a man and not a woman was because of the remnants of coat and tie that were still intact beneath his folded arms. His lower half was burned to a cinder. Scott figured the man must have been lying on his stomach when the fire scorched him.

"Help me, Mr. Scott," the man sputtered through cracked lips.

Scott looked at the man in confusion. "Do I know you, sir?"

"Don't you know *me*, Mr. Scott?" he croaked, every word an excruciating effort. "I am Lutzen."

Scott gaped at Gunther Lutzen. He would never have recognized the German.

Lutzen trembled as he raised his arms toward Scott, who thought the man was reaching out for aid. Instead, he lifted his precious notebook and held it toward Scott. Now he realized that Lutzen must have thrown himself on the notebook to protect it from the flames.

"I'm dying. Give this to my sister."

Scott did not want to see another man die, so he desperately searched for any signs of help coming to them. A cargo vessel he recognized as the *Roddam* was turning to port to head out to open sea, and he could see that the entire stern was on fire.

"Please, Mr. Scott," Lutzen said, drawing Scott's gaze back to him. "Ingrid Lutzen, New York City."

Seeing that there was nothing more to do for the man, Scott nodded and carefully took the notebook and tucked it into his waistband. "Of course, Mr. Lutzen. I'll see to it."

Lutzen couldn't smile, but he nodded in understanding. "Tell her I was there," he said with a pitiful wheeze. "I made the break-through. It will change everything. They shined like emeralds, as large as tree trunks."

He coughed violently, his body shaking from the strain. Scott tried to stand to go find him water, but Lutzen grabbed his sleeve and pulled him close so that Scott's ear hovered over his mouth. He whispered three words, then his hand fell away from Scott's coat. Lutzen became mercifully still, finally free from his pain.

Scott remained kneeling for a moment, confused by what he'd heard. Then more groans caught his attention, and he was on his feet. With the captain dead or mortally wounded, he was now in charge.

Scott gathered as many survivors as he could find, a total of only thirty out of the sixty-eight on board, and half of those would likely not make it through the night. Scott and three other crew members were the only ones not badly injured. They set about constructing a raft out of the remains of a lifeboat, but their efforts were rendered moot when the French cruiser *Suchet* arrived in the afternoon and took them aboard, leaving the *Roraima* behind to sink. The officer who gave him coffee told him that they feared not a single soul in Saint-Pierre had lived through the holocaust.

With nothing more to do now that he and his few charges were safe, Scott took Lutzen's journal from his waistband and flipped through it. As he'd suspected, he couldn't understand a word of it. Not only was every page written in German but the majority of the writing consisted of equations and scientific mumbo jumbo. Scott hoped Lutzen's sister would know what to make of it and vowed to keep his promise to return it to her.

Scott thought about what he'd tell her when he met her upon his arrival in New York, whether to save her from the horror of what her brother had suffered. He thought she deserved the whole truth, including Lutzen's last message to her.

He wanted to make sure he remembered it verbatim in the days it would take for the trip north, so he scrounged a pencil from one of the *Suchet*'s sailors and leafed to the first blank page. Scott scribbled the cryptic phrases he'd heard, Lutzen's raw voice in his head.

Tell her I was there. I made the breakthrough. It will change everything. They shined like emeralds, as large as tree trunks.

Scott paused, still unsure whether he'd heard Lutzen's final three words correctly. He shrugged and reproduced Lutzen's strange message exactly.

I found Oz.

Chesapeake Bay
Nine months ago

The X-47B prototype attack drone made a sweeping turn, only minutes away from the target eighty miles northwest of the Chesapeake Bay Bridge-Tunnel. Frederick Weddell adjusted the frequency-hopping algorithm of the jamming transmission. His mission was to block the control signal coming in from the drone's operator at Naval Base Ventura County in California and recode its onboard navigation system, causing the aircraft and its one thousand pounds of fuel to smash into a derelict barge.

Even without the two smart bombs it was capable of carrying, the drone could cause a deadly terrorist attack on the U.S.

Weddell relished the challenge. "We're gonna do it," he said to no one in particular, although there were two other men in the small room filled to the brim with electronic equipment and displays. The eighty-foot communications vessel anchored near the mouth of the Potomac was otherwise unoccupied except for its captain, who was topside on the bridge. Weddell adjusted his wire-framed glasses and looked up at the largest monitor to check the view from a camera on the deck. The drone was in its first turn after takeoff, a white wedge against the orange glow of dusk behind it.

To accomplish their mission, jamming the control signal wasn't enough. If the drone's contact with its controller was lost, it would revert to autonomous mode and return to its base at Naval Air Station Patuxent River, the Maryland flight center that served as the test facility for most of the Navy's aerial weapons systems. The key was to establish a new control authorization so that the coordinates for an alternative target designation could be loaded. In this case, the unmanned aerial vehicle would be instructed to crash into the barge at five hundred miles per hour.

This attack was the worst-case scenario for the Pentagon. No one—not the drone designers nor the Joint Chiefs—thought that the onboard systems could be hacked. But ever since a top secret RQ-170 Sentinel reconnaissance drone crash-landed in Iran, top brass had demanded that the Air Force and Navy prove that their communications protocols were unbreakable. Apart from losing a drone that cost hundreds of millions of dollars to build, the crash had given Iran a free peek inside one of America's most advanced pieces of technology. If the Iranians could bring it down, they might be able to wrest a drone's control away from its operator. The military was pouring funds into a program to make sure that never happened.

That was the reason for this hijacking simulation.

The call had gone out for the best and brightest in the drone community to put together a team to serve as the enemy infiltration unit. An electrical engineer by education and now the Air Force's top communications specialist, Weddell had jumped at the chance. He was an expert in all manner of signal transmission, encryption, and disruption, so he was chosen to head up the signal intercept mission. His team consisted of two other top-notch scientists.

Lawrence Kensit, a mousy fellow with a stooped gait and an acne-scarred face, was a computer scientist and physicist who had gotten his Ph.D. from Caltech when he was twenty. Despite his penchant for calling anyone he felt didn't rise to his level of brilliance "irredeemably stupid"—including officers who depended on his work—he nevertheless became the military's most brilliant drone software developer. He sat to Weddell's right, tapping away on a keyboard set in front of three screens winking with data.

The second man was Douglas Pearson, a hardware designer responsible for the technology that went into the most advanced drones in the military's arsenal. He was a bear of a man whose bombastic voice and enormous gut suited someone who didn't say no too much and wasn't used to hearing the word, either. He ruled his fiefdom with an iron fist and would argue loudly with anyone who disagreed with his viewpoint. He sat to Weddell's left with his feet up on the counter, a tablet computer in one hand and a coffee mug in the other.

If the three of them couldn't crack the drone's command system, no one else in the world could. After confirming that the drone would in fact proceed on an intercept path toward the derelict barge, Weddell planned to veer it from its course and have it waggle its wings over Patuxent in a final flourish before returning it to Ventura control.

Pearson slurped his coffee loudly before setting it down and tapping his tablet against the counter. "What's happening, Larry? I've got nothing on the linkup so far."

"Dr. Weddell," Kensit said without looking away from his screens, "please remind Dr. Pearson that I don't respond to that nickname. I prefer 'Dr. Kensit,' but I will accept 'Lawrence,' even though that privilege is usually reserved for people who could be considered equals." He paused before adding, "If it's not clear, I don't consider him an equal."

"Equal in what way, *Dr.* Kensit?" Pearson said with a mocking laugh. "We sure aren't equal in height."

"Or weight."

Pearson snorted. "Why don't I just call you *shorty*? Or how about *pipsqueak*?"

"My height is lower relative to yours, but close to average," Kensit replied without inflection. "Much like your IQ."

"Enough," Weddell said, fed up with their constant bickering. "We're not going through this right now." He had spent half of the last six months playing referee between them.

"We're about to win this thing," he continued, "so try to remain civil until we're done. We'll only have a direct line of sight for two more minutes. What's your status, Lawrence?"

Kensit pressed a final key with a decisive snap. "If Dr. Pearson's hardware calculations are correct, as soon as you are able to wrest the control signal away from Ventura, I will be able to reconfigure the onboard navigation protocols."

Weddell nodded and put his plan for blocking the transmission into motion. Spoofing the GPS navigation wouldn't work because all U.S. drones relied on inertial navigation to prevent just such a tactic. He had to be much more creative. Using an antenna of his own design mounted on the deck of the boat, he blasted the receiver on the X-47B with an overload spike that would cause the onboard systems to momentarily freeze. The sensitive part of the operation was to do it just long enough so that its receiver would immediately go into search mode again, but not so long that it recognized someone was attempting to compromise its protocols and cause it to revert to autonomous operation.

"Get ready, Lawrence," Weddell said. "Remember, you'll have only twenty seconds to acquire the signal."

"I know."

Of course he does.

Weddell turned to Pearson. He was responsible for disabling the drone's automated self-destruct, which would engage if the drone's sensors detected an unauthorized signal controlling it. "Doug, are you ready to go?"

"Let's do this," Pearson said, rubbing his hands together.

"Okay. On my mark. Three. Two. One. Mark."

Weddell pressed the ENTER button, and the pulse bombarded the drone. His screen confirmed that he had a direct hit.

"Go, Lawrence!"

Kensit began typing furiously. The seconds ticked by. All Weddell could do from this point was watch. He kept his eyes on the monitor above him. The drone remained on its original heading.

"Status, Lawrence." The countdown timer he'd programmed into his laptop gave them ten more seconds.

"I'm isolating the control subroutines," Kensit said, which was as close as Weddell would get to an estimate from him.

More ticks. The wait was excruciating. For the first time in the entire process, Weddell was completely powerless.

"Five seconds, Lawrence!"

More typing.

"You can do it, Kensit," Pearson said.

Kensit's fingers flew across the keyboard, and then he pulled them away like a concert pianist finishing a minuet.

"I know," he said. "We now have control." He looked pointedly at Pearson. "Try not to make my brilliance a moot point."

Although this drone wouldn't actually explode if Pearson couldn't disable the autodestruct, a switch inside the X-47B would trip in the event the autodestruct sequence wasn't terminated. The inspectors checking the drone later would know that the hijacking mission had failed. There would be no partial credit.

Pearson used the tablet as deftly as Kensit had manipulated his keyboard. Weddell was focused on entering new targeting coordinates into the nav system. He finished just as Pearson called out in triumph, "Take that, Uncle Sam! We done got your drone!"

Weddell and Pearson clapped and slapped palms. All they could get from Kensit was a raised eyebrow and a shrug, as if he shouldn't celebrate something that he fully expected to happen.

The festivities became short-lived when Weddell noticed the X-47B turning on the monitor. It should have been heading away from them on the course toward the barge. Instead, it was flying directly toward them.

And it was descending.

"What the hell is going on, Lawrence?"

Kensit shook his head in bewilderment. "This can't be."

Pearson took his feet down and stared at Kensit. "What did you do, Larry?"

"I didn't do anything to cause this."

"Cause what?" Weddell asked.

"The drone is locked onto the signal we're broadcasting."

"What?" Weddell tried to disengage the signal they were broadcasting, but the computer wouldn't respond. "How is that possible?"

"I . . . I'm not sure."

Weddell looked up at the monitor. The X-47B was growing larger on the screen every moment. They had less than a minute before the drone and its payload of fuel completed its kamikaze attack and blew the boat apart. "Can you reprogram it?"

Kensit just gaped at his screen, perplexed and mute.

Weddell rushed over and shook him by the shoulders. "I said can you reprogram it?"

For probably the first time in his life, Kensit uttered the words "I don't know."

"You've got to try or we're all dead." He wheeled around and pointed at Pearson. "See if you can engage that autodestruct."

Pearson nodded furiously and hunched over his tablet. Weddell raced for the door at the front of the room.

"Where are you going?" Kensit asked.

"If you guys can't reassert control, I can at least stop our antenna from broadcasting."

He threw open the door and ran up to the bridge, where he found the captain staring at the drone diving toward them.

"Get us moving—now!" Weddell shouted.

The captain didn't need to be told why and throttled up the engine.

Weddell climbed up onto the top deck above the bridge where the antenna was located. If he disconnected the power cable, the broadcast would cease. Even if the drone had locked onto their initial position, moving the ship would get them out of its path.

He reached the antenna and was about to reach for the cable

when the ship lurched forward. He was thrown back, tripped on a railing, and struck his head against the bulkhead.

He saw stars for a few seconds and shook his head to clear them before crawling toward the antenna. The black cable leading to the dish lay exposed on the white deck.

He glanced up and saw the slash of white wing plunging toward them, the drone's black air intake gaping like the maw of a manta ray. The banshee wail of the jet engine foretold a fiery end if he couldn't disable their broadcast. It looked like neither Kensit nor Pearson had been successful.

Weddell grasped the power cable with both hands and yanked it. The cable held firm. He braced his feet against the dish's rotating pedestal and put everything he had into it, his muscles straining in protest.

With a sudden pop, the cable flew backward in a shower of sparks, sending Weddell tumbling.

He picked himself up and saw the cable had completely disconnected from the antenna. There was no way it was still broadcasting.

The water splashed in whitecaps from the bow, indicating that they were now doing a good twenty knots. They'd have plenty of distance from the drone's impact.

Weddell turned his attention back to the drone so that he could tell the crash investigators exactly where it went down. But to his horror, the drone continued to make adjustments in its course.

It was still aimed straight at them, no more than five seconds away.

He scrambled to his feet in a mad dash to jump overboard, but he was far too late. Time seemed to compress as the drone plunged into the ship and exploded.

His last thought before the fireball consumed him wasn't of his wife or his mother or his German shepherd, Bandit. It was focused on the fact that this event was no accident. Frederick Weddell used his brain's final impulses to wonder who it was that killed him.

2

Puerto La Cruz, Venezuela
Present day

Harbormaster Manuel Lozada shook his head in disbelief as his boat approached the rusting hulk that he was about to inspect before it unloaded its cargo at the La Guanta docks. He shielded his eyes from the setting sun to give himself a better look. From a distance the pattern of mottled green paint on the hull seemed designed to camouflage the ship for a jungle cruise, but up close he could see that it was just a sloppy patch job, with various shades of puke green splashed on the sides to cover up bare spots, and even the newer paint was now flaking away.

As his boat passed by the stern, Lozada could make out the name *Dolos* on the champagne-glass fantail, the only mark of elegance on an otherwise profoundly ugly vessel. The flag flying from the jackstaff was of a Liberian registry, which matched the information he'd obtained independently.

The ship was large—560 feet long—but nothing compared to

the massive supertankers that berthed at the Pamatacual oil terminal only five miles away. The *Dolos* wasn't a containership, but rather an old tramp steamer that carried whatever needed to be transported between the less prominent ports of the world. This one in particular looked like it should have been sent to the scrapyard last century. If it ever got caught in even a minor gale, Lozada wouldn't be surprised if the old girl broke in half and sank.

Two of the five cranes on board were so corroded that they could not possibly be operational. Trash and broken machinery was scattered across the deck without a care. Twin funnels belched black smoke. The filthy white superstructure was situated between the six forward holds and two aft holds, and two bridge wings poked out from either side. The windows on the pilothouse were so dingy that Lozada could see the spot the pilot had wiped clear to see through during the five-mile trip into the harbor.

Lozada had served in the Venezuelan Navy for twenty years, and had remained a reservist since becoming harbormaster, and he would have been keelhauled if he'd let a ship of his reach this state of disrepair. Only the cheapest or most desperate shippers would trust their cargo to a vessel like this.

He motioned for the boat's operator to pull alongside the shabby gangway lowered from the *Dolos* and turned to the man sitting behind him, a former Chinese Marine named Gao Wangshu. With a high-and-tight brush cut and a lean, sinewy frame, Gao could have still been in the military.

"Well?" Lozada said in English, the language common between them. The admiral had handpicked Lozada for this task and wanted a definitive answer.

"I do not know yet," Gao replied.

"I can't report back to the admiral until you are sure. Your payment depends on it."

"I cannot be confident of my conclusion until I get on board."

"Either way, you'd better be right."

"Is that a threat?"

"A warning. Admiral Ruiz does not like to be made a fool."

Gao eyed Lozada's sidearm and nodded slowly. "I will share with you any doubts I have about its identity."

"See that you do. Remember that you are playing a trainee, which means you will be silent."

"I understand."

Once the boat was tied to the *Dolos*, the two of them climbed the gangway and were met at the top by a slovenly crewman sporting a battered cowboy hat. Tendrils of stringy brown hair jutted out at odd angles around the edges, and bits of food were caught in a handlebar mustache draped under his bulbous nose. The man's khaki shirt was dotted with coffee and sweat stains and strained to cover a generous gut.

"*¿Habla Español?*" Lozada asked.

"Nope," the man replied with a twang Lozada couldn't identify. "I sure hope you speak English."

"My name is Manuel Lozada. I am the harbormaster for La Guanta. Please take me to your captain."

A smile revealed the man's nicotine-soaked teeth. "You got him. Buck Holland's the name. Welcome aboard *Dolos*." He stuck out a hand and shook Lozada's vigorously.

Lozada could barely contain his surprise that this slob was the vessel's master, but he recovered quickly and introduced Gao as his apprentice, Fernando Wang. He didn't expect Gao's ethnicity to raise any red flags since Venezuela has a sizable Chinese immigrant population.

"I need to review your crew and cargo manifests, as well as your registration and shipping orders."

"You got it," Holland said. "They're up in the bridge. Follow me. Watch your step. We've got a few deck plates to repair."

Lozada almost laughed at the understatement. Rust was so prevalent on the warped steel plates that it was a wonder the ship held together, regardless of the weather. Chains stretched across breaks in the railings, and the superstructure was even more of a horror close up. Rotting plywood sheets were screwed over gaps in the bulkheads, and a third of the windows around the bridge were cracked.

Despite his research into the captain, he hadn't expected this degree of neglect, not only to his vessel but to himself as well. Although Holland's age was forty, drinking and sun damage had added fifteen years to his face. According to his file, the captain was a recovering alcoholic who had run a containership aground near Singapore. The only command he could get after that was this rickety tramp steamer, and by the looks of it Holland had completely ceased to care about his reputation.

They entered a narrow corridor, and Lozada was struck by the foul stench, a mixture of cigarette smoke, diesel fumes, and sewage. He practically gagged.

"Yeah," Holland said. "Sorry about the smell. The head's backing up again, so I hope you don't have to use it. I've got my boys working on it. You know, two weeks ago in the middle of the Atlantic we had to resort to using buckets." Instead of being embarrassed, he laughed at the memory.

Lozada suppressed the temptation to hold his nose and followed the captain inside. Gao kept pace beside him, taking in the awful state of the interior. Chipped linoleum squeaked under Lozada's rubber soles, and he took care not to rub his clean uniform against the grimy bare-metal walls. The overhead fluorescent lights flickered enough to trigger epileptic seizures.

They arrived at the captain's office, where the pungent aroma was even stronger. The rectangular room had a single porthole caked with salt, and creepy sad clowns painted in neon shades stared down at them from black-velvet paintings on the wall.

The office featured two other doors, both open. The first was to a captain's cabin, furnished with little more than a dresser bolted to the wall, a mirror, crazed as if someone had put his fist in it, and an unmade metal bed topped with discolored sheets and a worn blanket.

The second door led to a cramped bathroom that looked as if it hadn't been cleaned since the ship had been built. The odor emanating from the toilet was overpowering.

Holland went behind his desk and plunked himself into a chair that squealed in protest. Lozada was amazed to see him plug bare wires from a desk lamp into the wall, snatching his hand back and cursing when the inevitable sparks shot from the outlet. The lamp winked on anyway.

"Take a load off," Holland said, and gestured to a couple of chairs on the other side. Lozada perched himself on the edge of the seat to avoid a glistening spot of some unknown substance. Gao mimicked his uncomfortable posture.

Before they could get started, a huge black man rushed into the room carrying an enormous dead rat by the tail, startling Lozada and Gao.

"I found it, Captain!" the man yelled in victory.

"The critter was what clogged us up?"

The crewman nodded. "The heads should be working now."

"Be sure to get more traps while we're here. We're going through them like crazy." While Holland was distracted by the rat, Lozada surreptitiously took his photo with his camera phone.

"Aye, sir." The crewman left just as quickly.

"At least something's going right today," Holland said as he rummaged through his desk. He produced two binders, one containing the cargo manifest and shipping orders, the other the registry and crew manifest.

Lozada flipped through the cargo information to start.

"This says that you're carrying fertilizer," he said.

Holland nodded and picked up a toothpick from his desk that he stuck in his mouth.

"That's right. Five thousand tons from Houston. Only a thousand of it is for Venezuela. The rest is going to Colombia. We're also taking on some lumber while we're here."

"You're new to Puerto La Cruz. I haven't seen you before."

"I go where they pay me to go. Most of the time, it's the northern Caribbean, but I'm happy to visit your fine country for a change."

Satisfied that the cargo information was in order, Lozada next perused the crew manifest. Nothing stood out. It was just a mix of Filipino and Nigerian crewmen. The Liberian registry also checked out.

He passed the binders to Gao, who inspected them and then set them on the desk.

"How's it looking?" Holland asked.

"I'm afraid our dockworkers are very busy tonight," Lozada said. "I don't know if they have time to help with your cargo until tomorrow."

Holland grinned. "Maybe I can change that." He opened a drawer, withdrew an envelope, and handed it to Lozada. "That should cover any overtime."

Lozada riffled through the money inside and counted five hundred American dollars. Although he was here on a mission, there was no sense in letting this opportunity for a bribe go to waste.

"We all good?" Holland asked.

Lozada glanced at Gao. "Have you seen what you need to see?"

Gao gave a curt nod.

Lozada pocketed the envelope and stood. "Everything seems to be in order, Captain Holland. You may begin unloading immediately."

"That's mighty nice of you, Mr. Lozada. Let me walk you out."

They made their way back to the gangway.

"Nice doing business with you," Holland said with a tip of his hat. "Now, if you'll excuse me, I've been waiting to make use of the facilities for hours, if you know what I mean. *Adiós.*"

Lozada couldn't wait to get away from this putrid mess. He smiled wanly and nodded good-bye. When they were safely back on his launch and he could breathe fresh air again, he shrugged at Gao as the operator motored away.

"At least we know now this isn't the one," he said.

"You are wrong," Gao said. "This is the ship you're looking for."

Lozada looked at Gao in amazement and then up at the disgusting captain walking back toward his cabin. "You're joking! That thing isn't fit to be a garbage scow."

"It's all a clever disguise. I have been on that ship before."

"Look, we've all heard the rumors. A normal-looking cargo ship bristling with weapons that is used to spy on countries around the world. Some say it's British, some say American or Russian. No one knows its name. No one can agree on what it looks like. All we have are vague secondhand stories about the ship getting into sea battles with Chinese destroyers, Iranian submarines, and Burmese gunboats. Supposedly, it has missiles and torpedoes and lasers, armor three feet thick, and can withstand anything short of a nuclear blast. Does that barely floating embarrassment look like a warship to you?"

Gao's expression was deadly serious. "I didn't see any torpedoes or lasers, but I was stationed aboard the destroyer *Chengdo*, and I was one of the Marines sent onto that ship to capture it. We were repelled by a well-trained force armed with the latest weaponry."

Lozada laughed. "I could return with two men from the police force and seize that vessel without a problem."

"I advise against that. Your admiral has information that you don't. I suggest you call and report my conclusions."

Lozada narrowed his eyes at Gao. "Give me one reason why I should believe you."

"The ship's name—*Dolos*. Do you know what it means?"

"Of course. A 'dolos' is a molded concrete block. We pile them up to form breakwaters."

"There's another meaning. I did a search on my phone on the way here. Dolos is the Greek god of deception. You are meant to think it's harmless."

Lozada checked his own smartphone and came up with the same result. He frowned. It was flimsy evidence, but he could be in serious trouble if he didn't report back to Admiral Ruiz and then was proven to be wrong.

"All right," he said, and dialed the number he'd been given. He asked for Admiral Ruiz and was connected immediately. A distinct hiss came over the line before he heard a click.

"This is Admiral Dayana Ruiz," a female voice said in Spanish. "Who is this?"

"Admiral, this is Commander Manuel Lozada," he said nervously. "Señor Gao is confirming that this is the spy vessel."

"What do you think?"

"I think it's nothing more than a cargo ship two voyages away from going under."

"Did you take his photo as I ordered?"

"Yes, Admiral."

"Send it to me now."

Lozada messaged the picture to her.

After a slight pause, she said, "That's him. Holland is the same man as the one in my photo. We have intelligence identifying him as the captain of the spy vessel."

Lozada felt a rush of adrenaline. Admiral Ruiz was the most powerful woman in the Venezuelan Navy and next in line to be defense minister. He could write his ticket if he captured a foreign spy. "I'll have them arrested at once."

Her voice stabbed through the phone like an ice pick. "You will do nothing, Commander. I'm aboard the frigate *Mariscal Sucre*. We are currently three and a half hours from Puerto La Cruz. If the rumors are true, we will need all the firepower at my disposal. I plan to capture the vessel myself."

Lozada swallowed hard at her bloodcurdling tone. "I must warn you, Admiral, the *Dolos* is carrying four thousand tons of fertilizer. Ammonium nitrate is volatile. If a fire is started by gunfire, it could blow up and destroy the entire harbor."

"How long before she is scheduled to depart?"

"Four hours."

"Then we'll lie in wait outside the harbor. Let her get her cargo on board and set sail. We'll intercept her in open water."

"And if they do have all those mythical weapons on board?"

"It doesn't matter. *Mariscal Sucre* is more than capable of sinking her."

3

Once he was sure Lozada wouldn't be returning for an even bigger bribe, the man who had introduced himself as Captain Buck Holland returned to the office and set his hat and wig on the desk, revealing a blond crew cut.

"Okay, Max," he said to the air, removing the latex prosthetic appliances from his face as he spoke. "I think we're clear. You can turn off the odorant vents."

Silent fans kicked on and the foul smell was sucked from the room in seconds, replaced by a crisp pine scent. Max's disembodied voice said, "You like my new concoction?"

Next to go were the fake teeth and glued-on mustache. "'Like' is not the word I'd go with. If you were aiming for eye-watering, you blew right through it and hit vomit-inducing. I'm surprised the harbormaster didn't lose his dinner."

"But it worked, didn't it?"

Last to be removed were the brown contacts. His eyes were now back to the crystal blue that he had gotten from his mother. Juan Cabrillo smiled. "It sounds like he bought the story. I'll see you in my cabin in a few minutes."

He shoved the disguise—including the rubber belly that had covered a muscled torso sculpted by a daily hour of swimming—into a trash bag. He wouldn't be using it again.

The black man who'd barged in during the meeting returned, carrying the rat less gingerly this time. He tossed it on the desk, where it bounced against the wall. The stuffed animal looked so real that Juan could imagine it coming to life and scurrying away.

"Not a fan of rats, Linc?" Juan said, deliberately avoiding the implication that the former Navy SEAL was scared of them. If the massive Franklin Lincoln was afraid of anything, Juan sure never wanted to meet up with whatever that was.

Linc smirked. "Are you kidding? Back in Detroit, we'd call one this size a mouse. Ours were nearly as big as raccoons."

"They sound like they'd make great pets."

"Where do you think I got the name Charlie for this one?"

Juan laughed, and checked his watch. "We're scheduled to sail as soon as our cargo of fertilizer is unloaded in three hours," he said, leading them down the corridor, where he stopped at a tiny utility closet crammed with mops and cleaning supplies that had never been used. "What's our equipment status?"

"Everything is prepped and ready to go."

"Good. I'll check in with Max and then meet you at the moon pool."

"You got it, Chairman." He continued down the corridor, humming Otis Redding's "(Sittin' On) The Dock of the Bay" as he walked.

Juan spun the handles on the faucet of the nonworking sink in a specific pattern. With a sharp click, the back wall opened wide, revealing a hallway that would have been at home on the finest cruise ship. Recessed lighting glowed softly above mahogany walls and sumptuous carpeting, a far cry from the rust and grime the harbormaster had seen. He walked through the opening and down the corridor toward his cabin.

Juan always enjoyed the transition from the deceptively decrepit topside to the sleek and elegant world belowdecks. It symbolized everything he loved about the ship. Although her fantail currently bore the name *Dolos*, down here he never referred to her as anything but her original name—*Oregon*.

The *Oregon* was Juan's creation. As Chairman, he had conceived a ship that would not only avoid attention but would actually repel it. Few knew about the technological marvels hidden within the *Oregon*'s apparently crumbling hull. That trickery made her virtually invisible in the Third World ports that she plied. In reality, she was a fourth-generation, state-of-the-art intelligence-gathering vessel. She could travel where no U.S. Navy warship could go, enter ports closed to most commercial shipping, and transport highly secret cargo without arousing suspicion.

Juan entered his cabin, which was the antithesis of the fake one he'd shown to Lozada. Like all the members of his crew, he had a generous allowance to decorate it to his taste since the space served as his home. It was currently fashioned as an homage to Rick's Café Américain from the movie *Casablanca*.

Juan shucked his costume and removed the artificial leg that was strapped below his right knee, a disability he'd acquired courtesy of shell fire from a Chinese destroyer called the *Chengdo*. He rubbed the stump, but as usual the phantom pain wouldn't go away. He hopped over to his closet and placed the prosthesis at the end of a neat line of them that all had different purposes, some cosmetic, some practical. The one he'd taken off mimicked the look of a real leg, down to toenails and hair.

He picked up the one he'd dubbed the "combat leg" and put it on. The unique titanium prosthesis was packed with backup weapons, including a classic .45 ACP Colt Defender with a Crimson Trace laser sight—an accurate and reliable upgrade from his old Kel-Tec .380—a package of plastic explosives no bigger than a deck of cards, and a ceramic throwing knife. The heel concealed a short-barreled shotgun loaded with a single .44 caliber slug.

With the leg attached, he pulled on a pair of swim trunks, a breathable swim shirt, and fin boots for comfort.

He walked into his office and opened the nineteenth-century railroad safe, where he kept his personal armory. Most of the small arms aboard the *Oregon* were stored in a central armory adjacent to the ship's shooting range, but Juan preferred his own cache. Rifles, submachine guns, and pistols shared space with cash from multiple countries, gold coins totaling over a hundred thousand U.S. dollars, and several small pouches of diamonds.

Juan chose his favorite pistol, a Fabrique Nationale Five-seveN double-action automatic, loaded with 5.7mm cartridges that allowed the grip to hold twenty rounds plus one in the chamber. Despite their small size, the bullets were designed to drill through most ballistic armor but tumble once they reached their target to prevent overpenetration. Heavier weaponry wouldn't work for this operation, much as he wanted to bring some along.

A double-tap knock came at the door, and Max Hanley walked in without waiting for a response. The *Oregon*'s chief engineer had been Juan's first hire for the Corporation and Juan relied on his old friend's judgment more than anyone else aboard. Auburn hair fringed Max's otherwise bald head, and a paunch was the only other clue that the solidly built president of the Corporation was into his sixties, having .served two tours of duty in Vietnam.

"Lozada seemed to fall for the whole thing," Max said with a frown. He had seen and heard the entire exchange via the hidden cameras and microphones generously apportioned throughout the upper decks.

"You don't look happy about it," Juan said.

"It's not Lozada. I just don't like us being spread thin like this."

"Even though most of the plan was your crazy idea?"

"It was *your* crazy idea. I just came up with how to make it work."

The CIA suspected the Venezuelans of supplying arms to North Korea, defying a United Nations embargo of the pariah state. The U.S. didn't know how the weapons were being smuggled, but the shipments did correlate with known deliveries of diesel from Puerto La Cruz to Wonsan. Electronic eavesdropping pinpointed a warehouse along the dock of the oil terminal, which was less than a half mile across a mountainous peninsula from La Guanta Harbor, as a probable coordination point for the shipments. The Corporation's mission was to obtain evidence of the arms shipments while simultaneously dealing a blow to the fuel delivery that was critical to running the tanks and armored personnel carriers of the North Korean Army. Juan and Linc would be getting the evidence—documents, computer files, photos, anything they could find.

"And your plan is brilliant," Juan said. "So let's go put it in motion." He led Max out of the cabin and walked side by side toward the center of the ship, passing artwork that would have befit any of the world's great museums. Juan walked without a limp, the result of years of practice perfecting his gait with the artificial limb.

"Are we on schedule?" Juan asked.

"Everyone has checked in and is ready to go."

"See?" Juan said. "Nothing to worry about."

"I get the heebie-jeebies when you say that."

"It's good luck, like saying 'break a leg' to an actor." Juan looked down at his own metal replacement. "Well, maybe the wrong choice of words."

"At least I know you won't break my ship, since I'll be in command while you're gone."

"Since she'll be tied to the dock, you shouldn't have any problems, either."

"Just be back on time," Max said like a worried mother hen.

"Johnny-on-the-spot as always."

"Unless you put one of your infamous Plan C's into effect." Max turned and headed back to the op center, where he could coordinate all of the mission activities.

Juan called after him, "You should only worry when I get to Plan D." A dismissive wave of Max's hand was the only response.

After a ride on an elevator down three decks, Juan reached a cavernous space amidships. A submersible was suspended by a gantry crane over a swimming-pool-sized depression that was filled with water at a level even with the waterline outside the ship. The sixty-five-foot Nomad 1000 could dive to a thousand feet with six people aboard, including the pilot and copilot. Its smaller sister, the Discovery 1000, was missing from its cradle, away on another part of the mission.

The moon pool allowed either sub to be launched undetected through huge doors below the pool that swung downward. The port was too shallow to allow the doors to be fully opened, so the Discovery 1000 had been launched before they entered La Guanta Harbor. Juan wouldn't need the Nomad for this mission, so it would stay in its cradle.

Linc was already donning his black neoprene wetsuit. Their scuba equipment lay next to him. Juan put his pistol inside Linc's waterproof weapons bag and slipped into his wetsuit. The water in the tropical harbor didn't require the suits, but the black color would render them invisible to any casual observers on the dock.

They both checked over their Draeger rebreathing units. Regular scuba rigs released the exhalations as bubbles that would rise to the surface, leaving a trail that would be easily followed. The Draeger consisted of carbon dioxide scrubbers in a closed-loop system that eliminated bubbles. Although the unit was dangerous to use below thirty feet, the restriction wouldn't be a problem in this case because Juan and Linc were using the gear only to exit the *Oregon* undetected.

Juan knew that the harbormaster would have the ship staked out and would follow anyone who left the dock area. He and Linc needed to get to their rendezvous without a tail, so underwater was the only option.

Linc nodded that he was ready. With his gear in place, Juan climbed down the collapsible stairs into the moon pool. He put on his fins, clamped his teeth over the rebreather's mouthpiece, and lowered his mask. He drifted out into the center, and Linc came behind him. Juan gave the A-OK, and the technician in charge of the moon pool dimmed the lights to a faint smolder so that nobody on the dock would notice anything unusual going on beneath the ship.

Juan felt a slight eddy tug at him as the doors below cranked open with a muffled thrum. After a few seconds, the sound stopped. The technician waved a flashlight, signaling that the crack in the doors was now wide enough for their departure.

They released air from their buoyancy compensators and descended until they were floating below the keel. Juan clicked on a wrist flashlight, just bright enough to see the ship's metal hull in the murky harbor water. He and Linc swam to the stern, where he shut off the flashlight and referred to the waterproof compass on his other wrist to guide them.

Fifteen minutes later, he grabbed Linc's arm and gave him a thumbs-up. He slowly kicked upward until his mask broached the surface with the barest of ripples. He silently patted himself on the back. They were only twenty yards from the ancient shed that the Corporation had rented for the month.

Juan scanned the perimeter and confirmed that they were alone. No boats were nearby, and the road along the shore was empty. They had chosen this part of the harbor because it was the least traveled.

Juan and Linc removed their fins and crept onshore. Sure that there were no oncoming vehicles, they dashed across the road and into the run-down shed.

Instead of a grimy storage place for rusty equipment and fishing supplies, it seemed as if they'd stepped into the dressing room on a movie set. On one side of the shed was a well-lit mirror, a counter spread with makeup and latex prosthetics, and a director's chair. Next to it stood a metal frame where two Venezuelan Navy working uniforms were hung—one for a master chief petty officer, the other for a captain, both in camo gray.

The other side of the shed was occupied by a hulking Humvee painted in the livery of the Venezuelan military. Leaning against it was a slim man with a thick beard. He threw each of them a towel.

"You're a minute early," Kevin Nixon said with a bright smile. "I wish my actresses had been so punctual. Often I was happy if they showed up at all. Sober."

Kevin had been an award-winning Hollywood makeup artist, but after his sister died in the attacks on 9/11 he felt the need to contribute his skills to the war on terror. He applied to the CIA but went with a much more interesting and challenging offer when he was guided to Juan and the Corporation. In addition to disguising the crew's faces for operations when needed, Kevin and his team also had racks of uniforms and clothing from every nation and built whatever unusual props and gadgets they needed, occasionally tapping Max's engineering expertise for the most technical items. Kevin was the person responsible for Juan's earlier disguise, the stuffed rat, and the combat leg he now wore.

Normally, Juan would have met him on board the *Oregon* in the Magic Shop, the name they'd given the workshop where Kevin crafted his amazing designs. But since Juan had to swim out of the *Oregon*, any appliances and makeup would have washed off before he reached shore. So they'd prepositioned Kevin in the abandoned shed with enough battery power to keep him off the grid. Linc had flown in the week before, liberated the Humvee from a naval armory near Caracas, and stashed it in the shed for tonight's use.

Juan spotted discarded food wrappers in the corner. Food used to be Kevin's Achilles' heel. At one point, he weighed almost two hundred and seventy-five pounds, but successful stomach bypass surgery and a special diet prepared by *Oregon*'s gourmet chef brought his now solid frame down to a slender one eighty-five.

"I hope you've been careful with the local cuisine," Juan said to Kevin. "Nothing like Montezuma's revenge to make a sea voyage unpleasant."

"Tell me about it," Linc said, rubbing his belly. "I hope I never go back to Mozambique."

"Nothing but bottled water and prepackaged food for me," Kevin replied. "Now, let's get you in the chair. We have some work to do."

Part of Linc's time in Venezuela the previous week had been spent observing the suspected warehouse from afar. Covered wide-load trucks went into the facility night and day—presumably with armaments on them—through a razor-wired security fence and a well-guarded gatehouse before disappearing into the building. Sentries walked the perimeter on random schedules, and cameras monitored both the dock and the fence, ruling out stealthy infiltration.

The only other option was to go through the front gate. Twice Linc noticed the same captain going into the facility. The long-lens photos were sent to the CIA, where he was identified as Captain Carlos Ortega. He spent most of his time at the main naval base in Puerto Cabello, where he was now. Although Ortega was similar to Juan in height and build, they looked nothing alike. Whereas Juan was fair-haired and clean-shaven, Ortega was swarthier, with dark hair, bushy eyebrows, brown eyes, a trim mustache, and a nose that looked as if it had been broken.

That's where Kevin came in. He had several of Linc's photos of Ortega taped to the mirror. He would transform Juan into the Venezuelan Navy captain.

Juan dried off and sat in the chair while Linc went over the Humvee to make sure it was in good running order. They'd need to depend on it to get back to the *Oregon* in a hurry once their reconnaissance was complete.

Normally, Kevin would put on laid-back alt-rock music while he worked, but the unusual location demanded quiet so as not to attract attention. With an expert touch, he applied the glue for the latex nose, weaved on a thatchy set of eyebrows, and dusted Juan's face with makeup. The final touches were the black wig and colored contacts. When Kevin was finished, Juan felt the odd sensation that a stranger was staring back at him from the mirror.

"Excellent work as usual, Kevin," Juan said. "I can't recognize myself."

Linc, who was already in his Navy kit, complete with sidearm and FN FAL assault rifle slung across his shoulder, clapped Kevin on the shoulder. "Wow! I don't know whether to salute him or recommend a plastic surgeon for that ugly mug."

"Don't listen to him," Kevin said. "You look perfect, if I do say so myself. Try on the uniform."

Juan put on the tailored outfit, including the cap. When he was fully dressed, Linc and Kevin appraised him.

"I'd say you're an inch or two taller than Ortega," Linc said, "but I doubt anyone will notice."

"Then we're set," Juan said. "You've outdone yourself again, Kevin."

"It looks like my work is finished here," Kevin said, and started packing up his cosmetic supplies. "I'll head back to the *Oregon* as soon as you go."

He'd leave the less portable items behind and walk to the *Oregon*. Though the Venezuelans were watching for anyone leaving the ship, they wouldn't stop Kevin from getting on, especially because he had all the proper documentation to rejoin the crew.

Since Linc was playing the lower-ranking officer, he would act as the driver. They got in the Humvee and Kevin opened the shed doors. Linc started it up and eased out onto the road.

They didn't have far to go. It was a two-minute drive to the warehouse and dock.

When they reached the gatehouse, a guard armed with an assault rifle similar to Linc's waved them to a stop behind the lowered bar. A second guard stood behind him. The first guard leaned in and saluted when he saw Juan's lapel insignia and face.

Juan returned the salute and handed him the ID card that Kevin had forged for him. Although the guard clearly recognized him, the check was required.

The guard handed it back and motioned for the other guard to open the gate.

"Welcome back, Captain," the first guard said. "If you're here to see Lieutenant Dominguez, he's in the security office." The guard pointed, leaving no doubt as to their destination. It was a door at the corner of the warehouse. The huge garage doors were closed and no light leaked from underneath. Aside from the arc lamps around the compound, the only other lights shone on the deck of the giant oil tanker docked behind the warehouse. Workers swarmed around the front of the ship, where they were connecting pipes to feed the holds from the nearby refinery, one of Venezuela's largest.

Juan used his Spanish to order the guard not to announce their arrival, and Linc pulled away from the gate.

"So we have a host," Juan said. "We were hoping for a skeleton crew at this time in the evening."

"You know what they say," Linc replied. "No plan survives contact with the enemy."

"True, but I'd hoped it would last longer than this. We may have to act more quickly than we expected. Follow my lead, and remember to let me do all the talking."

Linc just laughed. While Juan was fluent in Spanish, Arabic, and Russian, Linc could speak and understand only English. Using a parabolic microphone during his surveillance, Linc had captured enough of Ortega's speech to give Juan time to practice mimicking the Venezuelan's cadence, tone, and accent. Although limited to a Saudi accent when speaking Arabic, Juan could modify his Spanish with ease to match virtually any accent in Latin and South America.

But the usefulness of the makeup and mimicry was predicated on cowing enlisted sailors and noncommissioned officers. If this lieutenant was very familiar with Ortega, it would only be a matter of time before he saw through the disguise.

Linc pulled up to the front of the warehouse office door next to a second Humvee. They got out, and Linc looped the FAL over his shoulder in as nonthreatening a way as possible. It was common to see soldiers and sailors carrying around assault rifles in South America, and Captain Ortega's adjutant had been no different.

Juan flung open the door in the style he'd memorized from Linc's video and strode into the office, surprising four men, three of whom were sitting behind desks, the fourth in front of a bank of video monitors and ignoring them. A radio in the background was playing a soccer match.

The heads turned toward the visitors as one and the radio flicked off. All four men leaped from their chairs and snapped to attention.

Juan scanned the group for only a moment and focused on the sailor with lieutenant's bars on his epaulettes.

"*¡Teniente Dominguez!*" he bellowed. "*¿Cuál es el significado de está?*"—*What is the meaning of this?*

The chastened officer was caught off guard, his eyes wide with fear. He showed no sign that Juan's voice was anyone's other than Ortega's.

"Captain Ortega, I thought you were in Puerto Cabello."

"That's what you were meant to think. I see that I should con-duct surprise inspections more often. Despite your mistaken as-sumption, it is not your patriotic duty to listen to our national team play Argentina. Quickly—how many are on duty tonight?"

Dominguez practically spit the words out. "Myself and ten sailors. The four of us here, two at the guardhouse, three on sen-try duty, two guarding the payload."

"Only two in the warehouse?"

Dominguez hesitated for a moment. "I have no men in the warehouse. I could post some there, Captain, if that's your order, but since it is empty I saw no need."

"I see," Juan said. But he didn't. If the payload wasn't in the warehouse, where was it?

"We have intelligence to suggest spies may be trying to gain knowledge about this facility. I want two of these men to join the sentry posts."

Dominguez didn't hesitate this time. "You heard the captain!" he yelled at the two men. "Move!"

The sailors snatched up their rifles and donned their caps as they scrambled out of the room. The only one to stay behind was the man at the monitors.

"Get back to work, seaman," Juan said to him, and the man plopped into his chair. Juan shifted his gaze back to the lieutenant. "Show me the payload."

"Sir, Admiral Ruiz ordered that no one was to view the cargo once it was loaded."

"You will show us the payload or I will report that you dis-obeyed a superior officer."

Another hesitation from Dominguez. "The admiral's orders were very specific."

"His orders are immaterial. That is the purpose of a surprise inspection."

Juan was an excellent interpreter of people's faces, and something that he'd just said was wrong.

Dominguez's arm did nothing more than twitch, but Juan could sense that the lieutenant was attempting to be a hero. Juan drew his pistol and had the FN pointed between Dominguez's eyes before the lieutenant could even get a finger on his own sidearm. Linc moved even faster, whipping the assault rifle around in one smooth movement.

Dominguez froze, then slowly raised his hands above his head without being told. Linc disarmed him and patted him down before gesturing that he had no other weapons. The seaman, who'd watched the whole sequence motionless and agog, moved against the wall with his lieutenant.

"Don't make a sound," Juan said. "Either of you."

Slow nods confirmed the order.

"How did you know?" Juan asked.

"The admiral," Dominguez said. "She's a woman. You used the word 'his' when you talked about her orders."

Juan shook his head. Talk about playing the percentages. He didn't know how many female admirals were in the Venezuelan Navy, but it couldn't have been more than a handful. For once, the odds beat him.

"What did he say?" Linc asked.

"Apparently the admiral in charge of this operation is a woman. I will have to remember to look her up when we get back. Keep an eye on the lieutenant here while I collect what we came for."

Since Linc didn't speak Spanish, Juan would have to be the

one to scour the files and computers for anything relevant to the smuggling operation. He hit the jackpot when he found an encrypted computer. He didn't waste time trying to crack it. That wasn't his expertise, and they didn't have time. He'd let Murph and Eric, the Corporation's computer specialists, do their magic once he got the computer back to the *Oregon*.

A phone started to ring, but not one of the desk phones. It was the trill of a smartphone. Juan spotted it under some papers on Dominguez's desk.

Before either of them could stop him, Dominguez lunged for it and swept it off the desk, smashing it into the concrete wall.

Linc grabbed him and pressed the barrel of the assault rifle against his chest. "Don't do that again, *por favor*."

Juan picked up the pieces, making sure to get the memory card. Whatever was on there was important enough for the young lieutenant to risk his life to protect it.

Juan put the laptop and the phone pieces into Dominguez's briefcase.

"Let's see if we can get some pretty pictures," Juan said to Linc.

"What about him?"

"Hmm. Methinks he's not going to be very cooperative." Juan turned to Dominguez. "*¿Dónde está el baño?*"

The lieutenant reluctantly pointed to a door at the other side of the room. They slipped plastic ties around the hands and feet of both captives and used torn uniform fabric as gags. When the men were cinched up tight against the toilet with more ties, Linc locked the door from the inside and closed it.

Killing them, of course, would have been easier and safer, but that wasn't the way the Corporation did things. Although they were technically mercenaries, killing in cold blood wasn't part of their moral code. Juan created the Corporation to stop terrorists and assassins, not become them.

"Two minutes and we're back here," Juan said. "Nobody should need the potty that soon."

Linc nudged open the only other door in the room. After a quick sweep of his rifle, he said, "Clear. And I mean *clear*."

Juan followed him through into the main body of the warehouse.

"You weren't kidding," he said.

The vast warehouse was bare. Although the concrete floor was chewed up as if a rototiller had gouged it, the space was bereft of crates or vehicles. But Dominguez had mentioned a payload. There had to be more here than met the eye.

Then Juan saw it. The back of the warehouse—the side near the dock—had a large door identical to the one at the front. He looked up and saw a section of the ceiling above the door that was similar to the gantry crane above the moon pool on the *Oregon*. The difference was that instead of a submarine, this crane held a horizontal metal sheet that could be extended out beyond the door, large enough to cover anything moving the fifty feet from the warehouse to a ship from the prying eyes of a spy satellite.

Yet the only ship currently docked was a tanker named *Tamanaco*.

"I think I know what's going on here," Juan said. "Let's take a look."

He and Linc went to the back of the warehouse and out the person-sized door next to the garage door.

Only this close could Juan spot a modification to the *Tamanaco* and, even then, only because he'd made similar alterations to the *Oregon*. A dark seam etched the outline of a huge door in the side of the ship. They had been loading the weapons onto the tanker, which must have been modified to carry cargo as well as fuel. No one would think of stopping a tanker to look for embargoed arms.

Still, they had no proof. One look inside and they'd have all the evidence they needed.

Juan spotted a sailor standing at his post next to a gangway.

"We're going to continue the surprise inspection," he whispered to Linc.

"Sounds good to me."

They walked past the seaman, Juan returning the salute but saying nothing. Once they were on deck, they took the first flight of stairs they could find and went down until they saw another armed sailor posted at a bulkhead door.

"We're here to inspect the cargo, sailor," Juan said. "Open the door."

The sailor probably had the same orders not to let anyone inside, but he wasn't going to disobey a captain.

"Aye, sir," he said, and turned smartly. He swung the door wide, and Juan and Linc stepped through. The sailor flipped a switch and fluorescent lights flickered on.

The payload was here, all right, but it wasn't what the Corporation had been led to expect. The Venezuelans were suspected of shipping Russian technology to the North Koreans.

Instead, Juan counted twenty American Bradley Fighting Vehicles and a dozen of the latest M1A2 Abrams main battle tanks.

They didn't have time to snap even one photo. Without warning, the tanker's steel hull reverberated with the sound of a klaxon.

Someone had pulled the alarm.

4

Like a crocodile lying in wait for its prey, the submarine drifted at periscope depth as the supertanker cruised toward it. Two freighters had already passed by less than a thousand yards away. Few cargo vessels carried active sonar, so the sub remained undetected. As long as Linda Ross kept the Discovery 1000 below the surface, the oncoming 113,000-ton *Sorocaima* would have no way of knowing it was there.

The Discovery had been on-station for the past four hours since the *Oregon* had lowered it into the Caribbean fifty miles north of the Venezuelan coast. The shipping lane curved around the island of Nueva Esparta before turning east. The spot was chosen because it was along a well-traveled route for tankers from Puerto La Cruz heading to the Mediterranean.

The mini-sub was large enough to carry eight passengers to a depth of one hundred feet, but it currently held only Linda and the two men playing cards behind her. This would be a quick in and out mission, and more than two men infiltrating the tanker would increase the risk of them being seen.

Linda, a Navy vet who'd served aboard a guided-missile cruiser and as a Pentagon staffer before she was hired by the Corporation to be vice president of operations, was beneath only Juan and Max in the crew hierarchy. Her petite figure, upturned nose, and soft voice had once been a hindrance in her career, preventing her from being taken seriously enough to ever warrant command of her own ship. But she'd earned the respect and trust of everyone on the *Oregon*, to the point that she was tagged to lead some of its toughest missions. She had a habit of changing her hair color often and tonight her long ponytail was a fiery red.

Linda peered at the monitor showing the feed from the periscope camera. The full moon and starlight enhancement turned night to day, and the outline of an approaching tanker was unmistakable. Though she couldn't read the name on the side of the ship from this distance, there was no doubt it was their target. The tracking device Linc had planted on the vessel during his visit to Puerto La Cruz pinged strongly. The *Sorocaima* was right on schedule, only a mile off their stern.

"Here she comes, guys," she said.

Marion MacDougal "MacD" Lawless and Mike Trono looked up from their cards. The two gundogs, as Max called members of the shore operations team, had been playing gin rummy, and from the Cajun-inflected whoops of triumph she'd been hearing from MacD for the past two hours she guessed he was trouncing Mike.

"It's just as well," Mike said, and tossed his hand on the pile. "I was about to find out how this grunt was cheating."

As VP of operations, Linda knew the files of every crew member backward and forward. Sporting thin brown hair atop a slender frame, Mike had been an elite pararescue jumper for the Air Force, dropping behind enemy lines multiple times in Iraq and Afghanistan to save downed pilots. He left the military and got his kicks racing offshore powerboats before joining the Corporation when he realized the adrenaline surge of real-world operations was the only thing that would do the trick.

"Cheatin'?" MacD retorted in his molasses-thick Louisiana drawl. "Why would Ah have to cheat against a wing nut like you? Ah'm just good."

"Because that would make life really unfair. You can't be good at cards *and* look like an underwear model."

Linda had to agree with Mike on that. While Mike was cute and lean, former Army Ranger MacD had a physique sculpted in marble and a face fit for a movie star. He was one of the newest members of the crew, and his down-home New Orleans charisma and quick thinking in battle had charmed everyone on the *Oregon*.

"Now Mike, you and Ah are two sides of the same coin," MacD said.

"How's that?"

"Neither of us was stupid enough to become a swabbie."

They both turned toward Linda, the lone Navy person on the mini-sub, and pointedly stared before laughing heartily. Mike and MacD were the butts of good-natured ribbing on the *Oregon* for being the only two non–Navy vets on the ship, but now she was the one outnumbered.

She stared back at them stoically but with a twinkle in her eye. "That's it. I order the both of you to walk the plank."

"Yes, ma'am," they said in unison, and started donning their black night gear—sweaters, pants, gloves, boots, and hats. The final touch was black greasepaint smeared on their faces.

While they were preparing for their excursion, Linda engaged the motor and aimed the Discovery directly into the path of the oncoming *Sorocaima*, which was on its way to the North Korean port of Wonsan.

The tanker held ten million gallons of refined diesel, ready for use by the North Korean Army for almost every vehicle in their arsenal. With fuel embargoed by most other nations and having few refineries of their own, the increasingly belligerent North Koreans depended on regular diesel shipments from Venezuela, whose president was a personal friend of their leader. Without the fuel, the North's armed forces would grind to a halt.

The *Oregon* could easily sink a ship of even the *Sorocaima*'s size with the weapons at its disposal, but the mission was more subtle than that. Not only did the Corporation refuse to sink unarmed vessels but there was no shortage of tankers or Venezuelan oil, so at best the shipment would only be delayed. Instead, Linda, MacD, and Mike were going to ruin the fuel on board the tanker, laying waste to a huge swath of vehicles in the North Korean military.

At the back of Discovery were six thermos-sized canisters, one meant for each hold on the tanker. The canisters were loaded with bacteria developed in secret by the Defense Advanced Research Projects Agency, or DARPA. Mutated from a strain of the anaerobic bacteria *clostridium* and dubbed Corrodium by the biologists who created it, the microbe multiplied easily in diesel, contaminating an entire tank once it was introduced. It was colorless and odorless, so the contamination was undetectable without laboratory testing.

The bacteria changed the composition of the diesel so that it would burn much hotter. When the tainted diesel was ignited in engines, it would cause them to overheat and seize up, resulting in a total loss. With luck, the Corrodium that they had injected into the holds of the *Sorocaima* would go on to infect the entire North Korean supply, rendering it unusable and destroying the engines of any vehicles into which the diesel had been loaded.

The hard part was getting the Corrodium into the fuel without being detected. If there was any suspicion that the diesel had been tampered with, the *Sorocaima* crew would test it and find out the problem long before it reached Wonsan. Once the North Koreans knew about the potential for bacterial infection, they would have every delivery of diesel tested for it. Linda and her team had to get the mission right the first time because there wouldn't be a second.

The delicacy of the operation was also the reason for conducting it simultaneously with the Chairman's recon mission. If they were done separately and the initial one in the sequence failed, success with the other operation would be in jeopardy.

Linda's responsibility on this mission was to keep the mini-sub on-station while MacD and Mike climbed the side of the tanker with the Corrodium and delivered it into the holds using the ship's own deck piping system.

But they couldn't get on the ship while it was moving. Even if they could match the tanker's speed, maneuvering the Discovery next to it and keeping it stable while MacD and Mike tried to disembark was a recipe for disaster. They had to get the *Sorocaima* to stop.

Disabling the tanker in any way was out of the question. It might be tugged back to port, instead of going on to North Korea, and investigators might realize the damage was intentional, prompting questions about who had done it and why. Stealth was the only option, and it had a side benefit as well. If the North Koreans blamed the Venezuelans for the contamination, it would make them less likely to trust their suppliers for future diesel shipments.

It was Max as usual who had used his engineering expertise to devise a way to get a tanker to stop without hijacking or damaging it.

The Discovery's robotic arms cradled an apparatus the size and shape of a coffin, flat on the long sides, with watertight Plexiglas sealing the ends and an uninflated tube on top. A filament connected the object, which they called the beatbox, to a control system inside the mini-sub. When attached to the hull, the beatbox, which was equipped with a high-impact rotating hammer, would knock with each rotation of the propeller shaft.

No captain likes to be stranded in the middle of the ocean with a dead engine, so the mechanical systems are tuned and maintained rigorously to run at peak operating efficiency. If the engineer heard a pounding in the engine room that couldn't be located, he would recommend that they stop the ship until the problem could be diagnosed. Of course, in this case there wouldn't be a problem at all, and the onboard instrumentation would tell them that. Max estimated they would have thirty minutes before the engineer deemed the engines safe and cranked them back up.

"Hold on, boys," Linda said. "We're heading under."

She flicked the joysticks expertly and dived the sub, maneuvering the Discovery so that it was below the path the *Sorocaima* would take. The rush of water being pushed by the immense tanker's bow grew until it sounded as if the sub were a barrel floating toward Niagara Falls.

Using the onboard LIDAR, or light detection and ranging system, which relied on a series of reflected lasers that would recreate a three-dimensional image of anything they saw, Linda could see the tanker's hull soar over them like a zeppelin drifting through the clouds.

Linda clicked on her on-screen control and the tube on top of the beatbox inflated until it made the apparatus neutrally buoyant. She retracted the robotic arms and then backed the Discovery away, unspooling the filament control wire as she did. She stopped when she was a hundred yards away.

The positioning was perfect. The beatbox hovered twenty feet below the centerline of the tanker.

The tanker's gigantic single screw thrashed as it got closer. Linda would have to time this right. Too early and she'd get the beatbox too far forward of the engine room to be mistaken for a problem with the turbine. Too late and she'd get the beatbox chewed up by the screw or miss the tanker entirely. If that happened, there was no way the sub would be able to catch up and try again.

When the last hundred feet of the tanker passed overhead, she clicked another button, activating the powerful magnet on the beatbox. It flipped as the magnetized side was pulled by the steel hull of the *Sorocaima*. A loud bang signaled that the beatbox had made contact and was holding fast to the tanker only four feet from where Linda had been aiming.

The filament continued to feed out. She clicked another button and the hammer inside the beatbox started to pound away. She nudged the joysticks forward to the sub's maximum speed so that they would be as close as possible when the tanker came to a stop.

"Keep your fingers crossed," she said.

There was an agonizing wait as she looked for any signs that the tanker was slowing. A thousand yards of the filament had already played out. They had three thousand to go. After that, she'd have to cut it loose.

Another thousand yards came and went before she finally saw the unspooling of the filament slowing down.

"Good old Max," she said.

"I knew he wouldn't let us down," Mike said, rechecking the pistol that he was bringing along as a precaution even though their mission was to avoid any contact.

"Looks like we're going to have ourselves a cliff face to tackle," MacD said, and assembled their climbing gear.

When the Discovery caught up with the now stationary tanker, Linda's watch told her that they had twenty-five minutes left out of Max's thirty-minute limit. She surfaced the Discovery next to the bow, as far as possible from the engine room and bridge, where the center of activity would be taking place right now.

MacD popped the hatch and looked outside. When he came back in, he wore a grim expression.

"We've got something of a problem," he said.

Linda leaned forward and peered up through the mini-sub's front viewport. She immediately saw what MacD meant.

They were expecting the *Sorocaima* to be dark except for its running lights, the cloud cover allowing Mike and MacD plenty of pitch-black areas of the deck to move through unnoticed. That would be impossible now. From stem to stern, the tanker was lit up like a Christmas tree.

Red battle station lighting bathed the bridge of the frigate *Mariscal Sucre* in a hellish splendor that Admiral Dayana Ruiz relished. She had risen to her position as the top-ranking woman in the Venezuelan military not only because of her refusal to accept anything less than perfection from her subordinates but also because of her ability to command a ship in battle. She had never lost a war game exercise, and now she had the opportunity to show off her skills in actual combat.

She only hoped that the ship called *Dolos* was as formidable as the stories had claimed. The tip she'd received about the tramp freighter and its captain had come from an officer in the Libyan Navy she had met at an arms bazaar in Dubai. He told her that he had experienced the mythical ship's capabilities firsthand when it had nearly destroyed his frigate, the *Khalij Surt*—the *Gulf of Sidra*.

Although she'd heard secondhand tales of such a covert ship, she had previously dismissed them as fantasy. But the officer's eyewitness account was compelling. She spread word throughout the naval community that she would be happy to bag the mystery ship as a prize.

Then Gao Wangshu of the Chinese Navy had come to Ruiz with a story similar to the Libyan's. He had intelligence that the ship would be coming to Venezuela, although he thought the port of call would be Puerto Cabello. At the last minute, he gave word that La Guanta was where it would dock, and she sent him to the harbormaster there to get confirmation it was the right ship.

Now it seemed like she had even more reason to believe the *Dolos* was a spy ship. The call from Lieutenant Dominguez about the two impostors who had tied him up couldn't be a coincidence.

Ruiz finished her black coffee as she angrily waited for the phone call from Puerto La Cruz. She wanted to fling the mug against the window, but the rigid reflection staring back at her made her stop. Her short raven hair, tan angular face, and tall, ramrod-straight frame under an immaculately pressed uniform, projected the reputation she had as an ice-cold commander, ready to sacrifice anyone or anything for victory. Any histrionics would dispel that image and allow the macho Latin American men under her command an opportunity to question her ability. She would not let that happen, but these latest developments were testing her stoicism.

Lieutenant Dominguez was one of her brightest pupils and she had trusted him with some of the most valuable information about her operations that would propel her planned rise to power in the Venezuelan government. There had already been a female defense minister, but her ambitions were much higher than that.

Hugo Chávez had been her idol and she foresaw following in his footsteps.

But Dominguez had let her down and her empire was threatening to crumble.

She had called him to check on the status of her arms smuggling operation. When he didn't answer, she had called the guardhouse at the warehouse to check on him. Soon after the guards arrived at the security office, they found Dominguez and another man tied up in the bathroom. She immediately ordered the entire facility locked down so they could find the impostors who had sneaked in. She was now awaiting news that they had been found since no one had seen them leave the base.

The phone rang and she snatched up the receiver.

"Report," she snapped.

"Dominguez here, Admiral," he said. "We have them cornered."

"Where?"

He cleared his throat. "On the ship. They're in the cargo bay. They knocked one of my men unconscious and locked themselves inside."

Ruiz had to find out who they were, how they'd discovered her operation, and whether any other part of it was in jeopardy.

"I want them captured alive," she said.

"Yes, ma'am. We have all the exits covered."

"What about the cargo door?"

"We've cut power to that part of the ship. There's no way they can lower it. I have fifty additional men on the way. There's no way they can escape."

"Do you know what they were after?"

Another hesitation.

"Don't lie to me, Lieutenant. I will find out."

"They took the laptop and my phone." He added quickly, "The computer is encrypted and I destroyed the phone, so they won't be able to transmit any information from inside the ship."

Ruiz's hand tightened on the mug until it seemed in danger of shattering.

"You had better be right, Dominguez, or I'll use you for target practice."

She could hear him gulp. "Aye, Admiral."

"Describe these men."

"Both were dressed in Navy uniforms. One was a large black man. The second . . . well, I could have sworn he was Captain Ortega. But, then, he thought you were a man. I was about to arrest him, but he and the other impostor were so quick—"

"Enough. I'll read about it in your report later. Call me the moment you have them in custody."

She hung up without waiting for acknowledgment.

The news that they'd gotten hold of the computer and phone was the most disturbing part of Dominguez's report. She could survive the discovery of her arms smuggling operation, but if anyone outside her inner circle found out about the second aspect of her illicit activities her standing in Venezuela would be destroyed. She'd be executed as a traitor.

She retreated to her cabin. The next calls required more privacy.

Ruiz dialed a number that she had memorized. She erased the number after every call.

On the second ring, a clipped voice answered. "What?"

"We've had an incident, Doctor," she said in fluent English using the only name she knew him by.

"So?"

"I want to make sure it doesn't jeopardize my plans. Is the *Ciudad Bolívar* on schedule?" she asked.

"It will be in position in thirty-six hours just like I said it would."

"Have you detected any interest in our activities?"

"No," the man replied. "I expect the final payment to come through as soon as the *Bolívar* goes down."

"And in exchange you will hand over the encrypted software code for controlling the drones as we agreed?"

"Yes," the Doctor said.

"Then we'll proceed. Dominguez will report when the *Ciudad Bolívar* is sunk. Make sure the drones are ready by tomorrow night."

"Of course. That's why you're paying me."

He hung up. Ruiz wasn't used to being treated with such disrespect, but the Doctor's special skills demanded that she tolerate insubordination that would get a sailor sent to the brig.

Her next call was to the harbormaster, Manuel Lozada. She was afraid that the *Dolos* would cast off early and leave the spies behind if they knew they were cornered and would eventually confess to the covert ship's true nature.

"A pleasure to hear from you, Admiral," he said upon answering. "I was just about to—"

"Lozada, I want you to raid the *Dolos*. I will have thirty soldiers there in ten minutes to assist the police." She would redirect some of Dominguez's reinforcements to La Guanta Harbor.

"But Admiral, that's why I was about to call you. The *Dolos* has just cast off."

"What? You gave them permission?"

"Yes. You told me that you would capture them at sea, so I thought . . ."

Ruiz was steaming. She had idiots working for her. But she kept her voice calm.

"Lozada, do whatever you can to slow them down. If they leave Venezuelan waters before we get there, capturing them would cause an international incident."

"At once, Admiral!"

"And use any information that Gao can tell you about the ship. It might give you a tactical advantage."

"Excellent suggestion, Admiral. We will do everything in our power to keep them from leaving."

"I want regular updates about its location."

She hung up, and strode back onto the bridge. She checked their position. They were still forty miles from Puerto La Cruz. At their present speed, they would reach the port in a little more than an hour.

The *Mariscal Sucre*, a Lupo-class frigate, was the pride of the Venezuelan Navy. It was armed with a 127mm forward gun, eight Otomat Mark 2 surface-to-surface missiles, and twin Mark 32 triple torpedo tubes. Ruiz had no compunction about unleashing her arsenal on the spy vessel no matter how well armed or how defenseless it was.

She just had to make sure they got there in time.

"Captain Escobar," she barked to the ship's commander, "I don't care if you burn the turbines out. Give me all the speed you can muster."

After a smart "Aye, aye," Ruiz could feel the ship vibrate from the increased output, matching the adrenaline coursing through her system. She had never been more ready for a fight, and there was no way she would be denied her victory.

6

Juan and Linc had the cargo bay's stern door covered, occasionally taking shots to keep Dominguez's men from pouring through. The bow door was still locked tight, with a chain looped through the handle, but they could hear someone hammering away at it on the other side. It was only a matter of time before it was breached.

Bullets pinged off the armored vehicles around Juan and Linc as sailors with assault rifles poked their heads through the door to fire off a few shots. None came close. It was as if the men were simply trying to keep them pinned down.

Juan guessed that was exactly their plan. The Venezuelans had the high ground because the doors on either end, one toward the bow and one toward the stern, were at the top of the three-story-high hold, with stairs leading down to the floor, where the vehicles were lined up in eight rows of four. It was a stalemate;

Juan and Linc couldn't leave and the Venezuelans couldn't charge down the exposed stairs.

"How many rounds do you have left?" Juan asked Linc.

"Two magazines, but at this rate I'll be out in a few more minutes."

"I'm down to one on the rifle I borrowed from our friend who let us in here." A chop from Linc's hand had dealt the guard a blow that would have him woozy for days. That still left enough men to beat them by attrition alone. There was no chance they'd make it all the way back to the Humvee. They had to find another way out.

Even if they concentrated on one door and made a break for it, the only way off the ship was by sea. They'd be sitting ducks for anyone taking potshots from the dock.

However, they did have one possibility on this very cargo deck.

"Remember how gouged the floor in the warehouse was?" Juan asked.

Linc nodded. "Sure. The treads on the armored vehicles will tear concrete like that to shreds when they turn. The tanks weigh upward of sixty-five tons."

"Which means they have some gas in them. How hard do you think it would be to drive this?" Juan said, jerking his thumb at the M1 Abrams next to him. It was the tank closest to the dock side of the ship.

Linc was used to Juan's improvisation, so he didn't even blink at the suggestion. Instead, he said, "We've got to get the cargo door down first."

"So you've driven one?"

"I sat in the driver's seat of one back in the old days. A buddy of mine in the SEALs used to be a Marine tank driver. It looks pretty simple. Motorcycle-type handles for steering and accelera-tion, and a brake pedal. Not much different from my Harley."

Linc kept a customized Harley-Davidson in the *Oregon*'s hold for day trips at ports of call.

"So that would be a no."

Linc smiled. "I learn quickly."

"I like your attitude. Only one problem." Juan pointed at the battery-powered emergency lights that were on overhead. "I'd bet they cut off the power so the door won't go down."

"That *is* a problem. Even a tank can't smash through a ship's hull."

"But you did see the crates as we ran down here?"

A look of understanding crossed Linc's face and he turned to squint at the other side of the hold. Two metal shipping containers were placed end to end along the wall. Each of them was marked with yellow warning placards that said "EXPLOSIVES."

They held the ammunition for the armored vehicles. This really was a full-service smuggling operation. No sense in buying tanks that didn't come with ammo.

"Keep me covered," Juan said. "I'll be right back."

He felt extremely confident in Linc's ability to protect his flank. Linc was an exceptional sniper, and even in the dim light he could take down any sailor who tried to rush in as long as he still had a round in the chamber.

Juan sprinted between the tanks, keeping his head low as he ran. He felt the shock wave of bullets passing overhead, but they were few and hastily aimed thanks to Linc's expert covering fire.

Juan crouched behind the last tank and saw that the end of the freight container was exposed to the sailors at the stern door.

It was also locked.

A sizable padlock was looped through the handle. Either the North Koreans or Venezuelans didn't trust the sticky fingers of their dockworkers.

Juan hitched up his pant cuff and accessed the hidden compartment in his combat leg. He'd leave the pistol and knife there for now. The plastic explosive and detonator were what he needed.

The small amount of C-4 would take care of a padlock easily enough.

He removed the explosive from its package and readied its detonator.

"Give me ten seconds on the stern door!" he called out to Linc.

"Roger that!"

"Now!"

Linc concentrated his fire on the stern door, keeping the gunmen pinned outside.

Juan darted to the container door and mashed the C-4 onto the padlock. He stuck the detonator and pulled the firing pin, which would give him ten seconds to get cover.

"Fire in the hole!" he yelled.

The blast echoed through the hold. The padlock was blown to pieces.

This time, Juan didn't wait for the cover fire. The guards would be too surprised at the explosion to pop back in right away. He ran over to the container, unhooked the latch, and flung the door open.

Metal boxes were stacked up to his eyes for the length of the container. The boxes closest to the end were marked "M829A2." It was a sabot round. Juan knew the designations of every round the M1 Abrams used because the *Oregon* had an identical 120mm smooth-bore cannon hidden behind bow doors.

Sabots were uranium-depleted penetrator rods that were designed to go through tank armor. The shell around it was discarded as soon as it left the gun barrel. It would be no use to them. They would make a neat Coke-can-sized hole in the hull, and through anything else within a mile's range, but not near big enough for a tank to crash out.

What Juan was looking for was an M908, a high-explosive, obstacle-reduction round. It was designed to blow apart concrete bunkers. It should do nicely on the side of the ship if he could find one.

He pulled himself up on top of the crates and started making his way back, using the flashlight on his phone to check the markings.

He got a quarter of the way into the container before he found one marked "M908." He flipped the lid open and saw four giant shells nestled into their cradles, each weighing thirty pounds. He'd have to make do with two.

He slung his assault rifle over his back and hoisted two of the shells, one under each arm. He made his way back to the container door.

After carefully putting the shells down on top of a crate, he lowered himself to the floor, making sure to keep the door between him and the stairway. With the shells in hand again, he called out to Linc.

"Cover me!"

Juan dashed back toward Linc, knowing that if a stray round hit either of the warheads, there wouldn't be enough of him left to scrape off the tank treads.

He knelt beside Linc next to the tank closest to the cargo door.

"Getting in the tank will be tricky," Juan said.

"Too bad you didn't find any belts for that fifty-cal," Linc said, giving the machine gun mounted on the tank's turret a longing look.

"Sorry. I had my hands full as it was."

Linc nodded. As soon as Juan fired his shots, Linc leaped onto the front of the Abrams, flipped the driver's hatch up, and hopped inside, leaving only his upper body exposed. When he had the stern door above them sighted, Juan put the two shells on the turret and climbed up.

He opened the commander's hatch and lowered the first shell into the commander's seat. As he turned to retrieve the second shell, he saw the bow door above them slam open. Sailors poured through, their rifles at the ready.

Juan grabbed the shell and clambered through the hatch as gunfire rained down on them. One of the rounds grazed his shoulder, causing him to drop the shell. He cringed as it hit the floor, but the fuse didn't detonate.

Juan dropped inside and pulled the hatch closed behind him. He snugged it tight and engaged the locking latch, designed to prevent infantry from opening the hatch from the outside and tossing grenades in.

He put pressure on his shoulder to stop the bleeding while he checked his phone and saw that Max had come through. When they'd gotten stuck in the hold, he'd texted Max to cast off with the *Oregon* and that he and Linc would get out somehow and make it back to the ship. Juan had already had the idea of using one of the tanks to make their getaway, so he'd asked Max to contact their connections in the CIA to send Juan an operations manual on how to run an Abrams and fire its main cannon.

Max's message said *No need to contact CIA. Found this one on the Internet.*

When Juan opened the attachment, he saw that it was a PDF of a scanned Abrams operations manual.

He rapidly scrolled to the start-up sequence. His eyes flicked back and forth as they flew through the instructions. It seemed straightforward. He located the proper switches and started the engine.

The turbine behind him spooled to life with a whine that made it sound as if they were about to make a moon launch. Juan looked out of the viewport to see that the guards who had flooded into the cargo bay had stopped in their tracks, watching the tank with caution as its jet engine roar filled the hold.

Juan put on a headset hanging next to the commander's station.

"You with me?" he said.

"Loud and clear," Linc responded. "It's a tight fit but comfy. Like sitting in a recliner. I can't see much, so you'll have to let me know when to move."

"Believe me, you'll know."

Juan secured one shell in the magazine and loaded the other into the breech, a process as easy as shoving the shell in and slamming the back closed, which allows the Abrams to fire six rounds a minute.

Once the 1500-horsepower turbine warmed up and was at full speed, he settled into the gunner's seat. The sailors outside the tank had climbed on and were banging at the hull futilely trying to get inside.

Juan grabbed the two sticks controlling the turret and tested them out. The turret spun on its axis as easily as turning in his office chair. The guards outside tumbled off and ran for cover.

He put his eyes up to the gunner's sight and pointed the cannon directly in front of them at a five-degree down angle. His finger rested on the trigger.

"Get ready, Linc," he said. "This is going to shake you a bit."

"Let's get out of here."

Juan pulled the trigger.

The gun fired with a thunderous blast, rocking the Abrams backward, and was followed instantaneously by an even bigger explosion as the shell blew out the hull of the tanker.

The gaping hole now in the side of the ship sucked the smoke out, letting the lights from outside filter in.

"Let her rip," Juan said into his mic.

"You got it."

For a moment, the tank remained stationary as it tugged on the tie-down chains, but Linc gunned it and they snapped loose. The Abrams launched forward, its treads chewing the steel floor of the hold.

When the tank reached the gaping opening, its armor bent the jagged steel edges back as if ripping through an aluminum can.

The Abrams plunged six feet down onto the dock, slamming Juan into the seat when the tank hit the concrete.

The Abrams charged forward across the fifty feet separating the ship from the warehouse, Linc putting on speed as it approached the building's garage door. It blasted through without slowing, sending the door flying across the bare warehouse floor. The sequence was repeated when they ripped through the front door on the other side of the building. Getting through the chain-link fence wouldn't be any harder.

"Unless the Venezuelans can find someone to drive one of those other tanks," Linc said, "there's not much they can do to stop us."

Linc's comment gave Juan a devilish idea. "Hold up when we get to the fence."

Linc pulled to a stop at the fence. Sailors outside surrounded them, peppering the side of the tank with bullets to no effect.

Juan flipped through the manual until he found what he was looking for.

He keyed on the external loudspeaker and addressed the men outside in Spanish. "Hello out there, amigos. I just want to give you fair warning. Anyone who doesn't get off that ship in the next sixty seconds is going to have a very bad day."

He let go of the mic switch and spun the turret around until it was facing back the way they'd come. Through the two destroyed doors of the warehouse, he had a perfect view of the interior of the cargo hold.

He set the sight dead center on the ammunition container.

One of the sailors outside saw what was about to happen and yelled into a walkie-talkie. Men began careening in panic down the tanker's gangway.

"I can't see anything from up here," Linc said, "but are you planning to do what I think you are?"

"Might as well wipe out their smuggling operation while we have the chance," Juan answered.

"I'm all for that. Saves us another trip."

Juan loaded the second shell into the cannon and watched the seconds tick down on his watch. One minute was more than fair, he thought.

When sixty seconds ended, the ship looked as empty as the famous ghost ship *Mary Celeste*. Juan again pulled the trigger.

The cannon bucked, sending the shell straight through the warehouse and into the tanker.

The ammo detonated with a blast that dwarfed anything up to this point. The cargo bay disappeared in a flash of white flame, an enormous mushroom cloud rising above the dock. The warehouse next to it was blown down by the explosion. Even wearing the headset muffs, Juan's ears rang.

With a fire raging on board, the *Tamanaco* broke in two and began to sink immediately. They'd have a hard time selling the waterlogged vehicles if any of them survived the blast.

Juan glanced around and saw all of the men surrounding the tank had been thrown flat. They would need a few minutes to come around, but Juan spotted a column of what had to be military vehicles heading toward them from the nearby city.

"Where to now, Chairman?"

"Home, James." The Abrams lurched forward, plowing the fence down and turning onto the road.

"Any ideas for how we're going to get back on the *Oregon* now that they're heading out to sea? They'll have the docks locked down, so stealing a boat isn't going to be an option. Plan B is out the window."

They could have the *Oregon* send one of its lifeboats, but that would expose it to gunfire from the shore when it picked them up. Although the tank was impregnable, it was easy to follow, and it had only enough gas for loading onto and unloading off of the ship. At less than two miles per gallon, they were going to be dry in about fifteen minutes of driving.

Juan remembered the peak of the hill on the peninsula they'd sailed by when the *Oregon* was entering La Guanta Harbor. From the looks of it, it had enough elevation for what he was thinking.

"Max isn't going to like this," he murmured.

"Am *I* going to like it?"

"You'll love it," Juan said. "When has my Plan C ever failed?"

The *Dolos* had reached the mouth of the harbor by the time Manuel Lozada and his men had surrounded the lumbering ship in their four powerboats. The ship hadn't responded to his radio call to return to the dock, so Lozada had gathered Gao and fifteen other men to take the freighter by force, if he had to. He still didn't believe the rust bucket was armed with anything more dangerous than a kitchen knife, but he was going to follow the admiral's instructions no matter how ridiculous they seemed.

He raised the bullhorn and stood atop the launch.

"Captain Holland and *Dolos*," he called out in English. "You are required to return to your berth in La Guanta Harbor immediately. Your authorization to depart the harbor has been temporarily revoked because of safety precautions."

He waited, but there was no response. The dim light on the

bridge revealed no occupants. Lozada wasn't surprised considering how grimy the windows were. The *Dolos* continued to plod out to sea. He repeated the call with the same result.

"You're going to have to go aboard to stop her," Gao said.

"It's looking that way." Admiral Ruiz had told him to rely on Gao's experience with the ship and Lozada wasn't going to argue. His expertise was in sailing ships, not assaulting them. "What do you suggest?"

"I suggest you attack the ship with all four boats simultaneously. Two at the bow and two at the stern. Overwhelming force is the most likely tactic for victory."

Lozada agreed and radioed the other boats the plan. Each was equipped with a boarding ladder, and every man had been armed with an assault rifle. They weren't special tactics policemen, but they were able to handle the weapons well enough to capture a straggly crew.

"I would like to request a pistol to take with me," Gao said.

"Take with you where?" Lozada asked in confusion.

"I must go on board and guide your men. I know the hidden areas you have not seen. We may be ambushed unless we can find all of the crew."

"Why are you willing to risk your life for us?"

"Not for you. I must avenge the comrades from my own ship. These spies will be revealed for who they truly are."

Lozada considered the request. If the *Dolos* were nothing more than it seemed, letting Gao on board wouldn't be a problem. If it were a spy ship as Admiral Ruiz and Gao believed, Lozada would want Gao on board to help his men navigate through the ship. Either way, Lozada could justify himself to the admiral.

He nodded for one of his men to surrender his sidearm to Gao. "Use that only if fired upon. If you injure or kill a crewman who turns out to be innocent, you will spend a very long time in one of my country's prisons."

Gao took the pistol, checked the chamber, and tucked it into the waistband of his pants. "I understand. You will see soon enough."

They readied their ladder. Lozada signaled for all the boats to make their boarding attempt.

The harbormaster's launch pulled along the port side near the stern. One of his men latched the ladder's hooks over the deck scupper.

Before he could give the order, Gao leaped onto the ladder and began climbing. As soon as it was clear, the next man went after him. Lozada would go last, just to make sure the deck was secure.

He looked forward and saw that the boat at the bow was taking more time getting its ladder hooked on. Gao was nearly to the railing. He would be the first man on the ship.

He was about to call up and tell Gao to wait when a blast of water played across the launch, knocking Lozada and the rest of his men off their feet. The man on the ladder fell back under the pressure of the water, landing on the launch with a loud thump. Gao was high enough that he was above the aim of the fire hose trained on them.

The boat at the bow was hit at the same time and swung away. Lozada didn't have to tell his boat's driver to do the same. The launch swerved sideways, leaving Gao stranded on the ladder.

The fire hoses were often used by freighters to ward off pirates attempting hijacks. But there were always gaps. Lozada instructed his men to try again, keeping an eye on where the nozzles were located.

Gao leaped over the railing and drew his pistol. He motioned that he was going to try to disable the water jets.

He knelt over a valve and spun the wheel. The water flow lessened. In another few seconds he'd have it shut off and Lozada would be able to approach unimpeded.

The bridge door banged open and an Arab emerged carrying an assault rifle. Gao, who saw what was about to happen, rushed the gunman, but before he could reach him his rifle stitched bullets across Gao's torso. Blood spattered the deck, and Gao's momentum sent him tumbling into the gunman, his deadweight carrying them both back into the bridge.

Out of nowhere, crewmen aboard the *Dolos* popped up and fired rifles at the Lozada's boats. Tiny splashes erupted around them. They took cover and were about to return fire when the Arab returned and aimed a rocket-propelled grenade at them.

Lozada ran forward and threw the throttle to its stops. The launch lurched forward as the rocket fired. It overflew the launch and exploded only fifty feet behind them.

"Fall back!" Lozada yelled to the driver, and repeated the command on the radio to the other boats, which were also under attack from RPGs.

The mortally wounded Gao had been right about the spy ship. The putrid vessel's deception wasn't to conceal advanced weaponry. It was about hiding a crew of spies armed with handheld weapons aboard a ship so disgusting that it wouldn't arouse suspicion. Still, Lozada wasn't about to attack again. Although he didn't know if the ship had torpedoes and missiles and lasers, the *Dolos* with its assault rifles and RPGs was more than a match for his men.

Admiral Ruiz would now have proof that the ship was worthy of being hunted down. Even if she were still thirty miles away, Lozada was quite sure her frigate would easily catch the slow freighter before it escaped.

Max Hanley was pleased to see that Lozada had gotten the message and was retreating. He recalled the gundogs and shut down the remotely aimed water cannons.

Max was watching the huge flat-panel front display from his engineering station in the *Oregon*'s Operations Center, a high-tech room the harbormaster couldn't possibly have guessed was in the middle of the ship he thought was called *Dolos*. The op center was awash in blue from the innumerable computer screens, and antistatic rubber deadened footfalls on the floor. The entire room was colored charcoal, making the space a darkened analog of the bridge on the starship *Enterprise*.

Every aspect of *Oregon*'s operation could be controlled and monitored from this low-ceilinged nerve center, from weapons systems and helm control at the two front seats, to communications, engineering, radar, sonar, and damage control at the stations ringing the room's perimeter. The chair in the center was currently unoccupied. Dubbed the Kirk Chair, Juan Cabrillo's well-padded seat gave him an unobstructed view of the entire room, and he could control every function of the ship from its armrest, if necessary.

Max had to figure out a way to get the Chairman back in his proper place. He had protested mightily when Juan had told him to cast off, but the strange request for an Abrams tank manual made him believe Juan had something up his sleeve.

The door to the op center whisked open and Hali Kasim entered, grinning. The communications officer may have looked like an Arab, but the third-generation Lebanese American didn't speak a lick of the language. He took a seat at the comm panel.

"That was fun," Hali said. "I don't normally like leaving my

comfy chair, but I'll make an exception when I get to shoot him."
He pointed at the door and the man Lozada knew as Gao Wang-shu walked through without a scratch on him. Everyone on the
Oregon knew him as Eddie Seng, director of shore operations.

He had already changed out of his bullet-riddled shirt, which
had actually been perforated by squibs designed by Kevin Nixon.
Like the fake gunshot wounds Hollywood stuntmen used in ac-tion scenes, Eddie's were controlled by a tiny detonator hidden in
his sleeve. He was supposed to have "died" during a gun battle
while the *Oregon* was still tied to the dock, but Juan and Linc's
blown cover necessitated a change of plan. When Hali had come
out of the bridge firing blanks, Eddie had set off the charges in his
shirt, providing a convincing death for Mr. Gao. Harbormaster
Manuel Lozada would never know that he'd been duped.

Raised in Brooklyn by Mandarin-speaking parents, Eddie had
been recruited by the CIA as a field agent. His specialty had been
long-term infiltration of the Chinese government, so he was well
practiced at assuming a false identity in covert operations. It had
been his idea to insert himself as the final witness to *Oregon*'s true
nature, convincing the Venezuelans that it was the ship Admiral
Ruiz had been searching for. For months now, word had gotten
back to the Corporation that their cover as a tramp steamer was
starting to crumble, given the number of battles they'd fought over
the last few years. The Chairman had decided to do something
about it, to get their anonymity back, and implying that they were
no better equipped than Somali pirates was part of the plan.

Eddie's part in the mission was to keep tabs on what the Ven-ezuelans were planning and to make sure they discovered the *Or-egon*'s arrival at the proper time. Lozada and Admiral Ruiz were
convinced Gao had run into the *Oregon* before because a Chinese
destroyer called the *Chengdo* had been sunk under mysterious

circumstances. In fact, the *Oregon* had been responsible. It was during that battle that Juan lost his leg to enemy fire. A lie was much more believable if most of it was the truth.

"You look well for a dead man," Max said.

"It didn't hurt a bit," Eddie replied. "I'm just happy Hali is such a good shot."

"You taught me well," Hali said with a laugh. After an operation in Libya that resulted in Hali getting hit, he had asked Eddie for more combat training. Eddie held black belts in numerous martial arts and was one of the elite sharpshooters on the *Oregon*, so Hali had learned from the best.

"How are the Chairman and Linc doing?" Eddie asked.

"He's on to Plan C," Max said, knowing Eddie would understand that things had not gone as expected for them. He turned to Hali. "See if you can get Juan back on the line."

A hiss came over the op center audio system, followed by a click and a roaring background noise.

"Frank's Tanks here," Juan answered. "How's the ship?"

"Not a flake of rust out of place," Max said.

"And Eddie?"

"Good to be back, Chairman," Eddie said.

"Great. Now we just have the matter of getting me and Linc onto the *Oregon*."

"I wouldn't recommend commandeering a boat," Max said. "The harbor is full of angry Venezuelans with itchy trigger fingers. They're holding off from the *Oregon*, but you'd eat lead trying to get past them."

"My thoughts exactly. I've picked out a nice spot on the peninsula between Puerto La Cruz and La Guanta where we can meet you."

Max checked his satellite map for that location. "Are you

thinking of swimming? Because those rocks look pretty jagged. The waves would beat you to a pulp against the shoreline."

"I don't plan to get my feet wet. Bring the *Oregon* to three hundred yards offshore at the northernmost point."

"That won't be a problem. Why?"

"Remember when we tugged that containership off that reef in the Azores?"

"Yup. We couldn't get anywhere near it because of the gale."

"But we could get a line to it."

Max snapped his fingers. "The Comet."

"Eddie's the best shot. Get a disguise for him and get him up on deck. We need him to throw us a lifeline."

"On my way," Eddie said, and hustled out of the room.

Max shook his head. In this case, the expression "throw us a lifeline" was going to be the literal truth.

MacD Lawless clung to the port side of the *Sorocaima* in defiance of gravity like Spider-Man. Mike Trono was next to him, suspended twenty feet above the water. Linda Ross maintained her position on the Discovery, her face visible through the front window as she craned her neck up to watch them.

The tanker's hull was sitting low in the water with her holds full of diesel, but climbing the bare steel still presented a challenge. Not that MacD wasn't up to it. Taking on a demanding mission like this was one of the reasons he'd joined the Corporation in the first place.

He disengaged the electromagnetic handhold in his left hand and moved it up a foot, placing the rubberized flat side against the hull before reengaging it. The magnet, a smaller version of the one built into the beatbox still attached to the underside of the *Sorocaima*, adhered to the metal with enough force to support four times MacD's body weight. Shoes with high-friction toes allowed him and Mike to brace their feet against the side.

When they reached the lip of the deck, MacD nodded to Mike and they slowly lifted their heads to scan the area for any of the crew. A quick but careful look revealed no one in the vicinity. And since they were directly below the bridge's flying wing, no one stationed inside would be able to spot them unless they happened to look straight down over the railing.

The original plan was for MacD and Mike to access the holds via the emergency vents atop the deck, injecting the bacteria-laden vapor into each tank one by one. But once they had discovered that all of the tanker's lights were on, it was clear they would almost certainly be spotted from the bridge with that approach, and there was discussion of aborting the mission entirely. However, Linda pointed out that they wouldn't get this opportunity again and MacD and Mike had agreed.

They brainstormed alternatives for five minutes before Linda suggested a solution that had previously been rejected in the planning stages.

She told MacD and Mike that modern tankers used residual gas from the boiler flue to replace the air that was left in the storage tanks. The oxygen-deprived exhaust was inert, eliminating the chance that a spark could ignite the fuel vapor inside the tank.

A quick review of the *Sorocaima*'s schematics confirmed that the tanker was equipped with just such a system. If they could get to the purge controls inside the pump room, they could inject the Corrodium bacteria into all six holds at once.

With the deck still clear, MacD nodded to Mike and they hopped over the railing, leaving their magnets attached to the hull out of sight. The handles had enough battery power to last two hours, so it was simpler to leave them in place for a quick escape.

They pressed themselves flat against the outer wall of the superstructure next to the door leading inside. MacD felt naked in the bright light, and seeing Mike didn't boost his confidence. Clad in black from head to toe, including a greasepaint-covered face and a black backpack containing three canisters of the Corrodium, Mike might as well have had the word "Intruder" emblazoned on his shirt. MacD was dressed identically. Their only chance at remaining undetected was to stay quiet and out of anyone's sight.

Neither of them had to refer to a map. They had memorized the route inside the ship that would present the least chance of them being discovered. Once at the pump room, Linda would talk them through the process for injecting the canisters' contents into the air purge system. She would be able to follow their progress via head-mounted cameras and microphones and communicate with them through their earpieces.

He nodded to Mike, who eased the door open. They didn't have their sidearms at the ready. Gunfire would raise all kinds of alarms. If it came to a confrontation, their hand-to-hand combat skills would be more than a match for any crew member, and the crew on a tanker like this would be unlikely to carry any weapons.

MacD poked his head in and saw an empty corridor. With only twenty crew on board the *Sorocaima*, he hoped most of them would currently either be on the bridge or in the engine room, attending to the supposed malfunction. Of course, a crewman could pop out of a random door at any time, ruining everybody's night. The way MacD figured it, this mission was going to be at least fifty percent luck.

He and Mike crept along the corridor, using only hand signals to communicate. The path to the pump room was straightforward: the third door on the right was a stairwell, then it was four decks down to a hall leading directly to the room.

They reached the third door. MacD heard footsteps clanking up the metal stairs. He gestured to a utility room across the hallway. With no time to check if it was clear, they ducked inside. To MacD's relief, it turned out to be empty, and they got the door closed just as the stairwell door banged open. They listened as footfalls trudged down the hallway until the outer door slammed open and then closed. Silence descended.

"I hope we didn't use up all our luck on that one," Mike said.

"My daddy always said, 'Luck never gives, it lends,'" MacD replied. "Let's get this done before we have to pay it back."

"Amen, brother."

MacD pushed the door open and they stole across the hall. They didn't run into anyone else before they reached the door of the pump room. There was too much ambient noise on the opposite side of the door to be sure that the room was empty.

He cracked the door and, from his limited viewpoint, saw no one. He was tempted to continue inside slowly, but two voices somewhere behind them speaking Spanish made time a luxury. Even if the men simply passed by, he and Mike would surely be seen.

They moved through the door and immediately realized their luck was about to run out. Linda mumbled a curse in their ears because she could see the same thing they saw.

Two crewmen were hunched over a display, both with their backs to the door. Neither of them had heard MacD and Mike enter, and Mike, realizing that the door was closing quickly enough to be heard over the background noise, jammed his hand between the door and jamb to keep it from making a sound. He grimaced in pain but stayed silent. MacD moved the door enough for Mike to pull his hand away and then eased the door latch closed with nary a scrape of metal. MacD silently thanked the crew for being diligent enough to keep all of the hinges well oiled.

The two crewmen still hadn't noticed them, but one turn of the head and their presence would be known. They were only twenty feet from the purge valve that MacD and Mike needed to access. There was no way to reach it without being seen. Knocking them out wasn't the answer because it would reveal that intruders were on board.

They retreated behind a vertical pipe as big around as an oak tree and kept an eye on the two men from their hidden vantage point. All they could do now was wait and hope the crewmen would go on to other tasks in another part of the ship.

Five minutes went by. Then six. Then seven. The crewmen didn't budge.

"This isn't working," Linda whispered, knowing they couldn't respond. "If we wait any longer, the ship will get under way before you can do the job. Let's see if we can get them out of there."

Three loud bangs reverberated through the hull. Linda had reactivated the beatbox.

The crewmen's heads snapped up and twirled around, looking for the source of the noise. One of them raised a walkie-talkie and fired off rapid Spanish, shrugging and pointing to the display as he spoke. Whatever the problem was, it obviously wasn't in the pumping system because they had been monitoring it when the bangs were heard.

The crewman lowered his walkie-talkie and gestured for the other man to follow him out of the room. The door slammed shut behind them, leaving MacD and Mike alone.

"How did you know that would work?" MacD asked as they dashed over to the gas purge controls.

"I didn't," Linda replied, "but it was the only thing we had. They're probably certain the problem is in the engine room now."

Mike, who couldn't hold anything with his injured right hand, removed the canisters from his pack with his left. "What if the captain decides to turn back?"

"That's a chance I had to take. Unless his gauges are telling him something else, we'll hope that he'll assume the noise is incidental and report it to the maintenance crew when he arrives at his destination."

While Mike stood watch at the door, Linda talked MacD through the injection process. With her guidance, he attached each of the six canisters to the valve junction in sequence and in five minutes the Corrodium bacteria was multiplying inside the *Sorocaima*'s holds.

Like campers in a national park, they planned to leave no trace. MacD checked the work area to make sure it was clean and started putting the canisters back into their packs.

Before he was finished, he felt a vibration thrum through the floor.

"Is that you?" he asked Linda.

"Negative. They've engaged the engine. The tanker is getting under way. Get out of there now!"

MacD, with the shortened deadline, couldn't argue with that order. He jammed the last of the canisters into the pack and handed it to Mike, who put it on.

They retraced their way out. When they got to the main deck corridor and reached the end of the hall, three men were outside, smoking cigarettes and talking, apparently happy that they were on course again.

"Hurry up," Linda said. "You're already up to five knots. I won't be able to keep up with you much longer."

"We can't reach our climbing equipment," MacD said to her. "The port exit's blocked."

"I don't think we can wait them out this time," Mike said. He pointed at the other end of the corridor leading out to the starboard side of the ship. "How do you feel like going for a swim?"

MacD shrugged. "Why not?"

They sprinted down the hall, expecting at any moment to see a crewman emerge from a door right in front of them. When they got to the end of the corridor, MacD checked the door. It was clear.

Outside, the wind whipped across the deck as the tanker gained speed.

"Linda, we're about to take a dip on the starboard side," MacD said, knowing that their electronics would be fried as soon as they hit the water. "We sure would appreciate you coming on over and picking us up when you get a chance."

"Roger that," she replied. "I'm on my way."

With one last look to make sure they were alone, MacD and Mike climbed onto the rail. They launched themselves forward, competing to see who could make the better swan dive. Although they entered the water with splashes, MacD was sure that nobody on the tanker would have noticed in the darkness.

MacD surfaced and bobbed in the *Sorocaima*'s wake as it churned toward its destination in North Korea. Mike paddled beside him.

"How's the hand?" MacD asked him.

"Nothing an ice bucket won't cure," Mike replied.

In three minutes, with the tanker far in the distance, the Discovery broke the surface and Linda stuck her head out of the hatch.

"You look like you both made it through just fine," she said with a smile, "but I give you only a three on the dives. Let's see a gainer or a twist next time."

MacD turned to Mike and said, "Everyone's a critic."

"Especially a squid."

Like swabbie, squid was a nickname the other services used for a member of the Navy.

"Keep calling me that," Linda said, "and I might just leave you both behind."

In another minute, they were on the sub, with towels and coffee in hand, to begin the wait for the *Oregon* to return and pick them up.

The beatbox, now detached from the *Sorocaima* and with its tube deflated, was drifting to the bottom of the Caribbean. The only items they'd left behind were the climbing magnets still stuck to the side of the ship. Once the batteries discharged, however, they would fall away, disposing of the last evidence that any intruders had ever been aboard.

9

Juan Cabrillo grinned when he spotted the ill-advised roadblock ahead. Two tractor-trailers had been stretched across the far end of a bridge leading to the peninsula where Juan intended to rendezvous with the *Oregon*. Two Humvees with armed soldiers waited with the trucks, and three more Humvees trailed the tank, their occupants taking the occasional ineffective potshot.

Not wanting to reveal their final destination, Juan and Linc had led their pursuers on a stop-and-go chase around the city while Max got the *Oregon* in position. Max had just radioed that they were ready, so they were on the way to their hilltop objective.

"You see it?" Juan said into his headset.

"Unless those trailers are filled with lead," Franklin Lincoln replied from the driver's seat, "I think they're underestimating what a sixty-five-ton tank can do."

"Why don't you go ahead and show them?"

"My pleasure."

Linc gunned the Abrams up to its governed top speed of forty miles an hour. The tank bolted across the bridge, an implacable juggernaut charging toward what the Venezuelans must have thought were immovable objects.

Juan knew how wrong they were.

The Abrams plowed through the trucks like a linebacker tearing through a paper banner before a football game. Juan felt the tank barely slow as the empty trucks were pulverized, showering the nearby soldiers with metal shards.

Juan turned to see the Humvees crawling through the wreckage to continue the chase as the tank made its way down the shoreline road. He checked the fuel level. They were getting dangerously close to empty, and they still had two miles to go. If they ran out of gas in the middle of the road, the Venezuelans would be able to call in bigger weapons and either wait them out or blow the tank up. They'd be as good as dead.

Juan's escape plan depended on having a few minutes outside the tank undisturbed. If they were surrounded by soldiers with rifles when they reached the top of the hill on the peninsula, they'd be shot as soon as they opened the hatches.

That meant slowing down their pursuers, and the power lines strung along the edge of the roadway gave Juan an idea.

"Linc, I think there's going to be a blackout on this side of the harbor pretty soon."

Without hesitation, Linc answered, "Yes, those telephone poles look very unstable. They should be replaced. I'll help them with the demolition."

Linc swerved off to the side of the road and aimed for the nearest thick wooden pole. The Abrams snapped it like a twig and it fell across the road, its power line sparking on the asphalt.

The streetlights were immediately snuffed out, leaving only the illumination from the tank.

The Abrams continued along the roadside until they'd knocked over half a dozen poles.

"Nice driving," Juan said. "That should give us at least a few minutes' breathing room while they try to get those Humvees around them." With no parallel street and rocky terrain behind the houses lining the road on one side and water on the other, the soldiers would have no choice but to clear the obstacles before they could resume the pursuit.

The rumble of the tank's treads had brought out residents from their homes. The astonished onlookers made Juan feel like they were cruising down the street inside a parade float.

When they got to the end of the road, Juan used his phone's GPS to guide them up the bushy slope. The Abrams faltered briefly as its treads tore at the dirt for purchase and then climbed the hill, flattening shrubs and small trees along the way.

In two minutes they had reached the apex of the hill, where in the daytime they would have had an expansive view of the Caribbean. The cloud cover obscured the full moon, making it impossible to see the archipelago of small islands three miles away that formed a natural breakwater protecting Puerto La Cruz and La Guanta from storms.

But Juan could make out the lights on the stationary *Oregon* far below them, three hundred yards north of the rocky coastline. Max had put the ship exactly where Juan was expecting to see her.

Juan popped open the hatch and climbed out of the tank, glad to get a breath of fresh air after being saturated with the stench of burned gunpowder. Linc cracked his hatch and pulled himself up. He stretched his beefy arms wide.

"That space was definitely not designed for someone like me," he said.

"Is anything designed for someone like you?" Juan said as he phoned the *Oregon*.

Linc shook his head. "Why do you think my Harley is customized?"

Juan's phone clicked and Max came on the line. "So that's your Plan C, huh?"

"We like to travel in style," Juan replied. "Are you ready to fire?"

"Eddie's on deck with the Comet and has you in his sights."

"Then let her rip."

Comet was a company that designed line-throwing rockets required on ships by the Safety of Life at Sea convention, or SOLAS. They were used as fire safety lines to people who'd fallen overboard, and they could also send lines to other ships for passing back towlines or supplies.

Comet's normal product fired rockets with a range of two hundred and fifty yards, but the Corporation had asked them to double that range.

Juan spotted a flash from the *Oregon* and a red teardrop of flame flew at them. Eddie's aim was dead-on. The torch arced high over their heads and down the other side of the hill. The rope line landed right across the tank's turret.

Linc wasted no time knotting it around the Abrams's gun barrel to anchor it. He gave Juan the thumbs-up when it was tight.

"Tell Eddie that he was right on the money," Juan said to Max. "We've got the line hooked up."

"We'll get it tied onto a crane at our end."

The rope line went taut as Eddie reeled it in. The *Oregon*'s thrusters would keep the ship in place so that the line wouldn't go slack or snap.

Juan motioned for Linc to go first. Linc climbed onto the tank, wrapped the strap from the assault rifle around the rope, and looped each end around his wrists.

"Remember," Juan said, "we're a lot higher than the *Oregon*, so you're going to have a good head of steam when you get there." Eddie had half inflated a couple of rafts to cushion their landing, but it would still feel like a wrestler's body slam. Juan let Max know that Linc was on his way.

Linc nodded and stepped off the Abrams's front end. Zip lines for tourists are made of heavy steel cable so they will remain taut under load, but the nylon line had much more flex to it and sagged under his weight. He walked down the hill until he was suspended from the rope and gravity took over.

Juan's eyes were drawn away from Linc's progress when he heard the sound of vehicle engines. Headlights came to a stop at the end of the road several hundred yards away. Doors slammed as soldiers piled out and scrambled up the hill. It would be simple to follow the trail of destruction the tank had left in its wake.

Flashlights bobbed as the soldiers climbed. Officers shouted orders to take them alive, but Juan guessed those orders would be countermanded if they saw he was about to get away.

Max called to tell him that Linc had made it, and not a moment too soon. The clouds had parted momentarily, revealing the tank's silhouette in the moonlight. The soldiers had spotted the Abrams and were sprinting toward it, their rifles at the ready.

Juan repeated Linc's actions. When he was set, he jumped off the tank and ran forward. His arms extended until his feet came off the ground and he was sliding down. Wind buffeted his hair, and the smell of salt water grew stronger as he neared the coastline.

Gunfire erupted behind him but was quickly snuffed out. Juan thought he knew why, but he couldn't turn his head far enough to verify it.

They must have seen him flying through the air, puzzled as to how he was doing it, and snapped off some shots. Then some perceptive soldier had to have realized what he was doing and the race was on to find the line he was using. It would only be a matter of seconds before they realized it was attached to the Abrams.

Juan was still more than a hundred yards from the *Oregon*, but past the waves crashing against the rocks jutting from the surf. A vibration in the rope told him the soldiers had found it and were trying to shake him off. The next step was obvious.

The line suddenly went slack on the hilltop end, the victim of a sharp knife, sending Juan hurtling toward the sea. He straightened his body and entered the water feetfirst.

He plunged ten feet down. Before he released the rifle strap, he grabbed the rope and kicked toward the surface.

He breached the water and the line went taut again. Juan tightened his grip as he was reeled toward the *Oregon*. He could hear shots coming from the soldiers again, but at this distance in the darkness they might as well have saved the ammo.

The side of the *Oregon* loomed over him and a rope ladder was tossed over the side. Juan swam to it and climbed to the deck. Eddie and Linc pulled him up and Juan landed on his feet. ·

"Thanks," Juan said. "I wasn't planning to make that a water landing."

"The guys at the yacht club will never believe what I reeled in," Linc said with a smile.

"Good to see you again, Mr. Gao," Juan said to Eddie.

Eddie bowed his head an inch in response. "Captain Holland."

"Tell Max to get under way and that Plan C worked without a hitch. I'll meet him in the op center after I dry off."

As they walked, Eddie relayed Juan's command on his headset radio. A moment later, the *Oregon* began to turn away from the coast.

Eddie's face suddenly took on a more serious expression.

"What is it?" Juan asked.

"Max says we've just been hailed by a Venezuelan frigate twenty miles due west. Their captain is ordering us to surrender or be destroyed."

10

Juan wasn't going to captain his ship in combat wearing a soak-
ing wet uniform of the Venezuelan Navy.

"Tell Max to put Chimana Grande between us and the frigate," Juan said to Eddie. "That'll buy us some time."

Eddie nodded and relayed the message on his radio while Juan
headed to his cabin.

The *Oregon*'s destination was a small cluster of uninhabited
islets ten miles to the northeast. Though the *Oregon* was out of
torpedo and gun range, Venezuelan frigates were equipped with
Otomat Mark 2 surface-to-surface missiles, which had a range
of one hundred and eighty miles. The mountainous terrain of the
islands directly north of their current position, including the largest, Chimana Grande, would make it impossible for the frigate to
get a radar lock until the warship was past them.

Juan entered his cabin to find Maurice, the chief steward,

standing inside with a pristine white towel draped over his arm and a silver tray holding a steaming mug of coffee. The dignified septuagenarian was elegantly attired in a spotless black jacket, a crisply knotted tie, and shoes shined to a mirror finish. After having provided impeccable service to numerous admirals in the Royal Navy, Maurice prided himself on anticipating his officer's needs, so Juan was not surprised to see fresh clothes laid out on the bed just moments after he had been pulled from the water.

Juan picked up the mug and took a sip, savoring the warm shot of caffeine. "You're a lifesaver, Maurice."

In a British accent fit for the House of Lords, Maurice replied, "Shall I serve you a light meal in the Operations Center, Captain?" Despite the rest of the crew calling Juan Chairman, in deference to his position in the Corporation, Maurice insisted on using naval terminology.

"It'll have to wait, I'm afraid," Juan said, peeling off his dripping uniform and donning the blue shirt Maurice had selected.

"Very good, Captain. For your post-action dinner, I will bring you a filet mignon with béarnaise sauce, roasted Yukon potatoes, and sautéed asparagus. Of course, I will be pairing it with an appropriate Bordeaux." Maurice's skills as a sommelier were unparalleled. He displayed nothing but sangfroid about the upcoming confrontation with the frigate, his subtle phrasing letting Juan know the steward had every confidence the *Oregon* would neither be sunk nor captured by the Venezuelans.

Without another word, Maurice slipped out of the cabin as silently as a ninja. Juan finished changing and went to the op center, taking the coffee with him.

He took his seat in the Kirk Chair and asked Max for a situation report.

"We're in the shadow of Chimana Grande on a course bearing

zero-four-five. The frigate, whose captain identified her as the *Mariscal Sucre*, won't have a firing solution for another thirty minutes at their current closing speed." The display showed that the *Oregon*'s pace was a leisurely twenty knots, far below its top speed but in line with the capability of an ancient cargo ship pushing its engines to the limit. As a Lupo-class frigate, the *Mariscal Sucre*'s maximum speed was thirty-five knots.

"ETA to Isla Caraca del Oeste?"

"Thirty-two minutes."

"Cutting it close, aren't we?"

"Hey, it wasn't my idea."

The *Oregon* could easily evade the frigate, if Juan gave the order. Instead of typical diesels, revolutionary magnetohydrodynamic engines provided the power via a pair of gigantic tubes that ran the length of the ship. Magnetic coils interacted with the free electrons in the seawater to accelerate it through the tubes. With the ability to thrust water like air through a jet engine forward or backward with equal force, the *Oregon* could not only accelerate like a dragster and stop like it had slammed into the Rock of Gibraltar, but she could also outrun virtually anything on the ocean slower than a cigarette boat. Venturi nozzles made it possible for the ship to turn on its own axis, and because she got her energy by stripping free electrons from the water, no diesel engine or fuel tanks were required. Her range was essentially limitless.

Juan smiled. "Steady as she goes. What about the *Sorocaima*?"

"They had a few hiccups, but the bacteria were successfully injected into the tanks. Only one small casualty. Mike Trono has a busted hand, but Linda says a few aspirin will hold him until we pick them up. I've already let Julia know."

Juan had no doubt that Julia Huxley, the *Oregon*'s medical officer and a former U.S. Navy doctor, would be able to get Mike back on operational duty in no time. It wouldn't present a problem on a ship equipped with a hospital-grade trauma unit and operating room.

Juan glanced at the helm and weapons control, the stations closest to the forward bulkhead and just below the enormous front screen. They were occupied by other Corporation members instead of Eric Stone and Mark Murphy, who were away on their own mission. With Linda gone as well, Max at engineering and Hali Kasim at communications were the only senior officers staffing the op center.

"Are Eric and Murph finished?" Juan asked.

"They've got everything in place and are headed our way on the RHIB. We should rendezvous with them in ten minutes."

The rigid-hulled inflatable boat, the same type used by Navy SEALs, had a metal hull flanked by inflatable tubes, making it as seaworthy as Styrofoam. Eric had served in the Navy in research and development rather than a blue-water assignment, but since joining the Corporation he had become an expert helmsman, ranking just below Juan in his ship-handling prowess. He would be leaning on the throttle to get the RHIB back aboard the *Oregon.*

"Then I think we've kept our caller waiting long enough," Juan said. "Mr. Kasim, hail our Venezuelan friends."

After a few moments, Hali said, "You're on the line with Captain Escobar."

Juan switched to his Buck Holland drawl. "Captain Escobar, this is Buck Holland, captain of the *Dolos*," he said in cheery greeting. "What can I do for you?"

"I order you to halt at once," a heavily accented voice replied. "You and your crew will be placed under arrest and charged with espionage and sabotage, and your vessel will be impounded."

"Those are some serious charges. What's your proof?"

"Your crew has assaulted our harbor police, and you stole a tank, destroying a ship and dock in the process."

"Oh, those were just misunderstandings."

Escobar was practically apoplectic at Juan's cheeky insolence. "'Misunderstandings'? You will be lucky if you are not shot for your crimes, you piece of scum."

"Now, there's no need for name-calling."

"You will stop your ship immediately."

"Why should I do something like that?"

"Because if you do not comply, we will blow you out of the water."

"Hmm. Arrest or destruction. Neither of those choices sounds very appealing. I'll take what's behind door number three."

"What?"

"Don't you have game shows down in these parts?"

"I don't—"

The line went dead for a second before a woman spoke, staccato and more commanding than Escobar.

"Captain, drop the charade," she said with only a hint of an accent. "I know that you are responsible for what happened at the warehouse."

"Admiral Ruiz, I presume," Juan said, the drawl gone. "I was hoping you were on board."

"Whatever you think you have accomplished with your operation in Puerto La Cruz, I can assure you it is nothing more than a pinprick."

"Is that sunken fake oil tanker the balloon in your analogy? Because if it is, it popped pretty well."

"For that you will pay, one way or the other."

"Oh, right. Arrest versus destruction. Why don't you come and get us?"

"I plan to. I'd prefer to meet you face-to-face so that you see who it was that beat you. But I will settle for sending your ship to the bottom, if it comes to that."

"You can try."

Ruiz laughed. "I'll do more than try. It's been an interesting conversation, Captain. I hope to meet you someday."

"The feeling isn't mutual. *Adiós*." He gave the cut sign to Hali and the connection ceased.

"She sounds like a charmer," Max said.

"In addition to being a good ship commander," Juan said, "man or woman, you get to the admiral level one of two ways: charm or ruthlessness. My guess is Ruiz can wield either, depending on her calculations. We shouldn't underestimate her."

"I'm not. My first wife had the same tone right before her divorce attorney took me to the cleaners. And I'm not letting us split the *Oregon* in half for Ruiz." After three failed marriages, Max's true love now was his ship.

"Chairman, Eric's got the RHIB one mile off our bow," Hali said.

"All stop. Open the boat garage."

The *Oregon* came to a halt and a hidden hatch on the side of the ship at the waterline slid open to reveal a wide bay, where the *Oregon*'s complement of surface vessels could be launched and recovered. The op center's front screen showed the feed from the boat garage. When the RHIB reached the *Oregon*, Eric Stone expertly guided it through the opening and Mark Murphy threw a line to a waiting technician. Without fanfare, they jumped to the deck and exited the garage.

"Close it up," Juan said. "Juice the engines for a few minutes to make up for the lost time."

The hull purred as the cryopumps spooled up and water was blasted from the stern.

A minute later, Eric and Murph sauntered into the op center, both looking pleased with themselves.

The two of them were the youngest senior officers on the ship. Eric, an Annapolis graduate with gentle brown eyes and a serious demeanor, took off his windbreaker to reveal his usual white button-down shirt and khaki slacks. He had come to the Corporation by way of a recommendation from a commanding officer who had served in Vietnam with Max. On board the *Oregon*, his technical acumen and computer skills were surpassed only by the man he'd brought with him to the Corporation, Mark Murphy.

Murph hadn't served in the Navy but had worked with Eric on a top secret missile project as a civilian contractor, and he was the only member of the crew without a military or intelligence entry on his résumé. An arms development genius with a Ph.D. from MIT earned in his early twenties, Murph was a natural fit in his role as the *Oregon*'s weapons officer.

Disdaining any semblance of conformity, Murph let his dark hair sprout like a wild bramble, which was now further mussed by the wind. His chin sported the patchy stubble of a beard that refused to grow, and his lanky torso was covered by a T-shirt that read "Gorilla Biscuits," which Juan assumed was the name of one of the punk rock bands that Murph blasted from his cabin stereo loud enough to wake Davy Jones.

The young crew members ceded their stations and Eric took his place at the helm while Murph sat at the weapons control console.

"From those smug looks on your faces," Juan said, "I'd guess everything went as planned."

"Affirmative, Chairman," Eric replied. "We have everything in place."

"What he means," Murph said, "is that we've outdone ourselves this time. Wait 'til you see it."

Before Juan could respond, Hali said, "Radar contact. We have an aircraft ten miles out, bearing one-eight-nine, approaching at a hundred and fifty knots."

"That must be the *Mariscal Sucre*'s ASW chopper," Juan said. "Threat assessment?"

Murph, a virtual database of weapons information, piped up. "Lupo-class frigates carry a single Agusta-Bell AB-212. In its role as an antisubmarine warfare helicopter, it can be equipped with two Mark 46 torpedoes and four AS.12 antiship missiles."

"What's their missiles' range?"

"Max range is four and a half miles, but they could drop a torpedo at seven miles."

"It's unlikely they'd fire torpedoes in an active shipping lane, but let's keep them at a respectful distance. Wepps, paint the target."

Murph activated the targeting radar, which immediately locked onto the approaching helicopter. The chopper pilot would hear a high-pitched whine, indicating that a missile could be headed his way at any moment from the ship.

Juan didn't want to engage, but blowing the helicopter out of the sky would be easy if it came to that. The *Oregon* concealed a formidable array of weaponry behind retractable plates in the hull. A 120mm tank cannon was hidden in the bow, while three radar-controlled 20mm Gatling guns could be activated for aerial self-defense and small-ship attacks. In addition to the water cannons, remote-controlled .50 caliber machine guns mounted inside fake oil barrels on the deck could be deployed to repel boarders.

The ship also featured hatches that could be blown away to fire Exocet antiship missiles and cruise missiles for land targets, and Russian-made torpedoes could be launched from tubes below the waterline. Surface-to-air missiles were at the ready in case the chopper pilot didn't take the hint.

They hadn't battle-tested their newest weapon system yet, a one-hundred-barrel multi-cannon based on a design by a company called Metal Storm. Unlike the Gatling gun's six rotating barrels that fired a stream of rounds fed by a belt, the Metal Storm firing system was completely electronic, so there were no moving parts, making jams impossible. Rounds were loaded into the grid of barrels so that the projectiles lined up nose to tail. The electronic control allowed for a precise firing sequence that made the Gatling gun's rate of three thousand rounds per minute seem pokey. With each barrel of the Metal Storm gun firing simultaneously at forty-five thousand rounds per minute, the entire weapon could pump out tungsten slugs at a staggering rate of four and a half million rounds per minute.

"The helicopter is turning around," Hali said.

Juan wasn't surprised. The latest shoulder-fired surface-to-air missile would seem like just the kind of weapon to be used by a spy ship with small arms and RPGs, so the pilot was wise to keep his distance. He would have no way of knowing that the *Oregon*'s missiles were orders of magnitude more potent.

"Let us know if he changes his mind, Mr. Kasim."

The next twenty minutes passed without incident. The three islets they were heading toward curled around one another in two-mile-long angular ridges jutting from the sea. They lay directly across from a pair of uninhabited peninsulas. The islets were so close together that the spans of water between them were barely longer than the *Oregon.*

When Isla Caraca del Oeste was off their port bow, Hali called out, "Surface contact! Bearing one-six-eight at ten miles out. It's the *Mariscal Sucre.* She must have her engines running flat out."

With the *Oregon* in full view, the frigate's next action was predictable, but even so, Hali's next words got Juan's attention.

"I have a missile launch!"

Juan leaned forward in his chair, his eyes on the map displayed on the front screen that showed a red blip racing toward the symbol for the *Oregon.* A video feed next to the map showed the image from one of the deck cameras. The missile wasn't yet visible, but it would be soon.

"Wepps, time to impact?"

"Fifty-two seconds," Murph said. The missile's cruising velocity was just below the speed of sound.

"Ready the Metal Storm battery. Let's see what it can do. But spool up the aft Gatling gun just in case."

The Metal Storm multi-cannon rose into firing position from its hiding place behind the stern-most hold. The plate covering the Gatling gun flew open and the barrels spun up to firing speed.

"Both weapons have a radar lock on the missile," Murph announced.

"Remember," Juan said, "don't fire until it's only six hundred yards out." That would only be two seconds before impact.

"Ready and waiting," came Murph's confident reply. "The system is programmed to fire automatically at that distance."

On the front screen, a dot of fire bloomed in the night sky, growing brighter with each passing second as it skimmed low over the water. When the missile reached the six-hundred-yard mark, the Metal Storm battery fired without Murph having to lift his finger from the Gatling gun safety.

The Gatling would have taken ten seconds to fire five hundred rounds. The Metal Storm unleashed that many rounds in less than the blink of an eye. In fact, it was so fast that on the video feed it seemed to emit a single flash, accompanied by a sound like a jackhammer echoing through the ship.

The missile didn't stand a chance. Murph had programmed the Metal Storm to fire the rounds so that they formed an impenetrable wall of tungsten in midair. The Otomat met the rounds three hundred yards from the *Oregon*'s stern and exploded in a fireball that temporarily overloaded the deck camera's imaging system and blanked out the screen.

Despite the missile's destruction, the *Oregon* didn't come out unscathed. When the image of the outside deck returned, it showed a massive fire raging.

Admiral Dayana Ruiz smiled at the ship blazing on the horizon. The missile had done its job and the *Dolos* slowed to a crawl.

"Shall we finish them off, Admiral?" Captain Escobar asked. His face was bathed in red from the battle lights on the bridge of the *Mariscal Sucre*.

Ruiz lowered her binoculars. "No. I want to capture the ship intact. Well, as intact as it will be if they are able to extinguish the fire."

"At our present speed, we will intercept them in fifteen minutes."

"Hail them."

Captain Holland—or whatever his real name was—answered. "Calling to gloat?" She could hear coughing in the background, no doubt from the smoke pouring through the ship.

"You see now that you had no chance from the beginning," Ruiz said. "Surrender and I'll promise leniency for your crew."

"We're not done yet."

"Captain, your ship is on fire. It will either sink or the fertilizer in your hold will detonate. Think of your men."

"It's nothing that a new coat of paint won't fix."

"I admire your resilience, Captain, but you must realize that your position is hopeless."

"We'll see about that." The line went dead.

"He's a stubborn bastard," Escobar said.

"If he were in this Navy, I'd either bust him for insubordination or give him command of an entire squadron." Ruiz saw much of herself in her adversary. It would be interesting to see if his composure continued once he was in the brig at Puerto Cabello Naval Base.

The frigate carved through the swells for ten minutes until it was just three miles away from the target, which was lingering just south of the closest islet. It was apparent that the effort to fight the fire wasn't going well. The fantail was still ablaze.

"We'll wait here," Ruiz said, and Escobar brought the frigate to a halt. Any closer and they'd risk being damaged if the *Dolos* exploded.

Ruiz ordered a boarding party to be organized. If the captain changed his mind and decided to surrender, she wanted to be ready. That is, if he could save his ship.

"Are there any rafts in the water?" The blaze should have made it easy to spot them despite the darkness.

"None that we can see, Admiral," Escobar said. "Their crew must still be attempting to put out the fire."

"They're fooling themselves. It looks to me as if the flames have spread. It's only a matter of time before it reaches the cargo."

"Admiral!" the radar operator cried out. "The enemy ship is moving."

"What?" Ruiz rushed over to his console. Sure enough, the *Dolos* was moving away.

"Speed?"

"Fifteen knots and accelerating. She's rounding the southern point of the island and heading into the channel between Isla Caraca del Oeste and Ilsa Caraca del Este."

"Their engines seemed to be out of commission," Escobar said. "How did the crew get them fixed so fast?"

"It doesn't matter. Prepare to fire the main gun."

"But she's hidden behind the nearest island."

She felt like she was talking to a child. "Use their trajectory and speed to anticipate their position and fire over the island. Impress me."

"Should we follow?"

She paused as she considered the proper pursuit course. Following them through the tiny strait was hazardous. And if the gun didn't find its target, she wanted to be between them and the open sea.

"No," she said. "Plot an intercept course around the island. We'll head them off in the event that I'm not impressed."

The *Mariscal Sucre* accelerated to flank speed in its dash north. The forward turret slewed around to starboard, its gears whining as the 127mm gun rose to aim in a high arc.

"We have the trajectory locked in," Escobar said.

"Fire," she said calmly as her heart pounded.

Escobar relayed the command. The frigate was shaken by the thunderous blast of the cannon firing its seventy-pound shell. The first round was followed by three more in quick succession.

Their view of the freighter was blocked by the islet's rugged terrain, so they would only be able to see the effect of the shots.

Rounds that splashed into the ocean wouldn't be visible. Only if the target were hit would they see the flash of a fireball.

The frigate's weapons officer counted down the time to impact. The opening shot landed without effect. The second round likewise missed. When the third round fell with no apparent impact, Ruiz could see perspiration dripping from Escobar's brow.

The last round, however, made up for the misses: a bright flare briefly illuminated the clouds from beneath. The bridge erupted in cheers.

"Excellent shooting, Captain," Ruiz said. "I will be adding a commendation to your report."

"Thank you, Admiral."

"Now get us around the island. I want to see if there's anything left for us to salvage. Examining the wreckage may reveal who is behind their mission. And I still want to question any survivors. At dawn we'll get the helicopter into the air to see if anyone made it onto one of the islands."

In five minutes, the frigate came around the northwest point of Isla Caraca del Oeste, revealing the *Dolos* motionless in the channel between the neighboring islands.

The spy freighter would be going nowhere. Fire had extended to the entire back half of the ship, making it easy to see that the bridge superstructure had been destroyed by the frigate's shell.

Ruiz was disappointed. She couldn't imagine that the captain who had given her so much trouble had abandoned his post. He must have died on the bridge. They'd be lucky to find anything left of him.

"Your orders, Admiral?" Escobar asked.

"There's nothing to do but wait," she replied. "It's only a matter of time now."

Ruiz knew very well the sight of a vessel in its death throes.

Juan felt a stab of regret at seeing the ship aflame. The familiar outline made the sight even more poignant, but she had served her purpose and now they had to leave her behind.

"Be sure to keep the islets between us and the frigate until we're out of radar range, Mr. Stone," Juan said.

"Aye, Chairman," Eric replied. "Shouldn't be too hard. The *Mariscal Sucre* doesn't appear to be moving."

"I don't think she's going anywhere," Max said. "Ruiz is like an arsonist watching her handiwork burn."

"Then let's show her the grand finale. Mr. Murphy, ready the fireworks."

Murph rubbed his hands together in glee. "With pleasure, Chairman."

Just as they had planned, Ruiz thought she was looking at the *Oregon* burning and adrift when it was really dashing northeast across the Caribbean at more than forty-five knots. The video feed on the front view screen proved their success in fooling Ruiz. The image being sent from a tiny drone circling the warship at a safe distance confirmed that it was stationary. If she hadn't been deceived, it would have shown the frigate in hot pursuit.

Although the mission commissioned by the CIA was to sabotage the tanker diesel fuel bound for North Korea and to recover evidence of the Venezuelan arms smuggling operation, Juan saw it as a good opportunity to add a third objective: regain their anonymity.

For the last few years, they'd gotten into scrapes around the world with various Third World countries and battled the occasional naval vessel, sinking a few of them along the way. No incident in isolation was enough to reveal the *Oregon*'s hidden purpose and identity, but the rumors had started to make the rounds that there was some kind of spy ship cruising the seas of the world, although the stories conflicted radically on what the ship was called and what she looked like. But Juan and his officers agreed that it was only a matter of time before someone would make the connection and blow their cover. Which meant they needed to take action that would not only convince everyone this mythical spy ship was crewed by nothing more potent than a ragtag bunch of mercenaries but also that it was no longer a threat because it was at the bottom of the ocean.

Juan had gotten the brainstorm for how to do it when he learned that the *Oregon*'s only surviving sister ship was scheduled to be scrapped. Before being rebuilt as a technological marvel, the *Oregon* had been a sturdy lumber hauler, carrying loads between the Pacific Northwest and Asia. Four other ships of the same design were constructed, but service lives had ended for all but the

Washington, which continued to ply the waters around her name-sake state, ferrying supplies to Alaska.

When the *Washington* was headed for the scrapyard, the Corporation bought her for a pittance, setting Juan's plan in motion. His crew had spent the past week altering her appearance so that the *Washington* and the *Oregon* would appear identical. They also filled her hold with the ammonium nitrate fertilizer that was supposed to be inside the *Oregon*. Then they'd moved the *Washington* to her anchorage nestled among the isolated Islas Caracas and left Eric Stone and Mark Murphy behind so that they could make the final preparations.

The part of the mission to regain anonymity had all been meticulously planned to lure one of the Venezuelan frigates into battle. Eddie Seng's trickery had ensured that harbormaster Manuel Lozada would report the *Oregon*'s arrival to his superiors in the Navy, and Eddie stayed glued to Lozada so that he could apprise Max of the Venezuelans' activities. Langston Overholt, their CIA connection, kept them informed about the location of Venezuelan warships via satellite observation. The *Mariscal Sucre* was the closest frigate on patrol, so they knew their target would be coming from the west.

After getting the intel about the smuggling operation, it was just a matter of baiting the frigate to the desolate islands where the *Washington* was hidden.

Like the squibs Kevin Nixon had designed for Eddie's staged shooting, Murph had created his own giant squibs for the *Oregon*. At the moment the Metal Storm battery had neutralized the incoming missile, close enough to the ship to make Ruiz think it had hit, Murph simultaneously activated explosives on the deck of the *Oregon* as well as preset gas jets that simulated the look of a raging fire while posing no actual danger to the ship. He assured Juan that the paint wouldn't even be charred.

The *Washington*, however, wouldn't be as fortunate. With Eric's help, Murph had covered her deck with canisters that would spew jellied gasoline when they were detonated, mimicking the fake fire on the *Oregon*. Additional explosives were rigged throughout the ship including the bridge superstructure.

Juan had idled the *Oregon*'s engines until the frigate was close enough to use her gun, floating at a spot that would quickly put them in the lee of Isla Caraca del Oeste after she got under way again. Once the island shielded them, Juan ramped her up to full throttle, knowing that the *Mariscal Sucre* would target *Oregon*'s presumed position based on the slower speed they'd been sustaining. The shells fell harmlessly in their wake. When the last one plunged into the water, Murph activated the explosives on the deck of the *Washington*.

Juan thought the odds were even between the *Mariscal Sucre* following them into the channel or intercepting them on the other side and he had to be sure which way to go, backward or forward, to be out of visual and radar range by the time the frigate spotted the *Washington* in flames. George "Gomez" Adams was the ace up his sleeve that made the decision easy.

Gomez, who got the nickname because he'd once been the paramour of a woman who was a dead ringer for the original Morticia from *The Addams Family* TV show, was the *Oregon*'s resident helicopter pilot. The ship carried an MD 520N chopper secreted within the aft hold that could be raised into launch position within ten minutes, but this night Gomez was seated comfortably in the op center.

In addition to his duties as a rotary-aircraft pilot, Gomez was also their most skilled drone operator. The *Oregon* was equipped with an array of UAVs for aerial reconnaissance and Juan had ordered one launched as the frigate approached. The off-the-shelf design with a four-foot wingspan had been modified by Max to carry a gimbaled high-definition video camera whose signal was linked back to the *Oregon*. Gomez, sporting a mustache that would have made Wyatt Earp proud, and blessed with looks so striking that Murph had once suggested that they have a shipwide "handsome-off" between him and MacD, stared at his monitor as he expertly guided the drone just above the wave tops to keep it below the *Mariscal Sucre*'s radar.

Thanks to their eye in the sky, they'd watched the frigate race to the northern side of the island, so Juan ordered full reverse and the *Oregon* made it out of the channel and behind the next island well before the *Mariscal Sucre* came into view.

"Gomez," Juan said, "bring it around so we have a good shot of the *Washington*."

"No problem." The drone turned smartly. The running lights on the *Mariscal Sucre* were visible behind the blazing cargo freighter. "How's that for an artistic shot?"

"You'd make Spielberg proud. What's your distance?"

"Three miles."

"That should be far enough. I can't say the same for the *Mariscal Sucre*, but that's their problem. They know what the cargo is. Are you set, Mr. Murphy?"

"Say the word," Murph replied, his finger at the ready.

"Do it."

Murph punched the button.

Explosives carefully placed beside the ammonium nitrate inside the hold of the *Washington* detonated, setting off a chain reaction within the fertilizer. A cataclysmic ball of fire bloomed silently on-screen. The ship was ripped apart by the blast and cleaved in two. Pieces of her hull pelted the neighboring islands. Only her broken keel would be left to settle on the seafloor, leaving little to examine even if the Venezuelans sent a dive team down to investigate. As far as they knew, the ship that had blown up was the *Dolos*, and no proof would be left to indicate otherwise.

To Juan, it was like watching the *Oregon* herself sink, and the pang of regret returned. At least it was a nobler end for the *Washington* than to be cut apart and sold for scrap.

A minor tsunami washed up on the islet shores and rushed toward the *Mariscal Sucre*, which was rocking back and forth from the explosive concussion. Seconds later, the drone bobbed drunkenly.

Gomez struggled to maintain control. "Man, that was bigger than I expected." He pulled the drone up and leveled out. No doubt the frigate wouldn't be paying much attention to its radar signature, if their radar array had even survived the blast.

Gomez kept the camera trained on the frigate. There was no movement.

"Well, I bet that woke them up," Max said.

"And blew out their eardrums," Juan said. "I'd be surprised if any of their bridge windows are still intact."

"If they go anywhere, it'll be back to port for repairs."

"I agree. But Gomez, keep an eye on them until we're thirty miles out. Then ditch the UAV."

"You got it."

The hull clanged as the shock wave from the blast now fifteen miles away reached them.

"Max, change us back to the *Oregon*. The *Dolos* has served us well, but we'll consign her name to the sea."

"Gladly."

The name on the fantail could be changed at a moment's notice using its magnetized panel, which could be programmed with any name and font they chose. At the press of a button, Max de-activated the magnets and the iron filings clinging to the fantail fell away. He remagnetized the filings and nozzles sprayed them into place, spelling out *Oregon*. Once they were in the open ocean and away from the shipping lanes, the crew would repaint the hull in a new decayed pattern and color, deck equipment would be rearranged, phony cargo pallets would be added, and the second funnel would be removed, completely altering the silhouette of the ship. The *Oregon* would steam into the next port looking nothing like the *Dolos*.

"Good work, everyone," Juan said. "I'd say we just bought ourselves a few more years of anonymity. Drinks are on me next shore leave."

"I hear that," Max said. "For this bunch, it's gonna cost you."

"Happy to do it. Mr. Stone, once we're out of radar range, set a course to pick up the Discovery."

"Wait'll they see the video," Murph said. "MacD and Trono will be sorry they missed it."

Juan walked over to Murph and handed him Lieutenant Dominguez's phone memory card.

"Before you show off your pyrotechnic skills, the first priority for you and Eric is to decrypt this."

Murph turned it over in his hands. "It feels damp."

"I had it in my pocket when I went into the drink. Linc has a laptop for you as well, but that should be nice and dry."

"Too bad," Murph said. "I like a challenge."

"I have a hunch our new friend Admiral Ruiz doesn't want us to find out what's on this memory card. I want to know what else she's up to."

Panama City, Florida

It was the first time Major Norm Miller had seen every single pilot station occupied inside Tyndall Air Force Base's Gulf Range Drone Control System facility. Most of the time, only one target drone was being flown, but this morning was the final test flight before the actual mission the next week. Everything had to go perfectly or the demonstration could be scrubbed. Miller had no intention of letting the slightest detail be overlooked, not with his promotion to lieutenant colonel on the line.

"Give me system status," he said, and each station responded that all systems were operating in the green and ready for takeoff.

"Excellent. Then let's begin. Quail One, radio the tower for clearance to taxi."

Miller, a former fighter jockey with sunbaked skin and thinning hair, drank a Diet Coke while he watched the drone's camera feed as it eased toward the runway. He didn't have a chair in the room, preferring instead to spend his time moving between the stations to keep tabs on the operators. Each of the six simulated cockpits was occupied by a two-pilot team to handle the increased mental workload imposed from the lack of tangible feedback that an onboard pilot would experience. Normally, the computer, preset with the mission parameters, flew the plane, with manual backup ready to take over in case the computer malfunctioned. The ultimate fail-safe was the detached warhead of a Sidewinder missile installed on the drone. In the event contact was lost, the unmanned aerial vehicle would self-destruct.

The lead drone taxiing on the tarmac turned so that the camera on the following drone got a good side view. It was a modified F-16 Fighting Falcon, now called a QF-16 to distinguish the sleek fighter as a target drone destined to be destroyed someday by another plane or ship. Its tail and wingtips were painted a bright orange, and an external fuel pod was slung under its belly.

Miller never could get used to seeing a plane that had been designed for a human pilot take off with an empty cockpit, but that's exactly what Quail 1 did now, its afterburner spewing a glowing red tail behind it. Quail 2 continued the procession. Circling above were two manned F-15 Eagle chase planes armed with air-to-air missiles. They would act as escorts during the mission for observation purposes and as a final backup in case something went wrong with one of the drones.

This mission was not the typical flight out over the Gulf of Mexico test range. The eight planes—six drones and two escorts—were part of a live-fire drill for the UNITAS joint combat exercise carried out annually by nations in the Western Hemisphere and select NATO countries. Surface ships from the U.S.,

Great Britain, Brazil, Colombia, Mexico, and a dozen other navies would be converging in the Caribbean southeast of the Bahamas in a few days to simulate war games and undergo training on how to cooperate as a multinational task force. The highlight of the exercise was a live gunnery and missile drill against surface and aerial drones.

The QF-16s were to make a precision flyby to demonstrate their pinpoint navigation and handling prowess. Then one drone would peel away and serve as an elusive target for the Aegis guided missile destroyers in the fleet. The goal of Miller's team was to keep the drone flying for as long as possible before it was brought down. He aimed to make it a long day for the swabbies.

Today, they were simulating the long duration of the mission by flying the same course, but over the Gulf of Mexico. Everything went smoothly until an hour in.

"Major," Quail 4's lead pilot said, "I've got something odd here."

Miller answered. "What is it?"

The pilot hesitated and looked at his copilot before responding. "It seems we lost the link to the plane for a few moments."

"It *seems* you did? Did you lose telemetry?"

"No, the telemetry was nominal. But I could have sworn I saw the plane waggle its wings."

"'Waggle its wings'? Weren't you on autopilot?"

"Yes, sir. That's why I don't understand it."

"You're sure?"

"I was moving my eyes to the camera feed when I saw it."

Miller frowned and turned to the copilot. "Did you see the plane execute any unplanned maneuvers?"

"No, sir. I was checking the GPS data at the time."

Quail 4 was the rearmost plane in the formation, so none of the other drone pilots would have been able to see it. Only the left-most chase plane would have a view of it.

Miller radioed the pilot. "Chase One, we have a report of an unintended maneuver on Quail Four. Did you see anything un-usual?"

"'Unusual,' Tyndall Base? Like what?"

"Like a . . . waggle. It's wings waggling."

Miller heard a chuckle on the other end. "No, I didn't see a waggle."

"Roger that, Chase One. Out."

Quail 4's pilot had heard the exchange and tried to laugh it off. "Maybe my eyes are playing tricks on me."

Miller patted him on the shoulder. He knew how tedious it was to man a station like this. "Just keep an eye on it," he said, "both of you. If you see anything like that again, you let me know."

"Yes, sir," they both replied, but Miller didn't think he'd be hearing from them again during the flight, and he didn't expect to see anything strange in the postflight telemetry data, either.

Miami

Brian Washburn winked at the barista who took his coffee order. The pretty, twenty-something blonde turned red and grinned at the special attention, a response he was used to. It was the "Wash-burn charm" the newspapers had attributed to his winning elec-tion twice as Florida's governor.

Now that he was back in the private sector, he took care to cultivate the persona of a regular Joe, despite the wealth that the

Washburn Industries conglomerate had given him. Nothing could
better help him connect with voters than showing that he was
willing to do his own daily errands and rub elbows with the ordi-
nary people at the local coffee shop. It was his best chance of ever
sitting at the desk inside the Oval Office.

Every time he had to stand inside this grubby little place, he
stewed about the man who had defeated him in the primary and
then chosen James Sandecker as his running mate just because he
needed Sandecker's reputation in the Navy and at NUMA to distract from his own lack of military experience. Washburn was
forced to influence the political sphere with his money instead of
standing front and center at the podium where he deserved to be.

He didn't betray any of that discontent when his name was
called by the barista. He gave her a warm smile and took his coffee outside and around the side of the building, where he climbed
into the backseat of a black Cadillac Escalade. Two blocks away,
the driver let him out at the oceanfront high-rise where his company was headquartered. His cell phone rang as soon as he reached
the privacy of his palatial penthouse office. The screen showed
the contact listing for his attorney.

"What is it, Bill?" Washburn answered as he tossed the unfin-
ished coffee in the trash and picked up the china cup of rare St.
Helena coffee that his assistant had brewed for him. "I don't have
much time before my first meeting with the board."

"This isn't William Derkins," an unfamiliar voice said. "But I
do have some information that you will be interested in."

Washburn was startled and looked at the phone's display
again. It was definitely showing the number for Bill's personal
cell, and only a handful of close friends and advisers had Washburn's number.

He went to the floor-to-ceiling window that looked out on

the Atlantic and took a sip of his coffee. "How did you get Bill's phone?"

"I didn't. It's a technique called spoofing. I won't bore you with the details. You wouldn't understand them anyway. This was the only way I knew you'd take my call. Sit down."

"What?"

"You're going to want to sit down to hear what I have to tell you."

Washburn laughed. "How do you know I'm not sitting already?"

"Because you're standing next to your window."

Washburn froze with the cup halfway to his lips. He scanned the water for any sign of surveillance, but the array of boats dotting the water below him were too far away to make out details. He moved away from the window until he couldn't be seen from the water.

"Okay," he said, playing along, "I'm sitting now."

"No, you're not. You're standing by your extremely expensive pot of coffee, flown at a cost of a hundred dollars a pound from the island where Napoleon was exiled. I hear it's quite rich, no pun intended."

Now Washburn was truly alarmed. He was in the tallest building on Miami's coast, so there was no way anyone had a view from the outside this far into his office. He looked around the office wildly, searching for the hidden spy gear.

"How did you plant a camera in my office?"

"I didn't. I see everything."

"Who are you?"

"You can call me Doctor for now. If everything goes well, we may meet in person in a few days. Now, take a seat at your computer. I have something to show you."

"What if I call the police?"

"Then I will have to tell them what you did to poor Gary Clement."

At the mention of Clement's name, Washburn's knees weakened. To his credit, he recovered and said, "I don't know who you're talking about."

"I know that you *do* and I'll prove it. Check your email."

Washburn straightened up, walked slowly to his desk, and opened his laptop. He put the phone on SPEAKER and set it on the desk.

The most recent email was from Washburn's own address. The subject line read "From the Doctor."

Washburn was aghast at the breach in his security. "You broke into my email?"

"I thought the attached video was better coming from yourself than from my email address. You'll know why when you see it."

Washburn took a deep breath and clicked on the attachment. When he saw the first image, he was glad he was sitting down because he nearly fainted.

The video showed him and Gary Clement, a squat, balding man, sitting on the deck of Washburn's yacht. Other than the bright lights of the boat, it was pitch-black. Washburn would never forget the evening three months ago. They were forty miles off the coast, a location specifically chosen for its privacy. No other boat had been within ten miles. It was just the two of them on the boat.

Yet it looked like the camera filming the scene had been on board the yacht with them, cutting back and forth between close-ups of each of them. Even the audio was flawless.

"I can prove you falsified those reports," Clement said in his nasal whine. "I made copies when we were auditing your books.

You may have destroyed them since then, but the discrepancies are clear. You shipped that body armor to Afghanistan even though you knew the manufacturing process had rendered it brittle and inadequate against the firepower they were facing. Hundreds of soldiers were killed and wounded because of you."

Washburn had to admit Clement had the leverage. Not only would the explosive allegations end his political ambitions but the subsequent investigation would send him to prison for a long time if the real data surfaced. He would lose his company, his reputation—everything.

"What do you want?" Washburn replied coolly.

"You're not even going to try to deny it?"

"Why should I? You showed me what you have, which is why we're out here. I thought you wanted to negotiate."

Clement smiled. "Then I want ten million dollars."

Washburn nodded, as if he'd expected such a figure. "And next year?"

"What do you mean?"

"I mean, whatever number we settle on, you will always be out there lurking with the Sword of Damocles."

"If you give me ten million dollars, I guarantee I will never talk about this again."

"I think I'm the one who can make that guarantee," Washburn said. He pulled a Smith & Wesson revolver from between the seat cushions and shot Clement in the chest.

As Clement gasped for air, Washburn said, "I found your files before we came out here. Not much of a backup plan."

Clement sighed a death rattle and slumped in the chair. Washburn tossed the revolver overboard and disappeared from the picture for a minute. He came back holding four diving weight belts. He tied one to each of Clement's wrists and ankles and heaved the body over the side. After scrubbing away any traces of blood with the bleach he'd brought with him, he tossed that over as well. No one knew there was a connection between the two men, let alone that Clement had been on his boat that night. At the time, Washburn thought it had been the perfect crime.

Now as he stopped the video, he knew this Doctor could ask for anything and he would have no choice but to give it.

"I would delete that immediately, if I were you," the voice on the phone said.

Washburn did as instructed, his hand shaking as he worked the trackpad.

"How did you get that video?"

"I don't divulge my secrets. But my talents could be very useful to a man like you."

"What talents?"

"I told you: I see everything."

"How much do you want?"

"You think this is about money?"

"Isn't it?"

"Money I have, Governor Washburn. What I don't have is your charisma, reputation, and commanding presence. I couldn't buy those no matter how much money I had."

Washburn shook his head in confusion. "Then what *do* you want?"

"The same thing as you," the self-proclaimed Doctor said. "I want to make you president of the United States."

After stopping to recover the Discovery without incident, and now well out of radar range and in international waters, the *Oregon* shifted course northwest.

By the next day, a rested Juan sat at his desk and read each team's reports. Despite some hiccups in the execution of the plans, the outcomes were what they'd been expecting. Juan was consistently proud of the hard work his people put into their jobs, as well as their ability to think on their feet.

With a rap on the door and a curt "Enter," Eric and Murph joined Juan in his cabin. Stoney wore what seemed to be the same outfit he'd had on the previous night, but Juan knew he had multiple versions of white shirt and khaki slacks. Murph, on the other hand, had changed into a T-shirt that bore the image of a burning figure and the line "I tried it at home." After getting a few hours' rest last night, the two of them had dedicated themselves to cracking the laptop and memory card. They gleamed with triumph.

"I'm guessing you guys had no luck with your hacking," Juan said drily.

"*Au contraire, mon* Chairman," Murph said. "They didn't stand a chance."

"Pretty simple military-grade encryption algorithms," Stoney added. There wasn't a computer system Eric and Murph couldn't break into, as far as Juan knew.

"What did you find on the laptop?" he asked.

"That was the mother lode for the arms smuggling operation," Murph said. "Shipment manifests, payment schedules, the works. The guys at Langley will have a field day."

"What about the phone?"

"It took a bit longer to access those files because of the water damage," Eric said. "We found the usual text messages and phone logs, again related to the smuggling op. We also found a few files. One of them was particularly intriguing."

"Why?"

"Because it had dates. Four of them. Three dates occurred over the last three months. The fourth date is two days from now."

"We're still working on what they refer to," Murph said. "Below each date is some kind of code." He read off the list. "Alpha seventeen, Beta nineteen, Gamma twenty-two, Delta twenty-three."

"Obviously, the Greek letters are in order," Eric said, "but we haven't been able to decipher the numerical progression's pattern."

"Assuming there is one," Murph said. "They could also have been assigned randomly, although the continual increase suggests that's not the case."

"And you don't have any theories about what they mean?" Juan asked.

Murph shook his head. "We've scoured the laptop for anything that refers to these codes and dates, but there's nothing. Without more data, we're at a dead end."

"We'll hand the information over to Langston Overholt. Maybe his people can find a pattern for the dates in their intel. After that, as far as we're concerned, our job is done and we can collect payment, just in time for everyone's quarterly shares." Because all of the crew were partners in the Corporation, profits were shared after expenses based on position and length of service. Although the hours were long and the missions risky, everyone aboard could expect to retire to a life of luxury after their years aboard the *Oregon*.

That evening, the Corporation enjoyed a five-star dinner. As coffee was being poured, Juan said, "We've got a long trip to Malaysia coming up to bust that piracy ring in the Strait of Malacca, so I hope everyone has plans to make the most of their shore leave in Jamaica."

"I talked Linda into a girls' day at the Sunset Cliff Spa and Resort," Julia said. "I've read it's Montego Bay's finest new resort."

"In exchange for putting up with massages and manicures," Linda chimed in, "I talked her into taking windsurfing lessons with me."

"We'll see how you feel about doing that after you have a few glasses of good Sauvignon Blanc and a foot rub," Julia retorted. "What about you, Linc? A massage for you, too?"

"Are you kidding?" he said. "With all those great coastal roads? It's time to get my motorcycle out of the hold. And since there's a new Harley dealer in Mobay that rents bikes, Eddie's gonna come along with me."

"How about you, Hali?" Juan asked. "Any adventures for you?"

"I have a feeling I might find one. MacD and Trono are taking me to a bar on the Hip Strip called the Waterfront. They claim it's got the best mojitos on the north coast."

"Be careful with those two. I don't want you waking up wondering what happened to all your clothes." Juan looked at Murph. "Let me guess what you're going to be up to . . ."

"Oh yeah! Time to set up the skateboard park. Eric's going to help me construct a new half-pipe. I'm trying to invent a new trick called the Murph 720." Juan grudgingly let Murph transform the deck into his own playground, when the opportunity arose. It was a small price to pay for having such a technical wizard on the team.

"Don't worry," Eric said. "I'll be there to film it for everyone's viewing pleasure later when he wipes out."

"What about you, Juan?" Julia asked. "Is there a beach with your name on it?"

"No, I'm going to stay on board to catch up on paperwork and oversee the resupply."

"The hell you are," Max said.

"No, really. I'll be fine."

Max threw a look at Julia. "You were right. We're the only ones who know what's best for him."

Juan trained his eyes on the two of them, recognizing co-conspirators when he saw them. "What are you scoundrels up to?"

"We thought you might be reluctant to take a little R and R," Max said, "so I took the liberty of chartering a fishing boat for tomorrow. Throwing back a few Red Stripes and wrestling tuna will do you some good."

Juan glanced at each of them in turn and realized arguing

was useless. He put up his hands in surrender and laughed. "All right. I'll go. But then it's back to work."

"That's what we wanted to hear. You won't regret it."

Montelíbano, Colombia

As the helicopter descended toward the landing pad, Hector Bazin took in the sprawling estate hugging the forested hillside next to the village of Montelíbano. With its terraced gardens, tennis courts, and three swimming pools fit for a Hawaiian resort, the mansion and grounds seemed an ostentatious way to show that cocaine trafficking had been exceedingly good for its owner, Alonzo Tallon. But the lavish villa also indicated that Tallon could afford Bazin's business proposal.

The helicopter flight from Cartagena's international airport had taken less than an hour, nearly the same time it had taken for his private jet to get to Colombia from his home in Haiti. Due to Tallon's mistrust, Bazin and the three men accompanying him were forced to ride in Tallon's helicopter instead of chartering their own. Guards with RPGs made sure no other chopper would be allowed anywhere near the mansion.

When the helicopter settled onto the pad, Bazin and his men exited into the sweltering tropical air to find a dozen guards aiming Heckler & Koch G36 assault rifles at them. Bazin stepped forward and stopped in front of the only man not holding a rifle, Tallon's second-in-command, Sergio Portilla. Bazin recognized the beefy subordinate by his thin mustache and the tattoo of a flaming skull on his neck. Portilla did his own visual appraisal of Bazin, verifying that he was the same man as the one in the photo that had been sent.

Like most Haitians' skin, Bazin's complexion was a smooth ebony, and his hair was cut tight to his scalp. An inch over six feet tall and as lithe as a panther, he concealed a well-muscled physique beneath the contours of his tailored Armani suit.

"I must check you for weapons," Portilla said with a growl. Bazin noticed a bulge under Portilla's jacket, which meant that either his suit was too tight or the pistol underneath was too big.

Bazin's men grumbled, but he quieted them with a stern look. He knew it was all part of the ritual. New visitors normally weren't allowed inside the house, let alone those who hadn't been searched. He held his arms up high as Portilla patted him down thoroughly.

Assured that Bazin was unarmed, Portilla jerked his head for him to follow, leaving Bazin's men at the helicopter. A solo meeting was one of the requirements to get an audience with Tallon.

They took a serpentine path through the marbled halls and lushly carpeted rooms of the air-conditioned mansion. Bazin stifled a sneer at the lavishly gilded decorations. Tallon's taste went toward the gaudy and grandiose, a far cry from Bazin's own restrained inclinations.

When they reached Tallon's palatial office, it was more of the same. Gold leaf on every surface that wasn't teak or granite, the better to display his wealth. Against one wall was a well-stocked wet bar, replete with expensive scotches and ports. On the other wall hung an original Picasso from his Cubist period. A gigantic cherrywood desk squatted at the far end of the room.

Behind it sat a stoic Alonzo Tallon warily eyeing Bazin as he walked toward him. Tallon's silk shirt strained to cover a gut expanded by too much gourmet food and fine wine. His wavy black hair shined from the sunlight streaming in from the window behind him.

Tallon didn't stand, didn't offer a handshake. He simply motioned for Bazin to take a seat in one of the leather chairs opposite the desk and Bazin took him up on the offer.

"Thank you for agreeing to meet with me, Mr. Tallon," Bazin said in English. Though French Creole was his first language, he'd been taught English at an early age by American missionaries in Port-au-Prince. He did not speak Spanish, and he knew Tallon's command of English was quite good.

"Your demonstration was convincing, Mr. Bazin. Your intel about the raid by the DNE saved my organization a lot of money. We were also able to rid ourselves of five agents."

The Dirección Nacional de Estupefacientes, Colombia's anti-drug agency, had targeted one of Tallon's factories for destruction. Bazin's tip about the raid allowed Tallon to shut the factory down before the operation and set up an ambush in its place.

"Call it a goodwill gesture on my part," Bazin said. He smiled. "No charge, of course."

"You said you had a business proposition that would continue to provide me the same kind of intelligence."

"I do. It can be very lucrative for both of us."

"You've worked in this line of business for a while?"

"Although I was born and raised in Haiti, I moved to France with my parents. I went to school there and joined the French Special Forces. I was asked to leave under unfortunate circumstances, so I've spent the last three years paving a new road for myself. This opportunity I'm presenting to you is my latest venture."

"You are not even a citizen of Colombia, let alone inside the government. How are you coming by your information?"

Bazin paused for effect. "Mr. Tallon, do you believe in magic?"

Tallon's eyes narrowed. "What?"

"Magic."

"Of course not. It's nonsense."

"Too bad you feel that way. Because magic is what I'm selling."

Tallon did not look amused. "Is this a joke? Is this what you came all the way from Haiti to propose to me? Magic?"

"It is. Magic is what will keep your product flowing from Colombia and into Mexico, where the cartels there handle the difficult task of smuggling it into the U.S. Magic will alert you to drug interdiction operations before they occur. It will tell you when the Army is planning to torch your crops. It will inform you when your enemies are planning to take over your business. The intel about the DNE raid was just a taste."

Tallon chewed on his lip. "Suppose I believe you can get me this information, magic or not. What would it cost me?"

Bazin rose and walked over to the bar. He nonchalantly picked up a bottle of 1939 Macallan scotch and sensed Portilla tense behind him. He had to be concerned that Bazin was so casually handling a bottle worth over ten thousand dollars.

"I've never tasted this vintage," Bazin said. "I've heard it's very good."

"Pour yourself a snifter," Tallon said. "Consider it my thanks to you."

Bazin did so and swirled the peat-rich liquor in the glass before taking a sip. It coated his tongue like honey and went down smoothly.

"Its reputation is justified," he pronounced.

"I'm sure you want to charge me more than that bottle of scotch would cover."

"I do," Bazin said, draining the rest of the glass. "Ten percent of your gross earnings."

Tallon's eyes went wide and flicked to Portilla. Then they both started to laugh.

"To call that absurd would be an understatement," Tallon said. "I will decline your generous offer."

Bazin frowned. "That's too bad. Unfortunately, not contracting with me could leave you open to all kinds of business risk. Suddenly, raids could happen without your knowledge. Shipments could be disrupted. Bank assets frozen. Your whole operation could come to a standstill. Is ten percent such a high price to pay to ensure that these kinds of events don't befall you?"

For the first time, Tallon stood, bristling at Bazin's words. "Are you stupid enough to come into my office and threaten me?"

"'Threaten'? No, of course not. I'm offering a valuable service to you. Surely I can expect to be paid a reasonable wage for this service. You see, *I* make more money when *you* make more money. It's a very equitable arrangement, and we both have a vested interest in making as much money as we can."

"I make plenty of money as it is."

Bazin made a show of looking around the room. "I see that. But I can provide you with information that will make your life easier. And make no mistake, my intelligence-gathering capabilities know no limit." He nodded at the Picasso. "For instance, there is a safe behind that painting. You access it by sliding a lever under the bottom right corner and swinging the painting out to the left. The combination is thirty-six, eight, seventy-two. Inside are one hundred thousand American dollars, two kilos of cocaine, a bag of twenty diamonds, and a matching pair of ivory-handled Colt revolvers. I can tell you their serial numbers, if you'd like."

Bazin had been looking directly at Tallon as he recited the safe's contents and the drug lord's mouth gaped wider with the listing of each item. "I'm the only one with the combination to that safe. How do you know what's in there?"

"I told you. Magic. Or maybe I have X-ray satellites watching this house. Or perhaps drones circling around day and night. I could have sent workmen in here to bug every room and plant cameras where you'll never find them. Or . . ." Bazin paused for effect. "Or there's always the possibility of a traitor in your midst."

Bazin avoided looking at Portilla, but Tallon got the hint.

"You?" he screamed at Portilla. "You sold me out?"

Portilla had his hands up in supplication. "No, boss. I'm loyal to you, I swear. This guy is lying."

"He's not lying. He described every last thing in that safe. You betrayed me!"

"I swear I didn't!"

Bazin edged closer to the bar, putting his hand by the drawer beneath it. To Tallon he said, "At least when I want to share in profits from your business, I'm upfront about it. I don't want to skim it behind your back."

"Is that true?" Tallon asked Portilla. "Are you taking money from me after all I've given you?"

"No! Please, Alonzo!" But Portilla's eyes revealed the lie. With a look of pure rage, he pivoted and drew a nickel-plated Smith & Wesson from his shoulder holster.

Bazin didn't know who Portilla planned to shoot—maybe both of them—but it didn't matter. The instant Portilla had made the move for his holster, Bazin had yanked open the drawer and snatched up the Glock pistol that Tallon had placed there as an emergency backup weapon. With a motion honed from years of training, Bazin raised the semiautomatic and put one bullet through Portilla's forehead before Portilla had even finished aiming at Tallon, who was still dumbfounded by what was happening.

"You've suspected him for some time," Bazin said. "I just did you a favor."

Tallon stared at Bazin holding his hidden gun. "How did you—"

"I told you. Magic. Do we have an arrangement?"

Tallon nodded dumbly, then waved off the guards who had rushed through the door and now stood gaping at Portilla's corpse.

Bazin walked over to the desk and dropped the Glock on it. He withdrew a slip of paper from his pocket and laid it on top of the gun. "The first number is the Cayman account where Portilla was stashing the skim. The second number is my bank account. I expect to see monthly deposits. And I will know if you're holding back. By the way, he was also sleeping with your wife."

Bazin left the office and made his way back to the helicopter. While his men got back on, his phone rang. It was the Doctor, likely calling to check on his progress.

"Where are you?" the Doctor said without preamble.

"I've just finished the business in Colombia. Another success."

"Good. I've got another job for you."

"I'm planning to go to Mexico tomorrow to meet with one of the cartel members."

"It can wait. There's a bigger problem. An unusual ship. It's called the *Oregon*. They've got some information that could damage our whole operation, and they don't even know it."

"If they don't know it, why is that a problem?"

"Because it's only a matter of time before they *do* know. Can you have an assassination squad in Jamaica by tomorrow?"

Montego Bay, Jamaica

A light breeze ruffled the palm fronds above the outdoor section of the Sunset Cliff Spa. The idyllic setting had been carefully chosen by the resort to take advantage of the spectacular view of the Caribbean Sea. Tourists frolicked along the picturesque beach that stretched from the twenty-foot-high cliffs that gave the resort its name. During the day, white canvas tents were erected atop the grassy cliff so that guests could receive an open-air massage free from the prying eyes of passersby. Before dusk, the tents were removed, giving guests and sightseers an unobstructed view of the sun's red and orange hues as it dipped below the horizon.

Linda relaxed on a chaise longue and sipped from a champagne flute as a pedicurist attended to her toes. Julia sat next to her with her own dedicated attendant. The two of them had been the first ones off the *Oregon* when it docked in Montego Bay that morning. They were both swaddled in plush white robes.

"It has been forever since I've had one of these," Linda said, gesturing at the pedicurist's work.

Julia grinned at her. "Aren't you glad I talked you into it?"

"I could get used to this." Although the *Oregon* was equipped with a Jacuzzi hot tub and a sauna, it just wasn't the same as a full-service spa.

"We should ask Juan to hire a dedicated nail technician for the shipboard mani-pedis," Julia said. "As the resident doctor, I know personally that some of the guys could sure use one. Their nails are disgusting."

"Can you imagine Maurice giving a mani-pedi?"

They both laughed until they cried at the thought of the distinguished steward buffing Franklin Lincoln's nails. The fit of giggles continued until the pedicurists had finished their work and took away their kits.

"I'll admit you were right for us to go windsurfing first," Linda said, rotating her sore shoulder. "I'm looking forward to a good massage."

"And I'll admit I had fun. But this is better."

An attendant returned to escort them to the tents. Linda and Julia followed her to the two bays where they would get their massages. Light classical music drifted from hidden speakers, easily heard now that they were far from the tourists at the beach. Each was open to the ocean, and Linda could hear the waves crashing against the rocks below them. Privacy between the bays was provided by a white canvas drape. None of the tents were currently occupied.

The attendant said that their masseuses would be along in a few minutes and asked them to lay facedown on the tables. She told them there was a coatrack in each bay for their robes and left.

"You know," Julia said, "if they're going to be a few minutes, I might go for a bit more champagne to tide me over."

"Allow me," Linda said, taking her glass. "I could use another, too."

While Julia entered the tent on the end, Linda turned to leave. Out of the corner of her eye, she caught the movement of shadows against the white canvas. Not one shadow but two.

Someone was already in the tent with Julia. A muffled whimper confirmed that it wasn't the masseuse.

Linda's senses went on full alert. She tossed the glasses to the grass and flung the canvas aside to see a man dressed in black holding his hand over Julia's mouth and withdrawing a knife from his hip sheath.

Acting on instinct and relying on the weekly self-defense training everyone on the *Oregon* was required to take no matter their position, Linda grabbed the bamboo coatrack and swung it like a kendo stick. The assailant saw her at the last instant and released Julia to keep from being knocked out by the vicious blow, but even though he was able to get a hand up, the rack made solid contact with his shoulder.

"Get help!" Linda yelled. But before Julia could run, a second attacker rushed through from the adjoining bay, where he must have been waiting for Linda. He dived across the massage table and grasped Julia's ponytail. Linda shoved the coatrack in his gut and he grunted, let go of the ponytail, and dropped his knife, a mean-looking weapon with a serrated edge.

Julia teetered backward and pulled the massage table's headrest free in her attempt to keep from falling. She landed hard but still held on to the padded headrest, its long, thin steel mounting pins facing out.

The second assailant lunged for Julia, but he was still unbalanced from the blow to his stomach. Linda tripped him and he went down in Julia's direction. He landed on her and immediately went limp. One of the mounting pins was poking out of his side, the other was lodged deeply in his chest.

Before Linda could help Julia up, she felt her arms pinned against her sides in a bear hug. The assailant wrestled her across the tent toward the cliff, intent on casting her onto the rocks below. She took a deep breath to fight the instinctual panic that threatened to consume her and her mind flashed back to her training.

The man was too tall for her, so she couldn't slam her head back and crush his nose with her skull. Instead, she shifted her weight and stepped to the side, freeing her fist to strike down at his crotch. Just with the strength of her triceps, she was able to connect with a devastating blow.

The attacker let go, and Linda used the opportunity to smash her elbow into his chin. His head flew upward, spittle flying. Linda kicked him in the chest, and his momentum took him tumbling over the side. She ran to the edge and saw his dead body sprawled across the jagged volcanic rocks, the torso submerged in the water. A small boat bobbed in the cove below.

Linda returned to the tent to find Julia struggling to crawl out from under the other corpse. Linda pushed it aside and helped her up.

"Are you all right?" Linda asked.

Julia looked shaken but nodded. "How about you?"

"Nothing a massage wouldn't fix."

"I don't think we should wait around for one."

"Me neither. Let's toss this guy over the cliff, too. We don't want to be answering a lot of questions from the local police."

Linda searched the man's pockets and found only a small

amount of cash and a cell phone. Julia pulled the massage table headrest from his torso and they hauled the body to the cliff, where they threw it over. It came to rest next to the other one. By the time the police made sense of the strange configuration, they'd be long gone.

"What just happened?" Julia asked, folding the bloody headrest in a towel and tucking it under her robe.

"This was no random attack," Linda said. "We were targeted."

"For what? All our belongings are in the lockers."

"Exactly. This seems like an assassination attempt. They wanted to do it very quietly, so they anchored their boat down there and climbed up to wait for us."

"What in the world . . . ?"

"I don't know. Let me check the phone."

It was a disposable, probably purchased this morning and meant to be thrown in the ocean after the assignment. Its user hadn't even bothered to password-protect it. The contact list had only five numbers and no names.

"We were lucky to survive this," Linda said. "Those guys were pros." There was nothing to lead back to anyone. If the assassin had thought there was even a chance he wouldn't succeed, he would have entered a password.

She checked the text messages. Only one was still in memory. It had been sent to all of the contact numbers and was written in French.

Tous ont été aperçus. Attaquer dès que vous voyez une opportunité.

"Do you know French?" she asked Julia.

"I took French literature in college, but it's been awhile." She peered at the message, whispering the words as she read. After a moment, her eyes became as big as saucers.

"What does it say?"

Julia swallowed hard. "'All of them have been sighted. Attack as soon as you see an opportunity.'"

Not the two of them. *All of them.*

"We have to warn the others. Somebody's going after the whole crew."

She and Julia sprinted toward the locker room to get Linda's phone, nearly knocking over their approaching masseuses in their scramble to save the entire *Oregon* crew from being murdered.

The steel deck of the *Oregon* baked under the cloudless sky where it was moored against the dock of Montego Bay's Freeport terminal. Eric's shirt was already soaked with perspiration from helping Murph construct the portable ramps, grind rails, and eight-foot-tall half-pipe that Juan reluctantly allowed him to install, turning the ship into a makeshift skateboard park. Eric lowered his sunglasses so they wouldn't steam up as he peered at the screen of his brand-new video camera. He was kneeling to get the best angle for the shot, an enormous cruise ship providing the backdrop.

The lens was trained on Murph as he hurtled across the obstacles, bobbing his head to the beat of heavy metal music only he could hear in his headphones. Every time he whipped around in a turn, sweat flew from hair that poked from the edge of his helmet. Eric had caught some good tumbles already, but Murph, who was dressed in baggy shorts and a black T-shirt that said "Welcome to Nuketown" and was protected by kneepads and elbow pads, popped back up every time. Only a true face-plant would slow him down.

Eric's phone rang, and he kept the video recording as he answered it.

"This is Eric."

"Eric, it's Linda," she said, her voice breathy and urgent. "We're in trouble."

"What's wrong?"

"Julia and I were attacked."

"My God! Are you all right?"

"We're okay, but we have reason to believe the rest of the crew might be targeted as well."

"Targeted? By whom?"

She described her attackers, including her assessment that they were either French or Haitian, neither of which made sense to Eric. But the danger implied in the message was undeniable: *All of them have been sighted. Attack as soon as you see an opportunity.*

The hairs on the back of Eric's neck stood on end. He suddenly felt exposed on the deck.

"Contact everyone who's on leave and tell them to get back to the ship," Linda said. "When that's done, get the *Oregon* ready for departure. She's a sitting duck. Julia and I are on our way back now. We'll be there in ten minutes."

"Got it."

Eric hung up. He couldn't help looking around to see if he was being watched, realizing someone could be observing them from any of a hundred spots in the crowded port area.

He yelled for Murph to stop, but the headphones were pumped

to the same earsplitting volume that Murph blasted in his isolated cabin. Eric tried moving over and waving his arms, but Murph was so absorbed in his tricks that he paid no attention.

Eric felt more than heard a disturbance in the air. A hole appeared in the half-pipe above the spot where Murph had performed a particularly difficult twisting move. There was no accompanying rifle crack, but Eric knew a bullet hole when he saw one.

The sniper must have been waiting for Murph to pause but was prodded to act early because of Eric's waving. He had to be using a sound suppressor.

Murph was oblivious to the threat. He would be up the other side of the half-pipe and back into the sniper's view in moments.

Eric sprinted across the floor of the half-pipe. Murph was already curling up the opposite side, preparing to go into his next spin. Eric launched himself at Murph, who gaped in surprise when he saw his friend barreling toward him.

Eric tackled Murph around the torso and Murph's momentum took his legs up into the air over the lip of the half-pipe. The two of them flipped around and crashed to the floor. Murph's headphones were ripped from his ears.

"What the hell?" Murph yelled, grabbing his leg. "I think my ankle's twisted, you goober!"

Eric looked down and saw blood oozing between Murph's fingers. The sniper hadn't missed completely.

"Let me see," Eric said, lifting Murph's hand away. A bullet had punched all the way through his calf. Murph blanched at the sight.

"I've been shot?"

Eric tore off his shirt and wrapped it around Murph's leg, tightening it as much as he could to keep pressure on the wounds.

"Linda called," Eric said. "She and Julia were assaulted at the spa by two attackers. A text on one of their phones implied that the rest of us were also targeted."

"Why?" Murph asked, wincing as Eric tied off the bandage.

"Good question. We may be stuck here unless we can get that sniper off our backs."

"Where is he?"

Since the half-pipe was built on the flattest section of the deck, the nearest hatch to the interior was a hundred feet away, so running for it would make them easy targets. More holes drilled through the polyurethane half-pipe material. The frustrated sniper was firing blindly to flush them out or kill them where they sat. Eric guessed he was somewhere in the direction of the terminal's oil storage facility. He couldn't stick his head out without getting it blown off.

His video camera, however, was state-of-the-art, with a 100× optical/digital zoom built in. Eric edged it around the end of the half-pipe and watched the screen as he panned around, looking for the most likely place for a sniper to hide within range of the *Oregon*. The assassin would want to be high enough to have a good vantage point.

Eric zoomed in on the fifty-foot-tall oil tanks until he could see every detail. The first two tanks were barren, but when he got to the third, he could spot the faint outline of a man lying atop the tank. He still had the rifle aimed at the *Oregon*, waiting for them to show their faces.

"Got him," Eric said, showing the image to Murph.

"He planned that well," Murph said through clenched teeth. "No way we can take him out with the Gatling gun when he's on a tank full of oil."

"Not that we could open fire here in port anyway."

"Are you thinking what I'm thinking?"

Eric nodded. "I think it's time to call the police." He routed the call through an anonymous server so that it couldn't be traced back to them and reported that shots had been fired at the oil facility.

Moments later, police sirens wailed in the distance. The camera showed the gunman scrambling across the tower toward the stairs. He would be gone before the police could arrive, but that didn't matter to Eric anymore.

He needed to alert the others. He preferred to call Juan first, but since he and Max were at sea and out of cell phone range, the *Oregon*'s radio would be the only way to reach him. As he helped Murph limp to the medical bay, Eric used his free hand to dial Franklin Lincoln.

17

When Linc got the call from Eric, he and Eddie were approaching
Ian Fleming International Airport, named to honor northeastern
Jamaica's most famous resident. They were only a few miles away
from the GoldenEye resort, Linc on his custom-built Harley and
Eddie on a top-of-the-line model rented from Montego Bay's new
dealer. The plan was to get a prime spot at the pool bar, consume
a burger and a martini, shaken not stirred, and take in the view of
both the oceanographic and bikini-clad varieties. Instead, they'd
have to turn around and head straight back to the *Oregon*. But
they first had to contend with the tail they'd picked up.

During the winding trip along the coast, they'd tested the lim-
its of their bikes, dodging other drivers who paid only minimal
attention to the rules of the road. It was a laid-back ride until they
reached Ocho Rios, where two guys on a pair of Suzuki crotch
rockets had fallen in behind them, careful to maintain a respect-

ful distance. Instead of a T-shirt and shorts, each of them was wearing a black leather jacket that was far too heavy in this heat.

Linc and Eddie had spotted them almost immediately. It was certainly possible that they were simply motorcycle enthusiasts out for a nice jaunt like they were, but a little variation of speed confirmed that the Suzuki riders were mirroring their pace. Eric's call about the two run-ins with attackers made it clear that these tails would attempt to succeed where their colleagues had failed.

In this case, Linc thought the best defense was a good offense.

He voice-dialed Eddie. Both of them were equipped with cell phone earbuds under their helmets. Linc related the situation from Eric.

"That's what they get for underestimating Linda," Eddie said.

"Now we have to figure out what to do with our two buddies behind us. What do you think they're planning?"

"If I were them, I'd make it clean and simple. They're probably waiting for us to stop. Double taps with pistols. Those bikes lend themselves to an easy getaway."

"You think they know we're unarmed?"

"They're probably assuming it."

"True, but uncertainty is our friend."

"The sniper has to be making the same type of warning call to them that Eric gave us," Eddie said. "Which means whatever they're planning is going to happen sooner rather than later."

"What do you say we make it sooner than they think?"

"It sounds like you have an idea."

As they passed the airport, Linc outlined his plan to Eddie. They couldn't simply outrun the gunmen. The Harleys were quick, but the Suzukis were faster and more nimble. Shooting from a moving bike was a challenge, but if their pursuers got close enough, all it would take was a couple of lucky shots to take down Linc and Eddie.

"I give it a fifty-fifty shot at working," Linc said. Actually fifty-fifty might have been optimistic, but they didn't have many options.

"I'll take those odds when we're not even bringing knives to the gunfight."

"The map showed a hairpin turn about a mile before the resort," Linc said. "That'll be the best place to try this."

"It's all in the execution."

"When you put it that way, it doesn't sound so good."

"Let me rephrase. It's all in the *implementation*."

"Better."

They kept pace behind a produce truck that was puttering along. The Suzukis stayed back a hundred yards, two cars behind them. No doubt the two riders were talking about advancing their timetable.

No matter what they had in mind, it wouldn't be soon enough. The hairpin was just ahead.

"Ready?" Linc asked.

"Ready."

"Let's go."

Linc gunned his bike and snapped around the produce truck with Eddie hot on his heels. They pulled in front of the truck just in time to avoid getting smashed by another semi heading in the opposite direction. They continued accelerating around the curve until the Suzukis disappeared in his rearview mirror.

With one hand, he flipped open his saddlebag and snatched up two chains that he used to lock up the wheels of his bike when he went riding in more unsavory ports of call.

Eddie nudged close enough to take one of the chains from Linc. Fifty yards from the end of the hairpin, they skidded to a stop and made a U-turn. Since Jamaica's roads were left-oriented like the British, Linc got into the left lane while Eddie drove along the right shoulder so he could wield the chain while keeping his hand on the bike's right-hand throttle. Linc would have the tougher task of whipping the chain over his head. He could feel his knuckles crack as his left hand gripped the end of the chain.

As they expected, the Suzukis barreled around the hairpin ready to give chase. The surprise of seeing their targets heading toward them provided enough hesitation. Their hands plunged into the jackets and came out with semiautomatics, but it was too late.

Eddie spun the chain around sideways like a lasso and let it fly right as the Suzuki was passing him. The chain caught on the front fender of the bike and wrapped itself around the spokes. The Suzuki launched its rider over the handlebars into the air, cartwheeling end over end before it landed on the screaming gunman, who went silent.

Linc twirled his chain over his head as he rode at his pursuer. The gunman got off two wild shots that missed their mark before Linc's chain smashed him in the helmet. The man's head snapped backward and he somersaulted off the bike, which kept going as if it had a phantom riding it before veering off into the trees.

Linc returned to his assailant. If possible, they needed to find out who was behind these attacks and how they had known exactly where everyone in the *Oregon* crew would be.

When he got to the gunman, he saw there would be no interrogation. His neck was bent at an impossible angle for a breathing human being. Linc jogged over to Eddie and found him kneeling over the other Suzuki rider. Eddie had removed the rider's helmet.

"Is he alive?" Linc asked.

"Not for long."

Linc could see why. The Suzuki had crushed the man's stomach. The internal injuries had to be extensive.

"Who are you?" Eddie asked him.

The man spit back in French.

Linc looked at Eddie. "Do you know what he's saying?"

"I don't speak a word of French. But we'll find out." He subtly glanced at his phone. The recording light was on. The gunman babbled for another twenty seconds, then coughed up blood and gurgled out a death sigh.

Traffic was slithering around the carnage, and crowds had started to gather.

"Let's get out of here," Eddie said.

"I'd take the guns, but I don't think I want to explain how we got them if the police stop us."

"Good point."

Once they were on their Harleys and heading back toward Montego Bay, they called Eric.

"We got rid of our tail," Eddie said matter-of-factly. "No casualties on our side."

"Is everyone accounted for?" Linc asked.

"Mark's still trying to raise Juan and Max," Eric said. "Linda and Julia just arrived at the dock. That leaves Hali, MacD, and Mike Trono."

"Where are they?"

"Still at that bar on the Hip Strip. MacD texted me that they have a situation."

18

MacD stood up from his table and staggered backward, knocking into his chair and pitching sideways until Hali Kasim and Mike Trono caught him. Neither of them seemed much better off. Shot glasses littered their table along with three beer bottles. They'd been ordering rounds of whiskey for the last twenty minutes, ever since they'd spotted the guy at the bar sneaking glances at them.

The Waterfront Bar & Grill was filled with tourists from the cruise ship, college students on spring break, and young couples on vacation. Some were watching basketball games and cricket matches on the TVs that festooned the walls of the bar, but most were enjoying the breeze coming in off the ocean, over drinks and burgers, watching the bathing beauties on the beach to one side and the foot traffic on the street to the other.

It wasn't a place frequented by the locals, so when MacD noticed a solo guy at the bar who seemed to be invested in a West

Indies versus England cricket tilt, he assumed the man was a Jamaican there for the television. But during a couple of commercial breaks when the screen went dark, he saw the man watching their table in the screen's reflection.

The guy was obviously keeping tabs on the three of them, but they had no idea why until they received Eric's call. If they were targeted for assassination, taking them out inside the bar would be messy, leaving plenty of witnesses and making escape difficult. But if their attackers waited until they stepped outside, they could fire a few shots and get away quickly before anyone even knew what had happened.

Before they received the warning from Eric, they'd decided to have a little fun with the guy, in the event he was setting them up for some kind of scam. Every shot they took was followed by a slug of beer, and they got louder and more obnoxious with every round. But instead of swallowing the whiskey, they'd been spitting it into the half-empty beer bottles, an old barmaid's trick. The guy must have relayed the news to his buddies by now that their targets were completely sloshed.

What had started out as a lark was now deadly serious.

MacD headed to the bathroom, wobbling his way through the tables. The man at the bar was right in his path. MacD gripped the backs of the barstools as he passed, seemingly to steady himself. When he reached their observer, he misplaced his hand and pushed against the man's back instead.

The man instinctively whipped his head around at the disturbance. If MacD had been anyone else, the guy at the bar would certainly have yelled at him to watch his step. But since he was trying to keep a low profile, he said nothing.

"'Scuse me, pardner," MacD slurred. "Ah didn't mean to knock you over."

"*Mwen pa konprann,*" the man replied. Then he added, "No English," and went back to looking at the TV.

MacD's eyes went wide like he'd just met a long-lost cousin. He'd heard from Eric that the attackers might be Haitian and the man had said "I don't understand" in Creole. MacD, who'd grown up in Louisiana, had learned Creole and French from his grand-father, and many Haitians are bilingual. The Haitian and Louisi-anan versions of Creole have many similarities. MacD decided to catch him off guard.

"My friend," MacD said in Creole, "you speak my language! Are you from Haiti?"

The guy, who certainly didn't expect MacD to speak his native tongue, stammered, "I . . . I'm trying to watch the television."

"You *do* speak Creole! I'm from the bayous of Louisiana. That practically makes us related."

"I should be going soon." The Haitian nodded to the bar-tender for his bill.

MacD draped his arm around him. "Going? Now? Let me and my pals buy you a drink. What's your name?"

"I really have to be leaving."

MacD's hand brushed against a hard metal object in the small of the Haitian's back, which confirmed that he was armed.

"Come on, brother," MacD said, "one drink won't kill you."

The bartender put the check in front of the man.

"I have to go," the Haitian said.

"At least let me pay your bill."

MacD leaned forward and tossed a U.S. twenty on the check. As he did, he snatched the pistol from the Haitian's waistband and jabbed it into his kidney.

"I have no problem killing you right here," MacD said. "Got it? If so, nod slowly."

The Haitian did as he was told.

MacD grabbed a napkin and covered his gun hand. He nodded to Hali and Trono, who instantly gave up the drunk act and stood. The four of them retreated to the back hallway, where the restrooms were located. They took him inside the men's room and locked the door.

Hali kept watch while MacD and Trono frisked the Haitian. Other than a folding knife, the SIG Sauer .40 caliber pistol Trono now held was his lone weapon. He also carried a phone with the same French text message that had been relayed by Linda. Two more messages indicated that he'd been communicating with someone outside the Waterfront.

"Who are you?" MacD asked him in Creole.

"I'm saying nothing."

"You'll say a lot once we get you back to the ship."

"No, I won't."

"You're no amateur, but this isn't exactly what you're best at. You're a soldier, aren't you?"

The Haitian didn't respond.

"See, soldiers are good at attacking, not so good at the spy stuff," MacD continued. "We, on the other hand, have had a little training in those kinds of things. Things like interrogation."

The Haitian's eyes were defiant. "Do you think you can scare me?"

"We'll see. Who's outside?"

"No one," the Haitian said with a smile.

"So we can just stroll out the back?"

Without hesitation the Haitian said, "Go ahead."

"They've got men posted front and back," MacD said to Hali and Trono.

"Did he say how many?" Trono asked.

"No. And getting anything out of him won't happen here. We'll have to take him back to the ship to figure out who he is."

"How do we get out of here?" Hali asked. "Use him as a hostage?"

"They may not care about him," Trono said. "For all we know, they could shoot him along with us."

"Good point," MacD said. "Let me see that phone. Stay with him." He took the gun, leaving Trono holding the knife to the Haitian's throat. He also took a spare roll of toilet paper with him.

"What are you going to do?" Hali asked.

"Not sure yet. Keep your phone handy."

MacD walked back into the bar and edged up to the front window but stayed out of sight. He typed a text in French saying "All three are coming out the front in two minutes. Honk twice to acknowledge."

The text went through. Seconds later, two short beeps came from the left. He poked his head around and saw a Toyota SUV with two Haitians inside waiting at the curb. Both of them were staring intently at the front door.

MacD went up to a table of American college students who had a collection of beers on their table. One was wearing a Panama hat and a plaid shirt over his T-shirt. He and MacD were about the same size.

"Ah'll give you a hundred dollars for your hat and shirt," MacD said.

The student looked at his three buddies, then back at MacD. "Is this a joke, man?"

"No joke." MacD held out a crisp hundred-dollar bill. "Right now."

"Yeah!" the student said, laughing, and shucked the clothes.

He plucked the bill from MacD's hand and high-fived the other guys before ordering another round.

MacD donned the hat and shirt. The two men in the car wouldn't expect only one of them to come out, and the different clothes would make him invisible.

He sauntered out the door as if he were simply taking a stroll, keeping his eyes toward the open window and away from the Toyota, the hat shielding his face from view.

He passed the Toyota and another car before ducking and circling around. Through the side mirrors, MacD could see that the SUV hitmen were still focused on the Waterfront's door.

He strode up to the Toyota and flung the rear door open. Before they could react, he was inside the SUV with the SIG Sauer against the driver's neck.

"Don't move," he said in Creole. "You understand?"

They nodded. He sat back and put the pistol's barrel against the toilet paper roll.

"Poor man's silencer," MacD said. "Don't make me use it." Each of them had a Heckler & Koch MP7 submachine gun laying across their laps. "Now, as slowly as you can, take the magazines out of your weapons and drop them behind you. Then pull back the bolts and show me they're empty."

The two men exchanged glances, then complied with MacD's instructions.

"Good. Now drop them on the floor back here one at a time. We'll start with the driver."

The driver twisted in his seat and held the MP7 up. Then he shoved it down while the passenger lunged toward MacD with a knife he'd been palming.

The sudden attack left MacD with no alternative. It was him

or them. He shot the passenger first, then the driver, through the back of the seats, the blasts muffled by the thick toilet paper. Both men slumped forward. The smell of gunpowder filled the SUV. He checked to make sure they were dead, then scanned the street around him. No one had noticed the brief battle.

"Ah really hate that you made me do that," he said to the two corpses, then called Hali.

"The front's clear. You can bring him out."

"Do we have transportation?"

Even though MacD wanted to take the SUV, there was no way to remove the dead body from the driver's seat without being seen. "We'll have to cab it."

"We'll be out in a minute."

MacD strapped the two bodies into their seat belts and propped them up so that it looked like they were napping. Then he wiped down the SUV for any possible prints.

Trono and Hali exited the bar with the Haitian in front of them. Trono had the Haitian in a Krav Maga finger lock that allowed him to control his captive while he held the knife in his other hand.

MacD walked up to them and said in Creole, "Your friends didn't want to cooperate."

The Haitian gaped at his partners slouched in the SUV. His prior confidence evaporated.

"No," he said, panicked, "you cannot take me. They will kill my whole family if they think I am helping you."

"Who?" MacD said over the rumble of an approaching truck. "Who do you work for?"

"Please kill me now!"

MacD shook his head in bewilderment. Someone had total control over these men.

"He wants us to kill him," he said to Hali and Trono.

The two of them responded simultaneously, both incredulous.

"What?"

"You're kidding."

Before MacD could explain, the Haitian tore his hand away, breaking two fingers in the process, and darted out into the street directly into the path of the oncoming truck. He was crushed by the truck's grille and fell under its wheels. Several women screamed. Two men rushed to his aid but drew back when they saw the condition of the body.

They were all shocked by the man's willingness to kill himself rather than be captured.

"Let's get out of here," MacD said.

While they hoofed it to the next street to find a taxi, MacD called the *Oregon*. Linda answered.

"Where are you?" she asked.

"We're on our way back."

"Everyone okay?"

"We're all fine. I'll report when we're there."

"Get back as soon as you can. We're getting ready to set sail."

"Is everyone else back aboard?"

"No. That's the problem. We can't reach Max and the Chairman."

Juan couldn't remember the last time he'd taken a day off. He wouldn't have today, either, if Max hadn't insisted, but now that he was on the fifty-two-foot custom Carolina deep-sea fishing boat called the *Cast Away* with a Red Stripe in his hand and four monster yellowfin tunas already in the cooler, he didn't know why he'd ever resisted.

The boat was trolling ten miles off the coast, four poles stuck in the rotating pedestal fishing chair, the well-used leather fighting belt hanging from its armrest. Juan and Max were the sole passengers on the luxurious charter. Captain Craig Reed, a garrulous Boston firefighter who'd retired to Montego Bay to start his fishing business, manned the conn and served as the boat's only crew member. Juan and Max had nothing to do but savor the fine weather and beer until the next bite.

"You know, Reed's got the right idea," Max said, and took another swig from his bottle.

"The right idea about what?"

"About how to retire in style."

Juan tilted his head at Max. "Thinking about leaving the Corporation?"

Max shrugged. "Maybe not tomorrow, but someday. I've been on the water since I was assigned to that Swift Boat in Vietnam."

"And you love it."

"I do. That's why buying my own fishing charter has its appeal."

"The Corporation doesn't provide enough excitement for you?"

"Too much, sometimes."

"It keeps you young."

"I just wish it did something for my weight," Max said, patting his round belly. Julia was constantly on him to watch his diet, but Chef's pasta was too tempting.

"I could install a treadmill at your workstation in the op center."

"You do that and I'm definitely retiring."

"Then we have a deal. No treadmill, no retirement."

They tapped bottles and took another drink.

"Well, what do you know?" Reed called down from his chair on the deck above them. "Looks like we've got some competition for this prime spot."

Another fishing charter cleaved the water as it raced toward them at full speed about a mile out. It looked to be a sixty-foot Landeweer, a high-end vessel that outclassed the *Cast Away.*

"She's coming on pretty fast," Juan said.

"That's the *Oceanaire*," Reed said, his brow knotted. "It's Colin Porter's boat. She's a beauty, fully customized, the fastest charter in Montego Bay. Now, why is Colin out here? He told me this morning that he'd be trolling east of here."

"Seems odd that he would be headed straight for us," Max said.

"Let me ask him what's going on." Reed tried calling on the radio, but instead of a response, Juan could hear a sound like a high-pitched electric drill coming from the speaker.

"What's wrong with this thing?" Reed said, banging on the console.

Juan looked at Max. "Does that sound like a jamming signal to you?"

"It sure does." Max narrowed his eyes at the approaching boat when he realized the implication of what Juan was asking.

There was no use checking their personal cell phones. Even if they weren't being jammed, they were far out of range of any tower.

"Someone's jamming us?" Reed asked. He followed their gaze to the *Oceanaire*. "Colin? That's crazy."

Juan scanned the horizon. "There aren't any other boats in sight."

"It has to be a malfunction," Reed said. "He's probably just coming over to say hi or tell us where the best fishing is."

"Has he done something like this before?"

"Well . . . no."

"Seems like a strange coincidence, don't you think? They're coming at us full bore just after your radio went out?"

"But jamming our signal? Why would he do that?"

"That's the million-dollar question," Max said.

Juan leaned into Max and said quietly, "This seems all wrong."

"I've got the same feeling," Max answered back.

"If they have a portable jammer on that boat, it required some planning to bring it along. They didn't find one in their neighborhood hardware store."

"Which means they didn't want us calling for help."

"As far as I know, nobody even knows we're here."

"Then I'd say better safe than sorry."

Juan looked up at Reed. "You know, you're probably right that there's nothing to worry about, but it might be prudent to take some precautions. I noticed you have a speargun mounted on the wall with the rods and tackle."

"That old thing? I don't even know how to use it. I bought it because I thought some of my clients would want to spearfish, but nobody was ever interested. Now it's just a conversation piece."

"Do you mind if I keep it handy? Just in case?" Juan's combat leg was back on the *Oregon*.

"Are you kidding?"

"I like to be prepared for the worst."

"Have you fired one before?"

"A few times."

Reed gave him a dubious look, then glanced at the radio and nodded reluctantly. "Just remember that you can't sue me down here, so be careful with it. I only have one spear for it. To tell the truth, I'm not even sure it works."

Juan ducked into the cabin and went to where the spare rods were lined up on the wall. At the very top was the five-foot-long Riffe speargun with a pistol grip. In the water, its effective range was little over twenty feet. Even though the air provided less resistance, the range wouldn't be much greater, but it was better than nothing.

Juan plucked the spear and its gun off the wall. The spear,

which had a wicked notched steel tip, was propelled by three rubber tubes on either side of the teak shaft. Juan loaded the spear and cranked the tubes back until the clasp attached to the spear's shaft. He didn't bother with the spear's retractable line. If he ended up using it, he didn't plan on reeling anything in.

He headed back up and saw that the *Oceanaire* was closing on them. He leaned the speargun against the bulkhead, out of sight but within easy reach.

"Max, why don't you join Craig up on the bridge?" If things got hairy, Juan wanted Max ready to take the wheel. Max climbed up and stood next to the controls.

The *Oceanaire* slowed and turned so that it could come alongside. Less than a boat length separated it from the *Cast Away*. Both boats idled on the calm sea. Juan stood on the balls of his feet, his arms loose and unencumbered.

Four men were visible, two on the bridge deck and two on the aft fishing deck. While the one at the controls was dressed in shorts and a T-shirt, the three others were oddly out of place in pants and light jackets, not the attire Juan would expect tourists to wear. All of them stared intently at the *Cast Away*, not a smile to be seen.

"Porter, what are you doing out here?" Reed shouted to him.

Colin Porter, *Oceanaire*'s owner, had to be the one in the T-shirt. He looked at the man next to him as if he were contemplating how to answer. A muscular guy with close-cropped hair and a military bearing, the man stood with a posture that conveyed his status as the person in command. He had angular cheekbones, a jaw carved from marble, and a glare that could freeze molten lava.

Who was he? Juan wondered. A local policeman? Someone in

the Jamaican armed forces? Juan immediately discarded both those possibilities. Neither would use a radio jammer.

Before he could speculate further, the *Oceanaire*'s engine died. Porter yelled at the top of his lungs, "Reed, they're going to kill you!" He reared back and threw what looked like a set of keys overboard.

The man next to Porter turned and without so much as a flinch shot him in the head with a pistol. Porter's body tumbled over the railing and splashed into the water.

While he was shooting the boat's captain, his men snatched assault rifles from their hiding places in front of them and brought them to bear on the *Cast Away*.

At the same time, Juan grabbed the speargun and aimed it at the closest gunman. They all fired simultaneously.

The spear struck the aftmost gunman in the center of the chest, causing him to fall backward as his weapon spewed bullets into the air over Juan's head.

The gunman next to him was aiming at the bridge. As Juan dived for cover, he could see Max shove the throttle forward. The sudden movement saved Reed's life. A round hit him near the shoulder instead of in the chest. The remaining bullets stitched their way across the ceiling of the bridge.

They kept their heads down as more rounds raked the *Cast Away*'s hull. In less than a minute, they were out of range and the shooting ceased. The *Oceanaire* was dead in the water behind them.

Juan scrambled up to the bridge and found Max putting pressure on Reed's shoulder with a rag that was already soaked with blood. Juan took over so that Max could pilot the boat.

Reed was awake and alert. His shoulder was a crimson mess.

He didn't seem to be in shock. Probably had been through more dire situations as a firefighter.

Juan inspected the damage. Reed winced but didn't complain.

"No exit wound, and the bullet seems to have missed any arteries," Juan said. "You got lucky."

"Oh yeah," Reed said through clenched teeth, "I feel like I just won the lottery."

"If it wasn't for your friend, none of us would be alive. He threw the ignition key overboard to save us."

"I can't believe Porter is dead. He was a good man, and that animal murdered him in cold blood. Who are those people? Why are they trying to kill us?"

"I don't know, but we'll find out. First, we need to get you to a hospital."

"It'll take us at least thirty minutes to get back to Montego Bay," Max said. He glanced back at them, but his gaze settled on the ocean instead. The look on his face became grim. "Unfortunately, I don't think we've got thirty minutes."

Juan turned and saw that the *Oceanaire* was no longer stationary. Crests of water curled in front of its bow.

The assassins must have figured out how to hot-wire the boat and now had the engine cranked to full power. Not only was the *Oceanaire* on a pursuit course, she was gaining on them.

"Still no luck on the radio," Max said.

"We're on our own until we can reach port," Juan said, holding his hand on Reed's wound. The injury was more severe than it originally appeared to be. The ex-firefighter was having trouble breathing, and Juan wondered if a bone fragment had punctured his lung.

"I'd say we've got ten minutes tops before they're in range to start firing at us. That was a great shot with the spear, but it was our only weapon."

"Do you have anything else that we could use?" Juan asked Reed.

Reed, who was now ashen, merely shook his head.

"There's gotta be something we can defend ourselves with," Max said. "Once they're next to us, they'll either mow us down from their boat or board us if we try to hide inside. Either way, I don't like our chances."

"Then I'll have to figure something out," Juan said. He put Reed's good hand on the rag. "Can you keep pressure on this?"

Reed nodded weakly. Juan didn't like leaving him there, but there was nothing more he could do for him until they reached safety. *If* they reached safety.

Juan went downstairs and saw that one of the two remaining men on the *Oceanaire* was climbing out onto the open foredeck with his assault rifle while his companion drove the boat. He lay down and took aim at the *Cast Away* but didn't fire, apparently not wanting to waste ammo until they were in effective range. Max similarly delayed taking evasive action until the shooting started. Doing so now would only allow their pursuers to catch up more quickly.

The spent speargun rested on the deck next to the fishing chair where Juan had discarded it. Empty beer bottles that had fallen from their perches when Max gunned the engine now banged against the transom.

Juan ducked into the cabin and searched for anything that might prove useful. The well-stocked galley had plenty of food and drinks, but nothing more lethal than a dinner knife. Juan had his own pocketknife, but it would only be valuable as a close-quarters weapon.

He opened the hatch into the engine bay and climbed down to see what he could find. Although the smell of diesel fuel and oil was strong, the equipment looked well maintained. Juan discovered a tool kit, but it contained little more than a wrench and a few screwdrivers. Nothing that would stand up to an assault rifle.

He was about to leave the engine room when the noxious odor made him stop. He realized that they did have a weapon: the fuel itself. He needed a way to launch it at the *Oceanaire* but didn't know how until the memory of the empty beer bottles inspired a brainstorm.

He hurried up to the outside deck and picked up four Red Stripes. He also took the portable bilge pump and went back down to the engine room.

He uncapped the fuel tank and stuck the pump's hose in. It took him only a few pumps each to fill all of the distinctive squat bottles.

He took the bottles and the tool kit back up to the galley, where he rifled through the drawers until he found a cigarette lighter. Juan then retrieved a life vest from the storage locker, took out his knife, and cut the vest open so he could get at the foam inside. He quickly sliced off pieces of foam and jammed them inside the bottles, where they would dissolve, converting the diesel to a sticky jelly. Then he got some hand towels out of the galley to stuff in the necks. He turned each of the bottles over until their makeshift wicks were soaked with diesel.

Now he had four Molotov cocktails. The next step was to figure out how to deliver them to the target.

Throwing them was the obvious choice, but it would also expose him to gunfire. He might get one good throw before he was cut down, and the boats would have to be practically next to each other to assure a hit. He needed a launch mechanism with more velocity and suddenly realized the speargun gave him all the velocity he needed.

Up on deck, Juan stole a glance behind them and saw the *Oceanaire* perilously close. The gunman took a couple of potshots, but the bullets had little hope of hitting a moving target at that range.

"Whatever you're doing," Max yelled, "you better hurry!"

"Two more minutes," Juan replied as he placed the Molotov cocktails in the cooler for easy access.

"I'll do what I can."

"That's all I ask."

With the knife, Juan hacked the three elastic rubber tubes from each side of the speargun and tied them together to make a pair of longer tubes. With a screwdriver from the tool kit, he rapidly detached the back of the rotating fishing chair and dropped it on the deck. He tied each tube to one of the chair's metal armrests. He lashed the other ends of the tubes to the leather fighting belt, which he could fold together to form a perfect pocket for gripping a beer bottle.

His slingshot was ready. And because the chair rotated, he'd be able to aim anywhere in a one-hundred-and-eighty-degree arc. Now he could fire the Molotov cocktails without raising his head more than a few inches above the transom.

Of course, that assumed the thing actually worked. Only one way to find out, but he couldn't give away his element of surprise.

Juan sneaked back up to the bridge.

"Max, I want you to turn around."

Max was incredulous. "I'm sorry. I thought I just heard you say that you want me to turn around."

"Running away only delays the inevitable. I've got a little surprise for those pirates. Molotov cocktails, and I'm ready to launch them."

"That means we have to get them in close."

Juan nodded. "I'd say no more than fifty yards."

"Oh, good. I thought you were going to make this hard."

"I know you like a challenge." Juan went back down to the aft deck as Max brought the *Cast Away* about.

Juan would have two minutes at most before they were within

range. He loaded an unopened beer bottle into the pocket of his slingshot and pulled it back until the rubber wouldn't go any tighter without breaking. The well-oiled chair rotated easily when he moved the pocket back and forth.

With the *Oceanaire* directly in front of them, it was unlikely their attackers would be able to see what Juan was doing. He took aim on a mountain peeking over the horizon, held his breath, and released the slingshot.

The beer bottle rocketed away from the boat with a twang of the rubber tubing. It flew in a graceful arc and landed in their wake over sixty yards away. Juan practiced twice more until he had the hang of it. Now he needed a real target.

"Get ready!" Max shouted.

"Stay low!" Juan replied.

He pressed himself against the bulkhead and lit the first Molotov cocktail as the *Cast Away* slewed around in another half circle. The gunman on the deck was already firing his rifle in the careful three-shot bursts of a trained soldier rather than unloading his magazine on auto. Bullets peppered the bridge, his primary target.

The *Oceanaire* swung around on a pursuit course. When it was directly behind them, Juan placed the flaming bottle in the pocket and drew it back. He aimed and let go.

The bottle soared into the air, but he immediately saw that he hadn't compensated enough for the speed of the boat following them. The Molotov cocktail flew over the *Oceanaire* and landed harmlessly astern.

Juan lit another and lowered his aim. The gunman, realizing that he now had a more important target than the bridge, adjusted his fire to just above the transom. If the water had been smoother, he might have been able to hit Juan more easily, but the small waves made his rounds impact the bulkhead above Juan's head.

Juan loosed the second cocktail and this time his aim was too low. The bottle smashed into the prow of the *Oceanaire* above the waterline, but the flames were doused by the spray of water.

Either the driver of the *Oceanaire* didn't see the Molotov cocktails or he didn't care because he kept coming without deviating from his course. Juan had only two bombs left.

He lit the third and loaded it into the slingshot. This time, he took the risk of putting his head up higher to improve his aim. He released the bottle as bullets zinged past his head.

Both Juan and the gunman knew it would hit as soon as he let it go. The man got to his feet to dodge the tumbling bottle, but he was too late. It smashed into the deck a foot in front of him, splashing him and the boat with the flaming jelly mixture.

An inferno engulfed the gunman. His screams echoed across the water as he danced in agony. For a moment, Juan thought the man would ease his suffering by jumping into the water, but a single shot came from the *Oceanaire*. The burning gunman slumped to the deck, put out of his misery by the boat's driver.

Juan readied the final bottle, but he wouldn't be needing it. The hijacker must have realized the odds were now even instead of in his favor. The *Oceanaire* veered away and made a beeline for the closest beach. He'd be lucky to make it to shore before he could put the fire out or the boat sank.

The *Cast Away* wasn't in shape for much more of a fight anyway. The engine was sputtering in fits and starts. A few of the rounds must have penetrated the hull and damaged the engines or nicked a fuel line. They'd be lucky to limp back into Montego Bay themselves.

Juan climbed back up to the bridge.

"Nice shootin', pardner," Max said.

"Are you all right?"

"The back of my chair sacrificed itself for me." The thick leather had absorbed three rounds. "How about you?"

"Not a scratch."

Juan bent down and saw that Reed had lost consciousness during the battle.

"How does he look?" Max asked.

"Not good."

"I'm giving it all she's got, but if the engines seize up, we'll have to wait for rescue."

"Reed doesn't have that much time. Try the radio again."

The whine was gone. They were out of range of the jammer. Max sent a distress call out on the emergency band. The reply surprised both of them.

"Max, it's Linda. Are you guys okay?"

"Juan and I are fine, but we've got a serious injury on board."

"We left port fifteen minutes ago to come get you." She didn't have to say that the *Oregon* located them by homing in on their subdermal tracking beacons, which were inserted into the thigh of every crew member. "I've got the RHIB in the water. You should see it any minute."

Juan and Max looked at each other with concern. If the *Oregon* had left port so abruptly, there must be more going on than they were being told, but there could be no discussion about it on an open line.

"Copy, Linda. We'll fill each other in when we see you. Tell Julia to be ready for the casualty."

"Understood. Over and out."

The rigid-hulled inflatable boat raced toward them, closing the distance in a hurry. When it pulled alongside, Max shut down the *Cast Away*'s coughing engines.

MacD and Trono vaulted onto the fishing charter.

"Looks like you saw some action, Chairman," MacD said as he surveyed the damage.

"We did, but you should see the other guys."

"I think we can," Trono said, pointing at a trail of smoke nearing the shore. "Is that them?"

Juan nodded. "Is Gomez getting the chopper ready?"

"Since we were in port, he was doing routine maintenance on it this morning. It'll take another half hour before he can take off. You want us to go after them ourselves?"

"No, we need to get the boat's captain back to the *Oregon* ASAP. He's been shot."

As gently as they could, the four of them lifted Reed into the RHIB.

When he was settled, Juan said, "MacD, stay with the *Cast Away*. We'll send a couple of technicians back to get it moving again. Then we'll figure out what to do with it."

The RHIB took off, skipping across the waves.

"I can't wait to hear how you took on someone who plastered your boat with that many bullet holes," Trono said as he tended to Reed.

"I want to know why the *Oregon* departed early," Max said. "You two weren't the only ones to be attacked today."

"Any casualties?" Juan asked.

"Just Mark Murphy. He took a bullet to his leg. Hux said he'll be fine, though he won't be skateboarding for a while."

"Who else was attacked?"

"Everyone who went ashore."

Juan and Max exchanged worried looks. The crew had been specifically targeted with detailed knowledge of their whereabouts. That led to only one conclusion.

Someone had breached the *Oregon*'s security.

21

Hector Bazin jumped from the burning *Oceanaire* and swam to shore two minutes before it exploded and sank with the bodies of his men still on board. Armed with his SIG Sauer pistol, he carjacked the first vehicle that came along, a rusted-out pickup driven by a barely coherent Rastafarian who reeked of marijuana. One shot to the head and Bazin had transportation. He stashed the corpse in the trees and sped toward Montego Bay's Sangster International Airport.

His waterlogged phone was useless, and he couldn't risk using the dead man's to instruct his pilot to have the Gulfstream fueled and ready to take off. He didn't want to leave a connection between this murder and the jet. He had to hope his other men had been more successful and were ready to leave.

As he drove, Bazin stewed over the missed opportunity. With so many simultaneous targets, he wasn't able to get real-time intelligence from the Doctor or he might have anticipated Juan Cabrillo's defensive strategy. But that was no excuse. Bazin had known the Chairman would be on that boat unarmed and that should have been enough.

Bazin wasn't used to setbacks like this. From an early age, in the slums of Port-au-Prince, he'd shown a knack for thriving in trying circumstances. If Bazin needed something—whether it was food, education, or money—he found a way to get it. Like hundreds of thousands of other poor children in Haiti, Bazin had been a *restavec*, a child sent to be a servant for a richer host family.

Despite the access to education and enough food to grow strong, Bazin despised his new home with a high-ranking government bureaucrat in the Ministry of Foreign Affairs. Beatings were a regular occurrence for even the slightest offense. The other *restavec* in the household, an orphan a year older than he named Jacques Duval, was never subjected to the same abuse because he was the favored one, the adopted son the minister could never have fathered.

The physical punishment only got worse when they were all transferred to the plum posting of the Haitian embassy in Paris. After a particularly bad beating put him in hospital with a broken jaw, arm, and ribs, Bazin took the chance to seek asylum in France. Without any other skills, he joined the French Foreign Legion and went into its elite commando team.

Bazin loved the training and action of the military, but he chafed at the authority, which only served to remind him of his childhood as a *restavec*. He wanted control over his own destiny once and for all, so he left the military after a ten-year stint to hire himself out as a mercenary, eventually building up a vast network of contacts and training his own soldiers from the vast pool of young poverty-stricken men back in Haiti.

He knew that Cabrillo and his crew were mercenaries as well. But they seemed to have the mistaken notion that there was some noble calling to their missions. Bazin was in it for the money, pure and simple. He would take any job that paid well no matter what the operation called for. He only hired men who shared the same ruthlessness, some because they enjoyed it and others because they knew what Bazin would do if they failed or betrayed him.

His reputation brought him to the attention of the Doctor, who had contacted him through various intermediaries. The money flowed from the beginning, and had turned into a tsunami of cash in the last six months.

Bazin's debut mission for the Doctor had been to act as the go-between for the sale of stolen U.S. military technology to a Venezuelan admiral named Dayana Ruiz. It was for underwater drone hardware from the U.S. Navy, a project called Piranha. Bazin didn't know what the admiral planned to do with it and he didn't care. The sale price had been in the millions and Bazin's share had been considerable. So when the Doctor offered him an exclusive contract for a much bigger operation, Bazin didn't hesitate to take it.

The orders were to surreptitiously obtain an array of scientific equipment that was baffling to Bazin. Under the Doctor's guidance and with the help of engineers and technicians, Bazin went about building a secret facility that seemed to have no useful purpose. Only when it finally went into operation did Bazin understand the true scope of the Doctor's vision. He shared the breathtaking details with Bazin, making it clear that if the Haitian stuck with him, he would have more wealth and power than he ever dreamed.

The exploitation of the Colombian drug lords was merely a means to an end. Although the drone sale had been lucrative and had supplied the funds to put Phase 1 of the operation into motion, the Doctor needed millions more to bring his ultimate plan to fruition and the cocaine cartels supplied the money. After Bazin, who had since earned the Doctor's trust, had heard where Phase 2 would lead, he gladly agreed to be a part of it.

The only thing that seemed to stand in their way was the crew of the *Oregon*.

Bazin drove into Montego Bay and left the pickup in an abandoned lot. By now his clothes were dry. He hailed a taxi to take him to the airport's private jet facility, where he breezed through immigration and boarded the Gulfstream.

The only one of his men inside the cabin was David Pasquet, a former Haitian National Police SWAT officer and the sniper who'd been sent to take down Eric Stone and Mark Murphy.

"Where is everyone else?" Bazin asked him.

Pasquet solemnly shook his head. "No one else is coming."

Bazin stared at him in disbelief. "Dead?"

"According to the police reports I'm hearing. I barely made it here myself."

Bazin poked his head into the cockpit and barked at the pilot to take off as soon as he had clearance.

"What happened?" Bazin snapped as he changed into fresh clothes.

"I can only speculate," Pasquet began, "but I think at least one of the women at the spa survived the attack and warned the rest of them. By the time I was set to take my shot, my targets were taking cover. I believe I clipped one of them, but the police arrived before I could finish them off. The *Oregon* left the harbor over an hour ago."

Bazin told him about his sea battle with Juan Cabrillo.

"Including the two who came with me, that's nine men lost

today." Bazin shook his head in disgust. They weren't his best, but they were the best available on short notice. "This crew is formidable even when they don't have their magic ship. We've gotten complacent with our surveillance advantage."

"Do you think this jeopardizes the plan?" Pasquet asked.

"That's up to the Doctor."

Once the jet took off, Bazin braced himself for the phone call he had to make. It wasn't going to be pleasant.

When the Doctor answered, he was his usual curt self. "Well?"

"They got away."

"How many of them?"

Bazin grimaced. "All of them."

There was silence on the phone for a gut-churning moment. "I give you literally the best intelligence money can buy and you let them escape?"

"The plans were put together at short notice," Bazin said, a defense he knew was lame.

"You know we're only four days away from the drone intercept mission. We can't afford to commit unforced errors."

"I can assure you this won't happen again."

"If the U.S. military finds out that their Piranha drones were not only stolen but also put to active use, it could eventually lead back to you and me. If that happens before the mission, the whole plan could fall apart. Do you understand?"

"Should we warn the Venezuelans that their operations may be compromised?"

"No. I kept a back door into the code controlling the drones. Once they've done their work today, I'll set them to self-destruct. They'll sink, and that will be the last anyone hears of them."

"What about Admiral Ruiz?"

"What about her? The drones have done the job for her. Besides, this is her fault. If she hadn't let the *Oregon* go, we wouldn't be in this mess."

"And the *Oregon*?"

"I'll keep tabs on her just in case."

"They've left Montego Bay. They must be near where I had to abandon my pursuit of Juan Cabrillo's fishing boat."

"I can't surveil them unless I know exactly where they are. Have the jet circle the area and tell me the coordinates."

"They couldn't have gotten far in the time it took me to get to the airport," Bazin said. "We'll find them for you."

Bazin told the pilot where to fly, tracing the route the *Ocean-aire* had taken from Montego Bay Harbor to the fishing grounds and then adding on the distance the ship had time to travel since it left. The cloud cover was low, under three thousand feet, so the pilot had to dip below it to search for the ship.

They descended from the clouds, and Bazin was ready to transmit the GPS coordinates to the Doctor as soon as he spotted the ship. But when they reached clear sky, all they saw was an expansive carpet of blue stretching in all directions from the Jamaican coastline. The only visible vessel was a cruise ship on the distant horizon. Otherwise, the sea was unbroken. There wasn't even a sign of the *Cast Away*, which presumably meant it was now sitting on the bottom of the ocean. As for the freighter, Bazin was mystified.

The *Oregon* was gone.

Thirty miles east of Jamaica

Juan was sure the Jamaican authorities were asking a lot of questions about why dead men were cropping up all over the island and two charter fishing boats had disappeared. He didn't want to risk returning to Montego Bay.

Instead of repairing Craig Reed's fishing boat and returning it to Montego Bay without him aboard, they used one of the *Oregon*'s cranes to hoist it into the largest hold, where technicians would fix the engines and patch up the damage free of charge for all the trouble they'd caused.

As soon as the *Cast Away* had been secured, Juan ordered the *Oregon* at full speed to get out of the area as fast as they could in case their attackers had something more up their sleeve. Three hours later, they had Eddie, Linc, and his motorcycle on board via a side trip from one of the *Oregon*'s high-powered lifeboats into

Ocho Rios. The local Harley shop would have to send someone to retrieve Eddie's rental.

Once Juan had his crew back together and they were sailing out into blue water, he went to visit the medical bay. He entered to find Julia writing some notes on her tablet.

"How's our guest doing?" he asked.

She tossed the tablet on her desk and leaned back, running her fingers through her hair. Except for a slight weariness around the eyes, she showed no sign of the stress she'd been through. "The surgery went well. Internal bleeding was causing a pressure buildup around his pleural sac. I've removed the bullet, put in a chest tube, and sutured the wounds. He should be up and about in a few days. Six weeks for a full recovery."

"That's good to hear. Is he awake?"

"No. I'll let you know when he's up for visitors."

"Thanks. When he comes to, let him know that his boat is well taken care of."

"I will."

"What's the diagnosis for our daring skateboarder?"

"A few stitches and a walking cast. He'll have a nice scar to impress the ladies."

"He's cleared for duty?"

"He can certainly sit at his post in the op center, but I wouldn't make him run laps."

"Don't worry," Juan said, "we've already got his skateboard park stowed."

Julia rubbed her eyes.

"You okay?" Juan asked. "You're not usually in on the type of action you and Linda went through today."

"I'm fine. I'm just glad I could get back to saving people instead of killing them."

"If you and Linda hadn't defeated those guys, we would have lost a lot of crew today."

"It was all Linda. I just tripped in the right direction."

"Craig Reed is happy that you did. I'll be back later."

He left and went to Mark Murphy's cabin, far forward of any other quarters on the ship to isolate the meteor-impact volume levels that were blasted from the room. The door was ajar, so Juan gave a perfunctory knock and then stepped inside. If this had been during Murph's downtime, Juan would have expected to see him battling Eric at one of his video games on the giant television, but he found them glued to their tablets. Murph's leg was stretched out on the sofa and wrapped in bandages. The air cast sat on the floor next to him.

"I'm glad you didn't join me in the Long John Silver Club," Juan said. "I'm the only one on the ship allowed to have a peg leg."

"And I will gladly let you keep that distinction," Murph replied. "I've decided I don't like being shot."

"Have you finished the analysis of our computer security?" Juan asked, closing the door.

"We've gone over it three times," Eric said. "Nothing."

"If someone has been tiptoeing around our network," Murph said, "we should have found something by now. Our firewall is as secure as ever. No one is inside our servers that shouldn't be."

"What about eavesdropping devices?"

"No network besides ours is sending any signals from this ship," Murph said.

"And I've swept the op center, conference room, and mess hall with our bug detection equipment. They're clean."

Juan frowned. "We were attacked in five different locations at the same time. That took detailed intelligence to coordinate."

"Everyone could have been tailed from the ship," Eric offered.

"One or even two of us could have been followed. But all five groups? And they'd have to know where we were going to be ready for us in Montego Bay with considerable firepower to take us down."

"Besides," Murph said, "how could anyone know the two of us would be exposed on deck? Someone had to scout out that oil tank to snipe from."

"So we have no network penetration and no one listening into our meetings with bugs," Juan said. "I'm looking for any other explanation for how the information about where we'd be could have made it into the wrong hands."

Eric stared in disbelief. "You mean we might have a spy on board?"

Juan sighed heavily. "We haven't had a new crew member in over a year. We've vetted everybody, both financially and personally. I don't see how it's possible."

"Do you want me to start looking into the crew members who weren't targeted today?"

Juan shook his head. "Not yet. I can't accept that we have a traitor on the *Oregon*, and going down that path will start making everyone paranoid. We work and live together too closely to be suspicious of each other. It would destroy us as a unit. I want another explanation."

"But how could they have known where we'd be unless they were in the room when we were talking about it?"

Juan was grasping for any explanation that didn't involve a witch hunt, and it couldn't hurt to take precautions. "We might get more answers about how it was done if we knew who'd done it."

The two of them shrugged and Juan left. His next stop was the op center, where he found MacD and Hali Kasim listening to headphones with both hands on their ears.

Juan leaned against the console. "Is this the recording Eddie made?"

Hali nodded. "MacD thinks he can translate what the guy was saying."

"Anything useful?"

MacD shrugged, which seemed to be his crew's favorite new gesture. "It sounds like the guy was delirious. Eddie said he hit the ground pretty hard with his head before he died."

"What's he saying?"

"Just one sentence over and over. 'The doctor'—whoever he is—'promised the world would be different in four days.' He says it like he's sorry he wouldn't live to see it. Does that phrase mean anything to you?"

Juan joined in the shrugfest. "It sounds ominous."

"Maybe he was being treated for some condition," Hali said.

"Then why does he say 'the world would be different'?"

"Maybe he means *his* world."

"Nope," MacD said, "he's definitely saying *the* world."

"That still doesn't answer why he and his friends would want us out of the way," Juan said.

"Could be they think we know something about this doctor."

"Or about what happens in four days," Hali said.

"If anyone has any theories," Juan said, "I'm all ears."

Linda came up and handed Juan several sheets of paper. "We just got this from the CIA. It's a preliminary list of everything newsworthy that happened on the dates found on the phone you took from that Venezuelan Navy lieutenant. They're doing more in-depth analysis on it right now."

Juan saw the four Greek letters and codes, each paired with a date, but they seemed as inscrutable now as they were the day Murph and Eric hacked into the phone. Alpha 17, Beta 19, Gamma 22. Delta 23, the fourth in the series, corresponded to today's date.

"Did they find any correlation?"

"The CIA checked for every series progression they could think of. Nothing fit. And there doesn't seem to be anything that ties the dates together."

Juan scanned the list of events. It included a wide variety of possibilities and spanned the entire world: murders, traffic fatalities, political speeches and rallies, weather phenomena, terrorist bombings, sports events. None of them fit a pattern that Juan could see.

One item caught his eye: a ship sinking. Most of the general public doesn't realize how regularly ships on the high seas go down. During an average year, more than a hundred ships sink, sending two thousand sailors to a watery grave. Even in the age of GPS tracking, weather forecasting, and satellite communications, many of the ships disappear without a trace, falling prey to mechanical failures, fire, storms, and rogue waves.

The listed ship fit into the Gamma 22 spot. She was a cargo vessel named *Santa Cruz* that went down with all hands.

The number of crew was twenty-two.

Juan felt the hairs on his neck prickle.

"What about this one?" Juan said, pointing at the shipwreck listing.

"*Santa Cruz?*" Linda said. "The CIA thinks the fact that it had twenty-two crew is a coincidence. The analyst told me it's easy to find random numerical links to anything. On the Alpha seventeen date, there was a traffic pileup in New York that involved seventeen vehicles and a snowstorm in Calgary where they received seventeen inches of snow."

"It's the *Santa Cruz* name that bugs me. Humor me."

They went over to her terminal, where she had a remote link to a worldwide ship database. She punched in *Santa Cruz*.

"She was flagged Panamanian, but was owned by a Venezuelan company called Cabimas Shipping. The company's owner is one of the richest men in Venezuela, Ricardo Leal." She did a quick search and found thousands of mentions of his name. "Seems like Mr. Leal has political aspirations in his country. Many are expecting him to use his wealth to run for president next year."

Juan looked at the list again and realized what the link was between them.

"Linda, check the database for all the ships that have sunk in the last three months."

"Even though there aren't any other ships on the CIA's list?"

"The dates that they sunk and the dates they were reported missing could be different. Sometimes a ship isn't considered missing for a couple of days after it misses a scheduled check-in."

Linda brought up the list and they compared it to the numbers on the phone list. She gasped when she saw how they matched up.

The numbers weren't a progression. The lieutenant was keeping track of how many crew members were on each ship.

Alpha 17—*Cantaura*, a containership lost off of Portugal with seventeen crew.

Beta 19—*Tucupita*, a tanker reporting missing with nineteen crew members as it was rounding Cape Horn.

Gamma 22—*Santa Cruz* and its twenty-two men disappeared in the middle of the Atlantic.

All of them belonged to Cabimas Shipping. The first two didn't broadcast any kind of Mayday or indicate anything was wrong before contact was lost. They simply vanished.

"Three ships disappeared in three months?" Linda asked. "That can't be chance."

"I'm sure Leal's insurer is saying the same thing. They must think he's deliberately sinking his ships or they've become so ill-maintained that they're falling apart. Either way, it would make him uninsurable. Without insurance, no one would send freight with his company ever again."

"Do you think Ruiz is targeting his ships?"

"It's possible. If she has political ambitions of her own, what better way to get rid of her biggest rival than to bankrupt him?"

"He must be teetering on the edge of that now," Linda said.

"One more sinking might do it," Juan said. "Check the crew complements on the rest of his ships to see if we get a match."

The answer came back immediately. Only one Cabimas ship had exactly twenty-three crew: a car carrier named *Ciudad Bolívar*.

"Where is she now?"

Linda queried the Marine Traffic database. "She departed Veracruz, Mexico, two days ago with a load of cars and construction equipment. Her destination is Puerto Cabello, Venezuela."

"Which would put her a few hundred miles due south of Jamaica," Juan said. "We just found our answer."

"To what?"

"To the question of why someone was trying to kill us," Juan said. "Ruiz is planning to sink the *Ciudad Bolívar* today and we're the only ones capable of stopping it."

23

Maria Sandoval was nearly done with her daily inspection of the *Ciudad Bolívar*'s vehicle decks. As the master of the ship, her responsibility was to make sure her cargo arrived safely, so she regularly checked the condition of the interior to make sure there were no leaks in the fully enclosed decks that could allow salt water to damage the shipment and to verify that everything remained in its proper place.

The *Ciudad Bolívar* was the pride of the Cabimas fleet. At 700 feet long and eleven stories high, she could transport up to five thousand cars, primarily serving the growing South American market. Her current load had significantly fewer vehicles because the ceiling of deck 10 had been hoisted to accommodate large construction equipment—graders, backhoes, mobile cranes, dump trucks, bulldozers—all destined for Brazil. The deck below this one was dedicated to cars and SUVs bound for Venezuela and Argentina.

The total value of her shipment was over one hundred and fifty million dollars, and Maria took her responsibility for its care seriously. Her short dark hair and round face made her look younger than her thirty-eight years, and burly new crew members tended to underestimate her when she met them, in her nondescript trousers and unrevealing light sweater. She ran a tight ship, for her first command, driven by the pressure to succeed as the company's only female captain. With the loss of three Cabimas vessels in the last three months, the crew was edgy, and Maria had spent plenty of restless nights worried about her ship, so she was especially attuned to anything that might pose a hazard.

The construction vehicles stretched out in long rows, parked side by side with inches to spare, maximizing the usable capacity in the cavernous, well-lit interior. Maria was the sole occupant of the hold. Even with the vibration of the ship's engines and the rumble of the air-handling system, the lack of any other sound in the gigantic space was eerie.

She tested the tie-downs on random vehicles, which had been driven into place on the roll on/roll off ship. She knew her men inspected them on a periodic basis, but she liked to go over their work to ensure that their reports were accurate. If any vehicle came loose in heavy seas, particularly ones like these that weighed upward of fifty tons, it could wreak major damage on the cargo or start a fire.

While the smaller vehicles were secured with canvas straps, those for construction were cinched down with heavy steel chains. Nothing short of a Category 5 hurricane would be able to budge them, and the forecast called for smooth sailing until they reached Puerto Cabello.

Maria finished her assessment and was pleased with the results. She expected a lot from her crew and they never let her down.

She was walking toward the stairs to the bridge when she heard a grinding sound. But it wasn't coming from the engine. It seemed to be emanating from the hull itself.

Before she could move, the shipwide klaxon shrieked, causing her to instinctively cringe. Instead of short bursts indicating fire, the horn sounded in lengthy peals.

There was a hull breach. The ship was taking on water.

The list would have been imperceptible to anyone not as familiar with the ship as she was, but Maria could feel the slightest tilt to port. She raced to the stairs, pulling the walkie-talkie from her waistband.

"Jorge!" she yelled over the wail of the klaxon echoing in the stairwell. "Report!"

She pressed it to her ear and could tell that Jorge, her executive officer, was responding, but the klaxon drowned out the words.

"All stop!" she shouted, and didn't listen for an answer.

Maria sprinted up the ten flights and flung the bridge door open, panting from the exertion as she entered. The ship was slowing, the controls set to stop as she'd ordered. Three men were on the bridge: Jorge; the navigator, Miguel; and the helmsman, Roberto. They were moving efficiently, no panic evident, but stress oozed from their pores.

Jorge, a balding man ten years her senior with a potbelly and a goatee, looked at her in utter confusion.

"What did we hit?" Maria asked.

"Nothing, Captain," he said. "There aren't any other ships in visual range, and the depth is steady at over two miles. We couldn't possibly have hit a reef."

"Rogue storage container?"

"Not likely."

"How big is the breach?"

"*Breaches*. We have compartments flooded in eight different locations of the ship."

"What?"

Jorge showed her the plot of the breaches. They seemed to be concentrated on the port side.

"Did anyone see what happened?"

"A crewman who saw a breach in the bow compartment said it was six inches in diameter and looked as if it had been bored with a drill."

Maria was astonished. That simply wasn't possible. A single large gash she could understand. But eight smaller holes opening in a double-hulled vessel was unprecedented.

"Was he able to patch the hole?" she asked.

"No, ma'am. The pressure was too great. He had to seal off the room. I've also shut the watertight doors to the engine room. We got major flooding in some of the holds before we were able to seal off the rest of the damaged compartments, but those closed-off areas are still filling with water."

The ship's list was at ten degrees and accelerating. Maria was already having to support herself with the console. If they did nothing, the *Ciudad Bolívar* would reach a literal tipping point. Once it did, it would capsize and sink in minutes.

They couldn't plug the holes, but they might be able to balance the ship enough to keep it from flipping over. The ballast tanks were already full, so they couldn't add water to the starboard side to equalize the vessel.

Maria knew she had to find a way to arrest the list. Like all other car carrier captains, she had heard the story of the *Cougar Ace*, an auto transport vessel like hers that nearly capsized when the captain was cycling the ballast water before entering U.S. waters off Alaska to avoid contaminating American shores with nonnative foreign species. A malfunction during the transfer sequence caused the *Cougar Ace* to keel over, but not so far that she completely capsized. It took the valiant efforts of a salvage team to right her again after thirty days on her side.

Unlike container vessels where most of the stowage is on open decks, a car carrier is fully enclosed. No other type of cargo ship could have survived turning on its side because at such an extreme list the lower outside decks would have let water into the hull.

Ever since the *Cougar Ace* accident, most large ships, including the *Ciudad Bolívar*, had been equipped with a load monitor computer application that helped her crew determine how to arrange the vehicles in the vessel for optimum stability. It also made sure that transferring ballast water was done as safely as possible.

Emptying the ballast tanks on the *Cougar Ace* had caused the accident, but perhaps Maria could save her ship with the same tactic.

"Miguel," she said, "send out a distress call. Jorge, input the flooded spaces into the load monitor."

"Why?"

"Because I want to know which portside ballast tanks to drain." When he looked at her like she was crazy, she prodded: "Hurry." The list was now fifteen degrees.

"Aye, Captain."

While Miguel transmitted the distress call, Jorge's fingers flew across the keyboard. Two minutes and another five degrees of list later, he said, "Ballast tanks three and four are our best hope. But if the numbers are wrong, we won't have time to abandon ship."

As much as the cargo was her responsibility, the crew was an even higher priority.

"Jorge," she said, "take Roberto and Miguel to gather the rest of the men at the muster station and prepare to launch the lifeboat." Since it was on the port side and closer to the water, they should still have time to lower it. At least there was no danger of dying from exposure in the tropical climate.

"We're staying, Captain," Jorge said. Miguel and Roberto nodded in agreement.

"No, you're not. It only takes one of us to do this. If it works and the ship is righted, I can bring you back aboard. But if it capsizes, there's no reason for us all to go down."

"Just you?"

"It's my ship. Now, go take care of the men. Let me know when you're away."

Jorge swallowed hard, but he could see that further objection was useless. With forced smiles and good luck wishes, the three of them scrabbled out, holding on to anything they could as they walked on the inclined deck.

By the time the crew had reached safety, she might not be able to hold herself upright or even climb out of the bridge. She wasn't suicidal or excited about a hero's death. She wanted to survive if at all possible. If things went wrong, she wanted a backup plan.

Maria went outside the bridge to the wall-mounted fire hose. She opened the case and pulled the hose out, unreeling it so that the nozzle snaked into the bridge and slid all the way to the other side. When it was completely unreeled, she went back in to the computer terminal and looped the hose around her waist.

Two minutes later, Jorge radioed that the lifeboat was launched and all crewmen were accounted for. They were motoring to a safe distance, ready to pick her up if she decided to leap from the ship. She thanked him and told him he'd know her choice when he saw what happened to the ship.

The list was now forty degrees, and the hose cut into her hip as the tilt threatened to make her lose her footing. If her plan worked, it would save the ship. If not, the new imbalance might turn it over before she had a chance to escape.

A faithful Catholic, Maria crossed herself and kissed her crucifix pendant. Then she pressed the command to empty ballast tanks 3 and 4, praying that the pumps were still working.

The immediate impact was anticlimactic. No sudden movement, no noise of machinery winding into action. But the screen indicated that the pumps were functioning. The levels of tanks 3 and 4 were declining.

A jolt rocked the ship, increasing its list by ten degrees in seconds, and Maria feared that she had made the wrong choice. Her last order would be the one that killed her and sunk the ship.

The soles of her shoes finally lost their grip and Maria's feet flew out from under her. Her shoulder smacked into the rubber-coated floor. The hose was the only thing that kept her from tumbling out the door and over the railing, spiraling to the metal deck below.

Like a climber rappelling down a cliff, Maria planted her feet against the floor and gripped the hose with both hands. She needed to get up to where it was attached to the exterior wall before the angle of ascent wouldn't allow her to use her legs to support her. She was strong, but her arms weren't muscular enough to pull herself up by her hands alone.

It was a race between her and the ship's tilt. She clambered up, making sure she had one hand on the hose at all times. One slip and she could smash her head against any of the consoles.

She was halfway up when the hose knocked against the radio on her belt. Before she could grab it, the walkie-talkie detached and tumbled gracefully through the air until it shattered against the railing, a fitting demonstration of what would happen to Maria if she followed it.

With renewed vigor, she climbed the final steps and hauled herself out onto the exterior metal wall of the bridge. She lay back and sucked in deep breaths, exhausted from the effort. It was only then that she realized the list had stabilized. Although the ship wasn't righting itself, it wasn't in imminent danger of turning turtle, either.

Maria estimated that the list was seventy degrees, making the whitewashed walls temporary floors. She untied herself from the hose, stood, and walked along the exterior of the crew's living area situated atop the ship, careful to avoid stepping on the windows. There was no point in going back inside the bridge and trying to adjust the ballast tanks further in the hopes of righting the ship. She could just as easily capsize it. Better to let an expert salvage company do the job.

Maria shielded her eyes from the sun blazing above the western horizon. It would be dark in a few hours and she had to decide whether it would be possible to descend to the port side safely so that she could join her crew. She could open doors into the interior, but navigating the upturned hallways would be riskier than it was worth. She'd wait out on deck until a rescue ship could arrive. Unless there was a naval vessel within range, the ship was too far from any shore for a helicopter to lift her to safety.

She put her hand over her eyes and surveyed the sea until she spotted the lifeboat coming around the aft end of the *Ciudad Bolívar*. Maria could only imagine the view the crew had of the green hull cocked at such an unnatural angle, the single propeller hovering above the water and the red underbelly exposed for the first time since dry dock.

She waved both arms madly until she saw the men waving

back. Their cheers carried to her over the water. When they approached as close as they dared, she shouted down to them that she had lost her radio and would stay on the deck until help arrived. As long as an unexpected squall didn't develop, camping out under the stars wouldn't be so bad, given the circumstances.

An hour went by. She lay down and took a siesta, during which she puzzled over the damage that had nearly sunk her ship. She couldn't think of any phenomenon—natural or man-made—that would cause circular holes to be gouged in the ship's hull.

Her thoughts were interrupted by the distant sound of an engine. She sat bolt upright and scanned the horizon for a vessel. Then she saw it coming toward them from the east, a gunmetal gray boat eighty feet in length. Too small for a cargo ship, but not the configuration of a pleasure yacht, either. Then she recognized it as an ancient fishing trawler.

It must have been in the vicinity and heard their distress calls. Jorge was probably on the radio with them now. As it approached, Maria was already thinking of ways that they could string up a belaying rope to lower her down.

She waved as it slowed and came alongside the lifeboat, but she couldn't see anyone on board. Her crewmen crowded along the open weather hatch, waving and shouting joyful greetings.

The door of the trawler banged open and eight men rushed out, all with black objects in their hands. Her crewmen's shouts of joy changed to cries of terror. She was baffled until she heard the unmistakable sound of automatic gunshots. Maria stood there, shocked into horrified silence, as muzzles flashed and her men were torn apart by the withering fire. It was over in seconds.

One of the men tossed two objects into the lifeboat and closed the hatch. Two thumps followed, and soon flames were consuming the boat. It would sink in minutes, taking her crewmen to the bottom and leaving no trace.

Maria was so horrifically mesmerized by the burning lifeboat that she wasn't paying attention to the fishing trawler. Someone on board must have spotted her because bullets began to ping off the metal around her.

Without thinking, she ran, dodging rounds, in a desperate attempt to make it to the nearest door. The bullets were getting so close that she realized she wouldn't have time to open it and climb inside before she was hit. She needed faster cover.

Maria leaped at the next window and braced her legs as she smashed its glass with her feet and plunged through.

24

Lieutenant Pablo Dominguez pulled himself up toward the bridge by a fire hose that conveniently swayed from its open door. If Admiral Ruiz found out that the *Ciudad Bolívar* was not sunk, it wouldn't matter if Dominguez got away from the scene of the crime. He'd already failed her once and had been given a second chance to make amends by overseeing this mission. If he failed again, he would be a dead man.

The hails from an approaching helicopter had been an unwelcome surprise. He certainly hadn't expected one so far from land. It had to mean that a ship was closing on their position, which was why he'd taken the risk of climbing onto the car carrier to find a way to sink it before rescue arrived.

The Piranha sub design had been purchased from a source of Admiral Ruiz, a man Dominguez knew only as the Doctor.

He had been part of a top secret U.S. drone program and somehow smuggled the designs away from the Americans. With the Doctor's expertise, Ruiz had eight of the miniature submarines built.

They were a stealth design, powered by battery-powered impellers that were virtually silent, so a swarm of subs could creep up on a ship without being detected. Once the subs were within range of the target and had spaced themselves out to maximum effect, they moved in and attached themselves to the ship's hull with powerful magnets and activated their only weapon: a rotating jet that fired a millimeter-wide stream of seawater pressurized to eighty thousand pounds per square inch. Industrial water lasers are used to cut aluminum, marble, and granite without the scorching of a cutting torch or the ripping of a saw. The Piranha's compact version used seawater itself as its cutting tool and could slice through the inch-thick steel of a ship's double hulls in seconds. The simultaneous hull breaches caused by the swarm of subs meant ships would go under before they even knew they'd been attacked.

Though effective, the Piranhas had drawbacks. Because they depended on battery power, their range and duration were extremely short. They could be used only once before they needed a full recharge. The fishing trawler had been specially outfitted to carry and charge the eight-foot-long drone subs. The trawler would place the subs in the path of the freighter to be attacked and leave them there to loiter until the ship was spotted by the subs' onboard cameras. The trawler, having retreated to a position miles away, would be nowhere near the scene of the crime when the ship went down. Dominguez controlled the subs from his handheld tablet, which allowed him to lock onto the target vessel. The subs would intercept the ship, sink it, and the trawler would recover the subs and eliminate any survivors.

The first three attacks went flawlessly. Each ship went down before lifeboats could be launched, and all Dominguez's men had to do was get rid of the few crewmen who'd made it overboard. But somehow Captain Maria Sandoval had arrested the capsizing of her ship. The Piranha subs were now recharging, but it would be another thirty minutes before they could be used again. If the rescue ship arrived before then, its crew might be able to save the *Ciudad Bolívar*, and Dominguez could not let that happen.

He knew he couldn't wait for the subs to charge. He had to find another way to sink the ship, which was why he was climbing toward the bridge. He'd considered setting fire to the ship, but the onboard CO_2 fire suppression system would extinguish the flames quickly. Besides, he had a more elegant solution. An experienced sailor himself, Dominguez knew that emptying the port ballast tanks should cause the ship to flip over.

He could have emptied the starboard ballast tanks, but the ship was already listing so far over that it might capsize before he had time to get back to the trawler. Instead, he would set the port tanks to drain in a trickle, giving him and the trawler plenty of time to get to safety.

He reached the bridge and pulled himself up to the computer terminal. He found the ballast tank controls and configured the port tanks to empty. When they did, the high side of the ship would weigh far more than the side in the water. It would roll back onto its keel and then keep on going, flipping over completely. When it did, water would flood into the hold through the air vents. As soon as the loading doors were compromised by the growing internal pressure, the ship would rocket to the ocean floor.

Dominguez smiled at his clever backup plan. Surely he would receive a commendation from the admiral for salvaging the mission.

After he activated the draining procedure, he drew his pistol and fired at each terminal until every one of them was destroyed. Now no one would be able to shut down the draining from here. The engineering station in the engine room was the only other location where the ballast tanks could be controlled. Once the list became less pronounced and the stairs became usable, he planned to send a man there to shoot up those controls in case Maria Sandoval hadn't been killed by their gunfire.

Dominguez cursed under his breath as the sound of the helicopter became a roar. The rescuers had arrived sooner than he'd expected.

Riding in the front seat of the *Oregon*'s MD 520N helicopter, Juan couldn't help but gawk at a sight he'd never before seen. The distress call had prepared him for the *Ciudad Bolívar* to be capsized, but he didn't expect the ship to be lying on its side, its keel facing them as they approached from the north. The shipping company's name, CABIMAS, was spelled out in huge gold letters against a forest green background along the ship's starboard side. The spectacle brought to mind the *Costa Concordia* cruise ship resting upon the rocks that had ripped through its hull, but this sight was even more incredible because the car carrier was floating motionless on the open ocean.

"That's not something you see every day," Gomez Adams said as he nudged the nose of the chopper down.

"At least we won't need the welding equipment," Eddie said

from the back, flanked on either side by Linc and MacD. A few months before, they'd come upon a completely capsized megayacht whose hull they had to cut into to save the passengers. They were ready to do the same with the car carrier, but the acetylene tank wouldn't be necessary now that they could see the ship's interior was accessible. The coils of nylon rope, however, might still come in handy.

The *Oregon* was behind them and approaching at top speed, but it would be thirty minutes before it arrived.

"Do you think you can land?" Juan asked Gomez.

"I can get the skids in contact with the hull so you won't have to rope down, but I can't see anything flat enough to keep us stable."

"How long can you loiter?"

"I can stick around until the *Oregon* gets here."

The *Oregon*'s helicopter, which was stowed in the aftmost hold, could be raised and lowered on an elevator platform for launch and recovery. The MD 520N was an unusual design because it lacked a tail rotor. Instead, exhaust vented from the turbine was used to turn the chopper and maintain rotational stability. It was so maneuverable that Gomez boasted he could outfly a hummingbird. He was a skilled enough pilot that Juan almost believed him.

They had launched the helicopter as soon as they'd received the distress call. The *Oregon* had been steaming south from Jamaica ever since Juan had realized the *Ciudad Bolívar* was in danger. Repeated calls to the shipping company warning them of the impending danger were met with wariness about their motives, and Juan couldn't blame them. Without a more concrete analysis of the threat, all the company could do was issue a vague caution to the ship's captain. By the time they were within range to radio the ship directly, the distress call was already being broadcast. When the Maydays abruptly ceased, no ship besides the *Oregon* was within five hours of the *Ciudad Bolívar*.

Juan had ordered the helicopter launched so they could get to the ship as fast as possible. Despite repeatedly hailing the ship during their flight, there had been no response. Although they didn't know if piracy factored into the equation, the fact that there hadn't been any survivors in the previous sinkings made Juan cautious. All four of the landing party were armed, and Juan had donned his combat leg.

"Let's find out where the lifeboat is before we set down," Juan said. "It couldn't have gone far." The unspoken concern was that if the lifeboat had launched, they should have heard from some-one on its radio by now.

"I'll give us a good look all around her," Gomez said.

He came in low, and details of the hull were now visible. The stern and starboard vehicle loading ramps seemed intact and in place. Juan examined the bottom, and his eyes settled on a six-inch-diameter hole in the red paint just above the waterline near the bow. It was the only obvious damage.

"Looks like they've got a gopher problem," Linc said.

"Or someone was drilling for oil in the bottom of the ship," MacD suggested.

Juan was the most experienced sailor on the chopper, but he couldn't come up with anything more realistic than their jokes. "Get some pictures of that, Linc."

Gomez paused for the snaps and then continued back and around the stern. It was only after they reached the port side that they saw a fishing trawler nestled against the car carrier near the bridge at the bow end.

Juan was surprised to see a boat, given the lack of a response to their hails. There was no sign of the lifeboat, but it could be under the water still attached to its davits. Juan's first thought was that the fishing trawler had come alongside to take the crew off, but as Gomez edged closer Juan knew that was the wrong conclusion.

Cables snaked into the water next to the trawler, eight of them, connected to objects floating on the surface, but Juan couldn't make out what they were. Ten men stood on the trawler's deck. One of them was belaying another, who gripped a rope on the ship's canted deck. Instead of a crewman dressed in work clothes disembarking the ship, the man was clad in black and scaling the rope toward the bridge.

As Gomez got closer, Juan could see that the man on the ship had an automatic weapon slung across his back and was balancing himself on a railing. He was facing the helicopter and speaking into a headset microphone. Juan recognized him instantly.

It was Lieutenant Dominguez from the warehouse in Venezuela.

"Those don't look like rescuers to me," Eddie said.

As if in response to Eddie's observation, the men on the trawler snatched up their own assault rifles and opened fire. Rounds pocked the helicopter's fuselage before Gomez was able to swing the chopper over the car carrier and out of view.

Juan checked the backseat. "Anyone hit?"

"We're fine," Eddie replied for them.

"That was the Navy lieutenant we tied up in Venezuela," Juan told Linc.

"I know. I think he recognized me."

"If they're trying to sink her," MacD said, "why is he climbing on board?"

"Their original plan must not have worked," Juan said. "Our hails spooked Dominguez because he didn't expect to see anyone out here. He could be looking for another way to send her to the bottom and get rid of the evidence."

"And witnesses," Linc added. "There could be crew still on board."

Gomez tapped the gas gauge. "We've got a new problem, Chairman. One of the rounds hit our gas tank. We're losing fuel. What do you want me to do?"

"Can you make it back to the *Oregon*?"

"I think so, but I'll have to leave right now."

"Is everyone up for an excursion?" Juan asked.

"Seems wrong to come all this way and turn tail," Linc said. Eddie and MacD nodded solemnly. They knew what they were signing up for.

"All right. Gomez, put us down on the stern right behind the funnel to give us some cover. Once they know we're on board, Dominguez will bring as many men as he can with him onto the ship. They'll probably post some men on the deck, so we'll have to go through the interior to get to the bow."

Gomez hovered over the fantail, making sure to keep the funnel between him and the trawler. He gently rested the helicopter's skids on the ship's railing, and MacD popped open the door, climbing down to the railing in one fluid move. Eddie tossed him several loops of rope and then he and Linc followed just as gracefully.

Before Juan could exit, Gomez said, "Take my life raft."

"You'll need it if you can't make it back to the *Oregon*," Juan replied.

"You'll need it if they sink this ship."

"No we won't. If this ship goes down, Dominguez isn't going to leave behind survivors. This mission is all or nothing. See you soon."

Without waiting for an argument, Juan took off his headset, climbed out, and slammed the door behind him. By the time he reached the nearest hatch to join the others, the helicopter was beating a hasty retreat toward the northern horizon.

25

Maria Sandoval gingerly tightened the torn sleeve of her sweater around her left biceps where she'd been gashed by the glass she jumped through. The crude bandage was soaked with blood, but she didn't want to cut off the circulation and render her arm useless.

When she leaped through the window, she had fallen ten feet onto the interior bulkhead wall of a cabin. She must have sat there for five minutes. Her mind replayed the deaths of her entire crew as she tried to rationalize the attack, the same type that must have been carried out against the company's other vessels. These were no pirates, not if they didn't take hostages. Obviously, their goal was to sink the ship with her on it and they weren't going to give up just because she had pulled off the miracle of saving it.

She couldn't return to the bridge to radio her situation. If the attackers boarded the ship, that would be their primary destination. After tending to her wound, Maria sought a hiding place until rescuers arrived.

Because of its extreme list, the ship she knew intimately was now foreign to her. She had to keep reminding herself that what used to be port was now down and what used to be starboard was now up.

The crew's quarters—including the cabin where she was now taking refuge—galley, mess hall, and offices were all located in the one-story accommodation block atop the ship behind the bridge. Every deck below it was dedicated to cargo or equipment to run the ship.

Maria wanted to put as much distance between her and the bridge as she could. She lowered herself into the corridor. Her foot slipped onto the opposing door's handle and it flew open, the dark room below nearly swallowing her in the process. She caught herself at the last moment and collapsed to her knees next to the yawning cavity.

Willing herself to her feet, she made her way down the hall toward the stern. Her first impediment was a corridor whose double doors were shut. To get across, she would have to stand on the doors. The frame at the top of the doors was too narrow to use at the ship's current tilt. Two light stamps with her foot confirmed that they would hold. She crossed, fully expecting it to snap inward and cause her to plummet a hundred feet to the other side of the ship.

During her traverse she heard a helicopter and thought she'd been saved, but gunfire scared it away before she could attempt contact with it.

After a few more leaps across open cabin doors, she reached the rear of the accommodation block atop the ship. She had three options: hide in one of the rooms she'd passed, go out onto the open weather deck, or try to make her way down the stairs, where she could hide among the thousands of cars in the cargo holds. Since she would be seen immediately outside, and the hijackers would expect her to hide in the crew's quarters, cargo was her choice.

It was only then that she noticed the tilt of the ship had lessened by five degrees, and it was continuing to decrease almost imperceptibly. The ship seemed to be righting itself.

At first, Maria was relieved, but then she had the horrible sense that something was wrong. She was sure she had shut the ballast tanks down. If some of them were now leaking, the remaining intact tanks would have to be rebalanced.

She had to get to the engineering station, though there was no way she could make it all the way to the engine room while the ship's list was so pronounced. She would have to climb down the stairs and then wait until the decks were navigable before she could complete the trip.

She sprung the latch on the stairwell door and it swung down with a bang that was much louder than she thought it would be. She poked her head through and saw movement down the stairs.

Someone was coming.

She stood and looked for anything that she could use as a weapon. The only item close by was a fire extinguisher. She took it from the wall and crouched, ready to spray her attacker with foam before smashing him with the metal tank. Her breathing was ragged, but she minimized the sound by sucking in through her mouth.

She wasn't sure if it was just one man or more, but it didn't really matter. She was in no shape to make a run for it.

To her surprise, it wasn't a head that poked out of the stairwell door. It was a mirror on the end of a stick. Her best chance was to rush the intruder, so she ran forward, stuck the fire extinguisher tube down the opening, and pulled the trigger.

A man below her shielded his eyes and dropped to his knees to avoid the spray.

"Hold your fire," he said, but he wasn't talking to Maria. He had turned to address someone behind him. The voice was oddly calm and controlled, and she even thought she heard relief in the way he said it.

Maria released the trigger and held the extinguisher up in a defensive posture. If they wanted to capture her alive, she wasn't going to make it easy for them.

She could now see that there were four men in the stairwell. The man she'd sprayed stood and put his hands up. A machine gun strapped to his shoulder dangled harmlessly by his side. He was a tall, athletic man with close-cropped blond hair. He beamed up at her with a smile, genuine and warm.

"It's okay," he said in American English.

"Who are you?"

"My name is Juan Cabrillo. I'm captain of the ship that responded to your distress call. This is Eddie, Linc, and MacD." The three men nodded greetings. All of them were as heavily armed as their captain.

"You were the ones in the helicopter?"

Juan nodded. "Unfortunately, the pilot had to get back to our ship. Your arm looks like it needs some first aid. Why don't you put that down?"

His story made sense, and she was desperate. She dropped the extinguisher. The four of them climbed out of the stairwell.

"Are you with the U.S. Navy?" she asked.

"No. Just Good Samaritans. Do you mind if one of my guys puts a new bandage on there?"

She nodded. Eddie sat her down, opened a first aid kit, and removed her slapdash bandage.

After examining the wound, he said, "It doesn't look too bad, but it's going to need a few stitches from Hux." Eddie began to wrap it with gauze and tape.

"I'm glad your injury isn't more serious. You're the captain, I presume?"

She narrowed her eyes at him. "Maria Sandoval. How did you know that?"

"When we received the distress call, we did some quick research about your vessel and I saw your name as the master. I don't imagine there are many other women on the crew."

"*My* crew," she repeated in a low tone.

"Where are they?"

"Dead. Those bastards killed them all after they escaped on our lifeboat."

A haunted look flashed through Juan's eyes. As a captain himself, he would be able to imagine what it would be like to lose a crew that way. "I'm sorry."

"Why are they doing this?"

"We'll talk about that later. First, we need to keep them from sinking this ship. We saw one of them on the bridge."

Maria went ashen. "Then he set more of the ballast tanks to drain. That's why the list is correcting itself. I emptied two of the tanks to keep us from capsizing."

"That was quick thinking to save your ship."

"When will your ship arrive?"

"It won't be here for at least twenty minutes."

Maria's shoulders sagged at the news. "I don't even know how they put those holes in my ship."

"It has to be some kind of submarine," Juan said. "We saw one of the holes when we flew in. It was a perfect circle."

"There were eight holes put in the hull at the same time, and we didn't detect anything on sonar. What kind of submarine can do that?"

"I don't know. There may be more than one. If so, they're probably remotely operated."

"Then we're dead. How can we stop them from attacking again?"

"They might be single-use weapons. The men outside wouldn't be climbing onto the ship if the subs were coming back."

"We need to stop the ballast tanks from draining completely," Maria said. "We'll be too top-heavy if that happens. Once we reach a critical angle the other direction, we'll flip right over." The list continued to decrease.

"Do you think they have explosives?" Eddie asked Juan.

"If they had enough to put a sizable hole in the ship, they would have planted it on the hull outside."

"They had grenades," Maria said. "That's how they sank the lifeboat." The vision was seared into her memory.

Juan turned back to her. "What stations can you operate the ballast tanks from?"

"Just the bridge and the engine room."

"What's your cargo?"

"Cars and SUVs on all the decks except the bottom one. We're carrying construction equipment there."

"Can we get from the cargo holds directly to the bridge?"

"Yes."

"He's probably sabotaged the bridge controls," Linc said.

"That's what I would have done." Maria didn't ask how he would know that, but given how these men were armed, she was quite sure they weren't from any standard commercial vessel. They had to be former military. But she didn't get the sense that they were pirates. Too helpful and concerned about her welfare.

"They're going to outnumber us at least two to one," Juan said, "so taking them head on is risky. We'll have to try outflanking them. Are you able to travel, Captain Sandoval?"

"*Maria.* And yes. Why?"

He took a small computer tablet from his pocket. To her amazement, Juan brought up a detailed layout of her ship on its screen.

"Where did you get that?" she said.

He grinned at her. "Remember that research I told you about? I need you to show us the fastest way to the engine room."

26

The accommodation block ended at the halfway point of the *Ciudad Bolívar*, and the weather deck covering the ship's back half was a flat expanse of metal ringed by exhaust vents. Juan and his group would have to traverse one of the vehicle decks during their journey. Maria stayed with them. Not only was it risky to leave her alone with Dominguez's team scouring the ship but she insisted on coming.

The list continued to lessen, which was fortunate because climbing down to the engine room in the aftmost bottom deck using ropes would take hours they didn't have. Maria knew her ship better than anyone else and she estimated that they would have ten minutes of relatively easy travel when the deck would be transitioning from thirty-five degrees aport to thirty-five degrees astarboard. If the pitch were any greater, they wouldn't be able to keep their footing without belaying ropes.

Of course, everything would be moot if the draining procedure caused an unforeseen imbalance in the ship's center of gravity or if one of the vehicles came loose and caused an avalanche of them to pile up against one side of the ship. Then the end could come so suddenly that they wouldn't have time to find an exit. The *Ciudad Bolívar* would become their tomb two miles under the surface of the Caribbean.

As they picked their way down the staircase by standing on the railings, Maria said, "Do you think the risk of sinking unexpectedly will keep this Dominguez from sending men to the engine room?"

Juan threw a look at Linc. "Unfortunately, we've met the lieutenant before and he recognized Linc from an encounter where we made him look bad to his superiors, so there's a personal angle. He's the type who'll want to make sure we don't get out of here alive even if that means risking his own life to do it. If he returns with anything less, Admiral Ruiz will have his head on a pike."

"Maybe literally," Linc added.

Maria's eyes went wide. "Admiral Dayana Ruiz?"

"You know her?" Juan said.

"I met her only once when I was serving in the Navy. She was three ranks above me. She's a brilliant tactician, but she has a reputation for being ruthless."

"Now you're finding out just how ruthless. We think she's been sinking your company's ships to put it out of business and bankrupt the owner for her own political gain."

"How do you know that?" Maria stopped climbing. "Wait a minute. You weren't just on a passing ship. You knew this was going to happen, that my ship was targeted."

"We tried to warn your company, but they wouldn't listen, so we made the trip out here ourselves."

"You're American, but you're not in the military. What's the connection?"

"I can't tell you that, but let's just say that Ruiz and Dominguez are not too happy after our business dealings with them."

Maria seemed content not to probe further, so they kept going down the stairs as the ship righted itself. When they reached the deck carrying the construction vehicles, Maria stopped them.

"It will be easiest to get there from this deck," she said. "We can take the ramp at the far end down to the stairwell that leads to the engine room. Once I'm at the engineering station, it will only take me a few seconds to stop the ballast tanks from draining. Hopefully, it will be when the ship is upright."

Although Juan was anxious to reach the engine room before Dominguez did, they waited to leave the stairs until the deck was walkable. Even with the ship listing at only thirty-five degrees now, they would have to be careful with their footing or they'd be somersaulting down a hill made of steel.

With his weapon at the ready, Juan took the first step out onto the vehicle deck. His rubber-soled shoes gave him plenty of traction, so he was able to take in the immense hold.

The hoistable deck above had been raised to accommodate the huge equipment. Bright fluorescent lighting allowed him to see the length of a football field in either direction. Only the interior loading ramps interrupted the view. Juan scanned the hold for a few moments but saw nothing moving. The immense space was eerily silent.

"All clear," he said to the others. "Maria, show us the way. Eddie, keep a hand on her. Linc, you take point."

Linc kept one hand on the deck as he came out like a roofer edging his way down slippery shingles. Eddie held on to Maria's uninjured arm as he guided her out of the stairwell. Once they were used to the angle of the deck, they started moving toward the ramp. MacD followed, and Juan covered the rear.

Now that they were on a more expansive surface, Juan could easily sense that the ship was slowly leveling. In a few minutes it would be dead even.

The loading ramp was only twenty feet ahead. Once they reached it, they'd be able to lean against the ramp's port wall for stability as they walked.

A clink from behind drew Juan's attention and he turned just in time to see Dominguez and five of his men drop into the hold from a stairwell near the bridge about a hundred yards away.

Juan yelled, "Down!" a second before the Venezuelans opened fire.

Bullets careened off the metal and shattered glass windshields. Juan returned fire and found out for himself how hard it was to aim while digging his feet into the floor at such an extreme angle. He took a bead on Dominguez but Dominguez slid down to find footing on a bulldozer. Instead, Juan's shot hit another man, who screamed and fell out of sight.

He looked ahead and saw his group unharmed. "Get down the ramp!"

Eddie grabbed Maria and scrambled forward behind Linc, but another volley of shots ricocheted off the floor next to Maria and the distraction caused her to slip.

She slid down the deck, but Eddie slid down below her, put his shoulder into her, and practically threw her to Linc, who enveloped her wrist in his huge hand and dragged her to him.

The effort caused Eddie to lose his own footing, but MacD wasn't close enough to latch onto him. Eddie scrabbled for purchase, but he was already accelerating and there was nothing to grasp. He went zooming below the undercarriage of a road grader.

Linc got Maria to the safety of the ramp, where he lay flat to take more careful aim on Dominguez. Now their attackers' shots were even more scattered.

Juan ignored the bullets pinging off the walls around him. He raced over to the road grader and braced himself against its wheel while MacD provided covering fire. Juan peered around the tread and was relieved to see Eddie clinging to a truck axle halfway toward the port side.

It would take him several minutes to climb back on his own. It was time they didn't have.

"Toss me your rope," Juan said to MacD.

"Ah'll anchor it up here," he replied, taking it off his arm.

"No, you and Linc need to take Maria to the engine room. If she doesn't keep the ballast tanks from emptying, we're all dead."

MacD grimaced at the order, throwing the coils to Juan, who caught them and shrugged them over his shoulder. Linc laid down a barrage, allowing MacD to join him and Maria.

They took one last look at Juan, who waved them to go on. He was shielded, at least for the moment, by the blade of the grader in front of him.

Juan activated his throat mic. "How are you doing, Eddie?"

"I scraped myself up pretty well, but I don't think anything's broken. Is Maria all right?"

"She's fine. I sent her ahead with Linc and MacD."

"You want me to come up there?"

"No, I'm coming down to you. We'll see if we can keep Dominguez occupied here instead of chasing after them."

Juan knotted the rope around the road grader's suspension so he could control his descent. It unspooled all the way to the opposite side of the hold. Eddie was able to put a hand on it and let go of the axle.

Juan kept his speed in check as he made his way down to Eddie. As he neared Eddie, he slowed more than he expected. But it wasn't him. It was the ship.

The speed of the tilt's correction had drastically accelerated. By the time he was under the truck adjacent to Eddie, the ship was undergoing a radical shift to starboard.

"I think we're—" was all Juan got out before bullets caromed off the truck's chassis and he had to take cover behind the wheel. Two of Dominguez's men had crawled under the equipment to get him in their sights.

The ship would be at a level beam in seconds and that meant there was an immediate threat more dangerous than the men shooting at them.

As soon as the sudden shift occurred, Maria knew what was coming. She told Linc and MacD to climb into the nearest SUV. All of the vehicles on the ship were unlocked, with the keys inside, for quick removal during unloading.

The wave of water rushing toward them was only four feet high, but it would be strong enough to knock them off their feet and send them flying if they didn't get out of the way.

They dived into the SUV and slammed the doors as the water enveloped it. For the moment, they were unscathed, but Maria's bigger fear was that the weight transfer would tip the ship over.

She held her breath as the water coursed down the loading ramp and settled against the starboard side. The list was only ten degrees—for now. Although the rapid shift had ceased, she could feel the *Ciudad Bolívar* continue to slowly roll. There must have been a sudden bulkhead failure on a lower level, but the ballast tanks were plainly unaffected and continuing to drain.

The right side of their truck was now submerged in water that was beginning to seep in. Linc turned the ignition key and unrolled the windows on the left side. They slithered out and stood on the hood of the adjacent SUV.

"This way," Linc said, and they made their way to the port side by hopping across the hoods of the row of trucks parked fender to fender.

In two minutes they were jumping onto the deck next to the stairwell that led to the engine room. The stairs were easier to take while the list was less pronounced, but the steps were dripping and slick from the water that had immersed them only a few minutes before. The lights had shorted out, so Linc and MacD flicked on flashlights for the short walk down.

When they opened the watertight door, their ears were assaulted by the roar of still-running engines. They stopped on the catwalk overlooking the two huge engines that drove the ship's screw and provided electrical power. The space occupied four stories and was crisscrossed by stairs, pipes, and ventilation ducts. Normally, the equipment was showroom clean, but rings of oil and grease were visible where the water had pooled and splashed before settling to the bottom. Obviously, a large amount of water had flooded into the engine room before it was evacuated and sealed from the bridge.

"Where's the engineering station?" Linc asked.

Maria pointed at the enclosed room at the stern.

MacD stared down at the water, which had to be at least seven feet deep. "Any way around that?"

Maria shook her head. "We're going for a swim."

Something floating in the water caught her eye. It was partially hidden in the shadow of the starboard engine on the far side. She held her hand out to MacD. "Can I borrow your flashlight?"

He shrugged and handed it to her.

She clicked the switch and pointed it at the object.

It was a foot.

Maria gasped and panned the light across the body, which was floating facedown. When the beam reached the holstered pistol, all three of them knew it wasn't a stranded crew member.

Linc shoved her down behind a vent at the same time MacD opened fire at a hidden figure. Bullets whistling past in response confirmed that they weren't the first to reach the engine room.

Juan's warning about the wave had come in time for Eddie to use his cat quickness to leap onto the dump truck cab's ladder and scale it before he was hit by the water. But because he was completely underneath his own truck, all Juan had time to do was loop the rope around the axle and wrap it around his wrist. He held his breath and rode out the rush of water like a fish hooked on a lure.

When the water had flowed to the other side, he could see that the two gunmen who'd been firing at him were bobbing on the water, limp and motionless. The one face he could see was caved in where it had met a metal protrusion.

Eddie called out. "Chairman, are you all right?"

Juan unwrapped the rope from his wrist and crawled out from underneath the truck beside Eddie. "I'm okay, but I have more sympathy for a marlin now. Dominguez is down at least three men. Do you see where he is?"

"I lost him."

"Don't worry. He'll find us."

The deck was still at a mild slant, but it wouldn't stay that way for long.

Maneuvering under and around the construction equipment, Juan and Eddie snaked their way to the starboard side. At the last row of vehicles, they would have to cross ten feet unprotected to get to the stairwell door.

They crouched behind a bulldozer. Juan poked his head out and sparks flew where bullets stung the metal. He pulled back.

"Dominguez was obviously expecting that," Juan said.

"Did you see where he was?"

"About thirty yards away. I couldn't tell if he was alone. I don't think we can both make it across without being hit."

"How desperate are we to get off the boat right now?"

Juan keyed his throat mic. "Linc, tell me you're about to shut off the ballast tanks."

A background roar in his earpiece was accompanied by the staccato pop of gunfire.

"I'm glad to hear you're up and about, Chairman," Linc replied, "but I'm sorry, they got here first. Two of them drowned, three left. We don't think they had time to disable the engineering station, though."

"Can Maria reach it?"

"Not yet, but we're working on a plan. We wouldn't mind some help."

"We're kind of busy ourselves," Juan said, "but we'll keep you posted."

"Roger that."

Juan dropped to his belly. His sodden clothes squished against the metal. He was certain one of Dominguez's men would be circling around in a pincer movement.

There. Feet scurried from the protection of one giant wheel to the next. Juan anticipated the path he was taking and placed the red dot sight on a spot five feet past the wheel.

On cue, the feet appeared. Juan led his target and shot a three-round volley. One of the bullets slammed into a knee and knocked the man to the ground, howling. He saw Juan and tried to get a shot off, but Juan cut him down with another burst.

"We know where you are, Dominguez!" Juan shouted in Spanish. "You can't stay there forever."

Dominguez didn't respond. Instead, a hand grenade bounced against the wall and skittered across the floor until it stuck against the forward chain anchoring the bulldozer to the deck. Juan and Eddie dived behind the dozer's blade, which rang with the blast.

Juan looked out and saw that the blast had severed the anchor chain. Nothing was holding the front of the forty-ton bulldozer in place except its treads.

"We need to take care of Dominguez and get down to the engine room," Juan said.

"I saw where he was when he tossed the grenade," Eddie said. "He's in the bed of a dump truck. Good sight lines and a stellar defensive position. A head-on attack wouldn't be the best idea."

The deck tilted farther and the bulldozer was losing traction. It skidded to starboard with a shriek of metal on metal until it came to rest against the dump truck next to it. Juan held his breath, thinking this might be the start of a vehicle avalanche. The truck's anchor chains squealed in protest at the added weight but held.

"That's not going to last long if the list gets worse," Eddie said.

"I agree." Juan radioed Linc again. "I don't mean to put pressure on you guys, but we've got a loose bulldozer up here that is getting ready to take half the cargo with it to the starboard side. If you don't stop this list in the next few minutes, none of us are making it out of here."

Maria's heart pounded as the gunfire echoed through the engine room. She had no idea how Linc and MacD stayed so calm.

"We've got two men left behind those pipes above the engine," MacD said, before snapping off another shot.

"The Chairman says the situation up there is critical," Linc said. "We need to get to the engineering station now. Do you think you can make it?"

"Maybe, but I wouldn't have any idea what to do when I got there."

"Maria could tell you over the radio how to turn off the ballast drains."

"No, I have to do it," Maria said. "It will take too long to talk MacD through the procedure."

She added, "This is my ship. I'm not going to let Ruiz sink her."

Linc grudgingly relented. "Okay. They don't have a good angle on the lower level, but even with our covering fire you'll be too exposed to use the stairs from the catwalk. They'll pick you off before you get fifteen feet." He pointedly looked down at the pool of water and Maria understood what he meant. Instead of using the stairs to get down there, she was going to have to dive over the railing directly into the water.

"I can make it," she said more confidently than she felt.

"We've got another problem," MacD said. "I'm down to my last magazine."

"Me too. Make every shot count. Ready?"

Maria took a deep breath and nodded.

Linc said, "On my mark. Three, two, one . . . Go!"

MacD and Linc snapped up and shot three-round bursts in rapid succession. Maria didn't wait to see if the suppressing fire worked. She jumped to her feet, pivoted around the ventilation duct, and launched herself over the railing, praying that the water was as deep as she thought it was.

She plunged into the pool feetfirst and stopped herself against the deck. There was just enough light to see the steps ahead of her, but the oil in the water stung her eyes.

Maria had the impulse to close her eyes and surface, but the less exposure to the gunmen, the better. She used a dolphin stroke to propel herself all the way across underwater. Her lungs were screaming for air by the time she reached the stairs to the engineering station.

She lunged out of the water, half expecting a bullet through her brain as soon as she hit the air, but the fire was still concentrated at the other end of the engine room. She sucked in a breath and heaved herself up the stairs. Those three steps were the longest of her life, but the moment she flung the door open and dived inside she nearly let out a victory cry. The door shut behind her, blocking out the sounds of the engine and gunshots.

Maria raced over to the terminal and tapped on the keyboard to bring up the ballast controls. She was so intent on shutting down the draining tanks that the reappearance of the noise from the engine room barely registered. Someone had opened the door.

Maria didn't bother to see who it was, but she didn't need to when she heard the man yell, "¡Alto!"

She ignored him and tapped on the mouse. The screen confirmed that the tanks were closed, and then the display exploded in a hail of bullets.

She closed her eyes and prepared for her own end, but the death blow never came. She turned to see the gunman staring blankly, a bloody third eye drilled through his forehead. The rest of his body knew he was dead a second later and slumped to the floor. Behind him, a neat hole had penetrated the glass, and Linc stood beyond it with his pistol raised.

He charged through the door and made sure the man was dead.

"Are you hurt?" he asked her.

"No. I was able to shut off the ballast tanks before he destroyed the terminal."

"Good. This guy went after you, so I came after him. MacD took out the last guy, but he's clearing the rest of the engine room to be sure."

The dead man's radio squawked. Linc picked it up. He listened but shook his head.

"I don't know Spanish," he said, and handed it to Maria.

She translated as she listened. "A ship has arrived. It's traveling at a fantastic rate of speed."

"The *Oregon*."

The discussion went on, and she went rigid when she heard the next sentence.

Linc tensed as well. "What?"

"He said the subs are charged and ready to attack. But they're not aimed at the *Ciudad Bolívar*. Lieutenant Dominguez has some kind of controller. He's sending them to sink your ship."

When Linc radioed with the news about the sub controller, Juan told him to warn the *Oregon* to be on the lookout for any subs.

But without any intel on them, he didn't know if they would be able to spot them or outrun them. He had to get the controller away from Dominguez and deactivate the subs.

Eddie had circled around behind the dump truck where Dominguez was hiding. Juan was waiting behind it in the shadow of another truck's fender. Eddie prepared to flush Dominguez out.

"I'm in position," Juan whispered into his radio.

"So am I," Eddie replied.

Juan unloaded half his magazine into the side of the truck's enormous bed. Dominguez and another man poked their eyes above the lip and returned fire. At the same time, Eddie used the distraction and noise to climb into the cab. He activated the bed's hydraulic lift.

With a whine, it started to raise. Juan was hoping Dominguez would scrabble to stay in the truck, but he jumped over the side near Juan while the other gunman went over the opposite side. Eddie would have to take care of that guy.

Juan sprinted after Dominguez on the angled deck. He could see the controller device in the lieutenant's hand, its screen illuminated. Dominguez stopped to turn and fire at Juan, but his footing failed him and he lurched to catch himself.

Juan tackled Dominguez, sending their weapons flying. The two of them locked together in a vise grip and tumbled until Juan's back hit the tread of another bulldozer, knocking the wind out of him. But in their fall he'd snatched the controller from Dominguez's hand.

Juan could see three dots on a grid. Two of them were side by side and labeled "Ciudad Bolívar" and "Bahia Blanco," which had to be the fishing trawler. The third dot was labeled "Unknown." It had to be the *Oregon*. Crosshairs hovered over it.

Dominguez drew his knife from a hip sheath. Not wanting to drop the controller, Juan blocked the knife with one hand while he kept hold of the device with the other. That left an opening for Dominguez's other hand to squeeze Juan's neck, cutting off his air.

Juan was intent on the controller. Dominguez had his knee atop Juan's arm, but he could still move his hand. His fingers shook as he moved his thumb to "Bahia Blanco." He tapped once and the crosshairs now centered on the trawler. An on-screen button said "Confirm target." Juan pressed it and with a flick of his wrist tossed the controller away. It slid down the deck and out of sight.

With his free hand he jammed his thumb into Dominguez's left eye. Dominguez released the grip on his neck and yelped. Now that he could breathe, Juan whipped the knife around and shoved the blade into Dominguez's chest. The lieutenant gasped in shock, then with a final choking wheeze he fell on his side.

Juan got to his feet in time to see Eddie approach.

"Your timing is impeccable." Juan nodded at the limp body.

"Mine is history, too. The *Oregon*?"

"Safe. But the trawler should be heading to the bottom any moment."

"Then there's no one left to answer why someone wanted to keep us from saving this ship."

"I don't think it has anything to do with the *Ciudad Bolívar*," Juan said. "I think whoever sent those Haitian assassins in Jamaica didn't want us to find out about the subs. When we recover them, we'll get some answers."

28

Juan and the others got up on deck in time to see the smoking ruins of the fishing trawler slip beneath the waves. Max told him that the trawler had exploded, possibly when one of the subs lanced into a fuel line. It was long past sunset. The *Oregon* swept the sea with searchlights but found no surviving crew.

They left the bodies of Dominguez and the others where they were on the car carrier. Because the incident happened in international waters on a ship owned by a Venezuelan company but flagged in Panama, jurisdiction was hazy at best. Any investigation would likely be carried out by the insurer, but all of the viable evidence would lead back to the Venezuelan Navy.

Gomez had the MD 520N fuel tank patched up and he ferried the five of them back to the *Oregon*, which had been temporarily renamed the *Norego* in case they were still around when other rescue ships arrived.

After Maria's injuries were tended to, Juan suggested that she change into a fresh set of clothes and go to the public mess hall for food and coffee. He then joined Max and Murph on deck to oversee the retrieval of the subs.

Three of them had survived the explosion and were floating on the surface, awaiting their next command. Juan had searched for the controller, but it seemed to have been lost in the standing water in the *Ciudad Bolívar*'s hold. The car carrier was still listing, but it was stable for now.

Juan studied the subs with binoculars while his crew readied the crane to haul them up. The sleek design made them look like tiny jet fighters, with short wings, a rudder, a water intake on the front end and an exhaust port at the stern. The subs were topped with a dorsal protrusion that housed whatever was used to anchor it to the hull and cut through it. A short antenna jutted from the body to receive the controller's instructions.

"I can't wait to take one of those babies apart," Max said, rubbing his hands together with glee. "I might be able to build one for ourselves. You never know when it could come in handy."

"Have you ever seen a design like that?"

"No, but it seems way too sophisticated for the Venezuelans to create. I'm guessing they bought it from the Chinese or Russians."

"Or they stole it," said Murph, who was taking photographs of the floating subs. "When I was a systems developer, we had to assess potential technologies for the military. One was an underwater stealth drone for attacking ships, but it was barely on the drawing board when I left. These could be based on that design."

"If they're based on American technology," Max said, "the CIA is going to want them back. I predict Langston Overholt is going to be writing a big check in the near future." Juan had to agree that this discovery would be riveting news for his old CIA mentor and liaison.

"Speaking of checks," Juan said, "did you call Atlas Salvage?"

Max nodded. "They'll be on their way shortly with an ocean-going tug from Kingston. The owner, Bill Musgrave, is negotiating the contract with Cabimas. As a finder's fee, he's cutting us in for ten percent."

Salvage was a lucrative and dangerous business, so the payouts were usually a percentage of the ship and cargo value. In this case, it would be more than one hundred million dollars if they were able to get the ship back to port intact, so the Corporation's split would be handsome.

Not bad for a day's work. And they were about to bring in even more.

The crane lowered its net toward the water, and divers in the RHIB would wrap it around each sub to pick it up.

Without warning, the first sub sank below the surface.

Max blurted. "What the . . ."

Another sub disappeared. Then the third.

Juan radioed to the op center. "We're losing the subs. Are they preparing to attack? Report."

"Negative, Chairman," Linda replied. "Sonar shows they're aiming straight for the bottom."

Juan called for the divers to try to snag one of them, but it was too late. All three were shooting two miles to the seafloor. Even if they could eventually recover the subs, at the rate they were descending little would be left on impact.

"Get those pictures to Overholt," Juan told Murph. "I'm going to talk to our guest."

Juan entered the fake mess hall and got a cup of coffee for himself before sitting down with Maria.

"Is my crew treating you well?" he said.

While looking around at the dingy room, she said, "Everyone has been wonderful. I'd never imagine that a ship in this, uh, condition would have such excellent food."

"It's all for appearances. The ship is cleaner than she looks. We spend the money where it counts. Listen, I have a favor to ask."

"Of course. Anything. You saved me and my ship."

"We'd appreciate you not mentioning our involvement."

"Why? You and your men should get a medal for what you did."

"Because of the cargo we tend to carry, we don't like a lot of attention." There was no harm in giving her the impression that they were smugglers. The fact that they had been experienced with guns and fighting tactics would only enhance the notion.

Maria gave him a knowing look. "Ah, I see. What about the dead men on my ship?"

Juan was ready with a story. "Pirates. They attempted to take the ship when it foundered and killed your crew."

"And who killed all of them?"

"Intragroup rivalry. No honor among these thieves, who will eventually be identified as rogue Venezuelan Navy sailors. The rest of them took off in their boat when they couldn't get the ship under way."

Juan could see her gears working as she pondered his story. Finally she said, "That all makes sense. It's the least I can do for you."

"Thank you. In the meantime, I think you should stay with us. It's your decision, of course, but if Admiral Ruiz is really behind this, you may be in danger. I don't think she likes loose ends. That is, if you don't mind going missing until this blows over."

"I don't think I'll be commanding my ship for a while. And

my ex-husband certainly won't care. But I should at least report in to Cabimas."

"Tell them the truth, that you're afraid for your life because the attackers got away. When they're caught, you'll feel safe enough to return."

She thought about the suggestion, then said, "All right. I think they'll understand that. They'll be more concerned about recovering the ship for now."

"Fine. I'll have my steward Maurice set you up with a suitable cabin."

"Thank you again, Captain Cabrillo."

He gave her a smile. "Glad to help."

Juan left her in Maurice's capable hands and went to his cabin, where a call from Langston Overholt had been routed.

"You've set off all kinds of alarms here with those photos, Juan," the gruff octogenarian said. "Nobody expected to see them surface—no pun intended."

"So this is a U.S. design?"

"The Navy was working on it for years until a virus set back the program. All of the controller software was corrupted and the design files were wiped clean. Only someone on the team could have done it."

"So it was an inside job. Why would you expect that the design hadn't already made its way into foreign hands?"

"Because we identified who stole them. It had to be a weapons designer named Douglas Pearson. The files were recovered from his home. He must have planted the virus."

"Is he in prison?"

"No, he's dead. Or at least we thought he was. He was participating in a training exercise when his boat was destroyed by a malfunctioning aerial drone. His body was never found, but we assumed it was incinerated in the crash and washed out to sea."

"Now you're not so sure?"

"Oh, we're sure he has to be alive. If these subs were built by the Venezuelans, there's no way they could have done it so quickly without his expertise. He was one of a handful of people who had intimate knowledge of the program. Two of the others were killed in the same incident and the rest are still employed with defense contractors here. We don't think they're responsible, but we're re-checking them just in case. I think Pearson is our man."

"Then I want him just as much as you do," Juan said, and told him about the attempts to kill the *Oregon* crew.

"How did he know where you were?" Overholt asked.

"That's a question I would love an answer to. But I think there's something more going on. He seems to have an army of Haitian soldiers at his command and may be planning a larger operation."

"He's probably the one who sank the subs. Do you think he has more?"

"I don't know, but one of the Haitians said that the world is going to change in four days. If Pearson is part of this, it sounds like he has the means to pull it off."

"It's bad enough that a stolen U.S. weapons design was used to sink three ships and damage a fourth. We can't let him use it for a terrorist attack."

"Since you thought he was dead," Juan said, "I'm assuming you have no leads on his whereabouts."

"No, and we can't go internal with this. You know Washington. The story would leak in about five seconds. I'm tasking you with finding Pearson. If you find evidence of a credible threat, I can use that to warn the appropriate agencies."

"Then I guess the best place to start is the last place he was seen alive. Maybe there are some clues in the boat wreckage that were overlooked. Did Dirk Pitt handle the recovery?"

"NUMA raised the boat from the bottom of the Chesapeake, but Dirk hired a disaster analysis firm to do the forensic investigation into the accident. A company called Gordian Engineering."

"Who's my contact?"

"Their chief engineer was brought in because of the sensitive nature of the technology involved. He has all the top security clearances." Juan heard some paper shuffling in the background. "Here it is. He's still at Patuxent reconstructing the wreckage. His name is Dr. Tyler Locke."

With the sun now long set, Hector Bazin could make out nothing past the reach of the headlights of the Toyota SUV that David Pasquet was driving. Because Haiti was the poorest nation in the Western Hemisphere, its rural citizens couldn't afford power generators, and night lighting was no more sophisticated than a wood-fired stove. The extreme darkness of the hilly central part of Haiti they were now passing through was so profound that the border between Haiti and its wealthier neighbor to the west, the Dominican Republic, was easily visible in night satellite photos of Hispaniola, the island comprised of the two countries.

As they rounded a hillock, the sudden appearance of high-intensity arc lights brightly illuminating a cement factory—in the middle of nowhere—was jarring. Nestled between the hills and Haiti's second-largest body of water, Lake Péligre, the plant consisted of a dozen buildings, a pattern of cantilevered conveyer belts, and a dome where the raw limestone ore was piled for processing.

If the buildings looked ancient, it was because they'd gone unused for more than fifty years until Bazin reoccupied them. They served as the base of operations for his mercenary force. It was the perfect location, miles from any town that would raise questions about the sound of guns being fired.

There was no chain-link fence to keep the curious out, but motion sensors had been placed at strategic intervals around the facility, setting off alarms the minute any intruders set foot within the property's perimeter.

Pasquet rolled to a stop in front of a large building closest to the hill behind the plant. Bazin took his duffel bag and entered the building.

Inside, he found sixty men, all Haitians, kneeling with their hands over their heads. His men circled them like wolves, their G36 assault rifles at the ready. Two bodies lay on the floor.

The phone call he'd received on the way from the airport had prepared Bazin, but he was enraged again by this further setback.

"What happened?" Bazin asked the senior officer he'd left in charge.

His officer nodded in the direction of a man kneeling in the front row. Blood dripped from a fresh wound on his forehead. He glared back at Bazin with grim determination.

"While they were digging, he and the other men jumped two of the guards and killed them," the officer said. "We were able to subdue them before they got to the weapons."

"The guards should have been more careful," Bazin said. "I told them Jacques was clever."

Jacques Duval turned his head and spat blood that had trickled into his mouth. "You can't keep us here forever, Hector."

Bazin cocked his head at his old housemate and until recently deputy commander in the Haitian National Police before he was abducted and brought here. "Who says I'm planning to?"

"We won't keep digging for you."

"You will if you want your families to live."

Duval laughed ruefully. "Don't you see the irony of all this, Hector? You're keeping us as slaves in the first country that threw off the shackles of slavery and became an independent nation."

"You're not slaves, you're traitors. I offered you a chance to join me and you tried to take me down."

Duval looked at him with pity. "How did you grow up to be this way? You and I were *restavecs* in the same household. We both joined the French Foreign Legion. We were the same. And now you're a monster."

"We were *not* the same." He addressed the rest of the kneeling group, many of whom had served in the Haitian government alongside Duval. "This man that you revere, that you *worship*, is nothing more than a sniveling dog who would let a boy younger than he suffer beatings every single day of his life."

Duval sighed. "You're right, Hector. I should have done more. But I was just a child. And now I'm trying to change all that, the whole system, to make Haiti a better place."

"It won't change. Never. That's why I brought you here. You and the rest of these men are deranged to think it could ever change. The only thing that changes is who holds the power. Well, now I hold the power. Because of what we're doing here, I will hold more power than you can possibly imagine."

"Why don't you just kill us? We're both military men, so be honest. That's what you're going to do, isn't it? You can't let us leave after what we've seen."

"We still need you to install an emergency escape tunnel, so there's more digging to be done. But you're right, I don't need all of you. There needs to be consequences for what you've done."

Bazin took the assault rifle from the nearest mercenary. Duval straightened up and looked Bazin in the eyes as if he knew what was coming.

Bazin shook his head and grinned. "Such a noble gesture. But no. As a military man, you should know that your men always pay for your failures."

Bazin shifted the rifle and fired shots through the foreheads of the men kneeling to either side of Duval.

Duval yelled, "No!" and jumped to his feet, ready to charge Bazin.

"Shall we make it three?" Bazin said.

Duval halted, sneered at him, and then knelt back down.

"Good," Bazin said, and threw the rifle back to his man. "That was just a small preview. If you behave from now on, I might let you live long enough to see the kind of power that can control the world."

29

Naval Air Station Patuxent River, Maryland

Juan threaded the rental car past concrete barriers that could stop a semi from barreling onto the naval air station property. He and Eric Stone, who Juan brought along for his technical expertise, were approaching the gate to Pax River, as it was known to the base personnel, now entering during the morning rush hour.

When Juan reached the gate, the guard's voice was drowned out by the thundering engines of a P-8 Poseidon submarine hunter coming in for a landing, but the intent was clear. He wanted to see their identification.

Juan wished they could have used the false IDs they normally traveled under, but to get into a Navy facility and access to a top secret project, at Langston Overholt's insistence, Juan and Eric had to rely on the security clearances they'd obtained when they were in the employ of the U.S. government.

While the guard examined their IDs, a sailor armed with an

assault rifle looked under their car with a mirror and inspected the empty trunk. Once they were cleared, the guard instructed them to drive to a hangar on the south side of the base.

As they passed a row of F-18 Hornets used for training Navy test pilots, Juan marveled at Overholt's ability to get them into such a highly classified military operation. The photos of the Piranha subs no doubt contributed.

Less than thirty-six hours ago, the *Oregon* had left the *Ciudad Bolívar* once the salvage company radioed that they were on the way. Not wanting to risk an encounter with the Jamaican authorities, the *Oregon* made for Santo Domingo, the capital of the Dominican Republic. There they off-loaded Craig Reed's repaired fishing boat and paid for his rehabilitation at the city's best recovery center.

Tiny Gunderson, the Corporation's fixed-wing pilot, had been waiting for Juan and Eric at Santo Domingo's airport with their private Gulfstream jet. Four hours later, they landed at Reagan National and were directed to a hangar that stood only a hundred yards from the shore of Chesapeake Bay. The sun gleamed on closed white doors large enough to engulf an airliner.

A man dressed in a leather jacket and jeans waved for Juan to park next to a side door where an armed guard in full battle dress uniform stood watch. Juan opened his door to a brisk chill. The civilian, an athletic-looking man with tousled brown hair and a warm smile, greeted him with a handshake. This wasn't the nerdy engineer Juan had been expecting.

"I'm Tyler Locke," he said. "You must be Juan Cabrillo."

"Yes, and this is Eric Stone. I understand you're the lead investigator conducting the forensic analysis."

"That's me. Dirk Pitt told us to expect you and authorized us to share all of our findings. What's your interest in the case?"

"Douglas Pearson. We want to know if it's possible that he survived the drone accident."

"'Accident'?" Locke said. "I can see we have to get you up to speed on our progress."

"So you've recovered the wreckage?"

"We've done a bit more than recover it. I'll show you."

Locke swiped a keycard and punched in a passcode at the door's security panel. An electronic bolt clicked and Locke pushed his way inside.

Juan's eyes took a moment to adjust from the blazing sunlight outside as he and Eric followed Locke in. When he was able to focus, he took in the incongruous sight of a half-dozen workers reconstructing a boat inside an airplane hangar.

Only the forward part of the vessel was intact. The rest of it had been pieced together like the world's largest jigsaw puzzle. A steel frame supported the pieces, most of which were blackened and bent out of shape, yet they had been fitted together so precisely that the boat's former silhouette was easily recognizable.

To the right of the boat was a smaller framework holding the remains of the UAV that had slammed into it. Fewer of these pieces were visible, but the drone's V shape was apparent.

A muscular black man holding a tablet PC was jotting down notes about the drone. When he spotted Locke and the two newcomers, he stalked over with something between the lumbering gait of a bear and the fluid motion of a panther. The overhead lights reflected off his bald head.

"We got the last of the fragments assembled on the drone," he said to Locke. "Another hour before we finish on the boat, but it shouldn't change our findings. For getting the job done so quickly, I told the crew you'd buy them unlimited pale ales and crab cakes at Clarke's Landing tonight."

"If you're included in that offer, I'll have to take out a loan to pay for it," Locke said, before introducing Juan and Eric. "This is Grant Westfield, Gordian Engineering's top electrical engineer and the bane of all-you-can-eat buffets everywhere."

Eric went slack-jawed as he shook Westfield's massive paw. "Grant Westfield? You're kidding! Murph is going to have a seizure when he finds out I met The Burn. We play you all the time in Pro Wrestling All-Stars."

"I sincerely hope that's a video game," Juan said.

"It's a real honor, Mr. Westfield," Eric said, ignoring Juan. "I admire your decision to leave wrestling to join the Rangers after 9/11, but it would be fun to see you in the ring again."

"I'm having too much fun on this job to go back to getting slammed in the head with folding chairs. So Tyler tells me that you have a pressing need to learn the results of our analysis."

Juan nodded. "It relates to an investigation of our own. The good doctor here implied that this was no accident."

"No way. The Navy's initial conclusion was that the drone locked onto the control signal emitted by the boat's antenna and homed in, but that's not possible."

"Why not?"

"Because we found that the cable to the antenna was disconnected before the impact. The boat was going over twenty knots at the time and using evasive maneuvers to shake it. The drone should have lost its lock once the signal stopped transmitting, but it hit the boat perfectly amidships."

"Do you know how it did that?" Eric asked.

Locke produced a charred piece of equipment. "By homing in on this. It's a beacon that was hidden inside a laptop. We think someone used it to guide the drone no matter what was done to dodge it."

Juan took the destroyed circuitry and turned it over in his hand. It was easily small enough to smuggle inside a computer case. "Do you think the saboteur was someone on the project team?"

"More than that," Westfield said, "we think it was someone on the boat. Whoever redirected the drone had to do it from a workstation on board."

"Pearson was on the boat at the time?"

"Four people were," Locke said. "The boat's captain and the three project leaders: Douglas Pearson, Frederick Weddell, and Lawrence Kensit. We found the bodies of only two of them, the captain and Weddell. Weddell was on deck at the time of the explosion and the captain was on the bridge. The control center was hit dead-on by the drone."

"Because of the intense heat, we were lucky to find any remains inside the boat after it sank," Westfield said. "Just a few bones, but it was enough for DNA testing of the marrow."

"I'm guessing you only found DNA evidence for Kensit," Juan said, "and Pearson's bones were nowhere to be found."

"That did seem to be the case," Locke said. "But we found a big inconsistency when we simulated the impact."

"'Simulated'? You mean you can reconstruct what actually happened at the moment of the explosion?"

Locke nodded. "My company, Gordian, developed the software. We create three-dimensional models of the craft involved. Then we input the deformities caused by the impact and explosion, the speed at which both craft were traveling, and the approximate locations where the pieces were recovered from the seabed floor, and the program crunches the numbers to produce a crude simulation of the event."

Westfield handed him the tablet and Locke tapped on it until the screen was showing a surprisingly detailed representation of the boat frozen atop the water's surface, trailing a wake behind it. The drone was suspended above it, poised in a dive.

"The video is slowed by a factor of one hundred." Locke pressed the PLAY button and the drone inched toward the boat until its nose crumpled against the deck. It continued to deform until it erupted in a fireball. Fragments of the boat flew away before it, too, exploded. The video ended when all of the airborne pieces had fallen in the water. Juan was amazed they could have recovered anything at all, let alone the substantial portion they'd fitted back together.

"Now that you know what the impact looked like from the outside," Locke said, "let's take a look at it from inside."

He pulled up another video, this one showing a re-creation of the control center that was nearly photo-realistic. Only one figure was in the room, a generic representation sitting in a chair.

"Where are the rest of them?" Eric asked.

"The captain is on the bridge, and Weddell had gone up to disconnect the antenna cable manually," Westfield said. "Our simulation shows that only one person remained in the control center."

"Pearson must have jumped overboard before the drone hit," Juan said.

"The DNA evidence did show that it was Kensit in the center," Locke said, "but watch this."

He started the video, and at the moment of the drone's impact, the person and chair were flung backward, smashing into the opposite wall, before disintegrating in the fireball.

Juan didn't see anything unexpected. "I must be missing something."

"Douglas Pearson weighed two hundred and fifty pounds," Locke said. "Kensit was one-sixty. If Kensit were the one in the chair, the impact profile would have been significantly different, at least six inches higher than where we found pieces of chair and DNA embedded in the equipment we recovered from that side of the boat. Kensit didn't die in that room, Pearson did."

"Are you sure?"

"I estimate the probability at eighty percent," Westfield. said. "We had a photo of the interior to work with, but we can't be sure of the exact configuration that day."

"But the Navy said the DNA evidence was a match for Kensit," Juan said.

"If Kensit was the one responsible for reprogramming the drone," Eric said, "someone with that level of expertise could certainly fake his own death by breaking into the computer records and switching the DNA profiles. I know Murph and I could do it, given enough time."

"That's exactly what our report is going to suggest," Westfield said. "The Navy should check the actual stored DNA sample, if they still have it. It's highly unlikely Kensit could have tampered with the original. They're kept in a secure deep freeze in Rockville, Maryland."

"When do you think the sample will be retested?" Juan asked.

"You know DoD bureaucracy. It could take weeks."

"We don't have that kind of time. Can it be expedited?"

Locke shrugged. "That's up to the Navy, although you must have some pull just to get in here. We'll deliver our preliminary conclusions before we leave tomorrow morning. We need to go to Cairo on an urgent project, so we won't be able to follow up for a week or two."

Westfield rolled his eyes. "I don't know why we can't go back to Seattle first. The Great Pyramid is five thousand years old and it can't wait another few days?"

"In the meantime, Mr. Cabrillo," Locke continued, "I would operate under the assumption that Lawrence Kensit is still alive. What he's doing now or where he went, I couldn't tell you. But if you're after him, I recommend you proceed with extreme caution."

"Why do you say that?"

The grim expression on Locke's face was chilling. "Kensit is a meticulous planner who was willing to kill people he'd known for years to make himself disappear. Two years prior to the incident, he practically forced himself on the project, which was interacting with every new type of drone the Navy had in development, both in the air and on the water. He learned everything there was to know about drone operations, from the security precautions to how they were controlled. He must have had a very specific reason for faking his death."

"Right," Eric said, "to sell the Piranha sub technology to the highest bidder without anyone realizing he was the one who'd stolen the plans."

Juan caught Locke and Westfield exchanging worried glances. "I'd be surprised if that was why he did it," Locke said. "We interviewed everyone on the drone project in the course of our investigation. Every single one of them said two things. First, Kensit, who earned Ph.D.s in both physics and computer science, was the most brilliant person they'd ever met, and this coming from some of the brightest minds in weapons development. Kensit and his intelligence weren't challenged on a project like this, they said. He disdained others for their inability to keep up with his mental acuity, but he stayed on the project anyway."

"And the second thing?" Juan prodded.

"Kensit didn't hide his contempt for how America was wasting its opportunity to fix the planet and squandering its technological superiority, specifically its advantage in weaponry. He thought world leaders were too corrupt or weak or beholden to uneducated constituencies to solve the problems that he felt had simple solutions. Crime, war, famine, pollution, disease, energy and water shortages—all of those issues could be solved if one person with the right technology, intelligence, and ruthless vision unencumbered by sentimentality could focus on the big picture and force leaders to do what he thought was best for the planet. One guess who that person should be."

Juan nodded slowly as the ramifications jelled in his mind. He now understood why the discovery that Kensit was the survivor alarmed Locke and Westfield. And while they knew he had killed three men to cover up his death, they didn't know he was now employing Haitian death squads that had nearly wiped out *Oregon*'s entire crew by using an untraceable means of spying on them. Based on the assassin's pronouncement that the world would change in less than four days, the physicist was either completely off his rocker or he was bringing to fruition a goal that was equally insane.

"Did Kensit have any friends at all? Anyone close that might have suspected his plans?"

"He had no family, and he didn't hang out with anyone outside of work. One of his coworkers mentioned overhearing Kensit speaking to Pearson about a diary he'd received as an inheritance. Pearson spoke German and Kensit wanted him to do some translation. The coworker thought it unusual because it was the only time Kensit talked about a personal matter. And he remembered there were just a few snippets of the conversation before Kensit abruptly shut Pearson down and never spoke about it again: something about a German scientist, a ship called the *Roraima*, and a reference to Oz."

"Oz as in *The Wizard of Oz*?" Eric asked.

"I asked the same thing," Westfield said. "He said that's what it sounded like."

"Kensit could have been referring to Australia," Juan said, meaning the nickname Aussies gave their own country.

Westfield shrugged. "It's hard to know without more to go on. We looked up the *Roraima*. There are three that we know of. One is a small cargo ship currently sailing under a Brazilian flag. The second was a nineteenth-century steamship that ran aground, but the vessel was saved and the captain subsequently built a Victorian mansion named after the ship. It's a bed-and-breakfast now."

"And the third?" Juan asked.

"That's the most interesting one," Locke said. "It sunk in Saint-Pierre Harbor in 1902 when Mount Pelée erupted. I understand it's a tourist attraction now. The question is why Kensit would be interested in any of those ships. We couldn't come up with a reason."

"I know someone who might be able to." And it was just their luck, Juan thought, that St. Julien Perlmutter was only a short drive away in Washington, D.C.

Port-au-Prince, Haiti

The stench from the harbor made checking the cargo an odious task, but this equipment was too important for Lawrence Kensit to leave to the crew of Russian scientists and technicians he had hired from a defunct nuclear fusion weapons laboratory. The contents of this container were critical if testing for Sentinel Phase 2 was to finish on schedule. He had to know right away if anything was damaged or missing, which was a distinct possibility considering he was buying all of his hardware on the black market.

The physicist called out the checklist to the team unpacking the crates that were to be loaded onto trucks for the rough ride over cracked and potholed roads to their final destination. Despite his small stature and reedy voice, Kensit was confident that his team would follow his orders to ensure the fragile instruments would make the trip intact and be ready for testing.

The barely functional harbor, severely damaged by the 2010 earthquake that killed a quarter of a million people, served as a strong reminder of why the world needed Kensit to take drastic action to save it from itself. Garbage was piled everywhere. Buildings that had crumbled in the temblor remained unusable. A gantry crane teetered in the middle of the harbor like the Leaning Tower of Pisa, its base completely submerged. Gaunt children rooted around in the refuse for whatever useful scraps they could find and sell.

The scene was representative of the laziness, corruption, and lack of will rampant in every country. Kensit thought of himself as too intelligent to believe in fate or destiny, but he did know an opportunity when it presented itself and the inheritance he had received nearly three years before was just that. If it had gone to anyone else, it would have been wasted; in his hands, the radical theories could usher in a new direction for civilization, with Kensit as its guide.

Lawrence Kensit had been unlike anyone else as far back as he could remember, which he saw as their deficiency, not his. His parents constantly told him that he was special, a fact that he considered self-evident in his ability to master calculus by the age of ten. He didn't connect with other children, and adults found him to be an oddity or an amusing diversion trotted out to perform tricks.

Kensit found the isolation strangely appealing. People were annoying and tedious, with their small talk and need to placate others' feelings. Instead, he immersed himself in online worlds where he could take on the persona of a powerful dark knight or sorcerer, someone equal to the stature that he could not hope to achieve in the real world because of his small build and meek appearance. In the real world, his towering intellect provoked jealousy and discomfort from those around him that radiated from their pores, but online he could make them submit to his will whether they wanted to or not.

After graduating from Caltech at eighteen with Ph.D.s in both physics and computer science, he had been recruited by the top universities. Although the idea of shutting himself away to ponder the deepest questions of the universe was intriguing, weapons design was far more fascinating to him. Drone warfare was in its infancy, but he saw the potential for transforming his video game experiences into reality.

The end result was more frustrating than he'd imagined it would be. His elegant software designs were used inefficiently by politicians who were more concerned about limiting civilian casualties than killing the terrorists or winning the wars the drones were meant for. Kensit's eyes were opened to all of the other problems that faced the planet. When he saw the answers in his mind, they seemed so simple to him, but when he explained them to others they seemed strangely repulsed by his solutions.

Then one day three years ago a lawyer called him up and told him that a great-aunt he'd never met had died. Because his parents had both succumbed to cancer at an early age, Kensit was his aunt's last living relative and she had left him a small inheritance that included a diary from her uncle, a German scientist named Gunther Lutzen who had died in the volcanic eruption of Mt. Pelée in 1902. Kensit nearly chucked the thing without reading it, but he casually flipped it open and found his uncle's equations, one of the few times in his life that he'd been truly stunned academically.

Kensit at once recognized that his genius had been familial. The equations he understood, but Pearson's prying when Kensit had asked him to translate some of the words made him realize he would need a professional translator to decipher the German text for him. When Kensit read the results, he knew he alone had to carry on his distant relative's work. If he turned the radical concepts over to his employer, the U.S. government, they would just waste them like they wasted his drone technology.

That was the day he began plotting to fake his death. It took two years to accomplish, followed by another nine months of eighteen-hour days, but he was nearly finished with the next step toward attaining the power to remake the world however he saw fit.

When the final checks of equipment were finished and the trucks drove off, it was time for his phone call. He found a quiet section of the loading dock and dialed Admiral Dayana Ruiz.

"Yes," she answered on the fourth ring.

"Admiral, didn't you see who was calling?" His voice was transformed by a modulator so that NSA eavesdropping software wouldn't recognize his voice.

"Yes, Doctor."

"Then you should answer faster next time. You waste our time when you play petty mind games."

"*I* waste our time?" she said. "You were the one who didn't sink the *Ciudad Bolívar*. I lost twelve men on the operation, and I'm having to answer questions about why Venezuelan Navy seaman were aboard her when she was discovered. And where are my drone subs?"

"I had to sink them."

"You what?"

"They were about to fall into American hands. I couldn't let that happen."

Ruiz shouted so loudly that Kensit had to hold the phone away from his ear. "When I find you, whoever you are, I will destroy you!"

"Your focus is on the wrong person," Kensit said. "You should be after Juan Cabrillo."

"Who is that?"

"You know him as Buck Holland, captain of the *Dolos*. His ship is actually called the *Oregon*, and you didn't really sink it. It was all an elaborate ruse."

"What are you talking about? How do you know that we sank the *Dolos*?"

"As I said, you *didn't* sink it. You sank a duplicate."

"Nonsense."

"Is it? Then how can you explain Lieutenant Dominguez and the rest of his men getting ambushed aboard the *Ciudad Bolívar*?"

"You. You're behind all of this."

"Why would I do that? Now I don't get the balance of the money you owe me. What would I have to gain? Admiral, this really isn't that difficult."

There was a pause. "How do I know you're not lying to me?"

Kensit tapped on the phone's screen, then said, "Look at the text I just sent."

It was a photo of Juan Cabrillo and Franklin Lincoln aboard the *Ciudad Bolívar* after it had partially capsized, standing on the railing, with the *Oregon* in the background.

"Do you recognize them?" Kensit asked.

"The blond man, no. But the black man was at my warehouse in Puerto La Cruz."

"The man you don't recognize is Juan Cabrillo, aka Buck Holland. The ship you see is the *Oregon*."

"It's the same dimensions, but it looks nothing like the *Dolos*."

"They can disguise their ship."

"That's ridiculous."

"I thought you might say that. Check your messages again." He sent her a short time-lapse video of the *Dolos* being transformed into the *Oregon*.

After watching it, Ruiz growled, "I will hunt those spies down and vaporize them."

"How? You have no idea where they are."

"But you do?"

"Yes, I do."

"I can't just leave Venezuelan territorial waters with a frigate. I need a reason."

"I know. In three days there will be a combined fleet exercise called UNITAS in the Bahamas."

"I'm aware of it. Venezuela was not invited to participate."

"Neither was Cuba," Kensit said. "But both of you can send your own ships to observe their operations. When you are near Haiti, you will divert your vessel and sink the *Oregon*."

"Why are you so eager to help me? What will this cost?"

"You have political ambitions. I'll make sure you achieve them."

"Why?"

"You're my type of leader. Direct, action-oriented, a little emotional for my tastes, but I can live with that. Once I help you sink the *Oregon*, I expect the rest of my payment."

"You're insane!"

"No, that's only fair. And if you don't sink the *Oregon*, I will reveal that her captain outwitted you. Your credibility in the Venezuelan Navy would be shattered. Then once your reputation is destroyed, you'll go to prison when I release details about your smuggling operation. Be there in three days." He didn't wait for a response before he hung up. Ruiz would come. She didn't have a choice.

He put the phone away and saw Hector Bazin walking toward him.

"Doctor, Brian Washburn arrived as you instructed. I've got him in the car. Shall I bring him?"

"Yes. Once we're on the boat, I need you to go to the United States. Captain Cabrillo is causing us more problems."

"Kill him?"

"If you can. But now that he's found out about the Piranha subs, the U.S. military may suspect that someone on my old weapons development program was responsible for selling the plans, so your highest priority is to eliminate any remaining links between me and the Sentinel project. I'll brief you about the target once you're in the air."

"Yes, sir."

"Get the governor."

Bazin returned with Washburn, who looked as if he didn't want his six-hundred-dollar shoes to be exposed to the air here, let alone touching the dock. When he got close to Kensit, he stuck out a hand and turned on the charm.

"You must be the Doctor," Washburn said with a smile. "It's a pleasure to meet you."

"No, it's not," Kensit said, ignoring the hand. "I sent for you and you came. There is no power balance in this relationship. You're used to being the one in charge. Not here. You work for me now."

Washburn's smile vanished, replaced by a sneer. "Who do you think you are, you little weasel?"

"I've been called every name possible during my life, so save the macho posturing. I have video of you murdering a man. You can leave now and face the death penalty or life in prison. You can try to kill me, and Bazin here will break your neck before you can reach me. Or you can do as I say and become president of the United States. Choose right now."

Washburn looked at Bazin, then back at Kensit, and realized he was completely outmatched, both physically and mentally. The sneer dissolved.

"All right. But why have you brought me to this godforsaken place? It literally reeks."

"That's what happens when you have a city of three million people with no functional sewer system. You would not want to swim in the harbor. We're going to take a ride on the *Victoire* over there."

Kensit pointed at a white, hundred-foot-long Lürssen yacht with a satellite dish on the foredeck.

"We're going on a cruise?" Washburn said.

"First, I'm going to show you my facility. A place called Oz."

Washburn's lip curled. "You're joking."

"Have you found me funny up to this point?"

Washburn put up his hands. "Okay. Oz. Where is it?"

"You won't know that, but I will show you my operation because I need you to believe I can do everything I say I can do."

"Which is what, exactly?"

"I operate a revolutionary surveillance system. One that needs to be seen to be believed. It's called Sentinel. I also want you with me when we complete our most important mission using Sentinel's capabilities. You gave your company the excuse I told you?"

Washburn nodded. "I'm here to review our aid for the Haitian earthquake rebuilding efforts."

"Good. That will survive scrutiny. Not that anyone will suspect you have anything to do with what's about to happen."

"Which is?"

Kensit ignored the question. "Who is standing in your way in the next presidential election?"

"No one's declared yet, but James Sandecker has a head start as the incumbent vice president if he wants the presidency. Are you saying you have dirt on Sandecker, too?"

"No, he's squeaky clean. But you'll need an edge to win in the primary. That's why we have to make you vice president."

"How are you going to do that?"

"I'm going to kill Sandecker."

Washburn's eyes bugged out. "You want me to be party to killing the vice president of the United States?"

"You've killed before. You'll have to kill again if you're president, you'll just have drones and soldiers doing it for you. You're all in, just like I am."

"You think killing him will make me president?"

"You were the second choice for vice president in the election. You're nearly certain to be selected as his replacement, making you the instant front-runner."

"But it's crazy! Even if I agreed to go along with this, you'd never be able to do it. The Secret Service protects him as well as they protect the president."

"You leave that to me."

Washburn eyed him with the implacable face of a career politician. "If I'm 'all in,' I think I deserve to know what you're planning."

Kensit sighed in annoyance, but he supposed it wouldn't hurt now to reveal the mission's goal. All of Washburn's electronics had been confiscated by Bazin, so there would be no way for him to convey any information until after the deed was done. By then it would be too late for him to chicken out.

"In three days the vice president will be returning from a summit in Rio de Janeiro," Kensit said. "When he is over the Caribbean, I'm going to shoot down Air Force Two."

31

Georgetown, Washington, D.C.

Juan had never met St. Julien Perlmutter in person, but he had consulted with him several times during past missions, most recently about a sunken Chinese junk called the *Silent Sea*. When Tyler Locke mentioned a potential link between Kensit and a ship called the *Roraima*, Juan's first call after leaving Pax River was to Perlmutter. The maritime expert was delighted to hear that Juan was in the neighborhood. A noted gourmand as well, he insisted that Juan and Eric join him for a late lunch at his home.

Juan's second call was to Langston Overholt, who told him that DNA analysis would take several days even if they could find original samples of Kensit and Pearson's DNA to compare the tissue found at the crash site. In the meantime, they had to operate under the assumption that Locke's forensic assessment correctly surmised that it was Kensit whose body wasn't found and that he was still alive.

Other than the ship connection, the only other lead into Kensit's motives was the German diary the coworker mentioned. After he brusquely ended his consultation with Pearson, Kensit would have had to find someone else to translate the document for him, a company or individual with expertise in scientific terminology. That narrowed down the list of possible translators considerably, and Overholt told Juan he'd get back to them when he had something.

When he reached Perlmutter's estate on a brick road flanked by hundred-year-old oaks, Juan wheeled their rental car around the circular drive of the three-story manor and parked on the side in front of a carriage house that rivaled the main house in size. Perlmutter had remodeled this building that once housed ten horses and five carriages, as well as upstairs quarters for stable hands and drivers, to accommodate his vast library. He was renowned for owning the world's most extensive collection of books, rare documents, and private letters about ships and shipwrecks. If there was any record of a German scientist aboard the *Roraima* when it sank, St. Julien Perlmutter would know of it.

With Eric at his side, Juan reached for the front door's anchor-shaped knocker, but before he could use it the door flew open, revealing a man who could have been Saint Nick's larger brother, dressed in a regal purple robe and matching paisley pajamas. His twinkling blue eyes were framed by shaggy gray hair, a full beard with a twisting mustache, and a tulip nose. Although he loomed at a gargantuan six foot four and four hundred pounds, Perlmutter was solid, without a jiggle of flab visible. A tiny dachshund gamboled around their feet, yapping happily.

"Juan Cabrillo!" he cried, grabbing Juan's hand and giving it a vigorous shake. "What a true pleasure it is to finally meet you!"

"It's an honor to be invited to your home, Mr. Perlmutter. I only wish I had brought something with me to share. I know you treasure regional delicacies."

"Where is the *Oregon* now? Not docked nearby?" Perlmutter was one of the few privy to the *Oregon*'s true nature and his discretion was unquestioned.

"No, it's currently in the Dominican Republic."

"Well, then send me some fresh conch and plantain when you get back. I have a fricassee recipe I've been dying to try. And this must be Eric Stone making friends with Fritz."

Eric was on his knees, rubbing the dog's belly. He rose and offered a hand. "Sorry. That's one thing I miss with shipboard life. We had a beagle when I was a child and he had just as much energy as your dog."

"Not to worry, Mr. Stone." With the attention gone, Fritz's barking restarted. "Fritz, behave! Or I will get a cat to set you straight."

"Please excuse our last-minute call," Juan said.

"Not at all. You're just in time to help me try my newest creation, a truffled lobster risotto and Precoce d'Argenteuil asparagus tips served with a bottle of Condrieu Viognier."

Perlmutter led them through hallways and rooms stacked with books and papers on every available flat surface. Juan knew that administrators in libraries and museums the world over salivated at the thought of acquiring the incredible trove of marine history that made up his unparalleled collection.

Eric gaped at the ancient maps and weathered tomes that seemed to be haphazardly strewn about. "It must be quite a task to catalog all of this. I'd love to see your database."

Perlmutter tapped his temple. "This is my database, young man. I don't think in computer language. I don't even have one."

Juan was amused to see Stoney's jaw drop even lower. "You keep track of all this in your head?"

"My boy, I can find any piece of information I want in sixty seconds. Like any good treasure hunter, you just have to know where to look."

They were escorted into an elegant sandalwood-paneled dining room, which looked decidedly bare as it was the sole room without a single book. They sat down at a thick, round dining table carved from the rudder of the famed ghost ship *Mary Celeste* and enjoyed the early-afternoon repast while Juan and Eric regaled Perlmutter with sea stories from their adventures, leaving out details that would compromise any classified information. Fritz was kept happy and quiet with regular pieces of lobster fed to him by Perlmutter.

When they were finished, Juan swirled the last of his wine. "Your reputation as an epicure is well deserved. I couldn't imagine a better lunch."

Eric nodded in agreement. "Maybe we can convince Mr. Perlmutter to share the recipe with the *Oregon*'s chef."

"Happy to! And perhaps he can send me one of his favorites in return."

"Done," Juan said.

"Excellent! Now, my cooking is not the only reason you came to see me, is it?"

Juan told Perlmutter about the missing physicist, the German diary he supposedly inherited, the mention of Oz and the *Roraima*. "Flimsy, I know," Juan said, "but we were hoping you could point us in the right direction."

Perlmutter patted his cheek with one finger for a few moments and then leaped up with startling agility and dashed into another room. He returned not thirty seconds later, thumbing through a thick book titled *Cyclone of Fire: The Wreckage of St. Pierre.*

"The eruption of Mount Pelée was the deadliest volcanic eruption of the twentieth century and it happened on May 8, 1902," Perlmutter said. "It's also unique in that we have such a rich historical record of the ships that were sunk in the disaster. I know of no other volcano that resulted in so many wrecked ships that can still be explored. Only one ship survived, the *Roddam.* Sixteen ships were sunk that day, including the *Roraima.* Many of them settled upright on the bottom and can still be dived on to this day."

"Do you think that's the *Roraima* we're looking for?" Juan asked.

"I know it is. This is the only remaining copy of a book that went out of print a hundred years ago. Remember that this was the biggest catastrophe in the Western Hemisphere. All but two people in a town of thirty thousand perished. Scores of books were rushed out about the subject. To take a different angle from the dozens that recounted the horrors visited on the city of Saint-Pierre itself, this one focused on the ships that were in the harbor that day. It was written by a newspaper reporter who took great care in interviewing shipboard survivors and relatives of those who died. Unfortunately, his journalistic thoroughness resulted in a publishing delay, so by the time the book came out the market was saturated. Most of them were pulped."

"Does it say something about Oz?" Eric asked, incredulous.

"Indeed it does," Perlmutter said, tapping the page. He read the relevant passage to them.

"*Ingrid Lutzen, a German émigré to the United States, lost her brother, Gunther, in the disaster. She sobbed as she recounted how excited he sounded in his final letter to her, sent from the ship's previous stop in Guadeloupe. He was searching for evidence in the Caribbean to support his postdoctoral research in physics that he was carrying on from his work at Berlin University and had made a recent breakthrough in the new field of radioactivity. Gunther was an avid photographer, even going so far as to convert his stateroom into a makeshift darkroom, and was planning to show her the photos documenting his work. The only keepsake she received was a diary of his scientific research given to her by the* Roraima's *first officer, Ellery Scott. He told Ms. Lutzen that her brother's last words were 'I found Oz,' a reference to a favorite story of Gunther's when she was teaching him English during his last visit with her. It gave her some peace knowing that he died thinking of their shared memory."*

Eric peered at Perlmutter as he processed the paragraph. "Didn't *The Wizard of Oz* come out long after this in 1939?"

"The film did," Perlmutter replied. "*The Wonderful Wizard of Oz* by L. Frank Baum was published in 1900 as a children's book. It's quite likely that foreign immigrants would have used the book to learn our language."

"But he said, 'I found Oz,' as though he'd actually been there," Juan said.

"Delusional perhaps? A hallucination in his final death throes?"

"Kensit seemed to think it was important. And the book references the diary that he inherited, so it definitely exists."

"And Lutzen was a physicist," Eric chimed in, "same as Kensit. But without knowing about the specific research Lutzen was conducting, we have no idea why Kensit would fake his own death to pursue it a hundred years later."

Nothing about this was adding up for Juan. "What kind of evidence would Lutzen have been searching for? Why would a physicist be scouring the Caribbean for his research?"

"Your answer may lie inside the *Roraima*," Perlmutter said. "Lutzen was an avid photographer."

Eric shook his head. "That film has been bathing in warm salt water for over a hundred years. It's probably mush by now."

"Not necessarily," Perlmutter said. "It's possible that the glass plate negatives, which he would have used at that time, are still intact if the seals on the container haven't been compromised. Frank Hurley, the photographer on the Shackleton expedition, saved photos that had been submerged in seawater because they had been stored in zinc-lined cases that had been soldered shut. If Dr. Lutzen was similarly prudent, the photos might have survived."

"If they're still there at all," Juan said. "Martinique isn't exactly off the beaten path. Divers have been picking over those Saint-Pierre wrecks for decades."

"Maybe not so thoroughly as you think. The *Roraima* sits in one hundred and fifty feet of water, below the level of most recreational scuba divers. Bottom times will be limited for all but the most technically adept divers, and few will have fully explored the interior, which is dangerous because of the rusting hull."

"It'll take a while to search the ship since we don't know where his cabin was," Eric said.

Perlmutter gave him a crafty grin. "I believe I can help you out there as well." He darted out of the room and came back with a roll of paper that he spread on the table. It was the deck plan for the *Roraima*.

"Okay, I'm convinced," Eric said. "No computer needed here."

Although he couldn't know which particular cabin Lutzen had occupied, Perlmutter pointed out where the passenger staterooms were located, considerably narrowing the search grid.

"May I take a photo of this?" Eric asked.

"By all means," Perlmutter said, waving at the plans. "And

when I finally get a chance to see that fantastic ship of yours, I expect a guided tour from you."

"Absolutely."

When Eric was finished with the snapshots, Perlmutter ushered them to the door. "Do come back someday. And let me know if you find Oz as well."

"I just hope we don't run into any flying monkeys," Juan said with a wink.

"Me neither," Eric agreed. "They always freaked me out." When he saw the looks from the other two men, he quickly added, "Back when I was a kid. Not now."

Perlmutter bellowed a hearty laugh, and after Eric gave Fritz one last scratch, he closed the door behind them.

No sooner were they on the road than Langston Overholt called back.

"Juan, we've found the translation firm. Global Translation Services."

"That was fast."

"They remembered it because it was such an odd job. Kensit had the translator transcribe the notes by hand so there wouldn't be a digital record."

"I'd like to speak to the translator."

"That's going to be a problem," Overholt said ominously.

"Why?"

"He's dead. Killed in a hit-and-run four months ago."

Juan grimaced. "That's not the kind of coincidence I like."

"Neither do I."

"Is there anyone else I can talk to there? They might remember something."

"The translator worked for a man named Greg Horne. He'd be willing to speak with you."

"Where are they located?"

"Manhattan. Midtown. They do a lot of work for the United Nations."

Juan checked his watch. "We can be there in two hours."

"I'll set it up."

After alerting Tiny Gunderson to fire up the jet for a New York flight, Juan made sure he had a secure encrypted phone connection before he called Max, who he'd left in charge of the *Oregon*.

"How are our guests?" Juan asked.

"Mr. Reed is being tended to at the rehab facility by some nurses that are so beautiful, I wish I was the one who had been shot. His fishing boat is fully repaired and ready to sail back to Jamaica when he's feeling up to it."

"What about Maria Sandoval?"

"She's been given our finest guest cabin and has an escort with her at all times to the exercise facilities, the mess hall, and the deck. I think she's still under the impression that we're a high-tech smuggling operation."

"Good. But she's free to go anytime she wants."

"I think she's okay for a few days. A friend told her that her apartment was ransacked, so she thinks laying low for a while is a good idea. So was your talk with Mr. Perlmutter useful?"

"More than we hoped," Juan said, and told Max about their discoveries concerning the *Roraima* and the connection between Kensit and the dead translator in New York.

"I think I see where this is going," Max said when Juan was finished.

"Get the *Oregon* under way for Martinique. You should be able to be there in twelve hours. When Eric and I are done in Manhattan, we'll fly directly there to meet you. But don't wait for us. Start diving as soon as you arrive. Eric will send you the deck plans for the search pattern."

"Already got them."

"Good. And don't tell Overholt where you're going if he calls. We don't know how Kensit's surveillance system works or how deep its reach is." Eric, Murph, and Hali had completely scrubbed their communications systems, so Juan was confident that no one was listening to this conversation.

"You think he might have penetrated CIA?" Max asked.

"Probably not, but it isn't a risk I want to take. Those photos in the *Roraima* could be our only clue to tracking down Kensit. If he learns about them and retrieves them first or destroys them, we may never find him."

Manhattan

It wasn't difficult to follow the white delivery van through the bustling New York traffic. The green-and-gray logo of tropical vines wrapping around skyscrapers on the back door served as a target that could be seen from several blocks away. Hector Bazin had been on its tail since the Urban Jungle courier service van had left its company's loading dock.

"Don't miss this light," he told his driver. "We don't have time to go back and follow another van if we lose this one."

"Yes, sir." The driver nosed the car around a stopped bus and goosed the accelerator. With the congested streets, there was no chance the van driver would suspect he was being followed.

After putting Brian Washburn and Lawrence Kensit on a helicopter to go visit the Sentinel facility, Bazin had taken one of their two private jets and headed straight for New York City on intelligence that Juan Cabrillo and his companion would be going there next. Bazin's mission was to intercept him and stop his investigation before it could go any further.

The van took a right on a quiet street in Greenwich Village and double-parked outside a brownstone with a shingle for an accountant's office. The driver, a white man an inch shorter than Bazin, dressed in the company's uniform of black trousers and green shirt, jacket, and cap, all emblazoned with the company logo, hopped out of the van with a package. He ducked his head against the chilly wind and rushed inside.

Bazin got out, hauling his own package, a box the size of a bread loaf. He casually walked up to the passenger side of the van and assured himself that no one on the street was watching. Like the deliveryman, the few people who were on the street had their eyes to the sidewalk out of the wind.

The driver had locked the van on exiting, but Bazin shoved a metal shim down the window frame and snagged the lock in seconds. He yanked up, then pulled the door open and slipped inside.

He relocked the door, took up position behind the driver's seat, drew a Glock semiautomatic, and waited. A minute later, he heard quick footsteps shuffling toward him. The driver's door opened, letting in a blast of air. The deliveryman settled into his seat with a squeak of springs and tossed his electronic signature pad on the passenger seat.

Bazin stuck the Glock into the driver's side.

"Hey!" the deliveryman yelled. When he looked down and saw the gun, he added, "Oh, God!"

"Go," Bazin said.

"Yeah, yeah. Okay, man. Just don't shoot." He put the van into drive and eased forward.

"What's your name?" Bazin asked.

"Leonard O'Shea. Where are we going?"

"I'll tell you where to turn, Leonard."

"Don't kill me, man."

"I won't hurt you as long as you do what I say," Bazin said in a soothing voice. "Do you understand?"

O'Shea nodded so violently that his skull banged against the headrest.

"Good. Keep going."

They drove for ten minutes until Bazin had O'Shea thread his way into a deserted alley in Hell's Kitchen. O'Shea parked and put his hands on the wheel. He eyed Bazin in the mirror with a pleading look.

"Listen, man, take anything you want. It's all insured anyway. It's mostly rich bankers sending each other stuff. They won't miss it."

"Unfortunately, Leonard, that's not why I'm here."

A confused expression was all O'Shea could muster before Bazin pistol-whipped his temple. The blow knocked him cold, but Bazin had to make sure he wouldn't come to and attract attention. He pulled O'Shea out of the driver's seat and snapped his neck before laying him on the floor among the packages.

Bazin was already dressed in black pants, but he needed the rest of O'Shea's uniform. He swapped clothes and was disappointed to find that the sleeves were a couple inches too short. Although they were close to the same height, which is the reason Bazin had selected the unfortunate man in the first place, O'Shea's arms were unusually short.

Bazin shrugged and donned the Urban Jungle cap. It was too late now to do anything about it. He had a package to deliver.

He rechecked the encrypted radio detonator in his pocket and secured the box on the passenger seat. The bogus packing slip on top, printed out with the Urban Jungle logo and a United Nations return address, read "Global Translation Services, Attn: Greg Horne."

Juan reached the offices of Global Translation Services fifteen minutes before they closed. He had Eric drop him off and circle the block so they wouldn't have to deal with Manhattan parking. The firm was a much smaller operation than the name implied. The front lobby overlooked Fortieth Street five floors below, and Juan spotted a dozen desks with translators listening to headsets busily typing away, three private offices, and a conference room.

A pretty, young receptionist informed Greg Horne of his visitor. Juan watched the traffic as he waited.

A short, dark-haired man, crisply dressed in a charcoal pin-striped suit, opened a door at the far end of the workspace. It was the largest office and had a plate-glass window with a view of the entire operation. The man quick-stepped toward Juan, a tight smile set beneath an upturned nose.

"Mr. Cochran, I'm Greg Horne, president and owner of GTS," he said with an outstretched hand. Juan had thought it prudent to use one of his aliases for this meeting.

"Thanks for meeting with me on such short notice, Mr. Horne," Juan said with a friendly grin, and adjusted the glasses he was wearing. "This is quite an operation you have here."

"We run a pretty lean business," Horne said as he walked Juan back to his office. "Most of the work is farmed out to independent contractors except for the most high-profile and sensitive jobs, which are kept in-house."

Horne ushered Juan into his office and closed the door. Juan took the proffered seat.

"Was the job for Lawrence Kensit in-house?"

Horne tented his fingers and peered at Juan. "I'm sorry, Mr. Cochran. What is your relation to Mr. Kensit?"

"So you remember him and Dr. Lutzen's diary?"

"Certainly. But the diary made no mention of him being a doctor. Although it was more than two years ago, it was a fascinating case. It's not often we translate a document that old. How do you know about it?"

"I represent a collector who is interested in buying it. I can't say who it is, but he's a wealthy tech entrepreneur who collects rare scientific journals. Mr. Kensit is thinking of selling it, so we wanted to verify its authenticity."

The glasses Juan was wearing contained a microcamera. If he could get Horne to let him flip through the original German or the English translation, he would have it all recorded so he could take it back to the *Oregon* for examination later.

"You do have a copy of the document," Juan said helpfully.

Horne's eyes briefly flicked to a file cabinet. "As I said, it was a special case. My translator, Bob Gillman, was not allowed to record his translation into the computer. Those were Mr. Kensit's instructions."

"But you have a physical copy in that cabinet."

"Of course not!" Horne exclaimed with feigned offense. "We were under strict orders to destroy even the handwritten copy."

Juan nodded and looked toward the lobby as if he were considering other options. A deliveryman in a green jacket and cap was dropping off a package with the receptionist. Urban Jungle, the back of his uniform read. Not a well-fitting outfit, either. The sleeves were comically short.

Juan turned back to Horne as if he'd gotten a sudden idea.

"May I speak to Mr. Gillman? Perhaps he can provide me with the information I need."

"I'm sad to say that Bob was struck by a car outside of our offices just a few months ago. Hit-and-run. The driver got away. Bob was killed instantly."

"Oh, I'm sorry to hear that."

"Yes, very tragic."

"It sounds like you were privy to the contents of the document."

Another eye flick to the cabinet. "I review the work of many of my employees."

"Mr. Kensit claims the journal outlines a radical new scientific development unknown at that time. Can you confirm that?"

Horne shifted in his chair. "Mr. Cochran, perhaps you should have Mr. Kensit contact me. I can't share confidential information without a release form."

Juan put up his hands. "I understand. I don't want you to divulge anything you shouldn't."

"Besides, although I can translate German scientific language, it doesn't mean I can understand the science behind it."

"That certainly makes sense. But if I could have a brief look—"

Horne suddenly stood. "Mr. Cochran, we don't have a copy of the document, and I resent the implication that we would violate a trust like that."

Juan got to his feet as well. Pushing further would accomplish nothing. But his assessment of the building's security made it clear that breaking in this evening and photographing the copy of the journal that obviously was in the file cabinet would be a simple task.

"I'm sorry I can't help more," Horne said as he ushered Juan out to the lobby. All of the translators had gone home, leaving the receptionist as the lone employee. "Please have Mr. Kensit send me a notarized request to consult on the translation authentication and I will be glad to assist you."

The receptionist handed him the package sitting on the counter. "This came urgent from the UN, Mr. Horne."

"Thanks, Jill," he said, and put the box under his arm. "Goodbye, Mr. Cochran."

Juan shook his hand, and Horne walked back to his office. Juan called Eric to find out where he was and looked down to the street below to see if he could spot him.

He didn't see Eric, but the deliveryman from Urban Jungle was still out there, looking up at the building. Now that Juan could see his face, he recognized the man immediately.

It was the assassin who'd been sent to kill Juan in Jamaica. For a moment, Juan thought the killer was waiting for him to exit the building.

Then he remembered the package.

Juan heard Horne shut the office door behind him. The assassin saw Juan staring down at him and waved with a wicked grin on his face. He held a small black object in his hand for Juan to see, his thumb poised over a red button. With a deliberate finality, his thumb stabbed down.

Juan dived over the lobby desk and tackled Jill before she could register what was happening, covering her body with his. The instant they hit the floor, a deafening blast blew apart Greg Horne's office, showering the cubicles with glass shards and chunks of the thick wooden door.

Juan shook off the stars circling his head and jumped to his feet to go to Horne's aid, but there was nothing he could do. Smoke billowed across the room as an inferno raged in Horne's office. The explosion was so powerful that it had damaged the sprinkler system, which sprayed haphazardly around the space.

Jill was cowering in the fetal position and screaming uncontrollably. Juan picked her up in his arms and carried her to the stairs, which was now crammed with the building's other tenants escaping the fire. She was able to walk down the stairs, so he put his arm around her shoulder and kept his head on a swivel, looking for signs of the assassin.

By the time he got outside, emergency vehicles were already arriving. He handed Jill off to a paramedic and jogged across the street.

The Urban Jungle van was gone.

Eric ran through the crowd of onlookers.

"Chairman! Are you all right?"

Juan nodded. "It was the Haitians again. They knew we were coming."

"How? We disabled our trackers."

"I don't know. Their surveillance system must be even more powerful than we thought. They must have cracked our communication encryption."

"I find that hard to believe."

Juan looked up at the flames licking from the fifth floor above him. "I think your evidence is on fire."

"You weren't able to get a copy of the diary?"

"It existed, but he wouldn't show it to me. Now it's up in smoke, and so is the only remaining person to read it besides Kensit."

Police were now screeching to a stop in packs.

"Come on," Eric said, "I've got the car stopped on the next block."

"I did get one piece of information," Juan said as they walked and rubbed the smoke from his eyes.

"What's that?"

"Lutzen's journal never mentioned that he was a doctor."

Eric thought for a second, then his eyes went wide. "Mr. Perlmutter's book said his postdoctoral research was continuing the work he did at Berlin University."

Juan nodded. "His doctoral thesis might still be in the library. We need to know what he was working on."

"And because his doctorate wasn't mentioned in the diary, Kensit might not know the thesis exists. I can do an online search to make sure it's still in the library."

"No. We don't know how far Kensit has penetrated our network or how his system works. If he knows we're looking for the thesis, his men might get there before we do and destroy it like he did Horne's copy of the journal."

"So we can't even tell the guys on the *Oregon* that it exists?"

Juan shook his head. "We'll tell them what happened here and that they might have company in Martinique, but our destination is between the two of us. I'm not even going to call Tiny. He isn't going to know until we get to La Guardia that we're flying to Berlin."

Saint-Pierre, Martinique

At the turn of the twentieth century, a dozen or more cargo ships would have been anchored where the *Oregon* now sat motionless, the only large vessel in sight. Although Saint-Pierre's harbor teemed with pleasure craft and sailboats, her days as a commercial and cultural jewel of the Caribbean ended the day Mt. Pelée erupted. The bustling city of thirty thousand had been rebuilt over the following decades with charming red-roofed cottages and stone churches, but its population had never topped five thousand since that fateful day.

Max Hanley couldn't blame residents for being reluctant to return. Not only did the now dormant volcano still loom over the town but Saint-Pierre had suffered catastrophe before the eruption. During the high-speed cruise from the Dominican Republic, Max found out that Saint-Pierre had been destroyed more than a century earlier by the twenty-five-foot storm surge of the Great Hurricane of 1780, the deadliest in Atlantic history. Over nine thousand citizens died in that disaster.

Nothing seemed to threaten the town today except the squall that was churning up waves in the harbor and pelting the town with rain. Mt. Pelée's silent peak, its slopes lush with the vegetation that had rushed back from its fertile soil, was veiled in gray clouds, but blue skies were forecast for the afternoon.

As dawn lightened the leaden sky, Max watched the local harbormaster return to shore in his tiny launch. Normally, Juan handled the local constabulary, but this time it had been up to Max and he thought he'd done a pretty decent job convincing the harbormaster that the *Oregon*'s crew was going to enjoy the scenery while they waited for their cargo to arrive at their berth in Fort-de-France.

In actuality, the *Oregon*'s crew had already been hard at work for two hours exploring the wreckage of the *Roraima*, acting as fast as they could while they had the dive site to themselves. Once the squall ceased, they'd have to suspend operations so they wouldn't arouse suspicion from the recreational scuba tours that would begin diving on the wreck in the afternoon.

Max took the stairs down to the moon pool, which was buzzing with activity. The latest group of divers was just surfacing through the keel doors. Mike Trono removed his mask and climbed out.

"Any luck?" Max said.

Mike shook his head and began to peel off his wetsuit. "The decks on the *Roraima* were all wooden. They rotted away years ago and collapsed. A lot of it was either destroyed by the volcano blast or crushed when the superstructure caved in. All that's left now is the steel frame and that's full of holes. Portions of the hull could collapse on us, if we're not careful. We're still looking through the section of the ship where Perlmutter told us the cabins would have been, but there's been a ton of coral growth over the last century so it's a slow search. The box could be buried in ten feet of debris."

Max smiled. "On the bright side, that means it might be intact. No hits on the Geiger counter?"

When Juan had mentioned that Lutzen's work had been about radioactivity, Max checked his history books and found out that radiation had been discovered only seven years before the eruption on Martinique, so it would have been a relatively new science at the time. If Lutzen had brought something radioactive with him and it was still with his belongings, detecting it might lead them to the photos. The *Oregon* was equipped with two Geiger counters, so Max sent one of them down with the divers, who were scouring the sturdier parts of the ship.

"Not a blip," Mike said. "If anything radioactive is buried down there, the radiation might not be able to penetrate the debris."

"Normally, that would be a good thing, but not in our case. Get something to eat before your next dive." Mike looked like he could use some shut-eye, too, since they'd been planning the op on the sprint here so they'd be ready to dive as soon as they arrived. "And maybe a nap."

"In that order," Mike agreed, and lurched toward the mess hall.

Max went to the op center, where Hali flagged him down.

"We got a hit on the Chairman's assassin," he said. "The CIA was very helpful."

"Finally some good news," Max replied.

Before the explosion went off in New York, Juan's glasses had been recording while he was looking down at the bomber. He sent the video to Max, who recognized the man immediately as the same person who'd attacked Reed's fishing charter. The guy definitely got around. Identifying him had been Hali's top priority ever since.

"Who is that unmasked man?" Max asked.

Hali handed him a printout with the key info. "He's a mercenary named Hector Bazin, a Haitian like all the others who tried to kill us in Jamaica. Former French Foreign Legion commando. Trains his own private security force now from a base somewhere outside Port-au-Prince. That's why they had both the skills and resources for an assassination attempt."

"Would he be the one tapping our communications?"

Hali pursed his lips in frustration. "I still don't even know *how* they're doing it, let alone *who* is doing it. We've got the most secure comm system possible. The NSA would have trouble breaking our encryption."

"Bazin is just the muscle" came a comment from across the room. Murph didn't even look up from his screen or take his hands off the joysticks he was manipulating. "Kensit has got to be the brains behind this."

"Email the info about Hector Bazin to Juan."

"Even if it could be intercepted?"

"If you got the info from the CIA, then Bazin might already know he's been compromised. I don't want Juan doing whatever he's doing completely blind. At least he'll know what he's up against." Max walked over to Murph. "Did you ever meet Kensit while you were working for the DoD?"

"No, but I heard about him. Everybody in weapons research did. Off-the-charts smart, but a real oddball." Murph looked away for the first time. "I wonder if they say the same about me now."

"Would it make you feel better if they did?"

"Probably."

"Then I'm sure they do. Now, do you have any theories about what this Moriarty's secret surveillance weapon is, Sherlock? Bazin's appearance in Manhattan just when Juan was paying that translator a visit couldn't be a coincidence."

"Isn't it obvious?"

"No."

"He knows everything we're doing."

Max rolled his eyes. "Well, that part's obvious."

"Which means he is able to hear what we're saying."

"You mean when we're on the phone?"

"Possibly. But that doesn't explain how he knew where we'd be in Jamaica. The only time we discussed that was on board the *Oregon*."

"Oh, come on! You mean Kensit has the *Oregon* bugged?"

"When you eliminate the impossible, whatever remains, no matter how improbable, must be the truth."

"We've swept the ship three times. No listening devices."

"Talk to Arthur Conan Doyle, not me," Murph said.

"In any case, I'm glad Juan didn't tell us where he's going. It's time for us to get a leg up on Lawrence Kensit."

"We're still not done searching here."

"Have you seen anything?"

Murph rubbed his eyes. He'd been going for three hours straight without a break. "Except for a few broken teacups and a pair of eyeglasses, nothing."

He was piloting the smallest remotely operated vehicle they had on the *Oregon*, the ROV called Little Geek. Murph was using it to explore the parts of the ship that were too dangerous for the divers to search.

An umbilical fed the video signal back to the *Oregon*. Even at a depth of one hundred and fifty feet, the vibrant colors illuminated by the ROV's lights were astonishing. Sea whips, urchins, sponges, butterfly fish, triggerfish, and a host of other sea creatures had taken up residence on the artificial reef. More than a hundred years of exposure to the warm seawater had rusted holes in the steel where it hadn't been covered by coral. The only traces of humanity that remained untarnished were the occasional ceramic or glass object, both materials that were impervious to the corrosive effects of saline.

Max thought Perlmutter's assertion that a photo container could still be intact was dubious at best. Their only hope was that the glass photo plates had been stored in tins with a zinc layer sufficiently oxidized to prevent the underlying metal from disintegrating.

Max watched as Murph steered the ROV through a tight cavity with little expectation of finding anything useful. He hoped Juan's end of the search would yield actionable data. He just wished he had a clue what Juan was looking for.

"Huh," Murph said, which got Max's attention.

"Did you see something?"

"A dull reflection. Let me back up."

He edged the ROV backward and turned it to the left. The camera panned across a zigzag crisscross of thin metal that was covered with green algae. Below it was the glint of glass in the shine of the LEDs.

"Something about that looks familiar," Murph said.

"I know what you mean. See if you can clear away some of the debris."

Murph used the ROV's small manipulator arm to pull away an encrusted piece of steel.

The needle on the Geiger counter jumped.

"Winner, winner, chicken dinner," Max said, and laughed. "Perlmutter came through for us."

They waited for the swirling debris to settle and saw that more of the glass had been uncovered, enough to identify it.

"That's a lens," Murph said.

"Perfectly circular and convex. Like one you might find in, say, a turn-of-the-century camera?"

Murph traced the zigzag outline of the metal next to it with his finger on the screen. "That's the collapsible articulation frame for a high-end camera of the time. You know, the thing they would use to move the lens in and out of the box? The canvas accordion material must have rotted away decades ago."

"There couldn't have been too many passengers with a camera like that one in 1902."

Murph rotated the ROV around the cavity. Three shattered glass jars lay in one corner. The needle on the Geiger counter moved again. Not enough radioactivity to be harmful but more than would be expected from natural background radiation.

"You said Gunther Lutzen developed his own photos in his cabin. Those look like chemical jars that would hold developing fluids."

The rest of the room was buried under debris. If they were going to see what else was there, they'd have to go through it by hand.

"I think we've found our spot," Max said. "Now we have to dig it out."

As soon as David Pasquet stopped the truck next to the isolated dock on the south end of Saint-Pierre, men poured from the back and began unloading the plastic shipping barrels stacked inside. The scuba equipment would come last.

Pasquet might have missed his targets when he was sniping the *Oregon* in Montego Bay, but he vowed to make up for the embarrassment with this mission. Bazin had put faith in him to carry it out and Pasquet had no intention of letting his mentor down.

Like most of Bazin's officers, Pasquet had received some of his training overseas before returning to Haiti. In his case, it was with the French Navy. The grunts were all locally recruited and trained in Haiti, with the understanding that they were to be completely loyal to Bazin. If there was any hint of betrayal, their entire families would be wiped out. Although most of the men didn't need such incentives because the money was so good, examples had to be made from time to time.

This mission had been hastily planned the minute the Doctor had learned about the possibility that evidence of the Oz facility might still be inside the sunken *Roraima*. Pasquet could see the *Oregon* already anchored in the distance not far from where his map showed the *Roraima* to be.

On the ocean, they were no match for the weaponry aboard such a ship, which was why an improvised solution had to be conceived. With the Doctor's unmatched surveillance skills, the plan had come together quite nicely.

After arriving in Martinique on the second private jet at the disposal of Bazin's company, they proceeded to a warehouse in Fort-de-France, where they stole twenty empty shipping barrels, plastic ones used to transport coffee and sugar. Then they raided a warehouse used by a company that was about to start drilling a new road tunnel through the southern part of the island.

Their last stop was at the dock of *Vue Sous* Tours. Tied up alongside the dock was the company's pride and joy, a white SC-30 diesel-electric passenger submarine. The unique design was perfect for Pasquet's purposes.

On most days, the sub was used to carry thirty tourists around Saint-Pierre Harbor so they could look at the dozen or so wrecks without so much as getting their feet wet. The main, tube-shaped cabin where the sub's passengers sat was perched atop twin flat-topped pontoons like a catamaran, with a large platform at the back that could host parties when the sub was on the surface. The pontoons were flared at the front and back, reminiscent of a Formula 1 race car down to the blue racing stripes that flowed along the fins.

Passengers sat facing the large windows on either side while the sub was piloted from the large glass bubble at the front. Unlike most pleasure subs that needed to be towed to their observation spots before being powered by batteries for the limited underwater portion, the SC-30's diesel engines let it motor out to the wrecks under its own power before diving.

As he dismounted the truck and put up his slicker's hood, Pasquet got a text that the jet had landed on the island of Dominica twenty miles to the north in preparation for their operation. Given how messy the operation was going to be, taking off from Martinique would be a problem once the mission was over. The safer solution was to steal a speedboat and take it to Dominica, where leaving the island by air would be considerably easier.

Two men were inside the submarine swabbing the deck in preparation for the day's tourists, the earliest arriving in fifteen minutes. Both of them wore white uniforms with epaulettes, the better to impress upon visitors that this was a professional operation.

The older of the two, who Pasquet recognized from the website as the owner and captain of the sub, set aside his mop when he saw half a dozen men unloading a truck by his dock. He put on a rain jacket and ducked through the hatch. His crewman followed suit. Pasquet smiled as they approached.

"*Bonjour, Capitaine Batiste,*" he said, and continued in French. "We are interested in using your vessel."

"I'm sorry," Batiste replied, "but we are fully booked today. And with the seas this choppy, we will have to postpone our first trip."

"What a shame. No matter. We will take it anyway."

Pasquet drew a pistol and pointed it at the captain, who automatically raised his arms. He was alarmed, but the old seadog wasn't terrified. His crewman, however, was shaking so badly that Pasquet thought he might throw up.

"What do you want?" Batiste said.

"I told you, we want your sub. And you're going to pilot it for us."

Batiste eyed the heavy plastic barrels that Pasquet's men were rolling onto the rear deck and pontoons of the sub. "What if I don't?"

"I will kill this quivering excuse of a man."

Batiste's implacable façade crumbled. "Please, don't! He is my son."

"Then do as I say and no one will be harmed." He turned to one of his men. "Take them inside. Make Batiste tie up and blindfold his son."

Pasquet supervised the placement of the barrels, distributing them evenly, before lashing them down. He had the last one taken inside the sub. He opened it and inspected some of the dynamite that had been destined for the tunnel project. The detonator on top was preset for sixty minutes, as were all the detonators in the other barrels. At the press of a button in his pocket, all would begin counting down.

His men carried scuba gear onto the sub's pontoons. They would be staying on the deck during the underwater cruise to tip the barrels over the side when it was hovering over the wreckage of the *Roraima*. All of them had the latest bone conduction headphones that could receive their vocalizations even with masks and regulators on. The transmissions were sent ultrasonically through the water to headsets attached to the straps of their masks.

"Bring me Batiste," Pasquet said to one of the men.

Pasquet showed him the barrel and the contents inside.

"This dynamite will be inside the sub with you and your son." Pasquet held up a device that he clamped to the submarine's hull with a magnet. "This is an acoustic transceiver that uses the metal as a speaker. I will remain outside on the sub's pontoon broadcasting my instructions to you as you pilot the sub. If you deviate from my directions in any way, we will simply swim away and set off the explosives. Do you understand?"

Batiste nodded numbly, and was taken back to the cockpit. Pasquet closed the barrel.

In reality, Pasquet had no way to remotely detonate the explosives once they were submerged. Radio waves couldn't travel underwater and he had no other way of broadcasting to the detonators, making the risk of a synchronized timer necessary. The barrels would be dumped all over the shipwreck, with the resulting simultaneous explosions reducing it to a jumble of steel that would take weeks to dig through and destroying any evidence of the Sentinel project that might lay within.

After all the barrels had been scattered on the *Roraima*, Pasquet would have Batiste settle the sub on the bottom. Pasquet had a small explosive charge that he'd stick to a window, blowing it out. The crew of the *Oregon* would attempt to rescue the drowning hostages while he and his men swam away. The barrel inside the sub would then explode a few minutes later along with the others, ripping the sub apart. It would be a perfect distraction for their getaway.

A tour bus stopped next to the truck. Pasquet smiled. Just who he was waiting for. Two hostages certainly wouldn't be enough if the crew of the *Oregon* decided to turn their weaponry on him and his men. Although the people of the Corporation called themselves mercenaries, Pasquet knew they wouldn't harm civilians, which made his job that much easier.

He went outside to watch twenty tourists pile off the bus. The tour guide got out of the driver's seat and Pasquet waved him over.

"Where's Captain Batiste?" the guide asked.

"He's inside the sub getting everything ready," Pasquet replied with a grin. "We have a very special trip in store for you and your guests today."

Pasquet mentally calculated how long it would take to tie up and blindfold the tourists and then motor out to the wreck. He didn't want to leave much slack time after they dumped the barrels. He thought now should be about right to start the timer sequence.

He clicked the button in his pocket. Simultaneously, the bombs in all twenty barrels began their countdown. Sixty minutes to detonation.

34

Berlin

It was only a few weeks to the official start of spring, but Germany's winter wasn't giving up easily. Three inches of fluffy snow coated the Berlin streets, and thick flakes continued to fall. The flight into Tegel Airport on the northwest side of the city had been bumpy, but Tiny Gunderson had put the Corporation's Gulfstream on the runway without a hitch. He planned to get some sleep in the cabin while Juan and Eric made their excursion to the Humboldt University of Berlin.

Juan got the last four-wheel drive on the rental lot, an Audi station wagon that had so far acquitted itself admirably. Only the highways had been scoured by snowplows' blades, leaving the thoroughfares and side streets caked and rutted. Buses and two-wheel-drive sedans were slowed to a crawl, but the trams that plied the city streets on rails moved easily, unhindered by the snowfall.

Now that they had arrived at their destination, Eric had to risk doing an online search of the library's catalog to find out if Lutzen's doctoral thesis was still at the university's main campus or in one of its multiple libraries located around the city. It would have been a long flight for nothing if the dissertation had been trashed, or destroyed during World War II bombing campaigns, or never filed with the library in the first place.

While Eric checked the library's database, Juan performed a series of quick turns through Berlin's streets to make sure they weren't being followed. Although they'd taken every precaution to prevent Lawrence Kensit from knowing where they were going, Juan couldn't help feeling that they were missing something, a piece of the puzzle that made it possible for Kensit to track their movements.

Max's information about Hector Bazin only confirmed that Kensit was willing to go to any lengths to keep his plans secret. To have a mercenary as skilled and brutal as Bazin at his beck and call wouldn't have come cheap, and bombing an office in Midtown Manhattan was a big risk.

"I got a hit," Eric said. "Gunther Lutzen. Real person. Physics doctoral student. Filed his thesis in 1901."

"Tell me it's still in the library," Juan said. "Tiny's going to be unhappy if we come back empty-handed."

"The dissertation is on file, but it's so old that it hasn't been digitized so we'll have to see it in person."

Juan nodded, happy that they'd flown to Berlin. If they'd done their search online, hoping to read the thesis back in New York, they might have tipped Kensit off about their intentions. "Where do we find it?"

"It's in the special collections at the Jacob and Wilhelm Grimm Center."

"A library named after the Brothers Grimm? How appropriate. Let's hope this fairy tale has a happier ending."

"It's a new building in central Berlin. They moved all of their natural sciences books to a different library, but most of the old theses and rare documents are at the Grimm Center. Lucky for us, it's only about ten minutes from here. I've got the route mapped out."

"Can we check the thesis out?"

"No. Because it's so old, it can be examined only at the library. Besides, we don't have a library card."

Satisfied that they didn't have a tail, Juan followed Eric's directions.

"What is Lutzen's thesis called?" Juan asked.

"I plugged it into my phone's translator, but I don't know how good it is with scientific terminology. We should get a more definitive translation when we're back on the *Oregon*."

"Spitballing is fine for now."

Eric furrowed his brow at the screen. "It says 'On the detection and perception of minor atom particles and radioactive decay.'"

"What are 'minor atom particles'?"

"I don't know. The abstract isn't online, if they even wrote abstracts back then. It could mean subatomic particles."

"It doesn't give us much to go on. Why would Kensit be so desperate to keep it secret?"

"When I was in college, I studied that era of physics experimentation, and it really was an exciting period in the science." Eric became animated as he talked about it. "In the span of ten years, from 1895 to 1905, some of the most critical discoveries and hypotheses in scientific history were made. In 1895, Wilhelm Röntgen discovered X-rays. The next year, Henri Becquerel and

Marie Curie found that certain chemical elements gave off rays that fogged unexposed photographic plates and called the phenomenon radioactivity. In 1897, J. J. Thomson discovered electrons. Ernest Rutherford built on their work in 1899 and determined that uranium gave off alpha and beta rays. And on and on until 1905, when a Swiss patent clerk published his special theory of relativity."

"I didn't know Einstein was Swiss."

"He was a draft dodger. He moved there from Germany to avoid Army service. Kind of ironic, now that he's considered one of the fathers of the atomic bomb."

"Where does Gunther Lutzen fit in?"

"At the time, Berlin University was one of the premier centers for theoretical nuclear physics and quantum mechanics. Max Planck was one of the first physicists to accept Einstein's theory, which was surprisingly controversial back then. Planck, who subsequently won the Nobel Prize in physics, was also a professor at the university. If Lutzen got his doctorate there, he was among some of the giants in the field."

"If Lutzen's work was so groundbreaking, why haven't we heard of him?"

Eric shrugged. "I just did a quick search of the physics literature. He never published, and his work was never referenced in anyone else's papers. If the work doesn't show up in a peer-reviewed journal, it essentially doesn't exist. Lutzen may have been preparing his findings for a paper when he died. That could be the journal that Kensit found. It's also possible that his work was *too* groundbreaking."

"'Too groundbreaking'?"

"It's possible Lutzen's ideas were so novel that he had trouble getting his work published. Enrico Fermi, one of the scientists on the Manhattan Project, submitted a paper to the journal *Nature* in 1934, explaining the structure of the atom as we know it today, and it was rejected for being 'too remote from reality.' If Lutzen's work was that far ahead of its time, he may have been trying to find more evidence to support it."

"In the Caribbean?"

"We won't know what he was looking for until I can see the thesis."

"We'll need just a couple of minutes with it," Juan said. He still had his camera glasses with him. When they reached the library, they'd request the thesis, which would be brought to their carousel. Juan would flip through each page to get a high-resolution image of the entire document and then transmit it back to Overholt for a complete translation by the CIA.

Juan found a parking space on the street in front of the Grimm Center, a gray concrete building that was all right angles and which had narrow slits for windows. Given the austere façade, he thought the name Grimm was fitting in more ways than one.

He and Eric hustled inside, brushing away snowflakes as they approached the main desk. They were directed to a librarian on the sixth floor who could help them with the special collections.

Their path took them through the building's central atrium, and Juan was momentarily taken aback. Unlike the center's cold and uninviting exterior, the atrium was a stunning architectural statement brimming with warmth and light. From the atrium's ground floor, terraced balconies of reading stations with forest green tables climbed to the sixth floor. The walls were clad in rich wood, and a grid of skylights provided much of the illumination. Thick carpeting muffled any rustling of paper or whispered conversations.

When they got to the librarian's station, a ponytailed student wearing a name tag reading "Greta" said something in German. Though Juan was fluent in Spanish, Russian, and Arabic, his German was minimal.

"I don't suppose you speak English," he said.

"English, yes," she said with a smile and a heavy accent. "A little."

"We would like to look at a thesis from 1901 by a student named Gunther Lutzen." Eric showed her the title of the thesis.

Greta furrowed her brow, then looked up at Juan. "You also want this document?"

Juan's muscles tightened. "What do you mean 'also'?"

"A man has come minutes ago to see it. The librarian, Herr Schmidt, has just taken him there."

"What did this man look like?"

"He is . . . oh, how do you say . . . *schwarz*?" She rubbed the skin of her arm and pointed at a black stapler.

"He has dark skin?" Juan said.

Greta nodded. "*Ja*. Very dark."

Bazin. He had anticipated their move yet again despite all of Juan's precautions. If he got the thesis and destroyed it, they might lose their last link between Gunther Lutzen and Lawrence Kensit.

"Where did they go?"

"To the archives on this level," she said, confused at Juan's sudden urgency. "It's there." She pointed toward the other end of the building.

Juan and Eric took off running down the hall. When they were alone, Juan stopped and pulled up his pant leg to access the hidden panel in his combat leg. He drew the .45 ACP Colt Defender and closed the leg back up. He hid the gun under his jacket. Eric wasn't armed, but he didn't have much use for a weapon since he wasn't trained for combat. Juan considered sending Eric for library security, but they would be unarmed. The police would be better, but this would be over by the time they arrived.

Still, Eric couldn't come with him empty-handed. Juan removed the C-4 pack, detonator cap, and activation switch and shoved them into Eric's hands.

"What should I do with these?" Eric asked.

"Not sure. You'll think of something. Stay behind me."

They continued on to a door marked "Archiv." Juan eased it open, the oiled hinges making no sound. He crouched and pushed his way inside with his eye on the Colt's iron sight. He swept the long room, which was filled with stacks of bound theses and rare books.

He crept along the row of shelves until he reached the end while Eric went the other direction. Juan swiveled around and saw Bazin behind a tall, thin man who had to be Schmidt. Juan would have had no compunction about shooting a murderer like Bazin without warning, but he was almost completely hidden by Schmidt, who had his back to Juan with his arms raised.

Bazin had a gun on Schmidt. The thesis was in Bazin's other hand.

Juan didn't have time to get a different angle on him.

"Let him go, Bazin!" he yelled, his pistol ready to fire.

Bazin pressed his gun to the bespectacled man's temple, making sure to keep the terrified librarian between him and Juan. Bazin's face was completely obscured behind Schmidt's head. Even with the Colt's Crimson Trace laser sight, Juan had no shot. The elbow of Bazin's arm made a motion that looked like he was tucking the thesis in his coat.

No one else seemed to be in the archives with them.

"You're quicker to get here than I expected, Cabrillo," Bazin said with a French accent as he edged toward a door on the opposite side of the room.

"How did you know I'd be here?"

"Ah, that is the question, isn't it?" Bazin inched closer to the door.

"You couldn't have tapped our communications to find out."

"It's definitely a puzzle. That was clever with the glasses, to get my identity."

Juan kept his aim on Bazin, ready for any mistake by him. Eric was poised in the next row with the C-4 and detonator, but Juan subtly shook his head to back off.

"You must realize you'll never make it out of Germany," Juan said.

"I'm not worried."

"What does worry you?"

Bazin was next to the door. "Nothing much, when you have the advantages I have."

"I know you work for Lawrence Kensit."

"And without this thesis, that's all you will know."

There was a polished metal plate beside the door with the name of the department in the next room. Juan could make out Bazin's face in the reflection. "Bazin, I see you."

Bazin looked at him in the mirrored finish. "You'll have to shoot him to get me."

"Not what I had in mind." Juan shifted the Colt's sight to the metal sign. He waited until Bazin eyed him with a sneer, then triggered the laser.

Bazin cried out as the powerful beam blinded him and he let go of Schmidt, who ran toward Juan in a panic. There was no way to fire again safely until he was out of the way.

"Down!" Juan shouted. Schmidt tripped over his own feet and

went sprawling, bashing his head against a metal shelf. Juan had his first clear field of fire at Bazin, who was still blinking away the dazzling effect of the laser.

The door to the hall flung open and another Haitian charged in, dual pistols blazing. The clever Bazin had been stalling, waiting for his man to arrive and outflank Juan. Juan didn't have time for more than a couple of wild shots as he dived for cover.

At the same time, the C-4 sailed over the shelf and landed on the floor next to the dual-wielding gunman. He looked with curiosity at the device before it detonated.

The blast hurled him like a rag doll against a shelf, knocking it over and causing a domino effect of tumbling shelves.

Bazin took advantage of the distraction and darted through the door next to him.

"Eric!" Juan yelled. "Are you all right?"

"I'm okay. Just buried under some books."

Juan pulled the dazed Schmidt to his feet and pointed at Eric. "Help him." Schmidt nodded, and Juan dashed through the hallway door in pursuit of Bazin.

As soon as he got outside, he saw Bazin running around the corner. When he saw Juan, he changed course and shot out the glass window into the central atrium. He jumped through and onto a table, past the students who were already rushing toward the exits in response to the blast and gunshots.

Juan chased after him. The masses of students in the background prevented him from taking a shot at Bazin, who vaulted down the terraces.

Juan was one terrace behind. Their jumps down to the next level were synchronized. When he reached the bottom, Bazin avoided the main entrance where the students were streaming out and instead crashed through an emergency exit.

Juan burst through the door seconds later to find near-blizzard conditions. Wind howled, and the icy flakes needled his exposed skin. The only good thing about the weather was that he could tell exactly where Bazin had gone.

Juan sprinted after the fresh pair of footprints.

35

Martinique

Max kept track of the recovery process from his engineering station in the op center. According to the latest reports from the divers on the *Roraima*, shoring up the collapsed steel girders was complete and they were beginning to dig through the debris where they'd gotten the radiation readings and found the camera lens. Eddie and Linc were about to go down for their second dive and join the search. If any photo tins were left intact down there, they should be relatively near the surface since the passenger cabins had been at the top of the ship.

"Max," Mark Murphy said with uncharacteristic alarm, "you better get over here and see this."

"Are the radiation readings spiking?" Max asked as he went over.

"Worse. I just got an email."

"From who?"

"That's problem number one. I don't know."

When Max reached Murph's station, he immediately saw the second problem. The email contained two photo attachments. The first was a picture of the interior of a tourist submarine with two rows of people, sitting back to back, with their wrists bound behind them and blindfolded. In the background was a plastic shipping barrel. The second photo showed what was in the barrel. It was enough dynamite to blast the sub to bits.

The message had only one line: *Stay away or they all die.*

Max frowned at the screen. "You don't know how you got this?"

Murph threw his hands in the air, flummoxed. "This is my private Corporation account. Nobody but the people on this ship should have the email address."

The breach was further confirmation that their security had been compromised.

"What does he mean 'stay away'?" Murph said.

Max turned to Linda. "Show me the harbor."

The main screen displayed the feed from one of the deck cameras. It panned left to right until Max spotted an odd white vessel in the distance moving slowly toward them.

"Zoom in."

Linda magnified the image until they could see a high-definition shot of a submarine that had catamaran pontoons on either side plowing through the rough seas. Armed men in wetsuits and scuba gear braced themselves on both pontoons amid dozens of barrels like the one in the email. Each of them had to have been filled with explosives.

"They're going to blow up the *Roraima*," Linda said.

"I'm getting really sick of Kensit knowing what we're doing and where we'll be," Murph said.

Max agreed. "This took some planning. They didn't just throw together dynamite and a sub hijacking at the last minute. They've known we were coming here as long as we have."

"Which means Kensit knows what we're looking for," Murph said. "Destroying the *Roraima* is the only way to keep us from finding it."

"He must also know at least some of our capabilities. That's why his men brought the hostages. They realized we would have torpedoed them the instant we knew it was them."

"We can't let them destroy the ship," Murph said. "We'll never find Kensit if that happens."

"What are our tactical options?"

"Offensive weapons are off the table with hostages inside."

"And we can't send divers to attack," Linda said. "Even with the rough seas, they'll be spotted long before they could sneak up on the sub. They'd kill everyone on board before we got within a hundred feet."

"They'll probably kill everyone anyway," Murph replied. Given what Max had seen about Kensit and Bazin's operations, he had no doubt the hostages were in grave danger no matter what they did.

"We have to do something," Murph said.

"What if we—" Max said and then stopped himself. He suddenly had an idea that might work, but if anyone really was listening in on their conversations, he'd have to risk putting it into play without conferring with anyone else.

"What if we what?" Murph asked.

Max shook his head as if he was frustrated with himself. "Nothing. It's too crazy. We need to back off."

"And just let them erase the evidence we're looking for?"

"We don't have a choice," Max said, hoping he sounded convincing. He called down to the moon pool. "Get me Eddie."

When Eddie was on the line, Max said, "We've got company coming, half a dozen hostiles on the outside of a sub carrying barrels of explosives."

"But we've got five men down at the *Roraima*, digging through it. They're about to come up for their decompression stops."

"I know. There are hostages inside the sub, so we need to make sure they're not harmed. I want you and Linc to take SPPs down with you just as a precaution."

Eddie sounded confused. "As a precaution?"

"I'm sorry but I can't explain right now. When you get down there, send your people up and you two hunker down inside the PUH." Max hoped that the portable underwater habitat would provide a safe haven for Eddie and Linc. "Wait for my signal that the hostages are no longer in danger. You'll know it when you hear it. You've only got about ten minutes before the sub gets here, so hurry."

"Roger that." He hung up.

"SPPs?" Murph said. "But you said—"

Max interrupted Murph before he could blurt out anything more. "I need you to trust me." He addressed everyone in the op center. "We are not going to let those hostages be killed. Do you understand?"

They all nodded, but Max could tell they were confused.

They did trust him, however. That's why no one asked why he had sent Eddie and Linc down with SPP-1 underwater pistols that fired deadly steel darts, firearms specially designed for Soviet-era Special Forces and acquired by the Corporation.

The crew knew Max was sending his men into battle.

36

Berlin

Juan followed the footprints around the building, where they disappeared under an elevated train platform. At the far end he caught sight of Bazin's silhouette as he approached a parked Mercedes SUV. He jumped in, started it up, and sped directly toward Juan.

Juan put two shots into the windshield before he had to roll out of the way. Neither bullet hit Bazin. Juan ran for the Audi.

Eric had successfully threaded his way through the students milling outside and was just arriving at the Audi wagon. Juan pointed at the SUV rocketing away. "Bazin's getting away! Get in."

The keyless entry chirped and Juan fired up the engine, dropping it into gear even before Eric had the door closed. The tires bit into the snow, Juan scraping the car in front of them with a screech of metal in his haste to get out of the parking spot.

The Mercedes skidded around the corner and out of sight.

Juan stood on the accelerator. The Audi spun all four wheels as it scrabbled for purchase on the slick road.

The Mercedes was heavier and had better traction, but the lighter Audi had the advantage of four-wheel drive. Juan closed within half a block before the Mercedes started taking a series of hard turns in an effort to lose them.

Even though the traffic was light, there were still plenty of cars to weave around. The Mercedes bounced off a Volvo as it overtook it, sending the sedan spinning into the path of the Audi. Juan wrenched the wheel around to avoid T-boning the screaming driver.

"He's going to kill someone if we don't stop him," Eric said.

"Working on it," Juan replied through gritted teeth.

They rounded another corner, the Mercedes banking off parked cars, and Juan put the Audi into a four-wheel drift like a rally car driver to make up the rest of the distance. He nosed the front of the Audi against the SUV's right rear fender and yanked the steering wheel to the left. The Mercedes skidded sideways, but it had enough power driving the rear wheels to keep from spinning out.

The Audi lost contact and Juan had to steady the wheel to keep it from careening into a light post. The Mercedes pulled a couple of car lengths ahead of them.

Juan had to put an end to the chase one way or another. He unrolled his window, drew the Colt, and aimed at the SUV's rear tire. He squeezed off three rounds. The third connected and the tire blew out.

The exposed rim bit into the snow, making the back end of the Mercedes fishtail back and forth. As Juan brought his arm back inside the window, the Audi hit a patch of ice and he had to slow considerably to regain control. The Mercedes was half a block in front, so he stomped the accelerator to catch up.

Bazin was approaching a red light, but he showed no signs of slowing. A yellow street tram approached on the cross street from the left. While the city's trams rode on steel rails embedded in the pavement, their seven cars were much more massive than a bus and took longer to slow down, especially on rails made more slippery by the snow and ice.

Bazin accelerated in an attempt to make it through the intersection before the tram got there. The three good tires churned at the snow, but the rim spun uselessly, slowing the SUV.

He didn't make it.

The tram slammed into the rear half of the SUV, missing the driver's door by mere inches. The Mercedes was crushed and then flew into the air in a neat pirouette. The tram barely shuddered from the impact.

Juan didn't want to suffer the same fate. He twisted the wheel to the left and feathered the gas pedal to maintain contact with the road. With the benefit of grip from all four tires, the Audi was able to maneuver across the intersection behind the slowing tram with millimeters to spare. Juan hit the brakes and the antilock system chattered as it strained to halt the car as it headed in the direction of a bridge over the Spree River, Berlin's main waterway.

The skewed angle across the road and the extra speed carried the Audi over an embankment and into a park leading down to the river beside the bridge. The snow on the hill was even deeper, and if the car stopped, Juan would never get it going again without a tow. He took his foot off the brake and accelerated left, risking a plunge into the icy river.

After zigzagging across the park, he crashed through a chain barrier and onto a road. He headed back to the scene of the accident.

His route had taken Juan all the way around the block. He came up behind the now stopped tram, which was surrounded by a snarl of vehicles that didn't allow Juan to get closer than half a block away before he had to stop as well.

He threw open the door and jumped out, running toward the scene of the accident. The tram's passengers had already filed off at the behest of the driver, who was helping Bazin out of his wrecked vehicle. Even from this distance, Juan could see that every air bag had inflated, sparing him any serious injury.

Bazin pushed the tram driver away and stumbled from the wreckage. He searched the crowd until he locked eyes with Juan, then scanned the traffic jam around him before settling on the tram itself. He ducked his head to use the milling passengers for cover and ran inside. The tram started moving despite howls of protest from the driver, who tried to get back on before the doors shut in his face.

Juan ran alongside the accelerating tram and shot the glass door at its tail end three times, shattering it. He pocketed the gun and latched on with both hands as his feet hit an ice patch. He slipped and was dragged along by the tram, the remnants of the broken safety glass digging into the flesh of his palms.

With all his strength, Juan heaved himself through the gaping hole where the door had been. As soon as he hit the floor, bullets ricocheted off the wall by his head. He took cover behind the nearest seat and returned fire, but Bazin was concealed too well in the driver's cockpit. Juan tried pulling the emergency brake above the door, but Bazin overrode the signal.

Bazin leaned out from the cockpit and took a couple of more shots. Juan did the same with his last two rounds, narrowly missing Bazin's head. Once again, Bazin poked his head out, but the slide on his pistol was locked back, indicating he, too, was empty.

At that point, Bazin placed what looked like the driver's bag on the deadman brake pedal, the safety device that was supposed to stop the train if the driver became incapacitated. Though Bazin left the cockpit, the uncontrolled tram continued racing along the streets, bashing any vehicle in its path. Bazin took the cockpit's fire extinguisher, went to the closest passenger window, and smashed the extinguisher against the glass. He was going to climb out, leaving Juan on the runaway tram and heading directly for a broad T intersection at full speed. If it didn't stop before it hit the curve in the track, the tram would derail as it took the corner and plow through the front lobby of an office building at forty miles an hour.

Juan charged forward and threw himself at Bazin, catching the mercenary's arm before he could tumble out. Bazin teetered on the edge.

"Not before I get this," Juan said, and plunged his hand into Bazin's coat. His fingers grasped the edge of the thesis and he pulled it free.

Except Bazin also grabbed part of the bound document, opening it wide. He leaned out and the weight was too much for Juan to hold with one hand. Bazin fell, still gripping the back half of the thesis, which tore right down the binding, leaving Juan holding the other half.

He watched the nimble Bazin roll through the snow and then spring to his feet before running toward a side street. Juan ran into the cockpit of the tram, kicked the bag off the pedal, and slapped a large red button that he hoped was the emergency stop.

The brakes squealed and the tram lurched and skidded on the rails. It slowed to twenty miles an hour when it reached the curve.

It leaned to one side but didn't derail and then came to a stop halfway through the intersection.

Juan opened the passenger door to see Eric pull up in the Audi.

"Are you okay?" Eric asked as Juan got in.

"I'm fine," Juan said, disgusted, "but Bazin got away."

"With the thesis?"

"Half of it." He showed Eric the ripped document.

"I can start translating that on the plane. Hopefully, it's still enough to figure out what Kensit has been working on."

"Let's get back to the airport before we have the entire Berlin police department asking us questions."

Eric drove away as the wail of sirens echoed off the buildings.

37

Martinique

"The sub is one hundred feet from the bow of the *Roraima*," Linda said, reading the scan from the passive sonar.

"What about our divers?"

"All recovered in the moon pool," Hali said. "MacD said he spotted what could have been a corner of the metal photo tin, but his air was exhausted before he could dig it up."

"What about grabbing it with Little Geek?"

"He said Little Geek won't fit where he saw it. It was a corner he had to reach his arm into. He said he told Eddie where it was when he passed them on the way up." The full face masks they were wearing let them communicate up close underwater.

"Where are Eddie and Linc now?" Max asked Murph, who was still operating Little Geek.

"Camera shows them inside the portable underwater habitat," Murph said. "They should be out of the sub's view." The PUH was an inflatable fabric dome that was anchored to the *Roraima* and contained an air bubble inside to allow the divers who were wearing regulators to rest, converse about the dive, or even get a drink of water.

Max knew curiosity about why they were down there was killing Murph, but he was glad Murph understood enough not to ask questions when he shouldn't.

The front of the sub was about to pass over the disintegrating *Roraima* twenty feet above its prow. Max couldn't wait any longer. It was the closest the sub would get to the *Oregon* before they started dumping the barrels of explosives.

"Linda, get ready to send a single ping."

All eyes whipsawed to Max. Linda was shocked by the command. "But Eddie and Linc—"

"Will be safe inside the PUH"—*I hope,* he thought, but didn't say. "It's the only thing I could think of to save the hostages. I'm sorry I couldn't tell you all before, but if our security has in fact been compromised, I didn't want any eavesdroppers to know what I was planning."

Linda nodded her understanding and raised her finger over the button that would activate a sonar ping.

Passive sonar detects submarines underwater using the noise generated by the sub itself. Active sonar sends out sound signals that bounce back to give a picture of the object, much like the clicks dolphins use to find fish. Dolphins are also thought to employ these clicking sounds to stun fish. At 220 decibels, their echolocation emanations are among the loudest noises emitted by any animal.

The active ping of the *Oregon*'s sonar registered at 240 decibels. If a diver were unlucky enough to be swimming next to the transmitter when a ping was sent, his internal organs would be jellied, killing him instantly. The sub was three hundred yards away, so the ping would only stun the divers, as if they had been hit by a flashbang grenade. Eddie and Linc would be protected inside the PUH because their lungs and ears would be above the water level and the sound pressure would be lessened by its transition from water to air. The hostages would be safe for the same reason. Eddie and Linc would have a few minutes to attack the dazed divers on the sub.

That was the plan anyway.

The sub was cruising slowly, likely to make it easier to drop the barrels in a regular pattern along the length of the *Roraima*.

"Linda," Max said, "send our surprise."

The deafening ping blasted forth, audible even in the op center.

"I hope you got the message, guys," he said under his breath.

Eddie and Linc had been discussing why Max was being so cryptic when the ping hit the dome's fabric so hard that it temporarily caved in. The sound inside the PUH was loud enough to make their ears ring. Eddie couldn't imagine how loud it would have been in the water.

"That must be the cue Max was talking about," Linc said.

They quickly donned their masks and drew their SPP-1 underwater pistols. "You take the port side of the sub and I'll take starboard. We should assume they're armed as well." The SPPs couldn't be reloaded on the fly, so each of them had brought a pair of the pistols that held four bolts each. The disadvantage was that at this depth, the weapons had an effective range of only twenty feet.

They ducked under the surface and emerged from the PUH to

see the white sub gliding fifty feet above them. Through the *Rorai-ma*'s remaining intact girders, Eddie could make out the silhouette of a scuba diver thrashing from the effects of the sonar disruption.

An object was tumbling down toward them. It looked unsettlingly like a depth charge, which meant it had to be one of the barrels that Max had mentioned. It crashed into a rusted girder, which collapsed and sent a pile of metal down with it. The tangle of steel landed on the barrel. It was only twenty feet from the location where MacD said he had spotted the object he thought might be the corner of the tin holding the photographic plates they were looking for.

There was no time to search for it now. Their priority was to eliminate the threat from the divers holding the sub passengers hostage. Eddie and Linc pumped their legs to intercept their targets before they regained their senses.

Linc angled away toward the port side of the sub while Eddie swam straight toward the scuba diver, who was still holding his hands to his ears. Blood tinged the water from the man's ruptured eardrums. He saw Eddie swimming toward him and fumbled with a small speargun that dangled from his wrist, but Eddie shot two bolts into his chest before he could fire. More blood, and the body went limp.

Eddie kicked for the sub, where he saw another barrel teetering over the edge of the stern platform. He caught the bottom of it with his shoulder and pushed it back up before it could fall.

The diver next to the barrel, who had been struggling to wrestle it over the side in his diminished state, was shocked by Eddie's sudden appearance. He reeled backward and managed to get his finger on the trigger of his speargun just as Eddie's bolt lanced through his mask. His spear fired harmlessly into the pontoon.

Eddie checked the diver and saw that his mask was outfitted with a bone-conduction communications device. Even with a ruptured eardrum, the man would still be able to hear a signal transmitted from another diver. Eddie had to assume all of the divers were similarly equipped.

He turned and spotted a third diver by the bow. The diver was paying no attention to him but was instead fumbling with a device in his hands. The light from the sub's interior illuminated him enough for Eddie to see that it was a shaped charge of plastic explosives.

The diver must have gotten the message that they were under attack and was attempting to destroy the sub.

Eddie dolphin-kicked toward him, the SPP-1 outstretched. He fired at thirty feet, but the bolt clanged against the sub's hull. He dropped the pistol and whipped the spare from his belt. He fired all four bolts in rapid succession, hoping one would hit before the diver could trigger the bomb.

Three of the bolts hit the target, one in the arm and two in the torso, but at this range they lacked the punch needed to disable him. The diver slapped the plastique against the sub and flipped the trigger.

The explosion was small but powerful. It ripped the diver to shreds and knocked Eddie back. He shook his head, and saw that the sub's hull hadn't been torn apart. In his haste and disorientation, the diver had placed the charge on an electrical conduit instead of the main body of the hull itself.

The sub was moderately damaged. A huge chunk had been gouged out of the conduit and the hull dented inward. Eddie didn't see any signs of a leak.

He went to the cockpit dome and knocked on it, startling the pilot. Eddie gave the thumbs-up, the diver's gesture to surface. The pilot shook his head and started babbling in French. He gesticulated toward the location of the explosion and then back toward the controls. Eddie didn't have to know the language to understand that the blast had disabled the sub.

He inspected the site of the explosion and found severed wires jutting from the hull. The sub wasn't going anywhere on its own.

The pilot ran from the cockpit into the sub's passenger cabin and Eddie swam along outside to follow. The pilot freed a groggy young man from bondage and then went over to the barrel of explosives. Eddie realized with horror that he was about to open it without knowing if it was booby-trapped.

He pounded on the window to get the pilot's attention. Eddie shook his head vigorously and made an exploding motion with his hands. The pilot got the message and backed off. He came over to the window and pointed to the barrel and then his watch. He flashed five fingers three times.

Eddie nodded. Fifteen minutes left before the barrel exploded.

Linc swam into view. Eddie waved him over and they touched masks.

"I took care of the three on the port side," Linc said. He saw the damage from the explosion. "That must have been the thump I heard."

"The sub's too damaged to move," Eddie said. "And we've got fifteen minutes until that barrel of explosives inside goes off."

"Which probably means we've got fifteen minutes until they all go off, including the one down inside the *Roraima*."

"We can't open the hatch this far down to evacuate the passengers."

"Even if we could they'd all drown before we could get them up top."

"Right. You hightail it to the *Oregon*. We're going to need help from them to get that sub surfaced."

"What about you?"

"I'm going to try to get the photo tin before the bomb blows."

"I'll be back with the cavalry," Linc said, and churned his powerful legs toward the *Oregon*'s moon pool.

Eddie turned back to the window to see the pilot's pleading face.

"*Aidez-nous,*" the man said.

Eddie understood that. *Help us.*

He smiled and circled his thumb and forefinger in the OK sign. *Help is on the way.*

Then he swam back down into the depths of the *Roraima.*

As Linc swift-kicked toward the *Oregon*, Max and the rest of the crew in the op center watched him on the big screen via the underwater camera lowered from the moon pool. Linc hadn't been down long enough to need a decompression stop so he swam straight up into the pool.

Max had the technician put him on the line before he was even out of the water.

"Where's Eddie?" Max asked.

"He's trying to retrieve the photo plate," Linc said. The view from Little Geek confirmed that Eddie was throwing up clouds of silt digging through the wreck. "But we've got a bigger problem. The barrel inside the sub is going to blow in thirteen minutes and the controls have jammed. They're stuck down there."

With that little time left, Max didn't have the luxury of debating the two primary ways of bringing up a submerged vessel: either floating it or pulling it up. It would take precise placement and synchronized inflation of air bags to bring it up without capsizing it. The best choice was to use one of the deck cranes to hoist it. They didn't have to raise it all the way out of the water, just enough to be able to open the hatch and not drown the occupants.

"Linda," Max said, "get us over the sub now. Put someone on the number one crane, and divers in the water to attach the cables." He radioed down instructions to Linc to attach the cables to the sub.

Linda rushed to the helm. There was no anchor to raise. The *Oregon* had been station-keeping with its thrusters. She nudged the ship over to the *Roraima*, expertly placing it so the crane's extended boom was directly over the sub.

Once the divers were in the water with Linc, Max ordered the moon pool doors closed. He didn't want the sub hostages seeing the unusual configuration as they were raised to the surface.

He wasn't worried about damaging the sub further. Speed was of the essence. He had a camera lowered with the crane's hook so that he could monitor what was happening on board. Five minutes later, Linc signaled that the hooks were secure. Max gave the order and the cable spooled up, grew taut, and the sub began to rise. The divers rode up on it except for Linc, who descended out of camera range. At the same time, Max had a lifeboat lowered to take the hostages aboard.

While the sub was coming up, Max checked with Murph, who was watching Eddie's efforts on Little Geek's monitor. The cloudy water made it hard to see any progress, but he was still digging.

"What's that?" Max said when he saw movement at the top of the screen. He thought it might be Linc coming to help Eddie. Instead, it was a piece of steel that must have been dislodged by the falling barrel.

Max went cold. "Warn him!"

"Not enough time," Murph said, and drove Little Geek forward into the path of the falling debris. Seconds later, the ROV lurched downward and the screen went dark.

Max and Murph looked at each other with dread, but there was nothing more they could do. They had to concentrate on getting the hostages to safety.

"Time?" Max said.

Hali had been keeping track. "We've got four minutes left, if the sub's pilot is accurate."

The sub's white pressure vessel broached the surface and the divers were already spinning its hatch open. The hostages, who had been untied by the pilot, hurried out and onto the lifeboat. When all of them had been evacuated, the divers joined them, the last one detaching the crane's cable before he got in the boat.

Rather than rendezvous with the *Oregon*, the lifeboat motored away to put as much distance as it could between it and the sub, which continued to float, the barrels filled with explosives lining the pontoons and rear deck.

"Linda, get us out of here."

Her eyes betrayed the same pain he had felt about leaving Linc and Eddie behind, but he had to put the safety of the ship first. Linda ran the engines up to full thrust and the revolutionary magnetohydronamic power plant accelerated the *Oregon* faster than any freighter had a right to go. Max watched the sub recede in the distance.

Hali had helpfully superimposed the countdown on the screen. When the timer read zero, they all braced themselves.

Nothing happened. A few more seconds elapsed. Still nothing.

Murph shrugged. "Maybe Kensit's men aren't as good at—"

He was interrupted by a huge geyser of flame that shattered the submarine, tossing fragments of metal hundreds of yards in all directions. The boom of the explosion reverberated around the op center two seconds later.

When the echo died down, Murph said, "I guess I spoke too soon."

"How's the lifeboat?" Max asked Hali.

"They report that they were pelted by a few pieces of the sub, but no damage or injuries."

Max nodded. "Linda, turn us around and take us back to the *Roraima*. Get some more divers ready to look for Eddie and Linc. Have the lifeboat meet us there."

She brought the *Oregon* about and headed back for the shipwreck. Only a few pieces of the sub remained on the surface.

As they approached the site of the *Roraima*, Max spied two heads bobbing in the water. Fearing the worst, he had Murph zoom the camera in.

Where he had expected to see lifeless corpses floating on the waves he instead saw Eddie and Linc waving to the *Oregon* and smiling. In Eddie's right hand was a shiny metal box the size of a paperback book. The lifeboat motored over to pick them up.

Max breathed a sigh of relief and patted Murph on the shoulder.

"That was a nice maneuver with Little Geek," Max said. "That probably saved Eddie's life."

Murph exaggeratedly cracked his knuckles. "All in a day's work."

"We'll just dock your partner fee until a new one is paid for."

Murph laughed until he saw that Max wasn't joining in. He eyed Max with a serious look and then grinned. "Funny."

Max winked at Linda and they shared a silent chuckle.

"Max," Hali said, "I've got a call for you from Juan."

Max went over to the comm station and picked up the handset.

"There's the mystery man," Max said. "You've missed all the excitement here while you've been gallivanting around to who knows where."

"I know. Hali gave me the highlights."

"Can you tell me your destination yet?"

"We were in Berlin, and we had a bit of a commotion ourselves."

"You and Eric all right?"

"We managed to make it to the airport under the radar. If the police come calling, we'll claim we were innocent bystanders to what happened."

"Can you tell me what this top secret mission was now?"

"That's why I'm calling. As we've been driving back to the airport, Eric's been studying the part of a thesis we recovered from the Berlin University library using his phone's translation app. The thesis was written by Gunther Lutzen, the scientist who was aboard the *Roraima*. Now that Stoney's had a chance to get a crude translation of some of the document, he thinks he knows how our security has been compromised."

"And it's okay to be discussing this on the phone? Kensit hasn't cracked our encryption?"

"He doesn't need to. Eric thinks Kensit has developed a neutrino telescope. At least that's what Eric is calling it for now."

Max frowned. He was an accomplished engineer and he'd never heard of such a thing. "How does looking at space help him eavesdrop on our plans?"

"Eric can explain all this better when we get back to the *Oregon*, but it has nothing to do with space. Lutzen developed revolutionary theories about how to detect subatomic particles. They were decades ahead of their time, and some of the equations in the thesis are so advanced even Stoney is having trouble understanding them. He believes Kensit used those equations to build a device that lets him see anywhere in the world."

Now Max was really confused. "What do you mean 'anywhere'?"

"I mean," Juan said, "with this telescope, he could be looking at you right now and you'd never know it."

38

Although he was fuming about the failures of the day, Lawrence Kensit couldn't help but chuckle as he watched Max Hanley look warily around the op center as if he could spy a camera hidden in someone's lapel. In fact, Juan Cabrillo was correct. There was absolutely no way for him to know that Kensit could see and hear everything Hanley was doing and saying. The control room on Kensit's yacht was hundreds of miles away from the *Oregon*, being fed the signal from the Sentinel array buried deep underground.

Despite the focus on his larger goals, Kensit enjoyed the Peeping Tom aspect of his design, based on Gunther Lutzen's work. With one giant observation screen, plus half a dozen smaller monitors and various keyboards, touch screens, and joysticks, Kensit could view anything he wanted anywhere in the world. It really was like he had a superpower and he felt like a god viewing his subjects from afar, ready to affect their lives at his pleasure or whim. Of course, he saw himself as a benevolent god, having humanity's collective best interests in mind, but he could be wrathful when it was required for his grand design. The lesser beings didn't need to understand why things happened the way they did. It was simply his will and they were his servants.

Before he brought Brian Washburn into his control room, he called Hector Bazin. As soon as the call went through, he read the GPS coordinates of the private jet just taking off from Berlin and fed them into the computer, which zoomed in until it found the right altitude for the plane and locked onto it to follow it. In an instant, he was looking at the interior of the cabin. Bazin was alone and answered the phone.

"Cabrillo got part of the thesis," he said.

"I know," Kensit replied, "I just heard him talking to the *Oregon*. What happened?"

Bazin recounted the chase through Berlin. Knowing that Kensit was watching, he began leafing through the portion of the thesis that he managed to save, giving Kensit an opportunity to see the pages.

Kensit nodded approvingly. "Good. At least he doesn't have the most important equations. Now I'm the only person in the world who possesses all of the secrets of the neutrino telescope. Burn it as soon as you land."

"Yes, sir."

"Your man Pasquet is dead." He stated it matter-of-factly even though he knew Pasquet was Bazin's closest friend. Kensit never understood why people insisted on soft-pedaling bad news.

Bazin looked away for a moment, his jaw tightening. "How?"

"He failed to destroy the *Roraima*. I told him exactly how to proceed, but once they were underwater, I couldn't communicate with them anymore to warn them. They didn't anticipate the

Oregon's tactics. All of them were killed, and the *Oregon* may have managed to recover some of Lutzen's photo plates."

"And if they discover where the Sentinel array is hidden?"

"That's why I want you to go directly to Haiti. The next forty-eight hours are critical. Your objective is to protect Sentinel at all costs. Once our mission is finished, Sentinel is expendable and we can move on to Phase Two. Do you have enough men to defend it?"

Bazin nodded. "I have two dozen mercs left, and I can call in a favor from the Haitian National Police if it looks like we might be overrun by a larger force."

"Excellent. Let me know once you're at the bunker. After you're there, no one else goes in or out until the mission is over, understood?"

"Yes, sir."

Kensit hung up, and called for Washburn to join him in the control room.

Washburn stepped inside and gawked at the technology that was beyond his comprehension.

"After showing you my operation in Haiti," Kensit said, "I hope you realize that this is not a small operation. I have the money and resources to back up my efforts to make you president."

Washburn rolled his eyes, then caught himself. "Yes, you've got impressive technology, although I have no idea where that cave is since you blindfolded me on the way there and back. I can't pretend to know how any of the equipment in there works, but it looked expensive. The question is, so what? How is this going to help me get elected? Even if you make me vice president, there's the primary and general election to get through. Being VP didn't help Mondale or Gore."

"True, but they didn't have me. Since you will be dependent

on me not only for the election but also when you're president, I wanted to convince you that there is virtually no limit to my power."

Kensit typed in some coordinates and the foyer of a mansion appeared on the big screen. Washburn frowned until he realized what he was looking at.

"That's my house in Miami! When did you get this video?"

"It's not a recording. This is a real-time feed. Let's see if anyone's home." He rolled a trackball and it was as if a camera were moving up the winding stairs until he was looking down from the balcony. He wandered down one hall until he reached a closed door. He pushed right through and a woman in lingerie was putting on a skirt.

Washburn lunged toward the screen. "That's my wife!" He wheeled around with balled-up fists. "You—"

"No, no, Governor. Remember, I have guards right outside this door. We can do this just as well with you tied up."

"This is a trick. You've planted a camera in my house."

Kensit nodded appreciatively. "Good for you. That would be a logical assumption. It is, of course, wrong."

"Prove it."

"I will. Tell me someplace where you are absolutely positive I could not have planted a camera."

Washburn shrugged, and said sarcastically, "The Oval Office."

"I was hoping you'd choose something more unusual, but that will do."

The White House was one of the easiest places on earth to locate. He typed the name in and a satellite view of the familiar white structure was displayed on-screen.

"Is that all?" Washburn scoffed. "I could do that with Google maps and an iPhone."

"Really?" Kensit said. "Can you also do this?"

He zoomed down, the roof of the West Wing racing toward them until the view plunged through. Kensit stopped it when it reached the most recognizable office in the world.

If the room had been empty, Washburn might not have been so flabbergasted. But Kensit had anticipated his choice and knew that the president was meeting with his senior advisers that morning.

"This farm bill is causing us all kinds of problems in the polls, Mr. President," his chief of staff said. "We can't cut subsidies as much as the Senate wants or our party will get killed in the next election."

"Let Sandecker handle it," the president replied. He looked as relaxed as ever, lounging in his chair with a mug of coffee in one hand and a sheaf of papers in the other, reading glasses perched on his nose. "He'll be back from Brazil in a couple of days."

"Do you think the vice president can talk them down?"

"Sandecker's a clever guy. If *he* can't convince them, they're certainly not going to listen to *me*. Now, what's on the agenda for the military briefing today?"

The chairman of the Joint Chiefs sat forward. "There was another terrorist bombing in northern Pakistan this morning. Six dead, twenty wounded. North Korea is moving a thousand troops to the demilitarized zone, but we think it's just a planned division reinforcement. And the UNITAS exercise has begun in the Bahamas. Seventeen nations are participating. The Cubans and Venezuelans are sending ships to observe, but we don't anticipate any problems."

"Good. What about the trip to California next week that . . ."

Kensit turned down the volume. "Satisfied?"

If Washburn's jaw were any lower, he could have swallowed an ostrich egg.

"They have no clue we're watching them?"

"No."

"And you can see anywhere you want?"

Kensit grinned. "I've already explored the inside of some of the most secure facilities on earth: NORAD, Area 51, the Kremlin, the Vatican's secret archives, NATO headquarters, Fort Knox. Do you want to know the secret formula to Coca-Cola?"

"How . . . How are you doing this?"

Kensit paused as he thought about how much he would have to dumb down his explanation. "It's called a neutrino telescope. I had been calling it a quantum receiver, but I like Eric Stone's name for it better. My code name for it is Sentinel, for obvious reasons. Do you know what a neutrino is?"

Washburn shook his head slowly, still gaping like a simpleton at the continuing video feed from the Oval Office.

"A neutrino is a subatomic particle created by nuclear reactions, such as those within the sun or from cosmic rays. Normally, they're very hard to detect."

"Why?"

"Because they are so small they can pass through matter without stopping. It would take six trillion miles of lead to stop half the neutrinos flowing through the earth, so the earth and everything on it are subjected to constant bombardment from them. But suppose we had a way to observe those few neutrinos that did interact with their surroundings. My long-lost great-uncle, a brilliant physicist named Gunther Lutzen, anticipated neutrinos decades before they were discovered. Not only that, he provided a basis for intercepting them and deciphering the spatial equations that would allow us to view the matter they had already passed through. If his work had been taken seriously at the time, he would have won the Nobel Prize and been mentioned in the same breath as Einstein."

"And the equipment in that Haitian cave is the neutrino telescope? That's Sentinel?"

"Yes. Uncle Lutzen theorized that he would need a very particular environment in which to build the telescope, a cavern that had the perfect level of natural radioactive ore and copper impurities to allow for the right conditions. He tracked a rare sample of the ore to Haiti and was about to return to Germany with his discovery when his ship was destroyed by a volcano. He called the cave Oz, but because of the green tinge from the copper in the cave's selenium crystals, I think he should have called it the Emerald City."

Washburn nodded in agreement. "So how are you seeing the images from here?"

"I have a transducer that uses the same technology to beam the images directly here from Sentinel, so I can be anywhere in the world and use it. I prefer to be mobile."

"But you could make millions of dollars with this technology," Washburn said in awe. "Imagine the potential."

"Billions of dollars, actually. Perhaps even trillions. And I *will* make that much. But you aren't imagining the true potential. I don't limit myself to thinking of what I can attain financially. Don't you realize that with Sentinel at our disposal, we can change the world? And I mean that literally. Shaping the future of the United States is only the first step."

"What more could there be?"

Kensit sighed. He supposed he shouldn't have been so surprised at such limited thinking. "In this day and age, there is only so much one country can accomplish on its own. Think what I can do when I have control of Russia, China, and the European Union."

"You? What about me?"

Kensit shook his head. "You still don't understand, do you? I am the only indispensable part of this equation. I'm the only one who knows how to build the neutrino telescope. And you're looking at Phase One. Currently, I can see only a single location at a time, a distinct disadvantage that I will improve upon soon. I've found a second underground cavern even bigger than Oz and I've already purchased the land around it for miles. Once Phase Two is built there, I will be able to view as many as a dozen locations at once. With advances in real-time translation software, I will be able to pass on secrets even the NSA can't deliver to you when you're president."

"And that's how you plan to get me elected," Washburn said, finally comprehending the possibilities.

"You will know every strategy your opponents plan to use, every secret they want to keep, every scandal they try to hide. You'll be able to anticipate their every move. Or *I* will, and then I will pass it on to you. So don't ever think about betraying me or getting the deluded notion that you could do any of this without me. Because I will find someone who does understand that I am the one making the rules from now on."

Washburn swallowed hard and nodded. He understood. Kensit had no doubt he would do as instructed.

"You said the first step is to shoot down Air Force Two. How, exactly?"

Kensit manipulated the controls so that the telescope descended on Tyndall Air Force Base in Florida until he had the orange-tipped QF-16 drones on the screen. Then he switched to the drone pilots' control room.

"Those are modified F-16s, with all the same performance capabilities of the actual fighter jets. I did a test a few days ago. I could take over any of the planes' command streams by mimicking the encrypted frequencies that the satellites use to connect them with their control base. The pilots couldn't tell anything was wrong even when I tried a slight maneuver to make sure I had control."

"You can fly those drones?"

Kensit nodded. "And they won't even be missed, because I can spoof the video feed and data relays. Air Force Two is currently sitting on the tarmac in Rio de Janeiro, having taken the VP there for a South American trade conference. In two days it will take off for its return flight to Washington. At the same time, this flight of six QF-16s will be flying toward the UNITAS exercise in the Bahamas for a demonstration. I will commandeer control of those planes and intercept Air Force Two when it's over Haiti."

Washburn leaned in, now more fascinated by than appalled at the prospect of killing to reach his goals. "I get it. You're going to use the drones' missiles to shoot it down."

"No, of course not," Kensit said, pausing for effect. "The drones don't carry any missiles. I'm going to fly them right into Vice President Sandecker's plane."

39

It was nearly midnight when Juan and Eric rendezvoused with the *Oregon* in San Juan, Puerto Rico. Juan felt proud of his quick-thinking crew as he read the after-action report about the events at Saint-Pierre. The *Oregon* had sailed from Martinique after Max and the crew gave statements to the local authorities, corroborated by the submarine passengers, that the ship's crew were simply innocent bystanders who happened to be in the right place at the right time to rescue the grateful hostages. When he assumed command again, Juan took a calculated guess as to where the evidence from the *Roraima* would lead them and ordered the ship to head west.

He and the rest of the senior officers had slept during their respective journeys, so he called a late-night meeting in the boardroom to plan their next move. Along the way, he stopped by Maria Sandoval's cabin. She answered the door wearing a pair of silk pajamas that Julia Huxley had loaned her. Juan thought they suited her well, but he made no comment.

"Thanks for seeing me, Captain Cabrillo."

Juan leaned against the door, creating the unspoken impression that this would be a short visit. "Are you being treated all right?"

"Every amenity I could ask for. Your facilities are marvelous. I wish we had them on my ship."

"The benefits of our chosen profession." He left it at that to keep up the appearances that they were simply smugglers. "I understand you called your company and your friends to let them know you're alive and safe."

"Yes, thanks for letting me do that."

"There was no point in holding back the news any longer. Your survival of the shipwreck is known to the conspirators by now." He didn't add how he came by that knowledge. "You're still free to go at any time, of course, but your life might be in danger until we resolve our current situation."

"I will have to go soon. My company is demanding to debrief me."

"I'm hoping we can get some more evidence that Admiral Ruiz was behind the attacks in a few more days. That should clear your name completely with your company."

"The admiral is why I wanted to speak with you. The shipping industry captains in my country are tightly connected and one of them told me he saw her at Carúpano, a minor port on the eastern side of Venezuela. I also talked to a few friends who are still involved with the Navy and don't have a particular fondness for her. They told me she had left headquarters with members of her staff to join the Cuban Navy in observing a joint U.S.–Caribbean exercise going on in the Bahamas."

"What was she doing in Carúpano?"

"He didn't know, but she was boarding a small cargo ship. She wasn't wearing her uniform. It was the government-issue car that drew his attention."

"Any idea what the cargo was?"

She shook her head. "Nothing but a stack of shipping containers."

"I appreciate the information. It's probably something to do with her smuggling operation. I'll let you know if we learn anything else about it."

Juan said good night and continued on to the boardroom. When he entered, Murph was recounting the events of the sub encounter to Eric.

"That's when I drove Little Geek under the falling girders on the *Roraima*," Murph said, his hands behind his head. "It destroyed the ROV, of course, but I didn't have a choice."

Eddie took up the story. "Although Little Geek kept me from getting crushed, I was still pinned. I had my hands on the photo tin but I couldn't get away, and I knew the bomb inside the barrel was ticking down. Linc's the one who pried me out of there. My legs were numb by then, so he had to drag me until I got blood flow back in my feet."

"I just wish I had gotten us fully behind that piece of coral before the bomb went off," Linc said, munching on an apple. "Doc said you won't be going into the water for a few weeks." The only injury among them was a perforated eardrum Eddie suffered.

Juan took his seat at the head of the table. "Good job, everyone. I'm going to have to stop taking excursions like this or you'll start thinking you can get along without me."

"Not a chance," Max said. "I was sweating fifty-caliber hollow points the whole time."

"That was a tough call to keep your plan a secret, but I would have done the same thing. Where are we with the fruits of your labor?"

"Kevin Nixon worked with the techs in the lab to open the tin," Linda said. "It was lined with zinc and sealed with paraffin, so it hadn't rusted through and water hadn't penetrated the gaps. We found four photo plates inside."

She removed a cloth covering a white canvas sheet on which lay the five four-and-a-half- by six-and-a-half-inch glass plates. The silver bromide emulsion had been perfectly preserved. Two of the plates had cracks down the center, but the others were completely intact.

"You can look at these originals, if you want," Linda said, "but I wouldn't handle them. Not only are they delicate but we found traces of radioactivity on them." When she saw Hali edge away, she added, "Not enough to be dangerous, but it doesn't hurt to be careful. They were transferred to digital so we can see them in more detail."

She lowered the screen and turned on the overhead projector. The first image showed a man standing on a dock in a dark coat and trousers, boots, and a wide-brimmed hat. He wore a serious expression, but his eyes shone with an intensity visible even in the old photo. The *Roraima*'s name was stenciled on the hull of a ship behind him.

"He's a happy-looking guy," Murph said. He looked at Eric. "Is that Gunther Lutzen?"

"I don't know. We never found a photo of him."

"It's probably him," Linda continued, "but there's no way to be sure. I'm showing these photos in reverse order to try to backtrack his travel from the time he reached the *Roraima*. As you can see, the numbers of the photo plates are noted on the bottom right corner. Unfortunately, there aren't any indications where this photo was taken. There's nothing distinguishing the port."

She moved on to the next photo. This one showed a jumble of crystals embedded in rock, the facets reflecting the camera's burst of flash powder. The image was marred by the crack through the middle.

"That looks like a geode," Eric said.

"Yeah," Murph agreed, "but without anything else in the photo, we can't get a handle on its size. The crystals don't look clear, though, like the quartz crystals in a typical geode. They look darker than that. It could be amethyst."

"Or they could be green. Lutzen's thesis mentioned that his detection method would rely on crystals of selenium, copper, and uranium, and copper impurities in crystals give them a green hue. The uranium would also explain why the plates are radioactive."

"Maybe he was collecting gems," Linc said. "Whatever this is could still be buried in the *Roraima*. Not that I want to go back to look for it."

Linda snapped to the third plate. Again the image was split by a crack, which bisected the interior of a cavern teeming with stalactites and stalagmites. A tunnel faded into black in the distance.

Juan felt a ray of hope. "Now we're getting somewhere. This narrows down our search area considerably."

"Why?" Hali asked.

"Because caves like that form only in certain limestone terrains, in what's known as karst topography. It rules out Martinique and any other volcanic island."

Linda nodded. "Juan's right. The problem is that it still leaves a lot of land to cover. Even if we're limiting ourselves to the Caribbean, it could be anywhere from Puerto Rico to Mexico and up through Florida."

"I think it's a good chance we're looking at Haiti," Juan said. "Remember, that's where tram enthusiast Hector Bazin hails from."

"The last photo might help confirm that," Linda said.

The final picture showed a flourishing jungle landscape of ridges, hills, and valleys. The same man from the first photo stood in the foreground, this time beaming with a smile, his foot jauntily propped on a rock. He pointed into the shallow gorge behind him where a cave opening yawned. A river wound through the bottom of the gorge.

"I don't mean to be a party pooper," Juan said, "but how does this photo help us? It shows us the cave entrance, but I don't see anything identifying where this is."

"The ridge in the background," Murph said. "See the distinctive outline? Given Lutzen's height—if that *is* him—based on him standing against the *Roraima*, whose size we know, I estimated how far away the ridge is. The river gives us another reference point. The measurements aren't exact, but they're close enough to run a comparison using our worldwide topographical map—you know, the National Reconnaissance Office one that has about ten times greater resolution than NOAA's."

"I'm sorry I doubted you," Juan said. "How long will it take?"

"It's been running for a few hours now and should come back with a list of possible hits any minute. Oh, and I decided to start with Haiti. If we don't find any leads there, it will take a lot longer if we have to look in the Dominican Republic, Cuba, and Mexico. At least Florida is out because it's as flat as a day-old beer."

"All right. Once we know where to look, we'll have to come up with a game plan. Remember, we only have a day left before Kensit puts into play whatever is going to change the world. However, our approach will be tricky because of the neutrino telescope that Eric thinks Lawrence Kensit has developed."

"Who came up with *that* name?" Murph asked.

"I did," Eric replied. "Although the existence of neutrinos was first proposed by Wolfgang Pauli in 1930, the particle Lutzen describes in his thesis much earlier is clearly a neutrino. He just didn't have a name for it."

"Yeah, yeah, great name," Linc said. "How does it work?"

"As far as I can tell, Lutzen theorized that intercepted neutrinos could be reconstructed to create the state of the place they passed through."

"Like an X-ray?"

"Yes, but far more advanced. It could show you literally any spot on earth. Not only that but you could also hear what was going on in that space because it would also intercept the air particles that are conveying the sound."

Murph said, "Think of what the NSA could do with technology like that. Say bye-bye to any secrets."

Linc scoffed. "You think Kensit actually made this thing? A telescope that can see through walls? And around the world? Has he also cracked the code to warp drive?"

"I know it sounds bizarre," Juan said, "but imagine explaining the idea of X-rays before they were discovered. We have to go under the assumption that this neutrino telescope exists. Kensit and Bazin have anticipated our every move. They beat us to Jamaica, New York, and Berlin, and they knew exactly where we'd be each time. Kensit could have been watching us type in log-ins and passwords, giving him full access to our communications and computer networks."

"That's why you had me shut down any external access to our main computer," Murph said, nodding.

"Right," Juan said. "In the case of Berlin, Bazin knew where we'd be even though I never breathed a word of it over any line of communication. It's very possible that he's watching and listening to this meeting right now."

Everyone paused to soak in the likelihood that their privacy was completely gone.

Finally Hali spoke. "Then how can we possibly defeat this guy? He'll know whatever plan we come up with."

"He's obviously not infallible," Juan said. "You proved that by foiling his sub plan in Martinique. Eric has a theory why."

Eric cleared his throat. "I think he only can see one place at a time. It lets him spy on our plans, but if there are multiple situations happening simultaneously, he has to choose what to observe."

"We have another advantage." Juan looked each of his officers in the eye. "Our shared history. If we talk in code, relating key information about our upcoming plans using past experiences that only we know between us, he'll never be able to decipher it even if he's listening in. That coupled with Max's idea to wait until the last moment to reveal our tactics gives us a fighting chance against Kensit."

Murph's tablet computer dinged. "The results are back. We got a couple of hits at more than fifty percent probability but only one that is better than a ninety-five percent match." Murph tapped on the screen, then groaned when he saw the results.

"What's the matter?" Max asked. "Is it a false lead?"

"No, it's a match. But you're not gonna believe where the cave is." He took over the main view screen from Linda and put up the map from his tablet.

A yellow dot was superimposed on a satellite image of the area, with the ridge outline in red. Instead of the dot appearing in a green valley, it was planted inside the blue water of a lake.

"Your comparison model must be wrong," Eddie said. "How could the cave be at the bottom of a lake?"

"Because that is Lake Péligre on the Artibonite River in central Haiti," Murph said with a dejected sigh as he read from his screen. "It was formed by the construction of the Péligre Hydroelectric Dam in 1956, more than fifty years after Gunther Lutzen visited it. The cave entrance is now under forty feet of water."

40

By midday the *Oregon* had reached the Dominican Republic's largest northern port, Puerto Plata. Lake Péligre was situated almost directly in the center of Haiti and would require travel over twisting and rutted roads; it would take Linda and her team seven hours to make the two-hundred-and-seventy-five-mile journey. The easier part was getting their transportation into the country.

Normally, prior approval from the customs office was required to off-load cargo, but greasing palms of the DR's low-paid civil servants took care of the "misunderstanding" that the clearance hadn't been preauthorized. Then after the thirty minutes needed to unload the PIG, the *Oregon* put back to sea. Crossing the border by land into Haiti unhindered would require another generous bribe.

Linda checked, but no one was following. Eric, who was riding shotgun in the truck's four-person cab, confirmed that they weren't being tracked electronically. If Kensit were watching them with the neutrino telescope, they'd never know. MacD and Hali sat in the backseat, rechecking their gear.

Since Max was the one who'd designed the vehicle, he was given the honor of naming it and he dubbed it Powered Investigator Ground, but, much to his chagrin, everyone else in the crew simply referred to it as the PIG. It was the Corporation's land-based version of the *Oregon* herself. To an outside observer, the PIG seemed to be nothing more than a beat-up cargo truck carrying fuel drums, down to the logo of the fictitious oil company on the side. The rear could even be opened by dockside inspectors, who could remove the six full drums that served as the vehicle's spare fuel and that could extend its range to eight hundred miles. Removing the first row of drums revealed a second row that was merely a façade hiding the rest of the PIG's interior. They took the calculated risk that no one would ever go to the trouble of completely emptying the cargo bed.

In reality, the PIG was an all-terrain platform built on a Mercedes Unimog chassis and featuring an 800-horsepower turbo-diesel engine with a nitrous oxide boost that could push it over 1000. The four-person cab and cargo area that could transport ten fully equipped soldiers were armored to deflect high-powered rifle rounds, and the self-sealing tires and fully articulated suspension with two feet of ground clearance meant it could conquer any terrain short of a cliff face.

The PIG could be configured to serve any mission required, from search and rescue to mobile command station to ground assault. Much of Max's attention had focused on its offensive and defensive capabilities. The front bumper concealed a .30 caliber machine gun, and hidden racks on either side of the truck swung down to launch guided rockets. A seamless roof hatch allowed the PIG to fire mortar barrages, while a smoke generator at the rear could belch out thick plumes.

The newest modification had been the addition of remote operation capability. The drive-by-wire system could be maneuvered by a handheld control with a range of five miles. The operator used cameras mounted on the front and rear that had both daylight and night vision settings.

Linda took several sharp turns through the city. If Kensit didn't have the neutrino telescope trained on them, there was no way he'd be able to find them now. Although she didn't often get the chance, Linda always liked driving the PIG the good old-fashioned manual way. There was nothing more macho than motoring along on its ultra-large tires, perched higher than any other vehicle, fully encased in a truck that could take on anything else on four wheels.

"You think Kensit's got his eyes on us?" Hali asked, the same question everyone else was thinking.

"Let's hope he's too focused on the Chairman," Linda replied as she steered the PIG onto the coastal highway.

That was the primary reason it was just the four of them and not a full assault team. The goal was to make Kensit think they were simply on a recon mission so that his attention would be elsewhere.

"Ready for the briefing?" Eric asked.

"Go for it," Linda said, not letting her apprehension show. She didn't like talking about this openly, but it had to be done eventually.

"Okay, the cave opening is underwater, but there is an old cement factory less than a mile away situated between the mountains and the lake, with just a dirt road leading to the highway. Limestone is the one thing Haiti has a lot of, and the cement made from it was used to build the Lake Péligre dam. Once the dam was completed, the cement plant went bust and was abandoned until it started operating two years ago under the ownership of an untraceable shell company."

"Too coincidental, if you ask me," MacD said.

"You'd be right," Eric said. "The factory is producing cement, but barely. According to CIA sources, the output isn't enough to profitably support a factory that size. And it's low-grade stuff. You wouldn't want your house built out of it."

Hali leaned on Eric's seatback. "So you think this is a cover for digging tunnels into the cave?"

"Right. Since the original entrance is now inaccessible, Kensit needed another way in. If Gunther Lutzen provided him with some kind of map of the cave system, Kensit could have drilled holes into the mountain until he found a way in and then bored a tunnel big enough to move his equipment. A cement factory would be the perfect cover to transport the waste material from the dig away without anyone noticing."

"Ah may not be the sharpest tool in the shed," MacD said, "but if the cave is underwater, how did Kensit build this telescope inside it?"

"Either he built a barrier to keep the lake water out and pumped it dry," Eric said, "or the cave he's using is above the level of the lake. Remember, cave systems can ascend and descend drastically."

"What about intel on the cement factory defenses?" Linda asked.

"Nothing. We have to assume Bazin has his forces ready for any incursions."

The scope of the "recon" mission was agreed to back on the *Oregon*. The planning had been extremely awkward because of the precautions they had to take. Without naming it, Juan referred to the sunken ship on their coldest-weather mission. Everyone on the team immediately knew that meant the *Silent Sea*, a Chinese junk that had gone down off the coast of Antarctica. Their mission go time tomorrow would be 1600 hours minus the number of letters in the ship's name. Nine letters meant that they all understood the mission start time to be seven a.m. Sunrise.

As for the role of their recon mission, Juan told them that they would be his *Aggie Johnston*. The *Aggie Johnston* was a super-tanker that had served as a screen for the *Oregon* so that it could sneak up on an enemy frigate off the coast of Libya. Linda's mission was to provide cover for the Chairman. She and her team were the distraction for what he was planning.

Juan proposed sneaking past the guards in the cement plant using the same method he did at Karamita, which Kensit would not know was a now defunct ship-breaker yard in Indonesia. Juan asked Linda and her team to place two sets of the equipment so that they would be ready for use when the mission started. They couldn't requisition the equipment from the ship's stores without Kensit seeing what they were acquiring, so they planned to buy it locally in the hope that Kensit would still have his eye on the *Oregon* by then. Linda didn't like using off-the-shelf equipment, but she would go over it with a fine-toothed comb to make sure it was all working properly.

"How far?" Linda asked.

Eric looked at his GPS, then craned his neck and pointed. "That should be it up on the left."

The sign above the shop read "Buceo De Diego." Next to the name was a red flag with a white diagonal slash through it, the international symbol for scuba diving. It had the reputation for the best equipment outside of Santo Domingo.

They all got out of the PIG and entered the shop. It wasn't a huge establishment, but the walls were lined with all of the latest tanks, regulators, fins, and buoyancy vests.

The athletic shopkeeper, who looked like a diver himself and was busy unpacking a box of masks, said, "*Buenos días*. Can I help you?" The four of them obviously weren't locals.

"Oh, good, you speak English," Linda said as if she were a tourist relieved not to have to break out her broken Spanish.

"We get many Americans here, of course. Are you and your friends interested in a dive trip?"

"We are, but we're planning to go on our own, so we'd like to buy our equipment." She withdrew a thick wad of cash from her pocket.

That made the shopkeeper jump to his feet and forget his unpacking duties.

"You will not regret it," he said, trying in vain not to stare at the pile of American dollars. "We have many of the best reefs in the world in the Dominican Republic."

"Actually," Linda said, pointing at a Nomad side mount tank rig, "we want to go cave diving."

Although the sky was clear, the deck of the aging 200-foot cargo ship *Reina Azul*, or *Blue Queen*, bucked in heavy seas churned up by a storm east of Nicaragua. Dayana Ruiz longed for her sleek frigate *Mariscal Sucre* to slice through the waves, but this mission required a covert command. She'd selected a handpicked crew of her most trusted officers who'd collaborated with her on the smuggling operation. Their naval uniforms had been left behind in Venezuela.

For her absence, she'd given the excuse that she would be observing the UNITAS joint exercises from the deck of a Cuban frigate. A Cuban admiral who owed her a favor would provide a convincing alibi.

They were ten hours from the coast of Haiti. The Doctor had assured her that the *Oregon*'s destination was somewhere along the western shore, although he wouldn't explain how he knew.

Ruiz found the entire situation oddly unsettling. She wasn't used to being kept in the dark about information. Information was power and in regard to the Doctor she had very little of either. However, the video images that he infrequently sent her showing the *Oregon* and her crew convinced her of the accuracy of his information but also enraged her every time she saw them. The most recent showed the ship departing from Puerto Plata on a westerly course toward Haiti, and she would make certain this would be their last rendezvous.

Taking the *Mariscal Sucre* into battle outside of Venezuelan territorial waters had been out of the question, especially when Ruiz was planning to attack so close to another country's coastline. Subterfuge had been the only alternative. With a top speed of just fifteen knots and no defensive capabilities, the *Reina Azul* was obviously no match for the *Oregon* in a one-on-one duel, but hiding on her deck in plain sight was a secret that would give Ruiz the opportunity to sink her.

She scanned the horizon and saw no ships. The rudimentary radar on board confirmed that they were alone.

"Begin the test," she said to the captain.

He relayed the orders, and Ruiz trained her eyes on a gray cargo container bolted to the deck. It looked exactly like all the other cargo containers on board, but this one held a hidden surprise.

"Raising to firing position," a voice on the intercom said.

The roof of the container pivoted up and four green tubes two-thirds the length of the container began to rise from beneath it, forced into place by a hydraulic ram. Encased in each tube was a Russian 3M-54 Klub-K antiship missile armed with a six-hundred-pound warhead. The turbojet engine enabled it to cruise no more than thirty feet above the waves until it got within three miles of the target, at which point its multistage solid-fuel rocket fired to propel it to supersonic speeds. Each missile was extremely difficult to evade or shoot down and she had four of them.

She had acquired the concealed weapons system to sell to a Hezbollah cell that planned to target Israeli shipping. One of the few pieces of hardware Juan Cabrillo hadn't managed to destroy in his raid would end up sending him to the bottom of the Caribbean.

"Report," Ruiz said after the tubes had stopped at their fully vertical launch position, conveniently hidden by the stacks of containers on either side.

"All systems functioning normally," said the missile officer inside the cargo container's tiny control room. "But Admiral, the targeting radar is completely dependent on the ship's system, which is too crude for a lock, especially if there are multiple ships in the area. The missile will have to make target acquisition once it's in flight, so we can only fire one at a time."

"What?" she shouted. "Unacceptable!"

"I'm sorry, Admiral," came the stammering reply, "but we're not very familiar with this weapons system."

"Fine," she said, stewing in anger. "Then we will have to attack when there are no other ships around the *Oregon*."

"Aye, Admiral."

"Good. Close it back up." She turned to the captain. "Have you heard from our escort ships?"

He nodded. "They will meet us in the Canal de la Gonâve near Port-au-Prince. All they know is that they are to sail alongside us."

"Excellent. When we are in launch position, have our escape boat ready. As soon as the *Oregon* is sunk, we will scuttle the *Reina Azul* and our companion ships. By the time anyone has figured out what happened, we'll be flying out of Haiti." False passports would be the last measure to erase any links.

Ruiz couldn't help but flash a smile, an unfamiliar expression that surely unnerved the captain. She savored the irony that she would be destroying Juan Cabrillo and the *Oregon* using their own stealth tactics against them.

As Bazin walked toward the exit of Sentinel's underground complex, the natural limestone caves with all their imperfections and protrusions made an abrupt transition to the smooth, rounded walls of the man-made tunnels. He would never admit it to anyone but the threshold always made him breathe a bit easier. The maze of caves went on for miles, as far as anyone could tell. No one had taken the time to explore them fully once the Oz cave had been found, and Bazin didn't relish the idea of getting lost in those dank confines.

Fluorescent lights buzzed at regular intervals through the tunnel. A massive electrical cable hung from the ceiling to provide power to the Sentinel telescope. The hydroelectric dam was the primary source, but it was so unreliable that it was supplemented by diesel generators, installed in one of the outbuildings, and by a battery backup inside the Oz cave itself that could run the telescope for more than two hours if all other power sources failed.

When he was close enough to the exit to receive a signal on his phone, which was routed through the Internet to make up for the nonexistent mobile service in the region, he dialed Kensit.

"Status," was the one-word greeting to his call.

"The engineers tell me that there are no mechanical issues they can foresee for Sentinel."

Although a large contingent of engineers and technicians had been trucked in to build Sentinel, only a few were retained on staff to maintain it. The rest were taken back out blindfolded, just as they had been brought in, with all paper and electronic records of their work left behind. Bazin knew that Kensit intended to use their skills again, but each of them was aware of only a small part of the design and none knew the software code used to operate the equipment. If they had known how it worked, Bazin would have hired them himself, killed Kensit, and taken over the operation long ago. Instead, he became Kensit's loyal right-hand man.

Bazin could live with being the second-most-powerful man in the world. For now.

"What about power?" Kensit asked.

Bazin walked past the humming generators housed in the building where the tunnel began. "The diesel generators are fully fueled and the batteries are at full capacity. Everything will be running for the operation in the morning."

"After that, we're going to close it up."

"How long will it take to get Sentinel Two up and running?"

"The tests yesterday were successful, so I'd say it will take less than three months, once we've dug an access tunnel to the new cave. We'll bring all of the engineers back, but this time they're going to stay permanently."

"And diggers?"

"You did well with the Haitians. I'm sure you can find plenty of Mexicans to do the same. Remember, keep Sentinel safe until nine a.m. tomorrow. That's when the intercept mission takes place." Air Force Two would be almost directly overhead when the drones brought it down in the morning.

"What's the latest about Juan Cabrillo's plans?"

"He's making it look like he's going to launch a direct assault, but I think he's going to try to sneak in."

"How?"

There was a slight pause. "I don't know. They unloaded a truck that looks like a big fuel transport. It's got an oil company logo on the side. I'll send you a photo so you know what to be on the lookout for."

"Where are they now?"

"I'm keeping an eye on Juan Cabrillo and the *Oregon*, so I lost track of the truck. There are only four crew members inside. They can't be a big threat."

Bazin had to bite his tongue. Kensit's reliance on his superpower made him overconfident. Bazin knew better than to underestimate an enemy, especially one like the crew of the *Oregon*, which had already outwitted him and his men.

"I will let you know when Cabrillo launches his assault. In the meantime, prepare your men and your defenses."

"Yes, sir. I have my own surprises, thanks to your friend Admiral Ruiz."

"I'll send you any updates by text. I won't call again until my drone attack begins." Kensit hung up.

Bazin stopped at the next building. The thick walls were built with cement from the factory's own output. He stepped inside to check on the two mercenaries who were standing guard in the vestibule. He put his face to the window and saw the pitiful forms of Duval and the rest of the diggers. Even through the cracks in the door, the place reeked from the stench of body odor and waste buckets that were scattered around the room. The men were in desperate shape, given the barest minimum of food and water needed for survival the past few days. Even Duval could do nothing more than glare at him. It was a look Bazin remembered well from their childhood whenever Duval didn't like something his younger housemate had done.

Bazin nodded in satisfaction. The deprivation had served its purpose. The men were no longer a threat, but they wouldn't die before they could be herded into the tunnels and sealed inside when Sentinel was blown up. The diggers who had made this first version of the neutrino telescope possible would perish with it.

Bazin had one more stop to make before gathering his team to go over the defense plans. He entered a large shed where cement mixers had driven inside to load their cargo. The mixers were long gone, replaced by four South African Ratel light armored vehicles, veterans of the war in Angola. They had been procured by Kensit, courtesy of Admiral Dayana Ruiz and her smuggling operation. Each of the six-wheeled vehicles was armed with a rapid-fire 20mm cannon and two 7.62mm machine guns.

Bazin had always thought his inaugural use of them would be when he rode into Port-au-Prince to take command of the government in his planned coup d'état. Now he'd get to test them in action against Juan Cabrillo and his crew if they were bold enough to attempt an attack, and he was looking forward to seeing how much damage the armor-piercing rounds could dish out.

He grinned at the thought of Cabrillo staring down the barrel of the cannon just as he pulled the trigger.

All Kensit needed was some popcorn. Sitting at his viewing station was like watching the most open-ended and unpredictable reality TV show ever made. And if it got boring, he could change the channel. Right now, he was tuned in to his favorite program, *The Juan Cabrillo Show*.

Cabrillo was currently in his boardroom talking with four of his men, Eddie Seng, Franklin Lincoln, Mike Trono, and Gomez Adams. The captain's efforts to thwart him were truly inspired, but they would ultimately come to naught since Kensit could simply watch their discussions and movements in real time.

"We'll take off in the chopper a half an hour before mission go time," Cabrillo said.

"I'll be ready," said Adams, the helicopter pilot. His dashing looks added to the sense that Kensit was watching a TV series, albeit one with an unlimited budget.

"Eddie, get us kitted out like we were for the Argentina incursion." They'd been speaking in this vernacular, referencing old missions, ever since they'd learned about the neutrino telescope. Kensit wished he could delve into them, but all remote access to the *Oregon*'s database had been locked out. Sentinel was unable to view computer code.

"I've got the techs working on putting our gear together," Seng said. "I'll get down there once we're finished with the briefing."

"Good," Cabrillo said. "We'll keep this op simple. I'll tell Gomez where we're going to land when we get close to the target. We'll split up and attempt our infiltration of the cement plant in two teams, Eddie and Linc on one and me and Trono on the other. Linda's team will be feeding us recon intel upon landing."

Kensit had already checked their radios, but they were using hardware encryption based on frequency-hopping algorithms, so Bazin wouldn't be able to listen in on their conversations without his help.

"Once we've captured Kensit and the neutrino telescope, we'll shut it down until we can figure out what to do with it."

Kensit smiled at that. Cabrillo had no clue that Kensit was hundreds of miles away.

Cabrillo scanned his team. "Any questions?"

"Seems pretty straightforward to me," Lincoln said.

Trono nodded. "No problemo."

Kensit admired the offhanded way in which they were all going to their doom.

"All right," Cabrillo said. "It's 2100 hours. We should be on-station in the Bahia de Grand Pierre in an hour. Make sure you get a few hours of sleep after you've prepared your equipment."

They all nodded. Kensit checked his map and saw that the Bahia de Grand Pierre was an isolated bay on the west coast of Haiti. It was well chosen. Cabrillo could launch his helicopter in daylight without being seen, and it was just fifty miles from the cement plant, about twenty minutes of flying time.

The men filed out, but Cabrillo stayed behind, studying the table as if he were contemplating a difficult decision. Then he looked up and stared right at Kensit as though he knew where the camera was.

"Lawrence Kensit," Cabrillo said, "I have something to say to you."

Uncharacteristically for him, Kensit was startled. He should have expected the direct address, but it was eerie all the same.

"I don't know if you're watching and listening to me," Cabrillo continued. "I may be talking to myself, but if you're out there, you should know something."

The surprise gone, Kensit leaned forward in his chair. The connection between the two of them was almost palpable.

Cabrillo's expression radiated malice, like a circus tiger prodded one too many times. The penetrating intensity shooting through the telescope chilled Kensit's blood.

"I'll only say this once," Cabrillo said, "and then you'll never hear me talk to you again. You may think you're a genius, Kensit, but you're not infallible. You made a huge mistake when you went after my crew. They're my family. Maybe a loner like you doesn't understand the importance of family, but your attacks made the situation between you and me personal. I don't care what advantages you think you have, I promise that I will find you. And when

I do, you'll discover that my retribution is swift and mighty." Cabrillo stood and grinned. "Spend this night well, Kensit. It just might be your last."

Cabrillo chuckled as he walked out of the room. "That was even more fun than I thought it would be."

But Kensit wasn't laughing. Try as he might to take Cabrillo's words as nothing more than tough talk, for the first time since he began to develop Sentinel Kensit actually felt uneasy.

The first shimmer of dawn peeked above the hills now denuded of the thick forest that Linda had seen in Gunther Lutzen's photos of the area in 1902. The vegetation that had sprung up in its place was a thicket of small trees and bushes that covered the gullies and ridges around Lake Péligre.

From their prone position on a rocky outcrop, she and Eric had a clear view of the cement plant five hundred yards to the east where it abutted the coastline. There was virtually no breeze to ruffle the water reflecting the scattered clouds being illuminated by the morning sun.

They had left the PIG a mile away and hiked to this spot through uninhabited country. Linda scanned the vista with a pair of Steiner 20×80 military-grade binoculars. There was enough light now for her to see the gravel road coming in from the west and paralleling the power lines from the nearby hydroelectric dam. She could make out several men on security detail and others walking between buildings.

"What's the force projection?" Eric asked.

"I count at least ten so far, but those buildings are big enough to house a regiment. How is the PIG looking?"

Eric tapped on his control pad, then looked at his watch. "Everything checks out, but I can't drive and operate the weapons systems simultaneously. If Hali and MacD don't get back soon, you're going to have to switch between observing the factory and firing the weapons."

A bush rustled behind them, momentarily sending Linda's heart rate into the stratosphere. She whipped around, bringing her assault rifle to bear.

"Our ears were burning," MacD said. Hali was right behind him.

Linda lowered her weapon. "Did you get the package set?"

MacD took up position next to her with a Barrett .50 caliber sniper rifle. "We put it where no one will spot it even if they're standing on it."

"The tracker is activated," Hali said as he lay down. "The Chairman shouldn't have any trouble finding it."

"From down there," MacD said, "this ridge looked almost like it did in Lutzen's picture. Except for the whole clear-cutting thing."

"Without any other fuel source, the residents have stripped the forests bare for firewood," Linda said. "With few trees to hold the soil, the lake is filling up with silt and causing the dam to lose power."

"Looks like they have plenty left over to light up that cement factory."

"And power the neutrino telescope," Eric added. He swept the area with the thermal scope. "I'm picking up excessive heat signatures pluming off that building next to the dome."

Linda raised the binoculars and saw what he was talking about. In the growing light, she could see crude vents cut out of the roof.

"That must be where the diesel backups are. They wouldn't be depending solely on the power from the dam, not when it's so spotty. According to the CIA, the turbines can go down for hours at a time."

"So that's target number two?" Hali asked.

"Yes." Linda looked at her watch. Seven a.m. on the dot.

She lifted the radio to her mouth. "Dragonfly, this is Groundhog. What's your position?"

"Dragonfly here, Groundhog," came the Chairman's reply over the sound of the MD 520N's pounding rotors. "We are right on schedule. The mission is a go."

"Copy that, Dragonfly. The package has been delivered."

"Understood. If you haven't heard from us in forty minutes after landing, abort the mission."

Not only was that a lot of time to keep Bazin and his mercenaries occupied but the Chairman's margin of error for his part of the mission was razor thin. Linda glanced at her team. MacD actually shook his head. She shared the sentiment, but she was also an officer. "Acknowledged, Dragonfly." It was bad luck in the Corporation to wish someone good luck, so Linda signed off by saying, "Happy hunting. Out."

"Okay, Eric," she said, "start the fireworks."

He nodded to Hali, who had his own control pad and screen at the ready. Eric pushed the stick forward and the camera showing the view from the front of the PIG slewed around until it was aimed dead center at one of the power line poles.

"Fire one," Hali said, and tapped on the control pad.

A rocket shot out from the PIG's launcher and blew the pole apart. The lines came down in a shower of sparks. The boom followed a few seconds later.

"And the light switch turns off," Hali said.

Linda trained the binoculars on the cement plant. The lights flickered off for a moment and then came back on. The few mercenaries who were visible milled around in confusion.

"Proceed to next target," Linda said.

Eric jammed the stick forward and the PIG's 800 horses propelled the truck at breakneck speed. Linda shifted her view to the road and spotted the PIG emerging from behind the hill.

"I've got target lock," Hali said.

"Fire," Linda ordered.

Two mortars were fired up through the PIG's roof opening. They flew in an invisible arc until they came down on the building housing the diesel generators. The fuel tanks must have been inside the building as well because the initial blast of the mortars was dwarfed by the explosion that followed.

The lights went out for good.

Mercenaries were racing in all directions looking for their attackers. It didn't even look like controlled chaos. Just chaos.

As the fire raged, Linda could make out the approaching throb of helicopter blades. The MD 520N swooped along the lake just above the surface.

When it was a few hundred yards from its landing spot, Linda said, "Launch at target three."

"Switching to smoke," Hali replied as his fingers danced across the control pad. "Firing."

Three more mortars thumped from the launcher, this time flying next to the plant to land on the side closest to the lake.

They landed right on target and began pumping out dense white smoke.

Linda was impressed. Despite being put together using code on the fly, the mission actually seemed to be going according to plan. They had provided the perfect distraction, and now Bazin's men would retreat to a defensive posture, waiting for an attack that wouldn't be coming.

She switched her view back to the cement plant, where movement at one of the buildings caught her eye. When she saw what emerged from inside, she knew the mission was *not* going to continue as planned.

She quickly spoke into the radio. "Be advised, Dragonfly, Bazin's got infantry-fighting vehicles and they're armed with twenty-millimeter cannons."

"Thanks for the update, Groundhog. Now tell us the bad news."

"One of them is headed your way."

Cans of Red Bull were scattered at Kensit's feet, and the only time he'd gotten up from his seat in the last twenty hours was to open the door when one of Bazin's men, who served as the yacht's crew, brought him his next meal. Luckily, he had plenty of empty water bottles to make trips to the head unnecessary.

The drone jets had already taken off from Tyndall Air Force Base in Florida and were winging across the Everglades, six unmanned QF-16s escorted by two F-15 manned fighters armed with air-to-air missiles. Kensit hadn't taken control of them yet, but the feed he was getting from the fighters' navigation systems on his computer showed him exactly where they were at any point in time, so he didn't need to use Sentinel.

He also knew the transponder code of Air Force Two and was tracking its movement as it flew over the West Indies. Its takeoff had been pushed up by a half hour, so his anticipated interception with the drones would now take place even earlier, at 8:30 a.m. Governor Washburn would join him to watch the destruction of the vice president's plane.

With both sets of planes converging on one screen, he was able to follow Juan Cabrillo's movements using Sentinel. Cabrillo, Eddie Seng, Franklin Lincoln, and Mike Trono had boarded the chopper, wearing green camouflage uniforms that matched the flora surrounding the cement plant, leaving Max Hanley and Mark Murphy as the senior staff in the *Oregon*'s op center. All four men on the helicopter had been heavily armed with assault weapons and several RPGs. Instead of having a close view inside the cabin where it would be difficult to listen in on the conversations because of the noise from the rotor wash, he chose to watch the helicopter from the exterior. Once it landed, he'd stay with Cabrillo to relay his movements to Bazin.

"The helicopter is headed for the eastern side of the cement plant," he said into his headset microphone.

"I've got a Ratel armored vehicle going there now. But shooting him down will be difficult with all the smoke."

Kensit sat forward. "What smoke?" Then he saw it as the helicopter spun around and flew toward the coast. Tracers from the 20mm cannon lanced across the sky, but the shots were nowhere close to the chopper.

The helicopter descended into the smoke before Kensit could close in on the cockpit. He zoomed in as it plunged into the opaque cloud spewing from the canisters.

Ten seconds later, the helicopter took off, emerging from the smoke without its passengers.

Kensit pushed his virtual camera from the neutrino telescope into the smoke, but it was like looking into a glass of milk. He occasionally saw the flash of clothing or an arm and then it disappeared again.

He rotated his viewpoint so that he was looking straight down on the landing spot, but the cloud had expanded to cover an area bigger than three football fields, all the way from the edge of the cement plant property to the lake and up the closest hillock, which was packed with enough foliage to cover a crawling person's movements. By the time he pulled back enough to see the Ratel armored vehicle approaching the edge of the smoke, he realized that Juan Cabrillo had vanished.

Juan and Trono had to get beneath the surface of the lake before the smoke cleared or the entire operation would be ruined. If Kensit even suspected what they were planning, he would instruct Bazin to triple the number of guards inside the cave with the neutrino telescope instead of committing all of his forces to repelling a raid that was literally nothing more than a smokescreen.

With Trono's hand on his shoulder to keep them together through the thick smoke, Juan used his phone's receiver to home in on the tracking signal from the package that Linda's team had planted. After skirting a few impenetrable brambles, they found it under a bush that had been carefully dug up and then replaced.

The equipment all specifically designed for cave diving had been prepacked so that it could be donned quickly.

The Ratel was randomly firing its cannon and machine guns into the smoke, chewing up the ground and trees nearby, so Juan and Trono carried their kits to the water's edge and hurried into them before a lucky shot found them.

In less than two minutes, they had the gear on and were stepping into the water. They sunk their clothes in the lake, leaving nothing behind to reveal where they'd gone. With weapons slung across their backs, they slipped underwater.

Juan was glad Linda had understood his coded instructions. On a mission in Indonesia, he had snuck into the Karamita shipbreaker yard by scuba diving underneath the gigantic door that admitted the cargo ships in to be illegally sawn apart for scrap. She knew he intended to do the same thing at the cement plant, swimming through the now submerged cave entrance to approach the neutrino telescope cave from the unprotected rear.

Juan was taking a big risk with this method of infiltration. Finding the cave entrance in the lake was going to be challenging, not to mention navigating through the flooded caverns to find the right passage leading to the telescope. He didn't even know if they had enough air to make the journey.

Any chance of success hinged on complete surprise. Being outnumbered inside a cave was a recipe for disaster, and retreat wouldn't be an option.

Finding the cave entrance might have taken them days under normal circumstances, but Juan was depending on the same device that had let them unearth the tin of photos. He took out the Geiger counter and descended to forty feet, the depth they estimated the cave to be below the lake's surface. They were hoping that radiation from particulates in the cave carried through the water would lead them in the right direction.

Poor visibility from the silt made it harder to see more than twenty feet in front of them, but that also made it impossible for anyone to see them from above the surface. The Geiger counter, which had been tuned for maximum sensitivity, didn't register anything above the level of the natural background radiation.

Based on the photo, Juan was sure that the cave was near the cement plant, so he kept swimming in that direction. He swept the counter back and forth, looking for even the most modest uptick.

They had traveled another hundred feet when Juan saw a slight bump in the reading. He stopped and moved the Geiger counter up and down.

There it was, ten feet above them. He kicked and a gaping maw rimmed by rocks that looked uncannily like teeth yawned before him, a black hole he would have missed without the radiation detector showing them the way. He signaled to Trono, who nodded in acknowledgment, and they switched on their dive lights as they were swallowed by the darkness. They were already ten minutes into the forty-minute deadline.

Linc, who had been hiding under a bush, waited until the Ratel was only a hundred yards away. At this range, he couldn't miss. He lifted the RPG-7, so commonly seen in newcasts around the world, and triggered the weapon. The rocket-propelled grenade shot from its tube and made a direct hit on the armored vehicle, igniting the ammo inside and setting off a huge fireball.

"One down, three to sizzle," he said, dropping down prone again.

"Nice shot," Eddie said as they crawled away, "although my grandmother couldn't have missed from this distance."

Linc paused to reload the metal tube with their one remaining RPG. "I didn't know your grandmother had a Navy rifle marksmanship medal, too."

"Oh, she's quite skilled," Eddie said, grinning.

Using the cover of some trees and the lingering smoke, they sprinted to a low hillock, where they found a depression.

Another Ratel was coming their way. The driver must have seen their new position and was pumping 20mm shells into the dirt in front of them, making it impossible for either of them to rise up and take the Ratel out with the RPG.

"A little help would be much appreciated," Eddie said into the headset radio identical to the one Linc was wearing. "We're right about where the Ratel is plowing a new field with its weapon."

"I see you," Linda replied. "We're on our way."

Seconds later, a piercing howl preceded the impact of a rocket from the PIG. It blew apart the second armored vehicle. Two down, two to go.

From farther in the distance came the sound of another cannon firing a murderous barrage. Linc peeked over the lip of the hillock and saw the PIG take a beating.

Two of the shells smashed right through its windshield and another took off part of the hood. Eric gunned the engine, followed by the whoosh of the nitrous oxide injecting into the cylinders. The PIG screamed down the road as cannon shells tore apart trees on either side of it. It went past an outcropping and found shelter from the onslaught.

The Ratel didn't pursue, likely expecting an ambush as soon as it was exposed. It waited out of range, its main gun trained on the spot where the PIG would have to come out.

It was a standoff.

"Linda, how's Max's baby doing," Eddie said.

"He's going to have a conniption when he sees what we've done to it," she said. "Eric tells me the targeting control is gone. He can fire the mortars, but they'd be blind shots. There's one rocket left, plus plenty of machine gun ammo, but the thirty-caliber rounds won't penetrate the Ratel's armor. He can shoot them, but he'll need line of sight from the onboard cameras to target them."

"That doesn't sound so good. Maybe we should—"

"Hold on," Linda said, "something's happening."

The smoke was lifting, and Linc could make out the central part of the cement plant. He raised his binoculars and could see armed mercenaries kicking and pushing scores of bedraggled men in tattered clothes from one of the buildings, assembling them in two rows in front of the plant. He estimated there were sixty of them in all. The fourth armored vehicle took up position behind them.

"Who are those guys?" Linc asked under his breath.

"Forced labor," Eddie said. "Believe me, I know it when I see it." Linc knew that wasn't an exaggeration because Eddie had experienced it firsthand.

The factory's PA system squealed. "Linda Ross," said a Creole-accented voice that had to be Hector Bazin, "you know who I am. And I know where you and your men are."

Eddie and Linc looked at each other. Kensit had spotted Linda with his neutrino telescope.

"Your assault is futile. Tell Cabrillo and the rest of his men to stand down from this pointless gesture."

"At least he doesn't know where the rest of the team is," Linc said.

"I have placed a call to the Haitian National Police," Bazin continued. "They will be here with a hundred more men within twenty minutes. Leave now or you will all be killed. If you attempt to continue your attack, you will have to go through these innocent men."

"Can you take him out?" Eddie asked Linda.

"Negative," she said. "MacD doesn't have a shot. Bazin hasn't revealed himself."

"Leave now or die," Bazin said. Another squeal signaled the end of the announcement.

"We gotta give the Chairman more time," Linc said.

"I don't think the part about the police is a bluff," Eddie said. "He could very well have a whole battalion on his payroll. I don't see many options for us unless we can get in there somehow, but the foliage stops long before we could get to the factory grounds."

Linc looked at the motionless Ratel and had a brainstorm.

"Kensit doesn't know where you and I are, right?"

Eddie frowned at him. "It doesn't seem so."

"Then we can sneak into the cement plant if we can get inside that Ratel."

Eddie's eyes flicked to the armored vehicle and then back to Linc in sudden comprehension.

"Return of the Jedi?"

"Right. Where Chewie and Han take control of the Walker and trick the base commander outside. If we can get inside the Ratel, we can do the same thing. Drive right up to them, take out the other one before they know it's us, and wipe out the rest of them with that big bad cannon."

"I like it," Eddie said. "Now we just have to figure out a way to get over to it without them seeing us."

"Maybe we can bring it to us," Linc said. He activated his radio. "Linda, don't say anything. We heard everything Bazin said and we've got a plan. I hope you've seen *Return of the Jedi*."

44

As Juan and Trono swam, the reading on the Geiger counter grew stronger, far below dangerous levels but enough to guide them in the right direction. Still, they ran into dead ends and passages that were too tight to traverse, requiring backtracking that significantly cut into the time they had left. If they didn't turn back soon, they wouldn't have enough air to make the trip. This was why cave diving is considered one of the deadliest sports in the world.

They reached an air pocket and surfaced. There was just enough room for both of their heads.

"How's your air?" Juan asked.

"Getting close to the halfway mark."

"Me too. The radiation signature is strengthening, but I can't tell how far we have to go. At least we're going up. If we don't surface anywhere else in the next five minutes, you're going back."

"You mean, *we're* going back."

"Kensit's planning something for today, so we need to get to his telescope before that happens."

"Then I'm going with you. If you think we can make it, that's good enough for me."

Juan saw that Trono wasn't going to let him continue on by himself no matter what he said, so he didn't argue.

"All right. If we don't find some dry floor in five minutes, we'll turn around."

They put their masks back on and kept going. Juan tried to imagine Gunther Lutzen climbing through these caves over a hundred years ago with nothing more than some rope and a lantern and carrying his bulky camera with him the entire way. He might have explored the caves for weeks before happening upon the one that would prove his theories correct.

Five minutes later, Juan still saw no sign that they were coming up into the cavern Lutzen called Oz. He continued going past where he should, counting on his and Trono's ability to conserve more air on the way out than they'd consumed on the way in.

The risk paid off when his light reflected off a mirror sheen where water met air. He kicked toward it, hoping it wasn't merely another tiny air pocket.

He poked his head from the water and instead of his regulator being muffled by the closeness of a bubble, its rasp echoed off widely spaced walls and a high ceiling.

He removed his mouthpiece, did a three-hundred-and-sixty-degree turn, and saw no signs of light. He signaled Trono. They crawled out onto the damp limestone and shed all their scuba gear except the wetsuits. They unslung their MP-5 submachine guns, equipped with suppressors, which were reliable close-quarters weapons ideal for the underground setting. After shaking water out of the barrels and receivers, they continued following the path set by the Geiger counter.

The winding caves often split off in multiple directions, but each time only one showed a stronger radiation signature. It was after the third intersection that Juan spotted a glimmer of light in the distance. He kept his hooded flashlight pointed at the floor so that it wouldn't be seen as they approached.

When they got within fifty yards, Juan noticed that his light was starting to be reflected by green crystals embedded in the limestone walls and ceiling around them. This must have been where Lutzen had taken his photo of crystals.

As they got closer to the ghostly green light spilling from the main cavern, Juan and Trono split up to opposite sides of the passageway and kept their backs to the walls to stay out of sight as long as they could. It wasn't going to be possible to sneak into the cavern when it was so well lit. They had to depend on total surprise and the expectation that most of the armed men would be outside at the cement plant.

Juan set aside the Geiger counter and held out three fingers to Trono, who had his MP-5 against his shoulder. Juan counted down silently with his fingers. When his fist closed, he and Trono rushed into the cavern.

At first, Juan focused on nothing but the men inside. Two Caucasians were seated in chairs at an equipment console, dressed in short-sleeved shirts and khaki pants. He immediately dismissed them as non-threats. His eyes then shifted to movement more than a hundred feet away at the opposite side of the cavern, which he was just beginning to realize was larger than he had expected.

Two men stood guard at a man-made tunnel entrance, which

had to be the one leading to the cement plant. Both were dressed in camo gear and carried assault rifles and both looked bored with their duties babysitting the cave.

Juan and Trono's appearance happened so quickly and unexpectedly that the pair of mercenaries had no time to react. Juan put a three-round burst into the one on the right and Trono took care of the man on the left. The muffled blasts echoed around the cavern but likely wouldn't travel all the way to the cave exit.

Juan scanned the rest of the cavern, but it was clear. The terrified seated men had raised their hands high without being asked, Juan finally able to take in the glory of the cave itself.

The center was packed with electronic equipment, stainless steel conduits, and scientific gadgetry that reminded him of the inside of a nuclear reactor. The entire apparatus stretched from floor to ceiling and was the size of a semi-trailer truck. The machine was surrounded by a metal grating that served as a floor to access the equipment from a level surface. Several large crates marked "Fragile: Scientific Equipment" were stacked near the tunnel entrance.

It had to be the neutrino telescope. The design was both complicated and elegant.

But as amazing as the telescope looked, it wasn't even the most awe-inspiring part of the cave.

The rest of the cathedral-sized space was crisscrossed with translucent green crystals. If Eric was correct, they would be selenium infused with copper impurities. It suddenly hit Juan that this was what Lutzen had photographed. It wasn't a geode that he'd documented. It was a picture of the cavern itself.

The reason they'd been misled was because none of them imagined the sheer immensity of the crystals themselves. Many of these crystals, beautiful and jagged diagonal pillars with edges as sharp as butcher knives, were the size of redwoods. Some of them hung from the ceiling, some went all the way to the floor, and scattered between them were huge piles of crystals jumbled like rock candy. Juan spun around, gaping at the splendor of a billion facets.

Gunther Lutzen had been absolutely right. It really was as if Juan had stepped into the Emerald City of Oz.

It took Linc and Eddie fifteen minutes of belly crawling to get in position around the corner just out of sight of the cement plant. They settled into a ditch thirty feet from the road, with the RPG now resting on Linc's stomach.

"I'm ready," he said to Eddie.

"Same here." Eddie radioed to Linda. "Show them the sacrificial lamb."

"Coming your way."

The PIG accelerated from its hiding space until it passed them, providing a rich target for the Ratel and its cannon. As soon as the armored vehicle was in view, the PIG's bumper-mounted machine gun chattered, but the rounds bounced off the Ratel's outer hull as expected. The PIG made a spinning U-turn in the gravel as the 20mm cannon shells sizzled past. It passed Linc and Eddie again and had nearly reached the safety of the rock outcropping when smoke began to pour from the rear. The PIG veered wildly off the road and disappeared down the embankment toward the lake.

That was the cue for the Ratel to give chase and it didn't disappoint. The vehicle's commander was obviously confident that he'd scored a mortal shot and wanted to verify his kill.

The Ratel roared past Linc and Eddie's ditch and came to a stop at the top of the embankment while smoke continued to rise from the wreckage of the PIG. The side doors popped open and four men in camo gear and helmets jumped out, aiming their assault rifles in the PIG's direction.

Linc and Eddie leaped from their hiding spot and rushed at the men.

"Drop your weapons!" they both shouted in the crude Creole that MacD had taught them over the radio.

Bazin's mercenaries were either brave or too stupid to realize when they were caught with their pants down. They crouched against the Ratel and raised their weapons to fire.

That was all the warning they'd get. Eddie expertly took down three of them while Linc got the fourth with his sidearm pistol. But the driver inside the Ratel didn't know when he'd been beaten. He backed it up and swiveled the main cannon around to fire at them.

Linc shook his head at the idiocy. He holstered the pistol, shouldered the RPG, and pulled the trigger before the cannon was in position. The antitank round blew the armored vehicle apart.

He dropped the empty tube and kicked the gravel in frustration.

"There goes our *Return of the Jedi* plan," Linc said.

"It was a good idea," Eddie said. He called to Linda. "What's the damage to the PIG?"

"Nothing at all," she replied. "With Eric's snappy driving, they completely missed. The smokescreen worked just like you thought it would."

The PIG powered its way up the embankment, the smoke now dissipating.

The two of them walked over and checked the mercenaries. All of them were corpses.

Eddie looked at the largest of the bodies and then at Linc as if he were comparing them.

"What's going on in that devious mind of yours?" Linc asked.

"You could pass for a Haitian from a distance."

"I suppose so, but we don't have the Ratel anymore."

"We still have the PIG. What if the mercenaries captured it and drove it back? As long as they thought you were one of the them, we could get within visual range of the last Ratel. The PIG does have one rocket left."

Linc thought about the plan and nodded. "I like the idea, but we need something to really sell it."

"Like what?"

Linc picked up one of the mercenaries's walkie-talkies and started pulling off the uniform of the least bloody soldier. "We're going to require MacD's language skills one more time."

Bazin tried to raise the third Ratel on the radio and got only static in reply. He peered from his concealed window within the main building, but all he could make out was a plume of smoke over the hill.

If the Ratel had been taken out, it still didn't change anything. For Cabrillo and his men to attack, they would be endangering the lives of sixty hostages. And a straight-on assault would be suicidal, with the Ratel he had left and the number of men still deployed outside.

A vehicle came around the hill, but it wasn't the missing Ratel. It was the truck that the Corporation called the PIG. He was about to order the remaining Ratel to open fire when he saw one of his men standing in the PIG's open roof, waving his gun and shouting with glee. He could see two more men inside the cab, driving their prize back to the cement plant.

The man in the roof had a walkie-talkie to his mouth. Bazin listened on his, but the voice was almost unintelligible with the wind and engine noise. He was shouting in Creole that they had captured the American's truck and not to shoot.

"Stand down," he radioed to the rest of the men.

Kensit had given him the intel on Linda Ross and her men, but he had been keeping an eye on them only in short spurts, when he could divert his attention away from the drone mission. Bazin didn't object since he had the situation under control and the Haitian National Police on the way as backup.

As the captured PIG approached, Bazin confidently called Kensit back with the intention of telling him his services wouldn't be needed anymore and to concentrate on destroying Air Force Two.

"What the hell is going on down there?" Kensit shouted when he answered, shocking Bazin, who'd never heard Kensit so out of control.

"What are you talking about? We've captured the Corporation's vehicle. It's over."

"It's *not* over! I can't see anything. Something happened to Sentinel. My screen went blank and I can't contact any of the techs. I'm trying to reconnect now. You get your butt in there and find out what's going on. And don't waste any more time. Set the self-destruct. I'll need an hour to complete the mission. Go!"

He hung up.

Bazin was about to turn and head for the tunnel when he realized that Kensit hadn't been able to watch what was happening in the battle between the Ratel and the PIG.

He looked out the window with dawning horror. The PIG was close enough now for him to make out the faces of the men and he noticed two things at once: the driver of the PIG had a bullet hole through his forehead and the man on top of the vehicle shouting in Creole was not one of his men. It had to be Franklin Lincoln.

He raised his radio to tell his forces to open fire, but it was too late. A rocket shot from the side of the PIG and hit the last Ratel, blowing it to pieces and his men around it to the ground.

Bazin heard Lincoln yelling for the hostages to get down. They dived to the ground as one and the machine gun behind the PIG's fake bumper chewed through the mercenaries like a meat grinder. Eddie Seng joined Lincoln on the roof of the PIG and added his firepower to the assault. Two more of his men fell to sniper fire. The rest scattered for cover. It was only a matter of time before they were defeated.

Bazin was furious that Kensit couldn't keep his precious machine running properly during the time when they needed it most. He knew a technical glitch in such a complicated device was inevitable. His only choice now was to get in to Sentinel, set the self-destruct, and escape in the speedboat he had stashed in one of the outbuildings along the water. Although he never expected the cement plant to fall, he always planned for the worst, so he also had a hidden SUV waiting for him on the other side of the lake.

As for his mercenaries, with the money he was pulling in from the drug lords, he could always hire more. And when Sentinel 2 was up and running, he could buy as many of them as he wanted. Haiti would still be his.

But he couldn't let them capture Sentinel 1 intact. Kensit had been clever to build in a self-destruct that was more than simply an explosive to obliterate the equipment. Equipment was replaceable. It was the Oz cave, with its unique natural properties, that was the real treasure. Someone could eventually clear it out and build a replica of Sentinel.

Kensit had rigged Sentinel itself to prevent that from happening. The device used a five-pound cobalt 60 core scavenged from used medical equipment to focus the neutrinos. The cave itself was slightly radioactive now, but nothing hazardous. However, detonating the core inside the cave would make the interior dangerously radioactive for generations. It would be impossible to build another neutrino telescope inside it.

As the battle raged outside, Bazin picked up an RPG from the weapons stockpile in case the Corporation helicopter tried to chase him across the lake. Armed with an Uzi submachine gun, he took off into the tunnel toward the Oz cave to start the sequence that would destroy Sentinel 1 forever.

46

The two techs had played dumb, responding to Juan's questions in Russian, but he shocked them when he asked them fluently in their native tongue where Kensit was. He was also very eloquent about what would happen to them if they didn't cooperate. Their bravery exhausted, the techs switched to English and told him that Kensit was on a yacht where he was monitoring the feed from the neutrino telescope that he had named Sentinel.

One of the screens on the control panel was slaved to the view that Kensit had from his remote location. Juan had been amazed to see it switch from a close-up of Linda to a shot of the PIG as it raced toward a Ratel armored vehicle.

Juan's first instructed them to deactivate the view altogether. Without it, his crew had a fighting chance at whatever they were attempting. The screen abruptly went dark, surely causing Kensit to go apoplectic. A phone on the console rang insistently, but he told the Russians to ignore it.

Then Juan had a better idea.

"Do you know how this thing works?" he asked them. When they hesitated, he and Trono pointed the barrel of their MP-5s in the techs' faces.

"We can operate it," one of the techs said, "but that's all."

"Do you know Kensit's location?"

He quickly nodded and pointed at a monitor showing the latitude and longitude. "That's where the signal is being beamed to," the tech said.

"Time for a demo," Juan said. "Show me Kensit's cozy little hideaway."

The tech nodded and eased over to the console, where he nervously manipulated the controls until a new image came up on the screen. It was an overhead view of a white hundred-foot yacht lazily cruising an azure sea. The image zoomed down as if it were a kamikaze dive bomber. The virtual camera plunged through the deck until it stopped in a room with a console that looked identical to the one in the cave.

"Pan around," Juan said. "Get a shot of this, Mike."

Trono held up his phone to video what they were watching.

The place was a sty, with empty cans and plates of food littering the floor. On the wall there was a map of Mexico with a pin stuck into a spot on the Yucatán Peninsula marked "Phase 2" in a sloppy scrawl. Papers with jotted equations and notes were strewn across the desk. A journal lay on the end of it. Gunther Lutzen's name was penned in neat letters on the cover.

The camera kept moving until it settled on Kensit himself. He stared wide-eyed directly at the screen as if he could see them.

But he *couldn't* see them. Kensit was monitoring the view from

Sentinel, so he was actually seeing himself on his own screen. His mouth began to move.

"Turn up the volume," Juan said.

The tech adjusted the sound and they heard Kensit's reedy voice: ". . . couldn't have gotten in there. If it's you, Cabrillo, I want you to know you're too late. If you survive the rest of the day, which I doubt, you'll see what little impact all of your efforts have made. Now it's time to say good-bye."

The screen went blank.

"What happened? Get it back!" Juan demanded.

"We can't," the tech said, backing away. "Kensit can control the software remotely from his location. He's probably locked out our ability to operate Sentinel and switched off the real-time feed to this console. But from his remote site he can still watch and control what Sentinel sees."

"What's he planning today?"

They hesitated again, but Juan could see that they knew. They backed up some more as if trying to edge their way toward the exit to make a run for it.

"Tell me," he growled. "Now!"

"Okay, okay," one of the techs said, his hands raised in supplication. "He's going to shoot down—"

A torrent of bullets tore into the chests of both techs. They came from the direction of the man-made tunnel leading to the cement plant. The only reason Juan and Trono were spared the same fate was because of the hulking mass of Sentinel machinery between them and the tunnel.

Juan and Trono scrambled behind one of the selenium pillars. Juan barely brushed against it and the razor edge ripped his fatigues. Diving for cover was not going to be an attractive option in this cave.

In the reflection of a huge crystal, Juan could see that it was Bazin who had killed the two techs. He was hunched over the console, typing with one hand while training his Uzi in their direction with the other. An RPG was propped against the console next to him.

Juan motioned for Trono to try to flank him at the tunnel's entrance by circling around the immense telescope.

"I know what you're doing, Cabrillo," Bazin called out. "I'd try to flank me, too. It won't work."

"Why?" Juan replied. "Because Kensit is telling you where we are?"

"It's an incredible advantage, isn't it?"

"I know my people are outside. You can't escape."

"I'd be more worried about this bomb if I were you."

Juan watched him typing and realized what he was enabling. "Have you got yourselves an old-fashioned self-destruct mechanism there?"

"It's state-of-the-art," Bazin said. "I suggest you go back the same way you came in here if you don't want to self-destruct as well." He made one last press with a flourish and said, "There. *Au revoir, mon capitaine.*"

Bazin picked up the RPG and backed away slowly, but Juan had no intention of letting him get away. He didn't have a direct shot at Bazin, but he wouldn't have taken it anyway. He needed Bazin alive to tell him what Kensit's target was.

He waited until Bazin was under a crystal stalactite dangling above like a chandelier. He unloaded his entire thirty-round magazine into it, showering Bazin with shards that cut him in a hundred places.

Bazin dropped the RPG to shield himself from further mutilation, but he kept hold of the submachine gun, shooting wildly in

Juan's direction. Blood gushed over his eyes. When the hammer clicked on an empty chamber, Juan rushed him.

He expected Trono to do the same, but more gunshots came from the tunnel. Some of Bazin's soldiers must have come to his rescue and Trono returned fire to keep them at bay, causing Juan to be one-on-one with Bazin.

Juan slammed into Bazin, throwing him to the metal flooring. Bazin leaned over and Juan gave him a solid punch to the kidneys.

What he forgot was that Bazin knew more about Juan than most any other opponent ever had.

While Bazin was absorbing Juan's punches, he grabbed for Juan's prosthetic leg. Bazin knew exactly how the combat version was strapped on and yanked at the buckles holding it to Juan's calf. It came free, sending Juan tumbling over. He was able to grab it away from Bazin, but giving chase would be impossible now.

Bazin wiped his eyes clear, scrabbled over to the Uzi, and popped the magazine out. Before Juan could snap the combat leg open to retrieve his Colt Defender, Bazin sprinted across the cave to find cover where he could reload and then finish Juan off.

Juan fired as Bazin retreated to keep him from ducking behind the closest crystal column. He thought he nicked Bazin in the leg just as he ran into the passageway where Juan and Trono had entered from the underwater cavern.

Juan heard the distinctive click of a magazine being rammed home and noticed that now he was the one under the chandelier of doom. If Bazin tried the same trick of firing into the cave ceiling, Juan would be a sitting duck.

Even though he wanted Bazin alive, Juan didn't have a choice. He rolled over and snatched up the RPG. Balancing himself on his stump, he aimed at the passageway and pulled the trigger.

The RPG lanced out on a tongue of fire and struck the ceiling, sending a rain of limestone down and collapsing the entire opening. When the haze cleared, there was no doubt that the passageway to the underwater entrance had been completely sealed. Bazin was gone.

Even as he was pulling the trigger, Juan thought that firing the RPG might set off a chain reaction of ceiling collapses. He held his breath as many of the huge crystals trembled and cracked. A few fragments fell harmlessly, then all was quiet.

Juan rushed to reattach his leg and help Trono fend off the remaining mercenaries, but as soon as he had it back on and was standing, he realized that the gunfire had ceased.

Trono cautiously emerged from behind the pillar.

"Special delivery for Juan Cabrillo!" yelled Linc's baritone from inside the tunnel to the cement plant. "We've got a box of chocolates for you if you don't shoot us."

"Come on in!" Juan yelled back. "We're starving."

Linc strode forward into the light and his jaw dropped to his chest as his gaze quickly took in the spectacle of Sentinel and the giant crystals of the Oz cave.

"That must have been what we looked like when we got here," Juan said to Trono.

"I don't know if I've ever seen him speechless before," Trono replied.

"Is everything buttoned-up out there?" Juan asked Linc.

"Five remaining men gave up after seeing the rest of their buddies go down. It's a mess. Bazin had sixty men digging tunnels down here. They were nearly starved to death. Linda is scrounging up what food she can find for them." He waved behind him. "I've got someone you should meet."

A disheveled but proud Haitian was escorted in by Eddie.

After gawking at the cave, he shook hands with a firm grip when he was introduced to Juan.

"Jacques Duval, deputy commander of the Haitian National Police," he said. "I understand you are the one I can thank for this rescue."

"You've got a whole team to thank," Juan said. "I'm not the Lone Ranger. Come to think of it, even the Lone Ranger wasn't the Lone Ranger. Not with Tonto around to save his skin all the time."

Duval cocked his head in confusion, not understanding the American allusion. "Where is Hector Bazin?"

Juan pointed to the tons of fallen rock on the other side of the cave. "Buried in there."

Duval nodded, both rueful and satisfied. "It had to be done. Thank you again. Now I must go and take command of the police that think they are coming to save Hector."

"Will they listen to you?"

"What choice will they have? There's no one else left here to command them."

He turned on his heel and strode away.

"Tough guy," Juan said.

"Other than some water," Eddie said, "he didn't ask for anything for himself, just for his men."

Juan nodded in understanding. He would have done the same. Those kinds of leaders usually win out over men like Bazin in the end.

"Get Eric in here," he said. "We've got another problem."

Two minutes later, Linc and Eddie were back outside, and Eric was sitting at the Sentinel console trying to ascertain how to deactivate the self-destruct, whose timer was already down to fifty-three minutes.

"Can you disable it?" Juan asked.

Eric shook his head. "I'd be afraid to try. Kensit could have it booby-trapped to explode if the wrong code is entered."

"What about pulling the plug?"

"No good. The outside power is already gone, and it looks like the battery backup is integral to the machine. Any attempt to disengage electrical power might also set it off. I'm afraid there's no way to prevent the explosion."

Juan ran his fingers through his hair, frustrated that they were out of options.

"The techs said Kensit was going to shoot something down. We have to figure out what and how he's going to do it."

"Well, it looks like the self-destruct is an independent system," Eric said. "Maybe we can see what Kensit is doing?" He moved over to where Juan had told him he'd seen Kensit's remote workstation.

Juan shook his head. "We already tried that. Kensit locked us out."

"Can you describe what the techs did?"

"I don't have to," Juan said, and waved Trono over. "Show him your recording."

Trono played back the video. Within a minute, Eric stopped him and tapped on the keyboard. The blank screen suddenly came to life, rewinding to show Kensit speaking again, but this time in reverse.

Juan gripped Eric's shoulder. "Nice work."

"I noticed in Trono's recording that the tech seemed to press a PLAY button on the keyboard," Eric said. "It only stands to reason that there would be other recording commands. Given our assumption that Kensit could watch just one location at a time, it's logical that he would have built in a feature to record everything he was watching so that he could go back and see it again in case he missed something in real time. We may not be able to see what Sentinel is watching now, but we can see what it has watched in the past."

"It's better than nothing. Keep going back until we see something besides us."

Eric sped up the reverse. It ran through shots of the PIG fighting with the Ratel, Linda and the team up on the hill overlooking the cement plant, the helicopter landing, and so on. Then he slowed when it switched to a shot of a plane framed against a brilliant blue sky.

Juan's blood went cold. The white and blue 747 was instantly recognizable as soon as he saw UNITED STATES OF AMERICA emblazoned on its fuselage.

He grabbed Trono's phone and sprinted for the exit tunnel, yelling over his shoulder as he ran. "Stay here as long as possible and find out everything you can about what Kensit was watching."

He didn't wait for a response. He was nearly to the other end of the tunnel before he could get a signal to radio Gomez for immediate pickup and a dash back to the *Oregon*.

He had a yacht to sink.

47

Kensit was shaken by the invasion of the cave and his continuing inability to get in touch with anyone at the facility, including Bazin, but he had a mission to complete. At least he'd retaken control of Sentinel—that is, until it self-destructed in less than thirty minutes. But once Brian Washburn was vice president, he would have a powerful ally in the government to protect him while he built Sentinel 2.

Unbeknownst to the ground controllers at Tyndall, he had been commanding the QF-16 drones for an hour, with the two manned F-15s following in close formation, as they approached the Bahamas. Now it was time to set them on an intercept course with Air Force Two.

He disabled the video and data feeds from all six drones to Tyndall. He wished he could see the operators' faces at losing their connection, but he couldn't take his eyes off the drones. His current viewpoint was following a quarter mile behind the rearmost planes. All eight planes were flying in a stacked V formation, separated by only a few hundred feet.

Surely the controllers were contacting the fighter pilots now, who would be telling them that they saw no change in the flight pattern, that it must be a communication malfunction.

Kensit took manual control of Quail 6, the drone closest to the F-15 on the left. Quail 6 suddenly banked left and rolled into the nose of the F-15, which sheared it off. The QF-16 drone exploded in a fireball as its external fuel tank ignited, catching the F-15 in the blast and blowing it apart as well. The pilot inside never had a chance.

Kensit quickly switched control to Quail 5 on the other side of the formation. He attempted the same maneuver, but this F-15 pilot was more alert. He loosed a volley from his M61 Vulcan cannon at Quail 5, but the rounds hit Quail 4 instead, chopping its tail to pieces and sending it into a rolling dive toward the Caribbean.

Quail 5 yawed to the right, catching the tip of the F-15's wing as it tried to bank away. The wings of both the drone and the F-15 snapped off, and they began to break up as fire streamed from their tanks. The pilot punched out, and his ejection seat disappeared from Kensit's view.

Kensit breathed a sigh of relief after the most difficult part of the mission was over. If one of the F-15s had gotten away, it could have brought down the rest of the drones with missiles. Now there were no fighters close enough to reach the drones before they intercepted the vice president's plane.

The three drones left were plenty to do the job. Even one should be enough to destroy the unarmed 747.

Pleased with himself, Kensit took another gulp of Red Bull and set the course for the three autopilots, and, with afterburners lit, sent the drones to their doom at greater than the speed of sound.

Thanks to a spare set of fatigues on the helicopter, Juan was out of his wetsuit by the time he, Linda, and Hali reached the *Oregon*. Juan had briefed Max and Murph during the flight in. The ship was ready to depart as soon as the chopper landed. Then he'd made a call to Langston Overholt to warn him about what he'd seen on Sentinel's screen.

They dashed to the op center, and Juan had barely taken his place in the Kirk Chair when he ordered Linda to set a course for Kensit's last-known location, a spot northwest of Haiti that was over a hundred miles from their current position. Based on the coordinates from Trono's phone recording, it looked like the yacht had been traveling east. But since Kensit knew Sentinel had been compromised and they could see his yacht's position from its connection to the neutrino telescope, he'd probably changed course to put more distance between them.

Juan glanced back at Max and grinned, happy to be back on board. "Are the engines revved?"

"She's champing at the bit," Max replied.

"Then give me all she's got."

"Flank speed, aye," he replied, and the magnetohydrodynamic engines spun up to full power, gushing jets of water behind them as the *Oregon* shot out of the Bahia de Grand Pierre.

"Wepps," he said, calling Murph by the nickname for the weapons station. "How long until we're in Exocet range?"

"At present speed, it'll be at least forty minutes. If we can't get an exact coordinate from Eric, we'll have to be even closer to make a positive ID on the yacht."

"Hali, get Eric on the line. I want to know if he has any more intel for us. Then, while we're talking, call Langston Overholt and let me know when you've got him."

Eric had previously established communications with them through the Oz cave's landline and his voice issued from the op center's speakers. "This thing is incredible."

"Man, you have all the fun," Murph said.

"I could spend weeks studying the technology."

Juan looked at the ship's chronometer. "You've actually got twenty-three minutes left, so give us the highlights."

"Right. Okay, we've been able to establish Kensit's location, but we'll only have that as long as we're in here and Sentinel is connected to his yacht. After that, he's a ghost." He passed the new coordinates on to Linda.

"He turned northwest," Murph said. "We won't be there for fifty minutes."

"That's a big problem," Eric said.

"Why?" Juan asked.

"Because Kensit took over six QF-16 fighter drones over an hour ago. They took off from Tyndall Air Force Base and are headed in our direction. They should be almost directly above Kensit right now."

Juan banged his fist in triumph on the arm of his chair. "That's how he's going to shoot it down."

"I've got Overholt on the line," Hali said.

"Patch him in." Hali nodded, and Juan said, "Lang, did you get in touch with the president?"

"It's not the president," Overholt said. "He's in Chicago this morning. But Vice President Sandecker is on his way back from Brazil."

"Where is his plane?"

"It just passed over Haiti."

"You need to get the pilot to turn around. Lawrence Kensit is about to bring Air Force Two down with drones he's hijacked."

"Oh, my God," Overholt said. "We just got a flash report that the data feeds from six drones were lost as they were flying toward the Bahamas for a demonstration at the UNITAS naval exercise. They haven't been able to make contact with either the drones or the chase planes."

"If the drones are modified F-16s, they'll be able to chase down Air Force Two unless their fuel is exhausted before they can intercept."

"Convincing the Air Force that the vice president's plane is about to be shot down by their own jets is going to be a tough sell, but I'll see what I can do."

The line clicked.

"Did you get that, Eric?" Juan said.

"Yes, and I might be able to help. I'm sending the transponder codes for both the drones and Air Force Two to Hali so you can track them. I got them off of Kensit's remote control panel."

"Good work."

"That shot from Trono's recording also might show Murph how to deactivate Kensit's connection with the drones if he can figure out how Kensit is controlling them."

Juan nodded to Murph and threw him Trono's phone. Murph caught it with one hand and began downloading the video from the phone to the ship's computer system.

"Before you go, I have another troublesome issue for you," Eric said.

"By all means," Juan said, shaking his head. "We're just twiddling our thumbs anyway."

"I found a video of Admiral Ruiz taken last night."

"Where?"

"I don't know. It starts with an overhead shot of three ships, then zooms down to the bridge and there's Ruiz talking on the phone. According to a sign on the bridge, the ship is called the *Reina Azul*. I think she's speaking with Kensit and he was watching her."

The *Blue Queen*, Juan thought. "Can you play back the conversation for us?"

"Yes, but you can only hear Ruiz's part of it. Here it goes."

Juan immediately recognized the dusky voice that threatened him just a week ago off the coast of Venezuela. Pauses interrupted her speech while she listened to Kensit.

They're launched from a container, she said. *No, even the* Oregon *will have trouble evading them. They're called Carrier Killers for a reason . . . Don't worry. The captains of the* Maracaibo *and* Valera *think we're going into Port-au-Prince to pick up a huge load of cement bound for Puerto Cabello . . . Through a shell company. They have no idea I'm on board . . . I had my men attach bombs to their hulls during the night. There won't be survivors or witnesses . . . Then I expect you to deliver . . . Yes, we'll be there on time.*

"That's it," Eric said.

"Not good," Murph said as he watched Trono's video. "Carrier Killer is the nickname for the Russian 3M-54 Klub antiship missile. It's very hard to shoot down because it accelerates to mach three during the final approach to the target and has thrust vectoring for high-angle defensive maneuvers."

This was sounding worse and worse to Juan. "Can the Gatling guns hit them?"

"If we're lucky, but it's not a sure thing. The Klub's speed is over three times as fast as our own Exocets. I'd say the Metal Storm gun is our best shot."

"Why the other two ships?" Max wondered. "Safety in numbers?"

Juan nodded. "Human shields. Ruiz knows we won't attack unless we know which ship to sink."

"But we'll know as soon as they launch. Those tailpipes spew out a lot of smoke."

"There's something we're missing," Juan said. "Linda, get on the radar and keep an eye out for any three-ship convoys. I'll control the helm from here. Wepps, be ready on the defensive weapons."

Murph lowered the false doors hiding the radar-guided Gatling guns and raised the Metal Storm array into place on the deck. "Weapons ready."

Juan thought about the names of the two ships Ruiz mentioned. Maracaibo was a large lake in Venezuela. It made sense that Ruiz would dupe cargo ships from her own country. It was possible that their guest Maria Sandoval knew one of the ship captains who was unwittingly serving as a decoy for Ruiz. She did say that the Venezuelan ship captains were a tight-knit group.

"Hali," Juan said, "ask Captain Sandoval to join us in the op center."

"After the great smuggling cover story we got her to swallow?" Max said in amazement. "She won't believe that after seeing what we've got in here."

"I have a feeling we don't have much time left, we need to get her on the satellite phone. We'll get her to pinkie-swear not to talk, if that makes you feel better."

Max shrugged in acquiescence. "That's a binding contract, as far as I'm concerned."

"She's on her way," Hali said. "I'm putting the transponders up on the view screen." A map of the Caribbean appeared with parts of Cuba, the Bahamas, and Haiti visible. Graphics of three red planes just north of Cuba was slowly converging with a blue-plane graphic northwest of Haiti. "That blue one is Air Force Two. The red ones represent three drones."

"What happened to the rest of them?" Juan wondered.

"They must have crashed or we'd be getting a signal from them."

"Murph," Juan said, "tell me you can disable those drones."

Murph was bent over his console in concentration and didn't respond.

"Murph?" Juan prompted again after a few seconds.

Murph finally raised his head. "It looks like he's controlling one of the drones manually and letting the other two fly on auto-pilot."

"Can you interrupt the signal?"

"No, and I can't take over the one he's controlling manually. I wouldn't have the right setup here to maneuver the plane anyway. But it's possible that I could reprogram the autopilot."

"Do it. At their current closing speed, we've only got ten minutes until those drones are on top of Air Force Two."

Maria Sandoval was escorted into the op center and her eyes went wide as she took in the high-tech command bridge.

"Who *are* you people?" she said in awe.

"We're the good guys, Captain," Juan said as he rose to greet her. "And I need your help. I can't explain everything that's going on right now, but it seems that your friend Admiral Ruiz is going to try to sink us and I need to know where she is. Do you know the captains of the cargo ships *Maracaibo* or *Valera*?"

"Not the *Maracaibo*," she said, "but Eduardo Garcia is the master of the *Valera*. I've met him a few times while we were docked in Puerto Cabello. He's a good captain, though he's a bit of an odd character."

"It's very important that we speak to him. I'm going to pass you to Hali and he's going to help you get in touch with Captain Garcia. What we have to ask him will be better coming from someone he knows."

"I've got an incoming missile!" Linda called out.

"What? From what direction?"

"It came over Île de la Gonâve to the south. Ruiz's launch ship must be on the other side of the island. Our radar couldn't see anything until the missile passed over the island."

Juan cursed under his breath. She was using the same tactic against him that he'd used against her with the *Washington* by putting the island between them. He couldn't fire back with his own missile because he didn't have a lock on the target while apparently she had a clear lock on the *Oregon* thanks to Kensit and Sentinel.

"Wepps! Get ready!"

Murph didn't look up from his furious typing. "I'm kinda busy trying to save the VP."

"Max, get on weapons."

Max rushed over and took Murph's usual spot at the weapons station. The missile was already on its supersonic final approach. He pushed the button to activate the Gatling gun.

Using the same technology as the Navy's Phalanx close-in weapons system, the six-barreled gun spun up to its full speed and fired 20mm armor-piercing tungsten rounds that sounded like an industrial saw ripping through a redwood. The radar, housed in a dome above the gun and looking uncannily like R2-D2, attempted to lock onto the elusive target, but at such a high rate of speed it had trouble connecting.

Max kept it firing, and fired the Metal Storm gun as well, unleashing five hundred rounds in the blink of an eye. The wall of tungsten finally made contact eight hundred yards from the *Oregon*.

Most of the missile disintegrated and plunged into the sea, but a substantial portion tumbled on, propelled by its supersonic velocity. Metal fragments smashed into *Oregon*'s hull.

"Damage report," Juan said.

Max consulted the exterior cameras. "No hull breach, but we've lost the Gatling gun's radar in the impact. Reloading the Metal Storm."

"Another missile on the way!" Linda said. "Two minutes to target."

"I'm turning us one hundred and eighty degrees to bring our starboard Gatling gun to bear," Juan said as he swung the *Oregon* about. "Be ready on the Exocet, Max."

"We need a target first," Max answered. "We could hit any vessel on the other side of the island if we don't have the coordinates of the ship that's firing."

Juan looked at Maria, who stared back at him with a stunned expression, the phone headset to her ear.

All he said was, "Hurry, please."

The captains of both the *Maracaibo* and the *Valera* were radioing desperate Maydays about a ship in their midst firing missiles as the second Klub rocketed over the island separating Ruiz from the *Oregon*. Ruiz saw, by her adversary's impotence, that her plan to hire ships to sail next to the *Reina Azul* had the effect she'd intended. Cabrillo didn't have the *cojones* to fire blindly back at her when there were two cargo vessels full of innocent crew members not a quarter mile to either side. Even with all that was at stake, he was too weak to risk sinking a noncombatant.

She watched the *Oregon* on the monitor feed from a camera planted on the other side of the eight-mile-wide island. Kensit had warned her that he would be too busy to provide real-time intel about the *Oregon*'s location, so in the middle of the night she'd sent two men to set up a camera with a high-powered transmitter on a remote beach on the opposite side of the island. When Cabrillo's ship sailed into view on the only course it could have taken out of Bahia de Grand Pierre, she'd attacked.

As her launch team had cautioned her, the missile control was limited by the container's positioning on the old cargo ship, so they could only be launched one at a time. Initially, she'd been furious about the restriction, but now she was rather enjoying seeing the *Oregon* flail away at the missiles. The high-tech ship wouldn't be able to shoot them down indefinitely. One of them would get through.

"Do you have the escape boat ready for evacuation?" she asked the captain.

"Aye, Admiral," he replied. "It's tied up on the port side."

"What about the bombs? I want to scuttle all three ships as soon as the *Oregon*'s back is broken."

"They've all been set and are ready to receive the detonation command." He handed her the remote detonator.

"Excellent work, Captain," she said. "You'll have a high place in my government when I'm president."

As the Maydays continued, she wasn't worried about any authorities coming to the rescue. Haiti had a token Coast Guard and no Navy, so the best they could do was send out a police launch or ask for help from the Dominican Republic. She and her men would be long gone before either could mobilize.

The second Klub darted toward the *Oregon* and she was sure this one would make it through, but the missile exploded off its stern in a hail of defensive gunfire, showering the ship with debris. Flames cascaded across the deck and this time she was satisfied they were the real thing, not the fakery she'd seen off the coast of Puerto La Cruz.

The only disappointment was that Cabrillo didn't know who

was about to sink his beloved ship. But *she'd* know and that's all that mattered.

Time to end this.

She radioed down to launch control. "Fire the third missile."

"The last one took out Metal Storm," Max said. "Only the two Gatlings left."

"I'm going to angle us so both of them have a shot at the next missile," Juan said, turning the *Oregon* toward Île de la Gonâve. "How are you doing, Maria?"

"I've got Captain Garcia on his sat phone," she said in triumph. "He's very upset. What should I ask him?"

"Can he get in touch with the *Maracaibo*'s captain, but not over the radio?"

She relayed the question. "Yes, he also has a sat phone."

"Good. Tell them to come to a full stop, and get me their exact GPS coordinates—and I mean down to the inch. And ask them if there are any other ships in the area." She looked confused by the request but asked Garcia anyway.

Juan turned to Max. "Get ready to plug them into the Exocet guidance computer."

Max furrowed his brow then nodded in understanding. "Tell it what not to hit?"

"Right." Juan checked the map and saw that the drones and Air Force Two were near to converging. "Murph, what's your status with the drones? We've only got five minutes left."

"Almost got it. I have to do this right the first time or Kensit will lock me out permanently."

"All right. Keep on it."

"I've got the coordinates!" Maria yelled, and told them to Max, who plugged them into the guidance computer.

"Missile three sighted!" Linda called out. "Two minutes to target."

"Ready on the Exocet!"

"Fire!"

The Exocet was ejected from its tube and its turbojet kicked in, sending the antiship missile skimming across the water. Its radar altimeter kept it a mere ten feet above the surface.

"The Klub is one minute out," Linda said.

"Max, try to get the missile in a cross fire with the Gatlings. It's our only chance."

An industrial-scale ripping sound echoed from two sides of the ship as the Gatlings spewed tungsten rounds at the approaching missile. The tracer streams danced as the missile bobbed and weaved to avoid the shells. But twenty seconds of uninterrupted fire eventually found its target and the missile erupted in an orange torrent of flame.

"Phew," Max said as he pointedly wiped his brow. "Gun two is down to thirty rounds left in the drum. I doubt we can take down another missile."

"Time to target on the Exocet?"

"I'm not sure," Linda replied. "It's over the island now, so we can't see it anymore on radar."

"Maria," Juan said calmly, "can you kindly ask Captain Garcia if he sees our missile?"

When Ruiz saw the missile fired from the *Oregon* on the shore-based camera feed, she assumed it was a last-ditch effort to shoot down her own Klub and that it had failed when they passed each other.

Now as it crossed the southern coast of the island and she had a better look at it, she recognized it as an Exocet antiship missile.

She had misjudged Cabrillo. In his desperation, he must have taken a blind shot, hoping that it would hit her ship merely by chance. Instead, it was traveling directly toward the *Valera*. She mentally patted herself on the back for bringing along the extra ships as decoys and prepared to order the final missile launched to finish off the *Oregon*.

Her attitude changed in one horrible moment. Guided by some unseen hand, the Exocet abruptly altered course and headed straight toward the *Reina Azul*.

The captain began to order evasive maneuvers, but she knew it was useless. With no defensive capabilities, her ship might as well have had a bull's-eye painted on its side.

The missile struck the hull amidships, blasting a gigantic hole in the side of the cargo vessel. Ruiz might have survived long enough to get to the escape boat if not for the scuttling charges she'd ordered planted on the ship. They rocked the ship as each was ignited in a cascade of explosions.

Ruiz's final emotion was a mixture of rage and jealousy at being the second-best tactician in what should have been a certain victory. Then the fourth Klub missile detonated in its launcher, vaporizing the bridge and every person on it.

Maria yanked the headset off, like she'd heard a deafening noise, and Juan's heart stopped for a moment, thinking the Exocet had hit the wrong target. Then she put the set back to her ear and tentatively said, "Captain Garcia, are you still there?"

After a tense moment, she jumped to her feet and shouted with joy. "Garcia says it's a direct hit! The *Reina Azul* was blown to pieces and is already going to the bottom. He and the captain of the *Maracaibo* will look for survivors, but he doesn't expect any."

Juan breathed a sigh of relief, but he wasn't ready to celebrate yet.

"Murph, you've got three minutes left."

"I get better the closer I get to a deadline," he replied with a lighthearted intensity. "And *voilà*!" Two video feeds showed up on the main view screen next to the map. Each of them showed blue sky and clouds flitting past below.

"Are those from the drones?" Juan asked.

"The two I control. Kensit's controlling one of the drones, but I've got command of the autopilots on the other two. The thing is he doesn't know that I do. But even so, the QF-16 on manual is too maneuverable. I'd lose a straight dogfight a hundred percent of the time. So the question is, how do I collide with his drone before it takes out Air Force Two?"

Juan looked at the map of the drones converging on Air Force Two northeast of Cuba and noticed they were near Kensit's location as well. He was probably excited to watch Air Force Two come down next to his yacht.

"Let's try a two-pronged approach. If one doesn't work, the other might. Do you think he'll notice the course change on one of the drones he's not controlling if it's subtle?"

Murph rubbed his chin in thought. "Probably not. Especially if there was something else to distract his attention."

"Then program one of the drones for a slow-motion collision, closing the distance between them by a foot every second. By the time he realizes what's happening, the drones will be colliding."

"I like it. What's the distraction?"

Juan smiled. "We'll make the other drone go into a sudden dive. Program it for an intercept course to the updated coordinates we're getting from Eric."

Murph looked up at the map, and when he turned back, his grin was even wider than Juan's as he input the data with gusto.

"Don't lean on my chair," Kensit said to Washburn in a tone not normally used to address someone who was destined to be the president of the United States. He didn't care. The former governor kept inadvertently pushing down on Kensit's seat back, disturbing his concentration. He was beginning to regret bringing Washburn in to watch the final destruction of Air Force Two.

"Sorry," Washburn said for the second time, and backed up to the wall. "How long until you shoot it down?"

"Not long now . . . There it is!" He pointed at a dot blooming against the blue sky on the lead drone's video feed. "It's five miles away. We're closing at three hundred miles per hour, so we'll be in range in sixty seconds."

"What if you miss?"

"The pilot will try to execute evasive maneuvers, but it won't work. A QF-16 can fly circles around a 747, and I have three of them."

One of the drones suddenly went into a nose dive. Kensit lost the video feed at the same time.

"Dammit!"

"What?" Washburn said, leaning forward onto the chair back again before quickly releasing it and saying "Sorry" again.

"We lost Quail Three. Must be some kind of malfunction."

"Can you fix it?"

"It's not worth pursuing this close to the target. We've still got a backup drone left in case this one doesn't succeed."

Kensit had Sentinel locked onto the cockpit of Air Force Two, watching the two pilots prepare to evade the approaching drones. They had received a warning about them from the Air Force controller and were trying to get away, but their efforts wouldn't make a difference. Being able to hear and see what they were planning to do, he could adjust with seemingly supernatural agility. The fuel gauge on each drone indicated fifteen minutes' supply left, so he might even toy with them for a few minutes before finishing them off. He wouldn't soon get another chance to play around like this with life-sized jets.

Then he thought no, he wouldn't take a chance. He'd been working nearly three years to get to this moment of opportunity. No sense in risking another glitch like the malfunction that downed Quail 3.

Air Force Two loomed in the drone's camera, easily distinguishable now for what it was. The pilots agreed to wait until the QF-16s were within a half mile before throwing the 747 into a tight right-hand bank, not knowing it would be a futile attempt.

Kensit wiped his sweaty palms on his pants and grabbed the controllers for the final approach. He was grinning maniacally at the sheer power literally in his hands at the moment. He was about to change the world just as he'd promised.

The smile vanished when he saw a strange image on the camera feed from the drone he was controlling. A narrow vertical edge was slowly rising into the frame from below and to the right, and the sight was so incongruous that he didn't realize what it was until he saw USAF stenciled on the side of it.

It was the rudder of the other drone.

"No," he said breathlessly. Then he screamed, "NO!" and rolled his drone sharply to the left.

He was too late. The air brakes of the drone in front activated, slowing it abruptly and sending it backward into Kensit's drone. He tried to cut the throttle, but by then the left wing of his drone sliced into the rudder of the drone that had snuck in front of it. The camera flared a bright white for a moment and then went black.

He changed Sentinel's view so that he could see behind Air Force Two. All that was left of the drone Kensit had been controlling was a huge fireball. The other drone, bereft of its tail, tumbled toward the ocean.

Kensit sat back in his chair, stunned at the loss of both drones.

There was only one explanation.

Cabrillo and his crew. But that was impossible. Ruiz was supposed to sink the *Oregon*.

"What the hell just happened?" Washburn asked, incredulous.

"Shut up!" Kensit shouted, practically pulling his hair out. "Let me think!"

He spun Sentinel's control all the way back to Haiti and the Gulf of Gonâve, where Ruiz's battle was to take place. He stared in shock at the *Oregon*, battered and smoking but still cruising along.

He zoomed into the op center. There was Juan Cabrillo, sitting smugly in his Kirk Chair. He waved at the map on the screen in front of him and said, "Bye-bye."

Kensit initially thought it was another spooky direct address to him, but then he noticed what was on the map. The Quail 3 drone hadn't crashed.

It was headed right for his yacht.

Kensit jumped out of his chair, sending it careening into Washburn.

"Get out of my way!" Kensit shrieked, and sprinted for the deck.

Maurice glided into the op center with a silver tray carrying a fresh Cuban Cohiba from Juan's private stock. Juan had no idea how the veteran steward knew the endgame was coming, but he thanked him and stuck the cigar in his mouth to watch the finale play out.

The white yacht grew exponentially on the screen as the drone dived toward the water at five hundred miles an hour, a speed low enough to maintain a precise lock as it converged on its target's constantly changing position.

Juan saw two Caucasian men burst out onto the deck as it filled the screen. Both stared up in disbelief at the diving jet, and Juan recognized Kensit's astonished and agonized face an instant before the screen went dark.

Murph threw both his hands straight up in the air and whooped "Touchdown!"

"You realize we just lost any chance of finding out how Sentinel actually works," Max said. "Lutzen's journal is now atomized."

Juan shrugged. "It's better than Kensit getting away and selling it to the highest bidder. Speaking of which . . . Hali, there's two minutes left on Sentinel's self-destruct. Tell Eric to get out of the Oz cave."

"He told me that he's taking photos of the machinery," Hali said.

"I don't care. He's had enough time. I don't want him anywhere close to it when it blows up. Tell Eddie and Linc to drag Stoney out of there if they have to."

Hali smiled. "Maybe I'll tell them to do that anyway."

As Hali made the call, Juan flicked open the silver lighter that Maurice had placed on his armrest and lit his well-deserved cigar.

Hector Bazin was shaken awake by a rumble that rattled his whole body. When it subsided, he sat up and rubbed his aching head, wondering how long he'd been unconscious. His hands and face were crusted with dried blood, meaning he'd been out for a while. He opened his eyes and saw nothing but darkness.

At first, he thought the concussion was so severe that it had caused him to go blind. He madly rummaged around in his pocket until he found the book of matches inside. Only two left.

He struck one and saw that his vision was still sharp. He was stuck in a cave, and the memory of how he got here came flooding back. The RPG rocketing toward him. The blast. The avalanche of rock. Then nothing.

He staggered to his feet and saw that the entire cave opening had been sealed by slabs of rock that would take half a dozen men days to move.

Terror gripped him when he realized the tremor that woke him was Sentinel self-destructing. The time on his watch confirmed it. Even if he could dig his way out in that direction, he'd be bathed with a lethal dose of radiation the moment he stepped into the chamber.

He stumbled back from the pile of rocks. The match burned down to his finger and he dropped it in pain. In his panic he stupidly lit the final one, then realizing his mistake, set fire to the matchbook itself for a few more seconds of precious light.

He was in his worst nightmare. The maze of passageways could go on for miles. Even with a light, it could take him days to find the entrance Juan Cabrillo had used to get in.

He turned and staggered in the opposite direction, desperate to find a path or markings. Before he went twenty feet, he tripped on a stalagmite and fell face-first to the floor. The matchbook went skittering across the cave and was snuffed out.

The darkness was so total that it was only seconds before Bazin could feel tendrils of insanity creeping into his mind. He would spend the last few days of his life trapped in his own tomb with no hope of rescue or escape.

Left with nothing but his own voice to keep him company, Bazin did the only thing he could think of.

He screamed.

EPILOGUE

One week later
Mexico

Juan swam leisurely through the submerged cavern that he and Max had entered through a cenote, a sinkhole that had filled with water. The state of Quintana Roo on the Yucatán Peninsula was so pitted with these sinkholes that there was an online database cataloging them. However, the cenote they'd dived into wasn't listed anywhere. As far as Juan knew, he and Max were the first to explore it.

According to Juan's inertial guidance computer that he carried with him, they didn't have far to go. He looked back and saw Max swimming along with wide eyes taking in the cave's blind albino fish, obviously out of his comfort zone. Or maybe it was the wetsuit stretched to the limit over his bulging stomach. Either way, it took some talking to convince him to join Juan on the dive.

Max would have rather stayed behind on the *Oregon* to complete the repairs to the weapons systems. The damage to the hull, the Gatling gun's radar, and the Metal Storm gun, were not as bad as they initially seemed, so Juan convinced Max that the rest of the crew could spare him while they finished up the job before taking their long-awaited shore leave.

Nonetheless, Max had to find something to complain about, so on the chopper ride to the cenote site he worried again about Maria Sandoval talking about the *Oregon*'s secrets. Juan, however, wasn't concerned. She was a ship captain who'd already been promised her command would be reinstated by the shipping company when the *Ciudad Bolívar* got out of dry dock, she owed Juan for saving her life, and she'd told him herself that she didn't think anyone would believe her story anyway.

Max certainly couldn't complain about their payment for the mission. In addition to their portion of the insurance company payout on the salvage recovery of Maria's ship, they made a tidy profit on the mission to track down Kensit. Once the entire operation report went to Langston Overholt and it was clear that the crew of the *Oregon* had prevented the destruction of Air Force Two, nobody balked at paying their fee, which took care of all their repairs and then some.

The fact that Kensit, Bazin, and Ruiz had been tied together had been a shock to the U.S. military and intelligence communities. But what had surprised Juan was when they discovered who the other man on the yacht with Kensit was. A single frame of the recorded drone video had been enough to ID Brian Washburn, former governor of Florida and logical choice to have been appointed vice president in the event Air Force Two had been shot down. A subsequent forensic search of his office computer files

turned up a deleted video of him killing a blackmailer, likely courtesy of Sentinel's all-seeing eye.

Of course, no one would be re-creating Sentinel's power anytime soon, particularly inside a cave that was now saturated with
deadly radioactivity. There had been some concern that radiation
would leak into Lake Péligre, but so far they'd detected no contamination.

Even if the cave had been intact, rebuilding Sentinel would be
impossible without Lutzen and Kensit's research and designs. But
Juan was under no illusions that the U.S. government would give
up. He was sure that simply knowing the technology was feasible
had spurred top secret research already.

The computer readout said they'd reached the proper coordinates. Juan shined his flashlight up and saw the silvery shimmer indicating there was air. He gave the thumbs-up to Max and
surfaced.

He hoisted himself up onto the lip of the cave floor and heaved
Max out after him.

Max peeled off his mask and spit out his regulator.

"You know," he said, his voice seemingly muffled by the black-
ness around them, "I could be on the ship knee-deep in repairs."

Juan laughed. "I thought you'd like to see this since you missed
Haiti."

"You thought I'd want to see a dank, dark cave? Do I look like
a Morlock to you?"

"Half Morlock. But the cave won't be dark for long."

Juan removed four high-powered LED lamps from his waterproof pack and arrayed them on the floor. When he lit them up,
Max leaped to his feet.

The cavern they were standing in was three times the size of

Sentinel's cave in Haiti, so big that it extended beyond the lights' reach. Brilliant green crystals sparkled in every crevice, some shaped like rosettes, others the circumference of cedars that had sprouted from the floor and grown through the roof high above.

"Holy Emerald City, Batman," Max said, rubbing his hands together in glee. "We've hit the jackpot here."

"They're not emeralds. They're selenium crystals colored by copper impurities. Not valuable as a mineral on its own, but for someone who has the means to create Sentinel—priceless."

"How did you know this would be here?" Max said as he turned in a gawking circle.

"The video we recorded of Kensit's office on the yacht. He had a map on the wall that said Phase Two. Underneath it had the exact latitude and longitude, plus a third number that I finally realized was depth. I was pretty certain he had found another cave. And if it was like the one in Haiti, it was a good bet that we could find a way in."

"For all we know, this might be the only other cave like this on earth."

"You may be right. The only similar cave that had been discovered is one in northern Mexico called the Cave of the Crystals, but those crystals are bone white so they don't have the same properties as these Oz crystals."

Max suddenly stopped gaping at the wondrous view and looked at Juan.

"You were afraid Kensit might sell his technology and let them build another Sentinel in this cave. That's why you destroyed the yacht."

Juan kneeled and picked up one of the crystals to examine its facets, careful not to cut himself. "I destroyed the yacht because

Kensit had to pay for attacking my people. But it did worry me that if he survived, he would buy his freedom with the secrets of Sentinel and the location of this cave."

"I can't blame you. I know I wouldn't trust anyone with that technology. If absolute power corrupts absolutely, wielding Sentinel would put almost anyone on the fast track to being a tyrant."

"As we've seen already. And if one man like Kensit could be corrupted by that much power, imagine what a whole government could do with it."

"Who knows about this place?"

"Just us. I figured what Langston Overholt doesn't know won't hurt him. Besides, it's on Mexican soil, so the U.S. government wouldn't exactly have a strong claim."

"But what if the Mexican government got in on the action?"

"Then it would get complicated. They could keep it themselves or sell it to whoever they wanted. A conglomerate with big pockets. A drug cartel."

"That brings up a good question. Who *does* own it?"

"Me."

Max regarded him with surprise. "You?"

"I discovered the name of the shell company that Kensit controlled to buy it. Since the company's owner is now deceased and left no decedents, I put in a lowball offer for this seemingly worthless piece of land, including the mineral rights. It's a matter of paperwork now."

"But how did Kensit find this place?"

"Who knows," Juan replied. "Geological survey. Or maybe he used Sentinel somehow. We'll never know what it was capable of with Kensit dead and the plans destroyed. Who knows if anyone will ever be able to re-create his work. For our sakes, let's hope not."

"Kensit was a psycho, but he was also a genius, wasn't he?"

"I'll grant that he was smarter than any single one of us, probably by a wide margin. But his mistake was thinking he was more brilliant than all of us put together." Juan took two Coronas out of his pack and handed one to Max. They clinked the cans together before sitting back to take in the sights.

"And I tell you what, my friend," Juan said with a contented grin. "I'll take a team of smart people over a lone genius any day."